THE FUTURE OF LOVE

also by SHIRLEY ABBOTT

Womenfolks: Growing Up Down South
The Bookmaker's Daughter
Love's Apprentice

THE
FUTURE
OF LOVE

A NOVEL BY

Shirley Abbott

ALGONQUIN BOOKS OF CHAPEL HILL 2008

Published by
ALGONQUIN BOOKS OF CHAPEL HILL
Post Office Box 2225
Chapel Hill, North Carolina 27515-2225

a division of
WORKMAN PUBLISHING
225 Varick Street
New York, New York 10014

This is a work of fiction. While, as in all fiction, the literary perceptions and insights are based on experience, all names, characters, places, and incidents either are products of the author's imagination or are used fictitiously.

Library of Congress Cataloging-in-Publication Data
Abbott, Shirley.
    The future of love : a novel / by Shirley Abbott.— 1st ed.
        p. cm.
    ISBN-13: 978-1-56512-567-4
    1. September 11 Terrorist Attacks, 2001—Fiction.   2. New York
    (N.Y.)—Fiction.   3. Psychological fiction.   I. Title.
    PS3601.B393F88 2008
    813'.6—dc22   2007046035

10 9 8 7 6 5 4 3 2 1
First Edition

SONNET 73

That time of year thou mayst in me behold
When yellow leaves, or none, or few, do hang
Upon those boughs which shake against the cold,
Bare ruined choirs, where late the sweet birds sang.
In me thou seest the twilight of such day,
As after sunset fadeth in the west,
Which by and by black night doth take away,
Death's second self, that seals up all in rest.

In me thou seest the glowing of such fire
That on the ashes of his youth doth lie,
As the death-bed, whereon it must expire,
Consum'd with that which it was nourish'd by.
This thou perceiv'st, which makes thy love more strong,
To love that well which thou must leave ere long.

—*William Shakespeare*

THE FUTURE OF LOVE

1 Mark

By September the grass of Riverside Park had been trampled to gray. Dead leaves (a few, only a few) rustled on low branches. He had his little girl in tow and was trying to make the best of things, in spite of his situation and the spike of pain in his left temple. The path to the playground sloped downward: he dug his toes in. The high residential façades of Riverside Drive facing the cliffs across the Hudson River were as harmonious and pleasing as certain glorious stretches along the Seine and put him in mind of Paris, where he'd spent a few months as a college student. (A positive thought. Yes. Surely.) The carefully planted esplanades and lawns in the park displayed a seasonal ripeness: city soot, a scattering of empty potato-chip packages, and an occasional smear of dog feces. Nearly everybody scooped these days, and poop existed in pretty much acceptable quantities. Still, it paid to look where you stepped or unfolded your picnic blanket. The river was no longer the cloaca maxima of New York state. The EPA had done its job upriver, and a new sewage plant was in place up around 135th Street.

One could measure a civilization by how well it disposed of excrement. Soon, according to the *New York Times*, the water would be safe for swimming; he already saw a canoe. Far above, a jet plane followed the channel northward. Traffic flowed on the double decks of the George Washington Bridge, and the morning light glinted off hoods and windshields, brilliant processions on the great span of steel.

Mark Adler planned to spend the day, or most of it, with his daughter at the playground. Pulling a battered wooden dog that quacked as it went, she bounced beside him, her brown hair thick as wild nettles, her toes in teal blue plastic flip-flops. The toy skidded over onto its back, and Toni patiently stopped and set it upright. "Now, doggie, don't get hurt. Come along. Don't cry." Mark held the stroller tightly with its cargo of sand pail, shovel, peanut butter sandwiches, two bottles of water, a box of tissues, a towel, and an extra pair of panties for her, just in case. It was a plain, light, proletarian stroller, a jalopy among the SUVs of infant transport that now clogged supermarket aisles and clothing stores and museums, took up entire elevators.

He himself had grown up north of here, at the end of the epoch when nosy landladies were still renting out rooms by the week to newcomers from Europe and the population was heavily Jewish. All that was history, one from which Mark felt utterly disconnected. As a child he had played in the same park system, though not the same park, to which he now escorted his daughter. His German-Jewish grandparents had changed their name, assimilated, and stagnated. His dad and his grandfather had both worked as guards at the Metropolitan Museum, and each had died of a heart attack at age fifty-nine, a Teutonic orderliness that their descendant hoped to escape.

Mark sucked at his water bottle and swallowed another ibuprofen, his third since arising, hoping it would soon ease his head and the agony between his shoulders. His innards had been too acidic even for soft-boiled eggs, the result of Scotch with the late late movie, all alone, while his wife and daughter slept. Meryl Streep was a doctor in a posh New England town, and her son had murdered a girl, and Meryl was protecting the guilty little bastard. It had felt good to be drunk and deep in somebody else's dilemma. But it had destabilized his gait and turned his hand into a bear's paw so that he had clatteringly knocked over Maggie's open bottle of herbal shampoo and the water glass at 2 a.m. as he groped for a toothbrush, creating a puddle of aromatic glop and broken glass that he dared not leave until morning, and of course he had cut himself cleaning it up. Why had she left the bottle on the sink? A long car trip tested a marriage, but sharing a bathroom was worse. Maybe he could be a better husband if they ever had separate bathrooms. Separate bedrooms.

Wait. Positive thoughts. He must count his blessings. One: his little Toni was a picture in a dotted-Swiss sundress over a bathing suit for the sprinkler in the park. A small grosgrain hair bow rode the pile of curls. Maggie believed in hair bows. Toni had always stopped traffic. Cute! A woman in the supermarket yesterday had advised him to get the child a modeling job. "Lots of money in that, and the child is sooo gorgeous." Where did the crones of the upper West Side pick up such ideas? And yet, what was he doing for her? Maybe he ought to send her out to work. He should have been able to take his family to the Hamptons in July and August. On hot Saturdays, instead of moldering in Riverside Park with its grimy sandboxes, he should have parked his new Range Rover at some members-only beach lot in Easthampton, and then guided his little family toward the shore, setting up the beach umbrella and opening the hamper, answering the smiles and waves of neighbors. No grime out there, no leaves black with soot, no concrete slabs sticky with Popsicle goo. In the Hamptons, dogs probably did not defecate.

A year ago he'd been an account exec at Grumple & Co. And had he not done their bidding? Worked long hours? Compromised and then forgotten whatever shreds of integrity he might have possessed? Pretended to be evaluating mutual funds when in fact he was merely arranging artful kickback schemes and hoping for a bonus? Neglecting the small investor, greasing the wheels for the large? His boss's boss appeared regularly on Louis Rukeyser's show on Public TV (paid for with the contributions of Viewers Like You), hyping the stocks he was dumping into his clients' portfolios while the smart money went elsewhere. Maggie had asked what a price target was, and he had explained that price targets were the product of much thought and research, no, in fact, they were a come-on, a wild guess, a con game, and the so-called little guy may easily be misled, but such was the nature of the business. Little guys should not trust big guys. Little guys should be looking out for themselves. Or putting their money in bank CDs. Only that wasn't what the ads said. The ads showed a kid graduating from college, clutching a diploma, with two proud parents at his side, all because they had done financial planning with hardworking account execs like him at Grumple & Co.

Mark had been ejected from that picture at precisely 10:30 a.m. one September Friday, when 25 percent of the staff was laid off. He had worn his gray suit to work that day, with the black loafers and the red print tie, had gotten in early because he meant to finally do something for that old guy who wanted to cash out the $21,000 in his IRA, and Mark had let the request sit in the basket for two months, being preoccupied with larger problems, and everything had gone down and there was only $17,000 and the man was threatening to report him to the SEC or sue Grumple. He had thought the summons to his boss's office had to do with this matter, but no, not at all. Those executive eyes, usually so warm and friendly, were cold and opaque. He remembered hearing "Please sit down" and "Have to let you go," followed by "Pack up and be out of here in twenty minutes." They gave him some kind of paper to sign—he hadn't been sure what it was. And a check for the salary he had coming, up through the previous day. There was severance, denominated in some way so that he could start drawing unemployment after three months. It was tagged as a layoff, not a firing. They reminded him once more that he no longer had access to the server, that his e-mails, address books, and all paper files had been impounded as the property of Grumple & Co., and that he was entitled to take only his personal possessions, whatever they might consist of. He was told, once more, that he had twenty minutes to clear out.

He did not remember cleaning out his desk. Indeed, perhaps he had not cleaned it. At Madison and Fifty-ninth Street half an hour later, he had stumbled, unsure where he was going or ought to go. And right there on the street, in broad daylight, he had begun to cry. So noisily that it attracted some attention, though no one stopped to inquire what the trouble was, since a grown man in a suit and tie weeping aloud on the street could only be a lunatic. Had anybody asked, he would have said that he was ashamed to go home before lunch. That it felt like third grade when he had broken out with chickenpox and been sent home by the school nurse. That his daughter would come home at three with her babysitter and his wife at six, and what would he tell them? Daddy's lost his job. And thus had he entered purgatory, a land where your closest associates, your drinking buddies, did not return your phone calls. The doors were locked.

Forget it, he was counting blessings.

Number two: the daily disgrace of joblessness might well be behind him, for on the coming Tuesday he was to interview at the biggest investment banking house in New York, his first crack at a real job in over a year. Of course, he had not been utterly idle. He had become the chief babysitter, and Maggie had fired the shy Honduran girl with no green card who'd been their part-time nanny. He had worked off and on for the last six months in Hammond's Fine Wines and Liquors on Broadway. They had paid him off the books, at first, so his unemployment checks would keep coming, and they put him on part time when unemployment ran out. In fact, unemployment had paid a little better than the job, but he liked the work, lugging boxes from storage in the cellar, stocking shelves, telling customers which red wines to try. It was a relief to be doing something physical. He liked his boss, a genial type, a born New Yorker like himself, who at least was not cheating people. He liked his customers. Mostly. He even liked the poor, old, stinking, stubbly guys who came in for a half pint. A supply was kept near the register so the bums didn't wander around the store. He treated them square. Would "sir" them as they counted out their dimes. There but for the grace of God.

He had applied for the job after a fight with Maggie. She said he had to do something, anything, retail sales, whatever, bag groceries, he could not just househusband anymore, because it was killing him, killing her. Plus, he never even did any laundry. She claimed he was terminally depressed. That he was making her terminally depressed. She accused him of not reading the want ads or looking on the Internet. (Not one response to any of his scores of e-mailed resumes had ever materialized. Unless you counted the autoresponses. Not one nibble. And yes, he had quit looking, and she would have quit, too.) Maggie said her mother would help out if they needed extra babysitting, but he had to do something or she was going to leave. So, okay, he had shut down the computer and gone over to Broadway to the liquor store. He got the job over another applicant who had clerked at Astor Place (a much better store) for two years but was short and fat and had acne. It never hurt, whether you were selling mutual funds or booze, to look like Michael Douglas, and Mark even had the hint of a cleft in his chin. It had felt so good to hear "Yes, when can you start?" Selling booze was more interesting than clerking at the Gap, for example, and required less training than driving a cab. And he knew a thing or two about wine.

It had been embarrassing, at first, lugging bottles off the shelves for Toni's playmates' parents, people he had in some cases entertained as dinner guests, or been the dinner guest of, back when they could afford dinner parties. People he had worked side by side with, as peers in fund-raising, at the Parkside Montessori Street Fair, where they all good-naturedly got out in the lovely spring weather, under the flowering trees, and raised a few thousand dollars for scholarships, just to keep affirmative action alive at the private nursery school level. He and Kevin Parker had hauled a kid-laden trolley up and down the street, a buck a ride. These days Kevin Parker was asking him, with only a hint of irony, to recommend a Burgundy, or what he thought would go with salmon, or which single malt was really worth the money. Maggie had at least pretended to be proud of him for having a job, though she never brought Toni into the store.

Most of these snooty parents at Parkside had never had to socialize with a liquor store clerk. In a liquor store in Gentry Land, a clerk needed to talk the talk. Mark had read up, and soon became an expert on red Bordeaux. He talked about "tannic structure," and compared the flavor of a certain vintage to chocolate, and told his customers that the 2000 was better than the 1999 but not as long lasting, talked of currants, plums, and tar in the taste, and of a lovely glycerinlike mouthfeel. He said solemnly that something was a "killer buy," or that it could be "attacked now, with no cellaring." As with stocks and bonds, you promoted belief and people gave you money, only with wine they had the pleasure of drinking their purchase. Sales improved. He got a small raise, more hours. Maybe he was meant to be a liquor-store clerk, a wine missionary among the yuppies. Every man an oenophile. Too bad it did not suit the expectations of his wife, editor of prize-worthy debut novels.

They approached the entrance of the baby park, and Toni broke into a joyous skip, abandoning her doggie. Mark lifted it by the leash and dumped it in the net bag that hung from the stroller.

Blessing three: this was a very good baby park. New landscaping, rubberized pavement under the swings and jungle gyms, and a whole herd of little bronze hippopotami. The toilets were perpetually stopped up, of course, but that was the curse of all kiddie parks. He wouldn't be living in this neighborhood at all without their rent-stabilized apartment on West End Avenue, acquired through a connection of his mother-in-law's. A dabbler in Marxism in his college days, he found it easy to think full time about money. The baby had caused this. The damn schooling. The public schools in this neighborhood were a few cuts above the prison system. He and Maggie gnawed themselves bloody about the future. Instead of curling up around her back, slipping his hand under her nightshirt, he would lie in bed, body rigid, dick soft, and opine, "Maybe she could do elementary school at P.S. 75. It isn't so bad. What matters is junior high, and we could save the money for that."

"No, what matters is early childhood. I guess we'll have to turn to my mother." Toni was only four. She could stay at Parkside through second grade, though the best people usually moved on to Brearley or Trinity by first grade. Sometimes Mark imagined Toni whizzing through junior high, up on Amsterdam Avenue, with top grades, energizing her classmates, winning the Westinghouse Science Award. He'd go to cocktail parties and tell his friends who were breaking ass to get $20,000 per to hand over to Dalton, "She's doing great in public school," and all those people would die of envy. But it was only a fantasy. They both knew that Antonia Pleasance Adler could never attend schools whose graduates came out equipped chiefly for retail jobs and burger flipping or screwing up your application at the Motor Vehicles Bureau while you waited an hour in line.

He watched Toni run straight for the sprinkler and wet herself down without taking off her dress. "Toni," he called. "Come here." She ignored him, and what of it? The dress would dry. He'd take it off her later. He sank down in the shade on an empty bench. Lots of daddies came to the park, but today the population was sparse—nannies, a couple of moms, a few kids. Everybody still on Shelter Island. In the Adirondacks. The Poconoes. The Hamptons. Dutchess County. The gazetteer of success. He sighted around the enclosure for one face, the one face he longed to see, or feared seeing. But she was not there. Just as well. He was in no shape to talk to Sophie. And yet if only Sophie would appear!

The sprinkler spurted, and a dozen children in swim trunks and ruffled britches danced around it, catching the spray in their buckets and wetting their heads. The heat was a good sign, perhaps. A surge of optimism told him he would get that job at Morgan Stanley, they would ask him to start work right away.

And then the year would finally begin, as years were supposed to begin, in September, and the failures would drag on no longer. The leaves would turn red and fall decorously off the trees, not just hang there, dry and whispery. He would go out every morning in a new suit and tie, on his way to Wall Street. Maggie could quit her job if she wanted to. They'd move to goddamn Mamaroneck. Would he find, with a few months' pay in the bank, that he could still love Maggie?

But at the bottom of the picture, like the cellar in a child's drawing of a house, there was another idea. If he did get the job, could he not escape this marriage altogether?

In the quandary his life had turned into, he often fantasized about his mother-in-law's death. That apartment of Antonia's was the main thing. . . . They could live in it, sell it if Maggie insisted on this stupid move to the stupid burbs. An apartment on a great street in a hot part of town. Hard to perceive Antonia and Fred as wealthy, really, just an ordinary New York couple, comfortably off, the old man had had a good job at *the* newspaper, which was not only the most important paper in the whole world but also had pension plans; the old lady, too, had worked and saved money. His mother-in-law had never invited him to evaluate her investments, but he would know how to handle them. Maggie's dad had been dead over a year. People said widows didn't survive long. Another positive thought. He had begun hoping, secretly, guiltily, for signs of morbidity in Antonia, pricking up his ears when Maggie reported that her mother had seen a doctor in July.

"Anything serious?" he had asked, adding, "Is she okay?" But Maggie had given him an ugly look. Ah, God, how vile he felt, and was. It was disgusting to be counting on your wife's inheritance. And yet, did that not have a long literary pedigree? How

many novels had been written about just that? The heirs lan-
guishing, mending their gloves, counting the years, and finally . . .
apoplexy . . . catarrh! The black armband, the downcast eyes at
the reading of the will. He had admitted freely to himself when
he married Maggie that her parents' wealth was a draw, a com-
pensation for her plain face and anxious temperament.

Toni stood at her father's knee, dripping. "Daddy, it's all just
babies here. Nobody to play with but babies. I miss Brittany."

"Yeah? Where is Brittany these days?" Turning her around,
he unbuttoned the sundress and pulled it over her head. The hair
bow, he noticed, was gone. He found the towel and rubbed her
head with it.

"Still in her country with her mom."

"Her country?" Was his the only Parkside Montessori family
that lacked a country house?

"Her farm place in the country. Way away. She says it takes a
really long time to get there. They have a horse and a pony. No, a
foal, a baby horse. She said she would take me there sometime to
see the horse and the foal. I think I will just sit here with you."

"But, Toni, the babies will make fine playmates. Look at those
little boys over there—twins, I bet you. They need you to show
them how to play in the sand. Run along, honey. What's the
point of coming down here if you sit on the bench with daddy?
We could have just stayed in front of the TV." That's what he had
wanted to do. She could have watched reruns of *Sesame Street,*
and he could have napped.

"Yeah, but mommy said no TV." She had his bone structure
but Maggie's wild hair, the hazel eyes. "I wish we had gone to
Grandma's with mommy. I hate it here. I'm so hot. You don't
smell good. You drank that whiskey last night." Her eyes darkened, and she scratched a scab on her shin until the longed-for

droplet of blood appeared. How did a kid that age notice whiskey? She had been asleep.

"I'm bleeding." She put her red-smeared finger into her mouth.

"No, you aren't bleeding very much. You scratched it yourself, didn't you? I didn't drink much whiskey. Anyway, how would you know? Run play in the nice water. Daddy needs a nap."

"I don't like it when you nap in the park. What if a bad man came and told me to get into his car and kidnapped me?"

Okay, he couldn't nap. What if she did get kidnapped, just because he had the worst hangover of his life?

"Honey, I am not going to let a bad man run off with you. I don't really nap. I just rest my eyes a bit. I watch you through my eyelashes like this." He leaned his head back, squinting. "See, there's always a little opening for my X-ray vision." She giggled. "And I am not going to drink any whiskey tonight or any night. That's a promise. Now run on and have some fun. We'll get you a Popsicle when the man comes. I remembered to bring some money this time."

He, too, would eat a Popsicle. Maybe it would be the magic turn-around moment in this hangover. The chill of the Popsicle, the sweetness, would go right to his headache and drive it out, as the ibuprofen failed to do. This was the last hangover. No booze tonight. No more booze ever. To what do you attribute your long and successful life, Mr. Adler? To forswearing alcohol when I was forty. Right after that, I got a job at Morgan Stanley, where I rose to a vice-presidency. I purchased a house for my family in Amagansett, a heartbreakingly old-fashioned and fragile house, so authentic it should have been in a museum; so endearing that our friends, such as they were, nearly died of jealousy. We lovingly restored it, put in a retro kitchen and period linoleum. My wife bakes bread every week.

"Look, daddy. Oh, look. It's Ashley. I can play with Ashley!"

And yes, there she was, materializing out of sprinkler mist. Ashley. From the other side of the park, walking past the sprinkler and the little bronze hippos, between the benches, around the parked strollers, a tall slim woman in jeans and an I Love NY T-shirt was leading the little girl by the hand. She bent toward the child, and her shining black hair fell over her face. Ashley, Kevin Parker's kid, glanced upward happily.

Blessing number four: Sophie, beautiful, kind, loving, desirable Sophie, Mark thought, a perilous, double-edged blessing.

"Hi, Toni, hi, Mark." Ashley and Toni greeted each other rapturously, like society matrons at lunch, kissing and squealing, and ran hand in hand toward the sprinkler. Sophie sat down on Mark's bench. Like a surfer on the crest of a roller, he was consumed by happiness. Things were going to go right.

2 Antonia

THE TEAKETTLE SHRIEKED. She took it off the burner and discarded her *New York Times* in the recycle pile, next to the glass bottles. She located the tea bags—herbal tea for Maggie, peppermint, apple spice, Yogi, chai latte—threw a few packets into the water, set the pot to steep. Two dollars' worth of designer water to make tea because her daughter was afraid of tap. New York City water had, among the urban "greens," been reclassified as a toxin, the subtext being that you couldn't trust the government because it didn't care if the water gave you cancer. With Bush in charge, the "greens" might be right. Antonia could just have lied about the water. She could have said she still believed it was disloyal and wasteful and undemocratic to drink bottled water rather than tap. But she wanted to be honest with Maggie, even about drinking water. She would use the Mountain Spring. At least they were of the same mind on greenhouse gases.

A bit of finery was needed, some linen napkins for a proper tea party, and Antonia excavated a couple of bulging drawers.

She must clean out this kitchen, the middens of Ninevah and Tyre. She found a stack of yellow napkins in the middle drawer under a blue tablecloth, needing washing perhaps, a bit faded at the fold. Under the napkins, like maggots under a bird's corpse, lay packets of coupons bound in a rubber band. Fred. She would never rid herself of the Things of Fred. Fred the prudent, the methodical, belt-and-suspenders, literal, practical Fred, the compiler of coupons for various loathsome cheese spreads and artificial whipped cream and vanilla wafers. Cereal fortified with vitamins, and nobody ate it. Fred would shop just to use up the coupons, and load the cupboards with stuff that fell out on you when you opened the door. And he cooked, too, or at least made a lot of pasta. An evolved husband, she supposed, before the term had been invented. Everybody had loved him, and she loved him the way they all did: generally, because he was too good a man to find fault with. "You are so lucky to have such a husband," Helen Mulcahy had never failed to whisper at the little dinner parties Antonia gave for Village friends long ago. Oh, yes, very lucky. The day after Fred died, Antonia began throwing things out. She took off her rings, a modest diamond set in gold that his mother had worn for forty years, the narrow gold band he had bought her at Tiffany's, and stuck them in the Tiffany box. She tackled the closet, put several suits in a black plastic bag, called Goodwill, and then lost her energy. These drawers, for example, had lain dormant. She grabbed the packets and threw them in the recycling after removing the rubber band.

Howard Mulcahy had died of an abdominal aneurysm a year ago, in August 2000. Whoop, he was gone, just weeks after the complications of diabetes had carried Fred off—"a long illness," as the obit said. (No photo, but a few inches of free space in the paper where he had spent forty years on the rewrite desk.)

Back in the early days, the dinner-party days, the child-raising days, Howard, a successful insurance agent, had taken pride in never taking out the garbage or changing a diaper. The kids were Helen's lookout, he always said. But at least he and Helen went dancing sometimes. Once, when they all were pretty drunk, he had done what anyone might have predicted of him—he caught Antonia alone in the kitchen and kissed her. With intent. She could still remember the kiss, and the sudden flash of desire. Adultery did not interest her at that moment; passing the Equal Rights Amendment did. Marching with Betty Friedan. As time passed, the seesaw tilted. Antonia went from ideological to social feminist. Why didn't feminists talk about the household help? Most women she knew hadn't even paid social security for the nanny. And what about black women? They didn't know about the feminine mystique. Who gave a rap about the ERA? The discussions lasted late into the night at her women's group, turned bitter and finally pointless. So she quit the group.

As newly minted widows, Helen and Antonia had tried companionship. Just the two of them. It did not work. Antonia insisted on the Truffaut festival at the Film Forum or documentaries about Chiapas, where, it might interest Helen to know, a true revolutionary movement was springing up with a Zapata-like leader, while Helen liked the multiplex on Union Square because the seats were comfortable; she sat through *Titanic* twice. Helen, who had marched across the bridge at Selma with Martin Luther King in 1965, was presently captain of the recycle team and president of the block association. She made sure that coleuses were planted around the gingko trees and saw to it that dead gingkos got replaced. One night last spring, after she and Helen had killed a bottle of wine, Antonia said she was sick of recycling, which in any event was the quintessentially feminine approach to politics. Pick up the mess and tie up the newspaper and everything will be okay. What about the jobless, what about raising the minimum wage? What about the stolen election, and the Supreme Court decision, events that stuck in Antonia's craw and left her permanently angry. And what about women getting stoned to death in Afghanistan? Stoned meant something different in Afghanistan than it did here, in case Helen had not noticed.

They had gone on for an hour or so like this, and then Helen had stormed out of Antonia's life, to their mutual relief. Of course, Antonia also planted coleus around the ginkgos, and she never failed to rinse out her dolphin-safe tuna cans. She also signed bulk e-mails to the Taliban, complete with her correct address and zip code, complaining about the shocking way women were treated under Muslim law. Did the Taliban have computers? When did they read their e-mails? Before or after they did the stoning? Silly, maybe, but the least she could do was to give a damn, she thought, not get orgasmic over the neatly packaged newspapers awaiting pickup.

Antonia folded the napkins atop straw mats, and set a vase of yellow mums on the table. She had picked them only last evening from Gregory and Arthur's garden below. A breeze stirred the gauzy white panels at the double doors that opened onto her terrace. She stepped outside and leaned out into the treetops, a fragrant inner-city jungle where green vines climbed the back walls, damaging the brickwork, and birds warbled and red squirrels nested in the A/C units. Two famous movie stars could often be glimpsed across the way on their plot of earth, their England, sunning their infant and rumpling the ears of their golden retriever. Within the block formed by Perry and Charles, Bleecker and West Fourth Streets lay a magnificent garden, secret and fertile, working synergistically with the movie stars to quadruple real estate values.

Five floors below Antonia's balcony, insulated from the nervous, nervy, hell-bent city, Gregory lay on a lounge chair reading, his brown torso bare, wearing khaki shorts, his bad leg propped on a pillow, while Arthur, in a green plaid shirt and jeans, sat on a low stool, thrusting a trowel into the flower bed. Time to think of bulbs, fall planting.

"Hey, honey pies," she called down, "the mums you gave me are still beautiful. What are you planting?"

Arthur looked up. The sweetest smile. A big man, Arty. Rangy, solid. Gregory was a tall man, too, but thin, so thin, and yet he still moved with the old grace in spite of bone loss and arthritic knees. The form and function of his dancer's body had eventually done him in. Such a devoted couple, quiet, mannerly. She forgave them for staying home on Gay Pride Saturday. They disliked the shouting, the corporate sponsorship of floats, the flaunting of it. Antonia went to the parade on their behalf.

"Tulips, tulip bulbs for the spring, dark purple ones. Where's Maggie? Is she bringing Toni?" Arty asked.

"On her way, I hope, and no, this is our afternoon together. Mark is taking Toni to the park." Toni, darling Toni, the hope of Antonia's life. Perhaps, when the child was old enough, she would learn from her Grandma, agree with what Grandma said. After all, this child was her namesake.

Greg put his book down. "Come for a drink this evening. Tell us how things are going. Join us for dinner. Bring Maggie if she'll come along."

"Are you going to tell her she may have a stepfather?"

"Arty, you know she isn't going to have any stepfather. But I am going to break the news about Sam. I guess she ought to know." Sam, her love. At her age. A widow of fourteen months, she already had a lover, confounding all statistics to the contrary. Okay, he was married, but that was a minor problem. Arty and Greg knew him, and Maggie must know him, too. And there was a connection: Sam's granddaughter, Alison, was the partner of Greg's niece Candace Johnson. A coincidence that delighted her, that seemed somehow to cement her relationship to Sam.

"How's Mark? Any prospects?"

"Oh, we're feeling good. He has that interview coming up next week. Morgan Stanley. Not too bad. There's hope. It's tough being unemployed, you know. I must go, guys. See you this evening. Get those bulbs in the ground, Arty."

Ice, she needed ice. Shoving aside a container of pear ice cream in the freezer, plastic-encased halves of baguettes as stiff as baseball bats, and hoary packages of peas, she located an ice tray. Empty. She'd have to go to the deli. Their ice cubes were made of spring water, or so it said on the package. She would tell Maggie.

Every week, she made sorbet for Sam, sometimes pear, sometimes apple, sometimes raspberry or mango. She put the fruit through the food processor, added sugar. She kept mint leaves around for a garnish. She made tiny ginger cookies. Feeding Sam was now her major preoccupation. "Food is love," he told her, as he worked at the range and chopping board. They walked to Chinatown for sea bass and whiting and fresh cilantro, to the east twenties for curry powder or preserved Turkish lemons, to Little Italy, or what remained of it after the second and third generation had moved to Manhasset and Secaucus, for arborio rice. Cooking with Sam was like making a fine tapestry, everything perfectly thought out, from prep to plating.

And now the Things of Sam were replacing the Things of Fred. Sam's shirt hung on a closet hook, his towel was in the bathroom, his toothbrush in the holder. The new goose-down pillow she had bought for him was on the bed. Secret things. Nobody would notice. She could not have kept Fred's old pillow, soaked with the sweat of illness. She had been faithful, a dutiful wife, until death, after a painfully long delay, did them part.

Gathering her keys, running a comb through her hair, applying a little pale lipstick, she calculated she had ten years before old age set in. She could still get out of a chair without groaning. She had just got a passing grade on her mammogram and her bone density test, and her colonoscopy had revealed pristine intestinal linings. Had she grown garrulous or dotty? No. She followed all the tips in the Health Section for staving off Alzheimer's: mnemonics, puzzles, use it or lose it. She tried to revive her knowledge of Spanish. She went to the gym three times a week and worked out for an hour. She sweated on the hip flexor machine. Ten years, maybe, and if Sam never divorced Edith, so what? But surely he, too, would seize the day.

She tucked a ten in her pocket and a few extra dollars, in case Charley was at his post near the deli, across from where small crowds gathered three or four times daily for AA meetings, balancing coffee containers and cigarettes. Young, beautiful alcoholics, mostly, and she wondered what had landed them in AA besides alcohol. Charley was tall and gaunt, a high-plains drifter, a Clint Eastwood of homelessness. He had once been part of the Metropolitan Opera chorus, soloed occasionally in small roles, and had lived in a Village rooming house. His voice failed and his building went co-op at about the same time, so he had moved to the street. St. Vincent's Hospital took him in sometimes, doctored him, and cleaned him up. And then he got filthy again.

Antonia used to think that if she voted for the right people and went to the right meetings, there would be no homeless wrecks on the streets. Here he was, intractable, with his sleeping bag rolled up under his arm—Maggie's old sleeping bag. The poor you have always with you. She could never accept that, no. The world could be fixed, surely. And though she was not religious, except for being a Democrat, she thought that if people had bothered—even a little—to listen to what Jesus had said, the world would be fixed already. All those evangelicals, so far as she could see, said nothing about rich men and camels and the eye of the needle, or of the meek inheriting the earth or doing unto the least of these their brethren. Instead, hounding homosexuals was the chief duty of Christians.

"Morning, Antonia." Today he looked fairly clean, and his scraggly beard had been trimmed. But his cheeks burned. And between his finger and thumb, a cigarette butt also burned. His one pleasure, he had said. Last year he told her he had pancreatic cancer, but when he changed it to prostate cancer, she quit believing him. Maybe he had both. Maybe he thought he had one or the other, on different days.

"You don't look so good, Charley. Have you had any breakfast?"

"Didn't want any. Don't feel good. No sleep, some bums they rolled me. I had five dollars. It's gone. No respect for the elderly anymore."

She gave him the ten. Elderly? He was younger than she was, by her rough calculation, but sleeping on the sidewalk did not promote a youthful glow. She sometimes toyed with the idea of inviting him home with her, for a bath and a rest. But Charley probably had lice, no telling what else. One couldn't go that far.

"You got anything to sell today, Charley? I can bring you something. I've always got books." Once in a while she bought back her own books from him. He did not seem to know.

"Thank you," he called after her as she headed toward the deli. "I really would appreciate it. I hate to take your money. You know I am not a true bum." No, he was not a true bum, and she was not a true income-tax cheat. On her tax return every year she listed the cash she had given Charley as a donation to the Church of the Ascension on Fifth Avenue, an architectural landmark where she and Fred had gotten married so many years ago. Was that cheating? She meant to e-mail that ethics columnist in the *New York Times Magazine* and ask what he thought.

A man and woman in identical Nikes stood at the corner with a map.

"Can I help you?" Antonia asked.

"Doesn't Nicole Kidman live around here? Do you know her address?"

"Uh, I don't know it. But if you stand here long enough, you might see her or Sarah Jessica Parker or even Monica Lewinsky. You might see Martha Stewart. That's what we've got these days. Matthew Broderick is around all the time. You'll see him any minute now, walking his dog. Lots of 'em are out here. But they look just like us. Anyway, good luck."

No beat poets around here anymore, no aspiring youths living five to a room and going to the Actor's Studio, no painters in rent-controlled studios passed down from the previous generation, no shy, crop-haired young lesbians from Kansas self-consciously holding hands in public for the very first time. Movie stars, investment bankers, and kids drinking in the White Horse Tavern, where Dylan Thomas got drunk sixty years ago, kids who never heard of Dylan Thomas or even, maybe, Bob Dylan.

Not the Village of her youthful imaginings. A few old coots and crocks and writers and former Commies and anarchists lurked about, but they were mostly invisible amid the glitter, or else their obits had appeared last year. Did New York still bestow the gift of loneliness and the gift of privacy, as E. B. White had written half a century ago? The grand gift of anonymity was why Antonia had come here, so long ago, from a sweaty little town in Mississippi, to escape, in White's words, the indignity of being observed by one's neighbors. Perhaps the city was still private, welcoming, in spite of the *anschluss* of money. White had written, in 1948, that "the city has never been so uncomfortable, so crowded, so tense," and it was always that way, eternally tense, poised to spring, and surely that would never change.

Back in the kitchen, making sandwiches (tofu egg salad on whole grain bread) in case Maggie was hungry, she forgot about gathering up the books for Charley. Maggie was an aspiring vegetarian, though frequently in relapse. Oh, why, when she had raised her daughter to be a socially conscious liberal, had it all come down to soy protein?

Maybe it was about money. Fred's death had left her the owner of a three-bedroom, two-bath apartment purchased in 1963 for thirty-five thousand dollars, now worth a couple of million, three bedrooms in a building so distinguished that you couldn't change a doorknob without permission from the Landmarks Commission. Fred's pension funds had done quite well besides, and his death benefits from his job had been considerable. She had earned some money, too. She had her fat, tidy little IRAs, and that didn't stand for Irish Republican Army. The more you had, the more deductions you got—that was the American dream. Antonia Blass had always been temperamentally a have-not. She had become a have. Odd, she herself had never had any sort of inheritance. Her parents, when they died, had left her a few victory bonds from World War II.

Antonia stowed the sandwiches in the refrigerator, along with the pitcher of cooling tea. She sliced a lemon (certified organic). She arranged her homemade ginger cookies on a blue-and-yellow painted Italian plate. She and Fred had bought that plate on their first and last trip to Tuscany. Fred was no traveler: they looked at the Botticellis at the Uffizi, and he said that was enough.

This was going to be a marvelous visit, a true mother-and-daughter tea with cloth napkins and secrets and giggles. Maggie would tell her about Mark's frame of mind. She would tell Maggie about Sam. Maggie would be thrilled. Bush would be kicked out in the next election, as he so richly deserved. Peace would prevail. The public schools would experience a renaissance. Maggie would have a second baby. The stock market would come raging back, and her mutual funds would once more earn 18 percent. Toni would attend one of those revitalized public schools, and then Harvard.

And, yes, she would take some books to Charley and he would sell them and get himself a room tonight. She had a stack of hardcovers on the hall table that ought to bring some money. And Sam would be with her this evening; they would lie in each other's arms. Antonia's hands nevertheless trembled as she refolded napkins and fussed with the flowers and waited for the visit to begin.

3   Edith

S HE SET OUT early, striding past the pond where frogs
cried *ribbet,* like the frogs in children's stories, past
the lacy, quivering willows, up the rise, into the meadow and the
deep forest. Her forest. And Sam's. Three hundred acres of it.
He seemed almost hostile to the property lately; it was a burden,
one mortal coil too many. Sam's passions shifted, of course. He
was restless, a malcontent. She herself was cultivating serenity.
She had bought the Dalai Lama's book, and while not exactly
an acolyte, she meant to make her walks a form of meditation,
strove to experience each step, each bend of the knee, each pebble
underfoot. Oh, striving wasn't the right thing, not the right Buddhist thing. Striving was the western thing, the Edith thing. How
she'd love to get away from the Edith thing. She must say her
mantra, cleanse her mind, but her mind was a caged gerbil on a
wheel. She was walking too briskly.

Five minutes into the woods, just as she had slowed down into
something like serenity, her right ankle gave way in spite of the
correctly laced high-top boot, casting her like a rag doll onto

a pile of leaves. She caught her breath and tried to collect her wits and rise. Then she saw the deer, a big buck with a rack of magnificent points against the sky, right in front of her, poised in the underbrush, taut and muscular under his gleaming, mottled coat. He faced her down, paralyzing her as if by injection. She stared up at him, aware of his ripe scent, his black eyes, broad chest, and ill-kempt majesty. A wild brute. The phrase came into her mind like a supertitle at the opera. Would he bite her? Stamp viciously upon her? After observing her—she thought she saw some kind of wisdom in his look, or at least forbearance, but not a trace of fear—he turned and ambled into the forest with a rustle and crackle followed by silence.

When you're seventy, a fall is not an accident but a harbinger. She had heard that sometimes a bone cracks and then you fall, rather than the other way around. Nothing in her interior seemed to have cracked. She felt okay. But it was too soon to stand up. She needed to reflect. An appreciative spirit in the presence of Nature was to be cultivated, and one should be pleased to encounter the untamed beast. And yet how brazen the creature was. Deer ate the bark off the trees, destroyed the blueberry bushes that she had so carefully netted against the birds, trampled the garden, caused fatal crashes on the highway. They carried those ticks that gave a person Lyme disease. Sam was thinking of putting up a deerproof fence around the gardens, a hideous, thick contraption costing thousands of dollars. Their neighbors had one. It spoiled the landscape, made one think of the state prison. Sam had spent unimaginable amounts of money on trees and flowers and rills and ponds, bushes and fruit trees. Landscape architects. Gardeners. And these animals trod mindlessly upon it all, leaving turds for people to step in. Always these irreconcilables, this push-pull, and the beauty of the deer against the damage they wrought.

Groping toward serenity once more, she reflected on her own common sense, her inner core, her quest for well-founded information. How to protect oneself against the natural world, against the course of things. Against Lyme ticks, for example. She always tucked her trouser legs into her boots and sprayed her clothing and checked her body afterward for the red aureola the nymphs were said to leave on your body. Imagine calling a bug a nymph! She had never found any such aureola. Attention to one's body was made up largely of routines now, routines to ward off morbidity and mortality—calcium supplements, vitamin capsules, sun block, DEET, the daily dose of baby aspirin, and the weekly bone-building pill—practices that had replaced her meticulous housekeeping (no longer necessary; she had servants) and the beautifying and grooming she had indulged in as a younger woman. Not that she had given up grooming, just that there was less point to it.

Well, she didn't mind. Nor did she mourn her life as mother of the household; though she did miss the children, was saddened in a secret corner of her heart by what they had become. Even her son, the eye surgeon, so rich. Who would not want such a profession for a son? And yet . . . the other day she had found Stephen's baby pictures in an album: there he was, two years old, burbling in his high chair, his little face needing a good wipe. She did not know who he was. It could have been somebody else's baby. In another person's album, would she have recognized him? That baby was gone, as surely as if he had been kidnapped. Like the Lindbergh baby, purloined from his crib. Time kidnapped your babies, transported them across state lines.

Raising three children had turned her into the quartermaster of a marching army: selecting, acquiring, storing, distributing, sorting, cleaning, refurbishing, and disposing of truckloads of clothing, furniture, toys, school shoes, books, hi-fi components, cosmetics, guitars, pianos and piano teachers, contact lenses, braces and retainers, birthday gifts, Christmas and Chanukah gifts, graduation gifts, wrapping paper, ribbon, suitable cards, luggage, eventually good jewelry and automobiles. All of it gone, mostly, along with the children, as though it had never existed. A lot of old, cast-off American stuff ended up in rural African markets where people thought that it had come from the dead, because the living would never discard such valuable things. The stuff from her family alone would supply many villages. Sam found her unsatisfactory, she knew, because she had never cared about politics or bothered to read the paper. But she had been a very good citizen, she reasoned, the tireless supervisor of so much consumption. The acquirer of goods. The donor to charity. She had kept the machine humming, boosted the Consumer Confidence Rating. How she had hated those feminists, who saw women like her as oppressed. They should be so oppressed!

But now she was merely among the fallen. Not certain she could rise. She must be serene. Put negativity behind her. She was not old. She was still beautiful. Her white hair was a cloud of curls around her face. Wrinkles, yes. Brown spots all over. But she was sleek and shapely still, a prime example of what they called, these days, successful aging, in spite of having been diagnosed with prehypertension and something called osteopenia, the prelude to dreaded osteoporosis. What ugly, frightening names they came up with, all these modern doctors. "Studies show etcetera" and then drug companies invented expensive medications to match the name. She had good legs, as always. She was never going to collapse into a bag of bones. In a slim black dress, high heels, and her mother's diamonds, she could hold her own. Ah, the family diamonds. Her French grandparents had arrived on these shores with their entire wealth, their family status, compressed into shining stones that could be measured in carats and carried across the ocean in a small case. They were her diamonds now. To which of her children would she bequeath them? Radical Anna wanted them, and pious Rachel, and wealthy Stephen would give them to his wife. They were more valuable than longevity genes. And the thought of them, wrapped in velvet, shut up in the safe deposit box at the bank, was restorative and bracing. Never mind the Dalai Lama.

She came fully back to herself, a sensible woman in hiking boots and jeans, a little confused, to be sure, solemnly assuring herself that she was youthful and glamorous still. Well, silliness was usually what got you through a crisis. She stood up. Perhaps, had she touched the deer's flank, she'd have caught the glint of gold brocade under the pelt. A prince in disguise. She smiled. No, only a vector for ticks and bacteria. A pest, but an enormous one with four hooves. She had no desire to finish her walk.

Five minutes later she was back at the house, settled on the wide verandah. Her left knee ached. Out of kilter. Tears filled her eyes. Why was she so alone? Sam was upstairs asleep; in some sense, he was never here. The day was warm, the leaves still green. Summer lingered like a houseguest after Labor Day, and a certain melancholy settled in on her—another year was inexorably beginning. And how many years were left? Painful to begin counting in fives and tens, rather than scores. Painful to realize that adding fifteen to your age got you a number you didn't want to get to. One day she might be counting in months. The change of seasons brought up the unpleasant question of how many more you could expect to see.

Masses of white petunias tumbled out of the flower beds around the porch. Mist rose from the ponds, one north of the house, on the hill, the other south of it, down the embankment, below the giant oak, its contours edged with lily fronds and iris spikes, the leftovers of a long and generous summer. The wide meadow beyond the pond stretched out of view. Her husband, who had created this artful landscape, or caused it to be created to his specifications, favored white, silvery, and purple flora, fuzzy lamb's ears, tall grasses, white roses or the blood-dark varieties. Something was always in flower. And in wintertime you had the berries, the evergreens, and the mysterious orange and burgundy hues of bare branches. He had seen to it all, an artist really, Sam was.

Sam had not created the mountains, but they formed a perfect setting for his landscape. They rippled gray and green, far away in the morning light; here on the earth, the rolls of new-cut hay in the meadow were the emblem of neatness, readiness, of duties performed in a timely fashion. The laid-stone walls that enclosed their property and ran like vasculature through their gardens reminded her, pleasantly, that she and Sam had provided a livelihood for local artisans who otherwise might have given up on rural life and be squatting in some slum in Binghamton or Albany. The flamboyant wealth of New York City bubbled up here like groundwater, irrigating the parched counties of rural New York, turning farmers into servants, causing four-star restaurants with wine cellars to spring up and the bed-and-breakfast trade to flourish. You couldn't eat a meal out anymore without reserving in advance. There were already hairdressers who charged $100 per cut, and Edith was the favorite customer of one of them.

Nothing like this had accrued to any of her relations, least of all to Vivienne and Adrienne, her twin cousins who were arriving this afternoon for a long visit (they knew no other kind), two dotty old maids, still struggling along in their parents' ancestral, dilapidated, rent-controlled apartment in Windsor Terrace, Brooklyn, whereas she might just as well be dubbed Lady Mendel. Who could have imagined she would rise to such heights, live such a life? Wife to a Major Publisher who was a member of the Century Club? Whose picture had appeared in the paper with Don DeLillo and his famous, formidable literary agent? Whose authors, over the years, had won Pulitzers and National Book Awards and the Nobel? Faulkner, of course, who when Sam was a junior editor used to stretch out on the reception-room sofa with a bottle of bourbon—it was one of Sam's standard stories. Author stories, told again and again over dinner tables. Sam was a fine performer. He really ought to write his memoirs. What would he say of her: "My lovely wife, a perfect mate, a zealous and protective mother, but at the dinner tables of my life, in the cocktail parties of my mind, Edith could hardly think of anything to say." He himself was quoted in *Paris Review* and *Le Monde,* but his partner in life was inarticulate, or at least cowed in the presence of all those so-called intellectuals at the center of Sam's life.

She went into the kitchen, all ceramic tile and Corian countertops, the sweep and gleam of stainless steel, a double built-in refrigerator and freezer, a restaurant-size espresso machine, the eight-burner cooktop. And it all fit together; drawers opened and closed soundlessly. Sam didn't skimp on kitchens. Or anything else. If any piece of equipment was missing, Edith could not think what it would be. It was almost eight o'clock. Surely Sam would be up soon. There was the matter of the swimming pool to discuss. The roof. The barn restorations. And the, well, party next June. Edith had had no idea things would go as far as they threatened to go. Much to talk about. Much not to be mentioned.

She must find that copy of the *Times*—there had been a nice dinner menu, with herbed lamb chops, chopped kale, and blue-berry cobbler. Some sort of cold soup to begin. Avocado? The perfect combination of fancy-dancy and down-to-earth that everybody liked, unsimple simplicity. Local ingredients, and enough property whereon to grow one's own herbs. Thursday's paper, had it been? She always did something special for Viv and Adri, poor loves, always torturing themselves with macrobiotic or diet-for-your-blood-type or low fat or high fat or entering the Zone. A wonder they were still alive. They dressed alike and were given to daisy-chain utterances:

"Did you know" (Vivienne) "that electric blankets . . ."

"Cause leukemia?" (Adrienne) "And maybe electric clocks do, too. They depress the, the uh . . ."

"Immune system."

"We read it in *Newsweek*. I put the electric clock on the other side of the room. We bought down comforters."

"Decommissioned our electric toothbrush. A hundred and fifty dollars wasted."

They debated whether one could dare eat peanut butter. "It has . . ." (Adri) "Aflatoxin." (Viv)

Edith made a double decaf espresso, foamed a pitcher of milk. Sipped. So calming. Mug in hand, she walked the long corridor from kitchen to living room, her beloved room with the sofas all done in floral chintz, the Persian carpet, the eighteenth-century Chinese silk paintings (cranes, chrysanthemums) she had found at an auction. It was her particular selection—Sam let her have her way with room décor. She had studied *Architectural Digest* for months. This room she could call her own. They seldom used it, except when large groups came, but Edith often sat there, relishing her taste.

A few newspapers were neatly stacked on the vast coffee table, but Thursday's was not among them. She went down the long corridor again, to his library and office at the back of the house. His den, all leathery and English clubby, lined with books, and a new computer open on the cherrywood table. Ah, the Thursday paper was right there on his desk. Well, yes. The very section . . . And maybe there was time for . . . He'd be up soon—but she heard no sound of him upstairs. Not a footfall. Not a flush. No shower running. She went to the foot of the stairs. Listened. Silence. He was still asleep. Once, when she was ten, she had found the key to a box her father kept hidden in the back of the hall closet. Wielding a small flashlight, she had shut the door behind her, opened the box in the dark, and found letters, six or seven of them. From a woman . . . Ah, it had turned out to be her mother! How very banal, how disappointing! And she felt the same childish guilt, terror, and certainty that she was wrong about Sam, as she had been wrong about her father.

She switched on his computer. Suspicious wives once checked suit lapels for hairs; now it was done with keyboard and mouse. She hated computers, refused to do e-mail. But she could find her way around in his private cyberspaces; she wasn't as clueless as he thought. A few months ago she had asked him for a computer lesson, which had come to naught, of course, as she grew increasingly ham-fingered and confused, but she discovered his password, which he had carefully noted on the inside page of an instruction book. Intimacy had come to this—a password.

She and Sam hadn't slept in the same bed, or room, these thirty years. Their sexuality, their lovemaking, energetic enough to engender three children, had faded and died. She hadn't minded when they began to sleep in separate beds. It was her choice, when during a bout of flu she had moved to her own room and had never gone back. He had always been kind, considerate, patient in lovemaking. He also sweated a lot. It had been like sleeping with an elephant, all those years. A restless elephant that thrashed about. That got up at odd hours. Three children were sufficient. She disliked gooey diaphragms and was afraid of the Pill. And then soon after she took up separate quarters, she was past all that, into a new, less complicated phase of life where her body was her own and need not be shared with anyone, apart from the affectionate kiss, the asexual embrace. She relished the cool sheets where nobody slept but her, the option of falling asleep immediately on lying down or reading until three, and Sam not making leading remarks or putting his hand on her thigh.

He had said nothing at the time—had hardly noticed. Perhaps it had hurt her a bit, though she could scarcely recall so much as a twinge, when he raised no objection to her sleeping alone, in another room. It was normal, to her, that a couple their age with three grown children would give up sex. But had he truly given it up? There was something about him these days, some black discontent, impatience with everything pertaining to his home. Like a caged adolescent. On a previous intelligence mission, Edith had noticed one odd address in his e-mail, a woman's name: Antonia77@earthlink.net. Of course, it could have been anything. Spam. A college classmate. A long-lost relation working on the family genealogy. An ad for penis enlargement, a stock tip; plenty of that going around. Edith clicked on the e-mail. And yes, there it was on the screen like a radioactive particle. A list of Antonias in the "sent" mail. Why did it matter? Well, his age. The property. The mess it could make. Her self-respect. His self-respect. And also, to her surprise, a stitch in her side. Wounded pride? Fury? The terror of discovering a Lyme tick? She had everything she could possibly want—why this stab of anguish?

She pressed the key. Dangerous. One's fingerprints went indelibly onto these electronic things. At least if you steamed a letter open, you could seal it up again. Six messages. Another from Stephen, their son, the eye surgeon in Dallas. Two from Alison, his daughter, the bride-to-be, oh, another stab of grief. Why did they always want to chat with Sam? Never with her. Despite all she had done for them, they found her wanting. Yes, her children, and especially Stephen, thought her boring. And it was true that she could hardly think of anything to say to any of them, especially now. It was as if they were supercilious strangers at one of Sam's publishing luncheons.

Ah, there it was, coming right in. In bold type right there on the screen. Subject: Tomorrow. Antonia77@earthlink.net. If she opened it, she would have to destroy it. He might know. But she clicked on the tiny box.

"Let me know if you'll be here for dinner. In or out? What would you like?" Dinner! Perhaps Antonia, too, was searching her living room for the herbed lamb chops recipe. Yes, no doubt. A brief electronic note, but it told the story as much as a shower of four-letter words. No, what story? It could be innocent. Sam had a lot of friends on committees, people who judged novels for prizes, that sort of thing.

Edith closed and deleted it. Then she noticed that Sam had left his cell phone beside the computer. Such an innocent old darling he was! She turned it on. Outgoing calls, a 212 number, no identifying name! She thought of pressing redial, to see if Antonia would answer, but then Sam might know. These treacherous little gadgets kept track of everything. There was no privacy, as many erring stockbrokers had recently discovered in court. Oh, she didn't want to deal with this, any more than with Alison's party.

Once again she went to the foot of the stairs and listened. Nothing. She fished around on the computer and found a folder labeled "Photos, England." It took time to figure out how to get into it, and she grew impatient. But finally she pressed the right keys, and a man in a vivid blue shirt filled the screen. A woman in a soft gray jacket, or was it a bathrobe? Roses, in a charming little basket, had been set on the table (they appeared to have been cut from some nearby garden), a silver coffee pot, cups, glasses, sunlight, a plate with bread and butter and jam. Who had taken the photo? Or had Sam set the camera on automatic?

He was laughing. A handsome man, a stranger. Sam. She had once thought of him as handsome, now she did not think of his features—or his body—at all. But this was a man with a body. Again, that sharp stitch in her side, and a sensation further down that reminded her what arousal had felt like, so long ago. And the woman—was it indeed Antonia?—was, if not beautiful, at least not bad-looking. Not a bimbo. That was something! An old lady, like herself. But that made it worse! Her hair was white, in one of those straight cuts that slanted over the ears. Not a beautiful face, nothing to compare with Edith. Damn him, he must have taken this woman to London when he went for that international conference of publishers. Antonia! And there they sat, in flagrante, roses, morning coffee, bread and jam in a hideaway. But maybe not, maybe not. Maybe it was not Antonia. Maybe it was only a secretary, an editor in some distinguished London publishing house. Yes, they'd been talking about a deal, or that prize that publishers set such store by. The Brookner, was it? Something like that. She had never read a single book that had won the Brookner prize. Who was that woman?

Edith heard a door close upstairs. She chose Quit. She chose Shut Down. She fumbled, thought for one horrid moment she had screwed the thing up, that it would freeze up as it sometimes did and never shut down. Oh, God, how long it took to black out! Beastly, self-willed, unforgiving thing! And she was sure that she heard a toilet flushing upstairs, footsteps. Her knee delivered a stab of red pain, the objective correlative for jealousy, rage. Summoning her iron will, she reprogrammed her inner self for serenity. She groped uneasily for the Dalai Lama. Where had he gone? Ah, the calm feelings reasserted themselves. That was the third or fourth time that morning she had lost her grasp on serenity, and it wasn't even nine o'clock.

4   Sam

H E AWOKE FROM brilliantly colored dreams and
the throb of a subsiding erection. Sleep was a creature fleeing through the leaves, Daphne evading Apollo or, more
likely, an incubus arriving at midnight and abruptly departing
at 2 a.m., a fiend that abandoned him, red-eyed and exhausted,
with a calf cramp to massage into submission. Ehh, he would
moan, leaning against the wall, twisting his toes upward, striving to quell the pain. Fully awake, he would open his book or
watch TV, debate whether it was too late to take a sleeping pill
(yes), or if a glass of warm milk didn't work (and why should it?),
he would have a shot of Scotch (Yes. No. Yes. What difference
could it make? How could he feel any worse?). By three o'clock,
his legs would be aching under the sheets, his thighs and calves
demonically twitching, as if they meant to abandon his torso
and run around the room by themselves. O Lord, you made the
night too long. And then, miraculously, emerging from her cave,
the goddess would descend and enfold him in her arms, give him
glorious, restful dreams that lasted until eight or nine. As had

happened this morning, and he was confused, and groped help-
lessly for the dream that had fled his field of vision.

He had been in England, the house in the Kentish hamlet
tucked so far back from the road that he and Antonia had been
hard put to find it the first day, after a perilous drive on the
wrong side of the road following traffic circles where your in-
stincts sent you in the wrong direction. Once off the highway,
they had gone up wrong lanes, had been forced to tangle with
surly householders and their suspicious dogs. In the dream he had
been asleep in that house, beside Antonia in that lumpy English
bed—did they never learn what comfort was, confound them,
the damned Brits?—dreaming another kind of dream in which
an enormous cat stood vigil at their bedside. He had leaped from
bed. The cat had stared at him. Not a menacing look, more like
a Cheshire cat. And what else? Oh yes, the next moment they
were at table, in the garden, eating pickled herring and ripe tomato and bread in the sunshine. The cat, of course, had been a
figment, but Antonia, the bed, the pickled herring, had all been
deliciously real last June. Awake but drowsy, he groped for his
compass points. He lay in bed alone, under an entirely different
down-filled comforter, on this side of the Atlantic in another
landscape, in another house inhabited by another woman.

This house and the woman whose name was on the deed,
along with his, were the central narrative of his life. He got out
of bed, naked (lately he had begun sleeping naked), and started
toward the toilet, fast. That terrible urgency, and then the slow,
sluggish drops. Goddamn, why were old men tortured with this
problem? It was worse than cataracts and thinning hair. Something wrong with your waterworks, a veritable indignity. At
length the last reluctant drop fell (there was always more of it
in the morning), and he washed his hands and splashed his face

with cold water. A fastidious man, careful about his person. He found his bathrobe on a hook behind the door, wrapped himself in it, and opened the window. On the surface of his lovely pond, out in the south garden, white lotuses lay like satin cutouts anchored by their ropey green stems.

Ah, this house, this island. Some people wrote poems and novels, biographies and memoirs. Some people created houses. A far humbler task, he truly believed, but here were gardens, beauty. Peace and grace on a September morning. The *New York Times* had begged for years to do a feature on it. *House & Garden* had proposed a photo essay, and a high-placed acquaintance of his at Condé Nast had tried to put the arm on him after he told the editor-in-chief no. The editor of *Elle Decor* had pleaded with him, but he had refused. Had not even answered the phone message from *Architectural Digest*. Never. No publicity. No tourists traipsing through, no drivers slowing down to gawk from the road. A hundred years from now, his descendants would remember who had built this house, laid out these magnificent gardens. Provided the immediate heirs didn't kill each other in their rage to acquire it.

He looked for his bathing suit. Wouldn't do to just saunter off to the pool in his bathrobe and swim naked. Edith hated that. Used to do it before they had so many workmen wandering about. The stonemason was here full time. Mustn't shock the stonemason, God knew where they would find another. Edith would be waiting for him below. The barn repairs. The commitment ceremony. Their amazing granddaughter, Alison, and her lover, Candace. Alison wanted to have the wedding in June because of the flowers—wild mountain laurel from the woods, banks of white rhododendron around the house, roses and lilies and irises, phlox and petunias. A hundred and fifty guests, and a caterer coming from New York. Next spring, engraved invitations would be in the mail, dear God, to all the family. It made him grin. No matter what Edith thought.

He found his swimsuit at last, on the floor, and pulled it on under his bathrobe. A swim. He would swim. The next best thing to sleep—fifty laps in his pool. Maybe he could dodge past Edith. But when he got to the top of the staircase, there she stood at the bottom, smiling her constant-wife smile. Only a churl, a person with no decency, could quarrel with a woman who smiled that way. The dutiful companion of his days, if not his nights. She had been studying a newspaper page, which she held in her hand, as if she had just lifted her eyes. Why did he think she had come from his office, where, possibly, she had been looking into his computer? But Edith the Luddite had no idea how to turn on a computer. She disapproved of e-mail. He paused to observe her, not without deep affection: in the last decade she had turned pink and silver. The curly cloche of white hair was meticulously cut and cared for. Her skin was mother-of-pearl-ish, with only a hint of fragility and collapse around the mouth, those little powder-caked wrinkles radiating from the lips. She wore pink lipstick, just enough makeup. Even in jeans and a white cotton shirt, she looked well dressed. Marry for looks and that's what you get: Mrs. America. He had always been too busy or too bored or too frightened or too honorable or too stupid or too hidebound or too distracted to wonder if they were happy together, well matched. Or if she were happy. Or he. He had upon occasion longed for a divorce. But he had been faithful all these years. Until now.

Ah, yes. You marry. Then it's children, schools, mortgages, taxes, hard work, and you feel you've got a successful marriage on days when you're speaking to each other. No time or energy

to ask why you haven't had sex with your wife for a year, and
then five years and then ten. You are a pair. Widely admired
as a successful couple. And then the children grow up and you
retire, and most of what kept you so frenetically busy for forty
years vanishes like the melting of ice and you are facing the
end of your life with a woman you never loved, and you hardly
know what love is. You hardly know who she is. But you cannot
leave her, because that would be dishonorable, folly, and have
you not enjoyed enough of life's gifts already? Must you ask for
love as well? He supposed that she was about to tell him that (a)
Vivienne and Adrienne were coming for a week or month or
maybe the rest of their lives and (b) mama don't 'low no commitment ceremonies 'round here. The usual game, and one of them
would be checkmated. She knew nothing of politics but was a
politician all the same. He returned her smile.

He felt her taking his measure, some odd sparkle in her eyes,
now that the smile had faded. An old man—you could not mistake him for fifty. Or even sixty. His skin bunched up and wrinkled around his knees like the muzzle of a bulldog. And his hair
was white, what there was of it. But he was fine, sturdy, straight,
not doddery. Not wobbly. Alive. She surely must know how alive
he felt. Could she have any idea that he was in love with another
woman, was, at his age, making love to another woman? No, she
would think it preposterous, impossible.

"Good morning, dear. Shall I make you some coffee?"

"Well, later, perhaps. I was counting on a little swim."

"Of course, darling. No hurry. But there is such a lot to discuss." After a long second's hesitation—but who could refuse
this silvery lady?—and although his swimsuit was scratchy and
creeping up into his crotch, he followed her into the kitchen, like

a dog lured by a biscuit. A puppy caught soiling the carpet. She seemed to limp slightly. Had she hurt herself? His jauntiness receded. Had she somehow guessed his secret? She probably wasn't as inept about his computer as she pretended to be. His whole life was in there, in that machine. Maybe she did know. Naughty puppy.

5 Candace

A T SIX THIRTY Alison Mendel had arisen, knocked a hairbrush off the night table as she reset the alarm for her bed partner, also life partner, banged around the kitchen and the shower, dressed herself in jeans and a jacket after a long search, and at seven let herself out the door. Candace Johnson had only pretended to sleep during this rattling about. Cradled by solitude and silence, warmed by the morning light behind the hand-embroidered bedroom curtains, she curled up and slept again. Around nine, just before the alarm went off, she sat up panic-stricken in the tumble of hemstitched linens and pouffy pillows. Alison wanted bed linens to look rich, and theirs had cost a lot and, in addition, had to be washed by hand and ironed, to the tune of $150 a month. Plus delivery. Well, that's what you got when you teamed up with the daughter of a rich doctor from Dallas. Fripperies. Luxuries. Big bills. Yet Alison Mendel was not some dope.

This morning Candace meant to disentangle her black ass from all this incipient laundry and finish a brief. She had taken the case of a man from the Dominican Republic about to be deported by the INS after being detained for six months in a holding tank. He was desperate to remain—his wife was here. The case seemed clear enough to Candace: family values. How could they refuse? This was Saturday work. She did her share of it. Six days a week you worked for the Man, and on the seventh you fought him. Six days for the Golden Calf, one for the Good Lord. Things might work out better in these pro bono cases if she and the Lord exerted themselves a little more.

Tying her bathrobe, she sank to the bed again, assailed by something like nausea. Her ailment, her secret, the thing that stalked her, often when she was at her happiest, her most secure. A weird sense of not belonging, seasoned by paranoia, a sudden onset of uncertainty as to where or even who she was. Anger. Take it a step further and it would be panic disorder. She was in control of it now, but the attacks had nearly caused her to flunk out in her senior year at Smith, had caused her to stay in bed when she should have been in class, had clotted her mind so that she could not tell one book from another in the library, and then it vanished, only to come on once more just before she and David had agreed to divorce. Well, anybody would have attacks, going through a divorce, especially when you loved the man but loved a woman better.

She had thought that Alison would be the end of panic, Alison, her stable lifetime choice and the love that she believed defined her. She had come out. Taken a stand, had emerged from the wilderness of bisexuality, the confusion of it, the duplicity, had forsworn males forever. But her mother, Mary, in Chicago, had been heartbroken. (Mary had hardly been thrilled when Candace married David, a white man, but at least it was a man.) Upon learning that his daughter had declared herself queer, Candace's father had said, "After all that you've come through. All we've done. All I've spent." Papa was an African, a Ghanaian, not a so-called African American like her mom. Africans were weirder about homosexuality than Americans were. They thought you should be crucified for it, for starters, whereas Mary took it as self-indulgence, stupidity, a poor choice for an ambitious black woman lawyer, and an insult to the civil rights movement. Another version of "after all we've done." Candace's father had never bothered to marry her mother—Candace was illegitimate, the old legal term, but the irony escaped them. They could do as they pleased but not she.

To hell with them. She already made more per annum than her father, and he was an actual diplomat with the striped pants and the parking places. She had earned all this luxury, dollar by dollar, and got past the co-op board, too. She'd be here even without Alison's dough and social position. This two-bedroom co-op overlooking the Hudson was hers because the board was scared to turn her down. She was smart and aggressive and worked forty-eight-hour stretches with no sleep and made partner when she was only thirty-two and was glad to be the token black lawyer and the token black lesbian. Two for the price of one. The token anything. Did they require a Buddhist? She would become a Buddhist. A black lesbian Buddhist. She was a feared litigator. She loved Alison Mendel. Was loved in return. So what if Alison was a rich brat? Mama—how would she handle this commitment ceremony? Mama didn't believe in that. Granny Mendel didn't either, oh boy, did she ever not believe in it. And now this crap from Alison about wedding gowns. A white dress with seed pearls. A joke, an act of deconstruction. Perhaps Candace should hold on to that idea, should position the whole thing as camp, irony. But for Alison it was also a fluffy, expensive bride-doll gown, a little American girl's dream. And, Candace had begun to suspect, an expression of anxiety.

"If all my friends spend ten thousand dollars on a white gown, why can't I?" Alison said. "Is this a real marriage or what? We have to wear jeans and sweaters because we're lesbians? Fuck that." Maybe it was Alison's way of apologizing to her family for not marrying a man. Anyhow, Candace did not want to wear a white gown. She had married David in a tailored suit; why not another business suit? "No, no," Alison said, "we're both women, we'll both dress like women. I don't want any of that butch crap. We're not like that. This is pure." And so Candace had promised to meet her later this afternoon at the bridal shop in Lord & Taylor. It felt like an appointment with the endodontist. "To realize one's own nature perfectly . . . that is what each of us is here for," Oscar Wilde had written. But what if the woman who opened the door to your own perfect nature wished to dress you like a Barbie doll? Well, Bosie, too, had been silly and flamboyant, but Oscar loved him.

Paralyzed at the bathroom mirror, Candace wondered why it was so important to pretend to get married. They could not have a license or a minister or any sort of legal joining. Maybe some sort of contract. Why should two women get married, even if it were perfectly legal, which it wasn't. Lesbians and gays should exist as outsiders, as exemplars of Other Ways. Marriage—a pathetic handcuff, joining two people together so that property could be passed on and children, if any, named and protected. She and Alison wouldn't even get a tax break. Half of all marriages ended in divorce, and thank God for that; otherwise the legal profession would be a lot smaller. Alison felt it was her right, because if straight people could achieve respectability, lesbians should, too. Really, Uncle Greg and Uncle Arty might be right:

lay low and don't make waves. But that was not Alison's way, or really even Candace's way. Candace was, by the nature of her profession, concerned with justice. So let it be done! And if 'twere done, why not lavishly?

Thus on to the bridal shop at Lord & Taylor. And if that did not produce the desired result, they were to visit that shop in Brooklyn where all the brides went—pawing and clawing one another to get at the designer gowns, standing in front of triple mirrors while the saleswoman pinned up the excess cloth in the back so that you could no longer breathe, or promised that the seams could be let out, in the event that already you weren't able to breathe. And Mama wrote out a check, nonrefundable, for twenty thousand dollars.

Candace washed her face and patted her gorgeous head, twisted Rastafarian curls piled upon curls, expensive blonde streaks following the twists. Maybe she should have her hair cut. Buzzed off. Her ex-husband, the old darling, had compared her to that luscious ivory mask from Benin, had been proud she was not some café-au-lait creature with white bone structure. Like Whitney Houston. Candace had her pop's face, the face of a chieftain. There he was, in her. Her face was her fortune. If she'd been a white kid instead of an out-of-wedlock black with a 4.0 GPA, her scholarships to Smith and NYU law would never have been so generous. Pop, the U.N. delegate, paid the rest. For her graduation present, he had taken her to Ghana for two weeks, shown her off in their village, where he owned the biggest hut, had dressed her in a caftan. They had sung the traditional songs, staged a three-day feast in her honor, and slaughtered a sheep. Now he said he was sorry he had ever helped her. Now, he said, he would never again take her home. She was dead to him. No cliché had ever been too tired for him to utter.

At Smith coming out had been easy. The love that dared not

speak its name in Oshkosh or Oklahoma City yakked day and night about it in Northampton, Massachusetts. At Smith you studied Queer Theory. You acquired the intellectual tools to disembowel any literary or political idea that proposed to shut you out or had ever shut anybody out. You busied yourself proving how wrong history had been written. Your critical apparatus had the power of a nuclear weapon. You summoned Wordsworth and T. S. Eliot and Camus before the bar of justice, exposing them as cryptoracists or fascists, the cringing tools of capitalism and racism. You skewered Jane Austen as the creature of British imperialism. You quoted Foucault and Derrida. You proved without a scintilla of hard evidence that Willa Cather had been a cigar-chomping Sapphic, bedding down the minor poetesses of American lit. You marched. You put up banners on campus. If somebody tore your banner down, you called it a hate crime.

Smith had been the world turned upside down: you got extra points for being black, and extra extra points for being lesbian, the unflagging solicitude of your profs and counselors, the certainty of grade inflation if you even half tried, fervent letters of recommendation when you graduated, strings proudly pulled on your behalf. Weirdly, though, the place was always packed with rich white girls who asked you, wonderingly, if they could touch your hair. Touch your hair! In those days she'd had a real Afro, and they wanted to pat it. Oh, can I feel it? It looks so wonderful! I want to run through it barefoot! What am I, she had answered, a sheep in a petting zoo? She had told them that what she truly craved was to make a lot of money on Wall Street, the way their dads had done. They loudly trashed what they called "the system," though they intended to marry some blond god from Princeton, get their M.A. at the School of Public Policy at Harvard, and rule the world, as usual. Maybe she, Candace Johnson, could do that, too.

In the kitchen she made lapsang souchong (the very fragrance anchored her) and checked her e-mail. Work stuff, looked like about fifty items. She'd just ignore that until this brief was further along. But what was this, a message from Tracey, who was teaching school in California. "Just checking in, think of you sometimes living your high-powered life, hope all is well." They had had breakfast together in April when Candace had been in the Bay Area, deposing a witness in San Jose for a stock fraud action. Such a fragile little soul Tracey, and the dorm room had been a rather romantic setting for their love affair. It happened in the spring, as love should happen; sitting with her first love on the hillside above Paradise Pond, a famous spot for lovers, she and Tracey, *jeunes filles en fleur* among the forsythia bushes, the trees bursting into leaf, the grass turning to velvet, the daffodils and hyacinths springing up in the carefully planned campus gardens. Candace knew it was all momentary, but Tracey fell hard, talked of a permanent partnership, of finding an apartment in the West Village, close to dear Arty and Greg. Happily ever after.

Candace knew better. Queer theory was fine in the academy. But if you wanted to get ahead, you had to make choices. Anyway, Greenwich Village was now as conventional as Scarsdale. Greg and his partner voted Republican and prayed at the Church of the Celestial Redeemer, a sanctuary that reeked of propriety. She broke off with Tracey, smoked a lot of pot, got depressed, and fell into the disorder that threatened her grade-point average. When she failed a midterm test, her econ prof suggested that she seek counseling. She sought it, got better, graduated summa. But she could never resolve the push-pull—her yearning for a woman and, sometimes, for a man, and her fear of ostracism or second-rung positions in the legal profession. She had dreamed of running for office. Maybe high office. Lesbians did not win elections; one or two might sneak into the cabinet, under a guy like Clinton. She also despised the slotting, the stereotyping, the lesbian bars, and the dykes. The assumptions people made if you were black along with it. She didn't want her sexuality to bar her from life's gold medals and rewards, which she felt very capable of laying her hands on. Why let your inclinations marginalize you? If you got elected senator, you might do some good for people like your mother. And here she was about to commit in a white bridal gown and probably get her picture in the *New York Times*. Well, if she ever ran for the senate nobody would have to hire a detective to dig it up.

She finished her tea and shot off a quick note to Tracey. She poured bran flakes into a bowl. Ah, here came something from David Ludlow. Not good. All her abandoned loves popping up on the screen. She would ignore David. He should not be e-mailing her. E-mail was like masturbating—an excuse not to work. It was eleven o'clock on a prime September morning, and she had accomplished nothing. She shut down her computer. From her neat and lavishly provisioned walk-in closet, she selected shorts and tee, running shoes, socks, and subjected herself to another fierce inspection in the bathroom mirror. She thought of going to the gym. Her membership charge showed up relentlessly on her credit card bills. Or she would go to the Hudson River park and run toward Chelsea Piers, at 23rd Street. Yes, that. Oh, heavens, the poor Dominican. This evening, this evening. It was a lovely morning. She'd be back in plenty of time to meet Alison at the bridal salon, do the brief, whatever. Lulled by the sunlight on the curtains, the silence, she was tempted to lie down once more amid the exquisite bedclothes, but she found her keys and sunglasses and headed for the elevator. Moments later she sprinted past the doorman, determined to do five miles.

6 Antonia

THE DOORBELL RANG. She pressed the buzzer and waited while the elevator cranked upward, two, three, four, five, six. Maggie emerged in T-shirt and chinos—no beauty, even Antonia knew that, but her hair was lovely, as people always said. She was holding an enormous bunch of roses.

"My darling, how sweet you are, bringing flowers to your mother!" Antonia took the bouquet, then held her daughter's thin body tight, aware of her ribs and hipbones. She oughtn't be spending money on flowers! God, nothing mattered, not even her vote for Ralph Nader, nobody could ever be as close as her daughter. Well, possibly Toni. But Toni belonged to her parents, and Maggie would always belong to Antonia. She would not trade her daughter for a regiment of lovers. Antonia kissed her, patted her brown hair. The dark, implacable hazel eyes came from Antonia's side of the family. There was so little of Fred in Maggie. Maybe she was blind to the genes of Fred. It hadn't been parthenogenesis.

Antonia banished Arty's mums to the hall table, settled the

roses in her Tiffany vase (a wedding gift decades ago, from Fred's boss at the *Times*) and filled it with water. It was much too big for the table, so she set it on the counter. She took the tea from the fridge. "You can have some ice cubes. I went out and bought the pure kind. And I have some tofu salad sandwiches if you're starved."

"No ice, Mom. I like the tea as it is. And I'm not hungry."

It wouldn't do to ask about Mark right off, let alone to launch into the story of her and Sam. Better let all that rest a few minutes. Better to let Maggie rest a few minutes, too. Maggie was angry about her job: the work load, the pressure to deliver, the multiple of her salary that her books had to earn to guarantee the job, let alone a raise, the mediocre quality of the prose that came into her hands. So Antonia started off with the op ed page. Tom Friedman was good for openers. Dear sensible Tom Friedman, who could disagree with him? He was decent. He had the answers. If she or Maggie started a fight about politics, Antonia resolved to be reasonable, flexible. Abortion. Palestine. Money for schools. Universal health care. She could discuss it all without getting pissed.

"Sure. You mean the piece about Bush. He's nothing but a right-winger. Compassionate conservative. Compassionate for CEOs, maybe. He doesn't care about the environment. Did you see what it said further down on the page about *Roe v. Wade*? It's a goner."

How quickly one stepped in mud that turned to quicksand. Maggie thought abortion was murder. Had always thought so. Could not be dissuaded. What about rape? Antonia had asked when this fight started twenty years earlier. If it was murder, then it was murder, no exceptions, Maggie had said. Antonia had told her about coat hangers, the kitchen table in New Jersey where her college roommate had almost bled to death and been rendered permanently sterile. "Why kill a baby? If she'd had the baby she wouldn't have nearly bled to death and ended up sterile." This opinion, from a child of fifteen, produced a slamming of doors and a chill lasting several days. Well, to her credit, perhaps, Maggie had never wavered.

"Yes, we're just one Supreme Court justice away from repeal," Antonia said. "Those bastards have worked for this for years, and they are going to get it. We thought we had it fixed. Guess the Emancipation Proclamation will be up for repeal. Maybe the Bill of Rights. "

Maggie joined right in. "I had to turn down a novel the other day because it was too anti-Catholic. About a lady who belongs to Opus Dei and her kid gets buggered by some priest. Pretty sordid, but it was very well written, moved along like a house afire. I recommended buying. The committee wouldn't touch it. Too inflammatory. Can't tread on the toes of Catholic women, they buy a lot of books. Another demerit for me. I mustn't lose this job. I have to be more careful."

"Maggie. That's . . . that's censorship! Well, the pendulum has certainly, certainly swung. Are you going to tell me how feminism has failed?"

"Oh, not failed. Just left women like me in the middle—a job and no day care. I can walk right in the front door of the Harvard Club. Only I don't make enough to support my family."

"Why blame feminism? What about Mark carrying more of the load? And what if Mark had been fired and you hadn't had a job? Then what?"

"God knows, Mama. God knows. Maybe Mark would have done a little better, I sometimes think, if he didn't have me—and you—to lean on. He doesn't like finance. He never should have gone to business school. He should have been a writer, maybe. He wrote a whole novel in college, you know. It isn't half bad. But what can he do? Half of him wants to be free, and half of him wants to be the steady earner. He dreams about a sports car, about a country house where Toni can play in the grass all summer and swim in her own pool. He says he'll get there one of these days, so long as I have faith in him. So I try to have faith. As long as at least some of his dreams include me and Toni, what can I do?"

"When do you think he might figure out who he is? Maybe a guy his age who hasn't found himself should look a little harder."

"Don't go there. Don't say that. It's mean. I love my husband. I don't care what you think of him. How about some lunch? I am hungry, starving all of a sudden. For God's sake, let's not fight. Sit still, Mama. I'll get the sandwiches. You know how little I care about politics, but I wish I could go on a protest march with you again."

"Once upon a time it did some good to protest. Now by the time you find out about anything, it's too late, they've already done it. When you were only three, we were in Atlantic City, throwing bras in the trash can outside the Miss America pageant. Well, I say 'we' but I never threw mine in. We never burned any bras, you know. We didn't have a permit to start a fire, so we didn't burn anything. Oh, the good old days! But you have to live with what is." In the 1970s Antonia had gone to Washington and the deep South in buses, slept in tents, hollered herself hoarse. Sometimes Maggie had held her hand as they sang. It drove Fred crazy. After shouting as she walked up Pennsylvania Avenue, she came home and shouted. Fred shouted, too. No wonder this child had turned into a strange green conservative.

Maggie laughed and looked at the ceiling. Why did kids always roll their eyes? "You were a good law-abiding little revolutionary. You meant no harm."

"Okay, forgive me. We were right about Miss America, and right about Vietnam. We were right about civil rights, you cannot deny that even if you question all the rest of it."

"Well, all you lefties weren't right about everything. Alger Hiss was a Commie and the Rosenbergs were guilty as sin."

"No they weren't."

"Yes they were, Mama. Don't you read anything? All those papers released from secret files in Russia. They were all on the Soviet payroll. Spies."

"Yes, I read, but I don't believe. Stop rubbing it in. Anyway, what does it matter now? All I do is read real estate ads and think about tax shelters. But never forget: property is theft. That's no joke. It was better to be out marching and at least hoping to set fire to one's bra." She drank her tea, folded and unfolded her napkin.

"And, uh, speaking of women's liberation, I have something to tell you. It's really very happy news." She tried not to sound tentative. "I am involved with a man. I mean, I have a friend, a companion. A lover. It's been going on awhile, and I ought to have told you sooner."

"Could I have more tea?"

"Another sandwich?"

"No. Thanks. Who is he, Mama?"

"You know him. Sam Mendel, my old boss, my old friend. You remember I quit my job at Sam's company when your daddy got so sick. But Sam sort of followed me, us, I mean. He was a big help with Fred. "

"Sam Mendel. How old is Sam, he must be eighty. And is his

wife still around? Edith, right? I remember you talking about Edith and their huge estate somewhere."

"Yes. Edith. He's only seventy-four. Only five years between us, that's nothing, like between you and Mark. Well, maybe it's a lot if you think of . . . well, life expectancy, but I'm not an actuary. He's in very good health right now, if that's what you're wondering. I mean, he has had some problems, sure. That's all anybody can say at my age, or his: that we're okay right now. Carpe diem is what I say. Tomorrow we die. Don't look so astonished. Or displeased. Or whatever it is you look like!"

"Is he going to get a divorce?"

"What a question, darling. Is that your first thought?"

"Well, why shouldn't it be? Otherwise, he's only playing around with you. You're my mother."

"It isn't playing around. You have no idea what you are saying. Or what this means to us. But, no, I doubt he will ever get a divorce. Why is that so important? I don't want his money or his house or his family. He is welcome to all that. I don't want to be Mrs. Mendel. Things are different when you're old. Different rules apply."

"Different rules don't apply. What are you talking about? Why are you so willing to settle for being the other woman? I thought you were a feminist. What kind of feminist are you?"

"A feminist who likes a man in bed with her. Likes to have somebody to eat dinner with. I like being a widow. And also, if you must know, I like sex. I never knew I did, but I do. Don't look embarrassed. It hurts my feelings." Antonia felt crazy, off base. She had had the speech all memorized. Maggie was going to be thrilled. "Anyway, he isn't going to divorce Edith, and that's the way it is. I can accept that."

"Mama, I don't mind if people in their seventies want to have sex. I am not embarrassed. Let's go back a few steps. Tell me more about Sam." She didn't mind if old people had sex, surely not, it just made her shudder. But okay.

"We'd known each other for so long. Remember, I worked in his company for ten years. Nothing ever happened. He is not some predator. I hardly saw him. I was doing publicity, press releases, getting gigs for writers at Barnes and Noble. Planning book tours. Getting novelists on NPR. And sometimes he would come to our business meetings. He often came. And I wondered if it was me that brought him. If he was coming there for me, not because he was interested in writer tours. Sometimes he would ask me to lunch. Which was a little strange. He should have been taking my boss and me to lunch. Which he did do, sometimes. Anyway, I got a crush on him. I guess you could say I fell in love with him. It felt good after all those years."

"Did Daddy know?"

"What was there to know? Fred met Sam at the office parties. I know it sounds like romantic trash, but I have always loved Sam. And he has always loved me. So much between us, so many people in common, the publishing business, almost as if we were relatives. I guess we finally admitted it to ourselves when I left my job. We went out for a drink after work the day I resigned. I had done such fine efficient things for the company that he couldn't lose me, he said, and it was a shame for me to turn into Fred's nurse. It wasn't right. He offered financial help, but I refused. I had to take care of Fred—how could I not?

"So he tried to help. Came to visit . . . spent time with your father, of course. You surely remember how he would sometimes send a car to take us to the doctor. Did errands for me. Sat with Fred, sometimes, so I could get away for a few hours. I was so grateful. And you know, I think Fred liked him. In his more lucid moments, he knew how tough it was. Maybe you didn't notice. Maybe you didn't think so much about it. You were struggling, and Toni was a baby. There was a limit, and Mark. . . . You remember how it was—you did all you could, even with Toni being so small and your job and all. Sometimes when Fred was in the hospital, Sam took me out to dinner. I needed it."

"You began to go out with Sam while Daddy was dying?"

Antonia ate the last ginger cookie. At this rate she'd be overweight. She knew she was beginning to lie. So easy to do, as Bill Clinton had found out.

"No. No, not go out. But I had already fallen in love with Sam before your father died. I couldn't help it. You know your father and I never were an ideal pair. You know, well, you know we hadn't shared a room or a bed for years. Diabetes and heart disease and failing kidneys and his reaction to it all didn't improve matters. He was not an easy invalid. He was demanding, angry. Maybe you didn't see it. I did."

"You seemed like an okay couple to me. You never could be satisfied with anything. That was the problem. You always want to fix things. Nothing is ever good enough as it is. There was nothing wrong with Daddy. I mean until he got sick. Sure he was boring. So what? Were you just waiting for him to die? When did you and Sam get together? How do you manage to see each other now?"

Oh, this was not the conversation she had imagined. How could she tell Maggie the truth? Antonia had started having sex with Sam long before Fred died, and it had begun one night here in the apartment, on the fat, tattered sofa in the living room, when Fred was in the hospital two blocks away. Sam had come home from the hospital with her one evening, had made them drinks: bourbon on the rocks, some rare brand. She had put in an eight-hour day at Fred's side, and she remembered that her hands shook, and the ice tinkled against the glass. Exhaustion, passion, or the onset of palsy? She had not been sure. She remembered the long swallow of whiskey, which went straight to her head, remembered that Sam had moved over close and kissed her. She had never known such kissing, not with any of her boyfriends in college, not Fred, not anybody. She went deeply into his mouth, did not bother to pretend she was reluctant, a married woman with a sick husband. He pulled her sweater up, unsnapped her bra, kissed her breasts. They managed to get halfway out of their clothes. The AARP magazine had a lot of stuff to say about thinning vaginal walls and lack of lubrication, flabby erectile tissue, and the necessity of creams and patience and oral methods and hours of foreplay, and the author of this advice, a well-known geriatrician, had reminded her readers that making love and having sex did not have to be synonymous for the elderly, but this expert from AARP did not know much about two starved people in their seventh and eighth decades who up until that moment had led chaste and proper lives but whose nerve endings and lust turned out to be in perfect working order.

Afterward they went into the bedroom, undressed, and made love again. They turned off the phone—if St. Vincent's Hospital called, too bad—and Antonia kept the lamp on. It was the first time in years she had seen a man naked, or allowed herself to be seen by one. It required a certain courage, almost as if they had never made love with anyone before. How beautiful he was, an old man had no right to be so beautiful. What painter ever caught the beauty of the aging face and body? Some had caught the horror of it, but not the vitality remaining. The objective correlative of life, or maybe death. A man can be very alive in his eighth decade.

And he had found her beautiful, too, and had said the things to her that young men tell young women. She loved his silky smoothness and warmth next to her, loved the noises and movements a bed partner makes, the snuffles and snores and turning. The hogging of the cover. The trips to the toilet in the middle of the night, and the return, both of them chilled and affectionate, applying skin to skin. She came to orgasm easily, intensely; for him it was slower, harder, and more ecstatic, more valuable and meaningful than the easy climaxes, the fast ejaculations, of the young.

Antonia would have liked to tell Maggie some of this, to hint at it, at least. As guidance, as good news: life doesn't end at fifty. As testimony that youth is not the only form of beauty. "Forever wilt thou love and she be fair," John Keats had said at age twenty-three, and he would have said the same at age seventy if tuberculosis had not carried him off. But Maggie's dark eyes were cool, unsmiling, Fred's partisan to the last.

"Look, Maggie my love, we manage to see each other. We enjoy each other. No point in going into the gory details. He's often in the city. We even went to England together. Remember my trip last June? I lied about it, I admit. I told you Sam was sending me to a publishers' meeting hoping I'd come back to work this fall. But it wasn't a business meeting. It was for us. And we didn't attend a single meeting. We stayed at a good hotel in Kensington, and then went out into the country for a week. Pretty heavenly."

"So as far as Edith is concerned, it's all just lying?"

"He's not chained to Edith. She doesn't care what he does. Sam and Edith don't sleep in the same bed, don't listen to the same music. They live different lives. They're there because they're there. Money. Appearances. Real estate. The wills are made. They don't want to scandalize their children. One of them has a grown daughter: Alison Mendel. We even have a family connection there. Her partner, Candace, is Gregory's niece. From Chicago. She calls him Uncle Greg just like you do."

Maggie did not melt at the news. "I have no right to ask this, but does he use Viagra?"

"No. You pull that disapproving face—I'm a dupe, he's an adulterer—and you want to know if the sex is good? Yes, good. You may not credit me with knowing the difference. You know it when you find it, even if you are almost seventy. This is a new world, a newfound land. Maggie, don't be so prudish! I answered your question. If I asked you about sex with Mark, you'd be out-raged. Does Mark use Viagra?"

"Mom, I love you. How can you settle for so little? Lies and sneaking around? What if he walks off?"

"It's not little. It's much. It's all I want. If he walks off, he walks off. I'm not thirty-five. I've done my bit. Anyway, do you want me entangling my finances with his, maybe endangering your inheritance? You'll need that money."

"I don't think of you as my inheritance. But I also don't want some man taking you for granted and giving you little bits of his time and making you his dirty secret. You're selling yourself too cheap. And you're lying."

"Well, Maggie, yes. Yes, I wish he would leave Edith, but not to marry me. I love Sam, and I have him on the terms he is able to offer. Whose happiness is it, anyway? We're not going to hurt anybody. Also, I want you to meet him. He wants to meet you, Toni, Mark. He's going to be around. He'll be here tonight, for example. I hope you can accept that. I don't want any more of your opinions."

Maggie pushed back her chair. "Okay. No more opinions. You look after yourself. It's time I went home. How is Uncle Greg? Wasn't he having a bunch of medical tests?" She opened the terrace doors, and Antonia followed her stiffly onto the balcony. The bucket on a pulley that Arty rigged up years ago so he and Maggie could send messages and books and flowers up and down still hung on its rusty hook by the railing. Maggie and her childhood friends had camped out in Arty's garden, and always, the next morning, after pancakes, Greg would put on his dancing shoes and teach the girls some steps.

This afternoon Greg and Arty were asleep on their double lounge.

"I won't bother them." Maggie said. "Just give them my love. I need to get home. I have to think of dinner. Thanks for the tea. Lunch. And thanks, Mom, for telling me about Sam. Sorry to be so negative. I only want you to be happy. I am a little crazy with the money worries. Hard to be positive about anything."

"I know there's the fall tuition bill from Parkside, honey. I'd love to pay it. I wouldn't miss the money. Maybe it would take some of the pressure off Mark in that interview."

"Mom, I don't know. Thanks. One problem is that I always turn to you, and then Mark gets mad. He says you infantilize us. He says you think he is a bum. I know it's unfair, but maybe it's partly so. Maybe he would get himself together if you weren't always there, wanting to paper things over. He feels we owe everything to you, and it shames him. Okay, we don't have the money for the tuition. But I want to wait until after the interview. If things go well, the school would wait a couple months, till we catch up. You mean well, Mama, but you interfere."

Antonia blinked. Extend your hand, it comes back with bite marks. Infantilize Mark, indeed! He was an infant without any help from her. "And if things don't go well?"

"I don't know what I'll do. A bank loan? No, I'll probably be asking for that check. We're your wards. Probably forever."

Maggie struggled into her backpack, and the two waited for the elevator.

"A hundred kisses and hugs to Toni. Tell her Granny wants to make gingerbread men real soon." Heartfelt as the invitation was, it sounded tired and phony. Oh, Maggie, how will you ever escape from this trap?

Maybe the world wasn't going to right itself. Maybe Bush would not be thrown out of office after one term. Maybe the public schools would simply vanish into hell, and that crowd of neocons would repeal the Voting Rights Act and overturn *Roe v. Wade* and even *Brown v. Board of Ed* and privatize social security, and the stock market would never, never come back.

The pile of books Antonia had meant to give Charley was still on the hall table. He had slipped her mind, as twenty things a day seemed to slip her mind. Maybe he wouldn't have a room tonight, he would sleep on the filthy sidewalk. Or maybe it was not too late. She could give him a little cash, too, and he could still get a room for the night. She put the books in a paper bag and went down into the street, but Charley was nowhere to be found.

7   Sam

Edith fiddled with a stack of envelopes. Bills.
Estimates. For the second time that morning, she
smiled at him, full wattage. Oh, God, forty-five years of this.
They would soon be planning their golden anniversary party.
He did not want to have a party or to have been married for fifty
years. He steamed milk, watched the espresso drip.

"I went walking this morning. Tripped and fell. And then
there was this deer. You'll never believe how threatening."

"Threatening?"

"In the woods. I fell down in the leaves. Turned my foot. All
at once there was this huge deer standing over me with its fierce
antlers. It looked so mean."

"A mean deer? But you're okay, aren't you? No sprains and
scratches?"

"No sprains. I admit my knee hurts a bit but nothing permanent. I thought it might attack me. It almost spoke. It almost said,
'This is my land, get out of here.'"

"But come on, glad you had a soft landing. What's to worry?

Deer are afraid of people. You needed only to clap your hands or yell at it. Tell it to shuffle off to Buffalo. That's probably the next thing we'll see—buffaloes. They sighted a moose down the road last week. Now, those fellows really are mean. If you see a moose, run like hell. Same for a bear."

He felt less like a naughty puppy. The fall had made her vulnerable. The coffee was as syrupy as chocolate under the foamy white, and he savored it like a martini. The caffeine calmed him. He loved caffeine. It should be reclassified as a vitamin. If, as old age overtook him (and he supposed it must), he had to give up breakfast coffee or his wine with dinner, which would it be? Maybe the alcohol. Coffee was country cottages. Antonia across the breakfast table, her shining head. Eyes. Mouth.

"I don't like having so many deer around."

Was that all? Was that a reason to keep him from his swim?

"I'll make a note of it, my love. They kill the trees. They eat the flowers and shrubs. They'll be gnawing my willows soon. I must look further into getting that fence." Would that do, he wondered? What was he supposed to do about her meeting a deer? Maybe he should tell her about the fierce cat in his dream. Maybe the animals of this world were about to avenge themselves on him and Edith. Cats and dogs, deer and raccoons, armadillos and coyotes, marching across his well-tended fields, intent on mayhem.

"Viv and Adri will be here this afternoon. I'm going to meet the bus in Margaretville. It gets in at three. Or could you possibly pick them up? Will you be around for dinner?"

"I'll be gone by early evening, latest. No dinner, thanks. Sure, I'll pick the twins up. Are you getting nervous about driving? Or is it a haircut?"

"No. No haircut. I'll just be busy. I want to make a special dinner for them, for us, if you'll stay. And to tell you the truth, I do dread driving these days. I hate making left turns. I hate parallel parking. And I worry about cyclists. Running over a child in some parking lot. Turning out in front of some eighteen-wheeler on the road. Not to mention the damn deer."

"Well, Edith. Do you want me to hire a driver for you?" He hated the thought, the expense, too. But if she stopped driving, it would seriously hamper him. She'd be a prisoner here. Not even able to go to the grocery store. He'd be a prisoner, too. Surely, Edith did not want him here full time.

"No, no. You have something to do in the city?"

Annoying to be asked, though his cover was impeccable. Awards committees to serve on, luncheons with the old boys, afternoons at the Century Club, swapping musty thrice-told tales as the waiter offered dessert menus. He served on the PEN/Faulkner Awards committee, made a few graceful remarks every year at the National Book Awards ceremony, was a trustee for two minor museums and the Beaux Arts Alliance, whose lectures on Art Deco he occasionally attended. He wondered, sometimes, if he should try to bring Antonia into this part of his life under some pretext. . . . What? Edith had never liked being his social partner, even when the presence of a Mrs. Mendel had been an advantage, but now that he was merely puttering around, she'd dropped out entirely. They had kept their apartment in Gramercy Park, a kind of dusty museum on its own. The Danish modern furnishings purchased forty years ago direct from Copenhagen now qualified as antiques. Edith wanted to sell the place but liked owning a key to the park, the ultimate Manhattan snootiness, though she used it perhaps once a year.

"I do. Yes, I do. A committee meeting tomorrow at breakfast." Sunday morning? she might have asked, but did not. "I'll be back in a couple days. So then Viv and Adri can tell me about every MRI performed in Brooklyn last week. God, what a life they do lead. Cancer and cancer scares and gall bladder surgery and hip replacements. CT scans, blood work. Herbal remedies, homeopathy. When are they getting their M.D.s? Those folks in Windsor Terrace will bankrupt the health insurance system." He had done his share to bankrupt it already. A heart attack, bypass. He had his own medical epics, which he refrained from describing. It only made you sound like an old fart. Who cared? The aches and pains of relatives bored him. Let alone the CT scans of their neighbors. Aging was a police state. You never knew when the goons would knock at the door and carry you off to some torture chamber or other. Why dwell on it?

"They'll be here when I get back next week, and I can hear it all then. They'll save it up for me."

"Well, I know they're a bit monotonous. But Sam, they're so forlorn. So sweet. We owe them."

"I love them. Have I ever been anything but a brother to them? If we owe them, we pay them. For all I care they can come and live here. What are those envelopes? More bad news? We owe everybody."

"I was getting around to that. The pool estimate. Really shocking: twenty-five thousand dollars to reline it, and he wants to start right away before winter sets in. Then there's the barn roof. I don't want to show you the figures. You'll simply screech."

"Let me have the estimates." Like inspecting a snakebite. He supported half the contractors in the goddamn county. "This place eats me alive. If it isn't one thing it's twenty. All I do is pour money into this hilltop. Our children will put it on the market the day after the funeral and then squabble about dividing up the furnishings. Rachel and Philip will somehow get title to it and turn the whole place into a Baptist church camp. Anna will commit bloody arson to keep her brother and sister from sharing in it. I can see it now."

He scowled, muttered just for show, thought of which assets he'd need to liquidate, and in the next breath imagined himself free of this heavy burden. He would turn the whole mess into cash, run away with Antonia. Italy. France. Scotland. Wherever the mood took them. He'd rent houses for them, villas. No computers, cell phones, or e-mail. Start in Sicily, in spring, one of the islands, Lipari, perhaps, eat the fish caught minutes ago in the blue Mediterranean and spring greens so crisp they shivered, tables laden with oily antipasti, Sicilian wines from around Mount Etna, unpretentious and plain and delicious. They would follow the fine weather and the blossoming trees up the boot of Italy, to the Aveyron in the mountains of France, by July, perhaps, *la France profonde,* if there was anything left of it, then a few days in Paris, London, the north country, all the way to Scotland. The Isle of Skye in September, the heather! Shrimp, salmon, lobsters from the North Sea. Single malts! How he would feed her, how they would eat. Far away from this farm in the Catskills that kept him from everything he now wished for! So he said the wrong thing.

"We're putting this place on the market. It's nothing but a ball and chain."

"Well, by all means, Sam, let's get rid of it. I never wanted it in the first place. Your idea, remember? Let's keep our greedy children from inheriting it. You said they were greedy. I can live out my years in that dingy apartment."

She was rolling out the fighter wing. It could get bad fast, but he wanted peace and pretended to take her remark as affectionate teasing. Not too late, perhaps, for diplomacy. A polite communiqué in the morning pouch.

"Well, you're a long way from that. I didn't really mean we

should sell this house. And I don't think they are so greedy. Well, maybe I do. Greed is a normal human emotion. Naturally they have to squabble about the property. We're leaving this big carcass to a tiger and a lion and a cheetah. They will tear it, and each other, apart. You know it's true. Christ, remember last Thanksgiving. . . ."

The meal had begun, agonizingly enough, with Rachel and Philip ostentatiously saying a Christian grace, in which they and their two children were the only participants. His dark-haired, brown-eyed, imminently sensible Rachel a born-again! Magna cum laude at Yale, destined for a post as financial analyst at some important firm such as Proctor & Gamble or Kraft. She had ditched her degree and married a damnable Baptist, and had turned into a housewife and a professed practitioner of what to Sam was the most reactionary, doctrinaire, and anti-Semitic form of Christianity. And now, hoping to bring the backslidden and the heathen to the fold, she prayed over Sam and Edith's poor innocent turkey. Anna, on the other hand, their youngest, who had just divorced her second husband and owed $35,000 on her credit cards, had converted to Orthodox Judaism in matters of diet if not womanly conduct. She insisted on eating off paper plates when she came home, wanted Kosher groceries. Sam always obtained them for her, of course. At least Stephen, their eldest, had remained secular—and why not? A Dallas ophthalmologist clearing a couple of million annually, even after malpractice insurance, by lasering the eyes of rich people eager to do without their eyeglasses, scores of eyes cured of astigmatism, presbyopia, and myopia every single day. Whew!

In the living room over brandy, the fireplace crackling and chestnuts ready to roast and twenty people recovering from turkey and stuffing and proper wines with every course, and the

air still redolent of sage and rosemary, and right in front of Viv
and Adri and a gaggle of other guests and the children and everybody, in this room where Edith had so successfully wedded
good taste to money, the subject of the Mendel estate had come
up, probably in some private conversation between Anna and
Stephen. Sam had been pouring cordials and Courvoisier, and
soft drinks for the children, when Anna said to her brother, in a
tone that silenced the room:

"I'd rather die than see you get this house. I'll pour gasoline
on it and strike a match before I see you here. If Sam and Edith
leave it to all of us, I'll fight you to the last ember."

"Oh, my God. Always the melodrama. Don't kid yourself, I'll
always have the dough to buy you out. And you and Rachel will
have no choice but to sell. I'll hire the toughest lawyer in Dallas.
Maybe I'll sick Candace on you, she's pretty tough!"

"Imperialist pig," Anna shouted. "Ruining people's eyesight
for money. You wouldn't care if they all went blind ten years
from now. You will never have this place."

Rachel intervened.

"What a terrible commotion you're making. Stop, you're up-
setting Mommy and Daddy. This is immoral." For some reason
everybody had exploded in laughter except Edith, who had gone
white. Sam had long ago stopped being a Jew in anything but
surname, and even that was *goyische* now. Casting off religion
had been a joy, like getting rid of his Brooklyn accent and suits
that didn't fit. But the Lord's vengeance had ridden wild-eyed
out of the desert, flapping its cloak: two daughters gone into the
arms of fanaticism!

"Yes, last Thanksgiving. Heartbreaking to hear them go on
like that. But it was just the wine talking. Anna runs her mouth.
Always did. She's a little crazy. They are my darlings. I forgive

them. You never had any patience with them. Not even when you were home."

"Have you any idea why she calls him an imperialist? And sometimes a fascist? Because he's rich and she's broke? Ah, children. Sharper than a serpent's tooth!"

"What do you mean, serpent's tooth? What do serpents have to do with it?"

"Oh, really, Edith. *King Lear* and all that. Shakespeare, Edith. I wonder why they all hate each other. One good thing about selling the house, if we did sell it, we wouldn't have to have that commitment ceremony next June. Wouldn't that tickle you?" Might as well get to the main course. He knew what Edith had on her mind.

"Yes, and the thousands of people trampling the grass, and a battalion of caterers in dinner jackets. I do dread it. But it isn't that. I can put up with all that. Anything else, I'd simply buy a new dress. But I do mind the idea . . ."

"Ah, yes."

"I've tried to go along with this because you and Stephen and Alison seem to want it, and I love Alison so much, but I don't approve of lesbians getting married. Not 'married,' how can one even use the word? Having public 'commitment ceremonies.' How can they? You make a commitment to getting a mortgage or something. You have a partner in a business deal, not a partner in a homosexual household. You have a law partner or a water aerobics partner, or a partner to help you rob banks. You don't have a love partner, for God's sake, especially not one of the same sex as yourself. How can they be so open about it?"

"But, Edith. It's how they are. They have a right. And if they want to make it public, why shouldn't they?" When he had learned for a fact, a decade ago, that Alison was a lesbian, he had been stunned but only momentarily. Edith had demanded psychotherapy all around. "It's not a disease," Sam had explained to her. "What the hell, she's a maverick. Be proud of your granddaughter. A groundbreaker, this girl. A warrior princess." But this argument had been as worthless then as now.

He needed food; the caffeine had rattled him. He sliced a bagel and dropped it in the toaster. A good bagel from New York, thank God, not the soggy old spare tires that passed for bagels around here. He rummaged in the refrigerator for cream cheese (the real one, not the rubbery fat-free she kept around for him) and jam. And some of that wonderful thick Greek yogurt. Like cream, like cheese. Heaven atop a peach, was there a peach? Thank God Edith bought the fat Greek yogurt. Damnit. There was no peach.

"Sam, what has happened to Alison? Do you remember when she was eighteen and we took her to Paris—her first trip abroad?" Ah, the tales families tell twenty times over, and this was Edith's set piece: "The Education of Alison." There had been the dinner at the Tour d'Argent: querelles and pressed duck. (For a high school girl!) Dior perfume, handmade underwear. Bribery. Stupid bribery, like taking some headstrong, daddy-defying debutante on the Grand Tour. The bagel scorched his fingers, but he managed to toss it onto a plate and pile it with forbidden substances, peach or no peach. He wished he could have some eggs.

"The most feminine child! We had such fun, we were buddies, pals. She talked about getting married one day in that beautiful little church in Saint Germain. What's it called? Saint Something of Something, the one with the ivory staircase. And now this. What could have gone wrong?" Sam handed her the tissues. How many times would she ask? It was only a couple of years later that Alison had come out—not at the debutante cotillion as Edith might have wished but the other way.

"Nothing went wrong. There's no wrong to it. I guess her taste for feminine things just goes a little further than you imagined. She is still quite feminine, if you want to look at it that way. You know I tried to talk to you about it before that trip, and you shut your ears? I knew already, or thought I knew. You thought you could cure her."

"That's not true. I was giving her a treat, showing her what she had to look forward to if she got an education and made a proper marriage. Sam, how can you condone such a thing? How can Stephen? And in our home! The people who work for us are mass-going Catholics. This will deeply offend our neighbors!"

"It's none of their business. If this is how Alison chooses to live, who are we to say she shouldn't? I approve of love. I am in favor of it. Love is wonderful. If everybody had love, if everybody went to bed with the right person every night, the world might be at peace." He knew this was self-serving New Age bullshit, but it caught in his throat. He believed it.

Your problem, dear, is that you disapprove of sex in any form. He refrained from saying it. Enough already. She had been an excellent wife and mother. And perhaps her aversion was his fault. Perhaps if he had been more skillful himself back then. . . . Perhaps if she had married somebody else. He spooned up more yogurt. Delicious. Another bagel? Perhaps. Even now, perhaps, with the right man, Edith could revive. As he had revived. Maybe he and Edith could get a mutually agreed-upon divorce, and they could sell all the property, and she could hook up with . . . whom? He didn't care. Whomever.

"You have a funny idea of love. This child, who might have had anything, any man, she wanted! I hear this black woman of hers wants to go into politics. Some politician she'll make with this around her neck! A black lesbian! A *schwartze,* as your mother might have said. And that's another thing. . . ."

"Damnit! Stop this disgusting talk! And leave my mother out of this." A nuclear strike formed in his brain. He would ask for a divorce. He would denounce her as a vulgar racist. No, he must keep his rage locked up. Otherwise the world would fall apart. She would back him right to the precipice; hadn't he thought a hundred times about what divorce would mean? And he would have to give in. Of course he and Stephen had bulldozed her about this party. What else?

"Edith, my dear, it's our beloved Alison. I could hardly refuse. Maybe I rushed into it without your full consent. Okay. But try to play along, do try. This big flashy party will be a kick. You can buy yourself a new dress, I don't care what you pay for it. You can get your diamonds out of the safe deposit. How about a pair of those five-hundred-dollar shoes? The ones with the ankle straps. You'll be the center of it. Betcha the *New York Times* will come. *Modern Bride.* All that remains is to choose a wedding present. I was thinking we could give them six place settings from Tiffany's. Think of them as society brides. And they are, sort of. Candace's father is some Ghanaian diplomat at the U.N. and her mother works at the Chicago Public Library. The main branch of it. Downtown. Is that so bad? It'll sound great in the write-up."

"I am not giving them six place settings. You have any idea what that costs nowadays? Oh, Sam, I don't really care about the cost of the place settings, but tell me what two women want with Tiffany silver. Are they going to entertain? Oh, dear, I suppose so. I don't want Alison living this kind of life when she could have led another, that's all. And it breaks my heart to think of the offense to our neighbors, to our families, to have this embarrassing thing take place here. Why don't they do it in Manhattan? Nobody cares down there!"

"Okay. I admit I was inconsiderate. I should have listened to you. I should have told Stephen no. Okay, okay. Stephen's paid ten thousand dollars down already. Maybe he could switch the caterer to someplace else, but I don't know. I'll call him this morning. You have to talk to him, too. And you have to call Alison. But you're right. It's your house, too. I thought you were at least going along with it. I never dreamed you were this upset. Morally, I mean. Maybe the housekeeper and the stonemason will gossip. They'll get over it. You think there aren't lesbians and gays up here, too? Ask around. Find out what the Dalai Lama thinks about commitment ceremonies. He probably is for them, as long as he gets to wear his rubber sandals."

She blew her nose. "Right. You want to put it all on me and make fun of me to boot. I have to play the villain. Why can't you ever be my teammate? Why are we always at odds?"

The eternal question, but he knew he had won at least for this morning. "We're not always at odds, my dear." He laid it out for her. "We have raised three children. Two crazy, one sane, all heterosexual, all interested in money. Four grandchildren, and only one of them, so far, is queer. We own property. Lots of it. You and I made all this money ourselves. Never inherited anything, apart from the diamonds. We have been married almost fifty years. We are collaborators in the deepest, most consequential way. I am in favor of love, whenever and however it occurs. Ours, such as it is. And Alison's such as it is. Not one of our own children ever wanted to get married here, and now Alison wants to. I say hooray. I don't care whom she is marrying. And yes, they will give dinner parties. So what? They have as much right to Tiffany silver as I do, if anybody has a right to such a thing, God knows. Decency, Edith. Decency is on my side, too, not just yours."

The man who couldn't bully Edith would be devoured by her. They were, militarily at least, a good match. It was midmorning, and he had eaten too much. The swim trunks cut. Well, surely he was entitled to his swim. As he headed for the door, she smiled an odd little smile. And once again he got that feeling. Naughty, naughty puppy.

SAM LOLLED ON his back, then turned face down and floated in the deep blue rectangle shielded by grape arbors on one end, draped in blowsy purple clematis, bordered by the curve of labyrinthine hedges on one side and by a row of majestic willows on the other. He'd planted the trees twenty years ago, hoping to see them waft their tendrils daintily into the water, as they were doing now. The property that half an hour ago had seemed a leg iron found its way back into his heart. His home, his social capital, his own. His pool—he loved it dearly, forgave it for costing so much to maintain. His irritation with Edith dissolved in the sweet waters, his exasperation over the stack of estimates and bills. Last night, in his insomniac fit, he had read a few pages of *The Rape of Europa,* an account of how the Nazis had ransacked the great art collections of Europe, shipped it all to Herman Goering's castle. They had stolen Jewish collections, killed the owners. Even the rich had been murdered, not just poor Jews like his cousins and aunts and uncles who had died, he knew, in the inferno of Europe. If, in 1910, Sam's parents had gone from Russia to France or Belgium instead of to Ellis Island and the assorted hardships of Brooklyn, they'd have ended up in Auschwitz, and if there had ever been a Sam Mendel here on earth, he would have been fed into the flames. Luck. A lot to be said for luck.

The water this morning was cool, exactly as he liked it. He shed his swimsuit. Who cared if somebody saw him nude? An old man with drooping haunches and reduced capacity, so what? Anyway, it was his pool. He could skinny-dip if he liked. The ambient peace was blissful. Not a sound came from the house, no cars labored up the hill, no mowers or hay balers clanked in his meadows, though some engine could be heard chugging, barely perceptible, in the distance. He had bought this property thirty years ago for nearly nothing, hardly knowing what he sought: an unlivable, unlovable, old farmhouse and three hundred acres of overgrown meadow and tangled forest, threaded with crumbling stone fences of nineteenth-century farms, with a couple of outbuildings and a heart-stoppingly beautiful barn. In weedy ditches, quite at random all over the property, were rusty heaps of car parts and tractor wheels and tools and the occasional icebox, bed springs that twisted agonizingly skyward, old bedroom sets—legacies of defeat and disappointment, of harsh lives harshly extracted from the rocks, of homesteads abandoned. The American dream all dried up.

Yet to him it had looked like virgin forest. He had never wanted anything so much. He perceived that his mission in life was to make it beautiful again. Edith had hated the place. Of course.

He had the junk carted away from the ditches and the high meadows. There were natural ski runs. The ancient cow barn, with stalls for sixty cattle and concrete sluices, was a treasure he set about reclaiming. Edith and Rachel had begged him to tear down the farmhouse. The roof leaked, there was one moldy bathroom. The upstairs bedrooms were jail cells. Everything stank. The farmer, a widower, had kept a pack of dogs indoors. Their urine had, over the years, seeped into the floor planks. Sam had nevertheless seen the essential beauty of the design: the stolid, useful porch, like a stage running round the house, the gaunt windows like insane eyes.

Only the spare lines of the old house remained, the shapes of the windows, the porch, the ghostly lineaments of poverty revised into a mansion, beautiful and vast, with a formal library in which Sam housed all the books his firm had published, among other things. He collected volumes on English, French, and Japanese gardens and other art history. Fresh shipments of books arrived weekly, and the local librarian came every so often to catalog and shelve.

Upstairs, once the big additional wing was complete, the stingy bedrooms turned into seven big ones and four luxurious bathrooms. Edith insulated herself from the grim Catskill winters with central heating backed up by energy-efficient fireplaces, cashmere shawls. It was the perfect monument to their marriage—Sam charging ahead, ignoring her objections, the dragout quarrels. And now he was a guest here, arriving, departing. Yet it was not hers. It was his.

Getting his second wind, he began to swim laps, slowly, confidently stroking from one end of the pool to the other. It eased the knot between his shoulder blades, the relentless weariness of insomnia, the ache in his head, which might have been caused by too much coffee or not enough. He imagined Antonia here, in her black bathing suit, her white hair dripping. She was an excellent swimmer, and their house in Kent last June had had a pool. But she would never be here, only Edith, his children, his grandchildren. He belonged to this property, not the other way around. Perhaps it was his punishment for having assimilated, made himself a prince of a profession in which, until recently, Jews had been as unwelcome as in investment banking and law firms on Wall Street, all those fellows with fine old came-over-on-the-Mayflower names. He, Sam Mendel, of City College, had asserted himself. He was his own Defender of the Faith—his faith in life and literary art, pleasure, the importance of generosity and kindness and intelligence. Was that not religion enough?

Still, for the sake of the children, he and Edith ought to have worked out a way to keep their religion, even if only for show. French Jews Edith's people had been, their Judaism, like his own family's, instantly diluted upon arrival in the New World. Ironic that as soon as you set foot on Ellis Island you shed the thing that had driven you here. Sam briefly imagined himself in ecumenical bliss celebrating Chanukah and Christmas, having Easter dinner and Passover, too, like some people he knew, or him becoming a Protestant or Edith a Unitarian. Would that have kept the girls from fanaticism? Probably not.

He hoisted himself from the water, wrapped his bathrobe around him, and crossed the flagstones through the grape arbor toward the back door. Edith, thank God, was no longer in the kitchen. Upstairs, no doubt, writing notes. Making lists. What did Edith do all day? Mrs. Allen, the housekeeper, had come to work and seemed to be sorting laundry. He'd shower, dress. Have a small lunch—or skip it after that one-thousand-calorie breakfast he had wolfed down. Go collect Vivienne and Adrienne in Margaretville. Maybe he should, after all, stay for dinner with Edith and the girls. He didn't wish to be disagreeable and could think of no reason to refuse. After dinner, he'd drive to New York. He could leave by nine. Antonia would be okay with that; he must find a moment to call her.

8 Mark

THE SUN HEADED WEST, shadows fell on Riverside Park. He and Sophie and the children had eaten their peanut butter sandwiches, strolled to the boat basin at Seventy-ninth Street and back. It was time to pack up and go home, but they lingered. The little girls flew around like hummingbirds ("Daddy, I hurt my knee"; "Sophie, she won't let me play with the beach ball, make her let me") and then skittered away. Mark's temple no longer throbbed; he worked up a distaste for booze, a resolve against the disorder of his life. He should forswear being his kid's twenty-five-year-old nursery-school teacher's lover. But she was irresistible, the only human except Toni who gave him joy.

Sophie's face was half-turned from him, as she wound her hair into a clump with pink-and-white-tipped fingers and fastened the chignon with a huge, toothy, tortoiseshell clip. Locks instantly escaped, making her look like the heroine of a pre-Raphaelite painting. On her salary, French manicures! The streets were lined with salons where Korean manicurists toiled over the fingers and toes of New York women. Where did New York women, who mostly had to live in closets, get the money for manicures and foot massages? Maggie never had manicures or pedicures. He had thought it wise to marry a plain, practical girl who adored him, the sort who would never crave silly luxuries. Now he wasn't so sure.

He had first met Sophie at the school, delivering Toni to her classroom mornings; had listened to her explain the mysteries of child-centered learning in the evening sessions for parents, where he and Maggie hunched up on schoolroom chairs. Sophie worked after school and weekends as Ashley Parker's part-time nanny, so it was natural for them to meet in the park. Kevin and Alicia Parker's nannies and au pairs arrived and departed before Ashley had time to learn their names. Nobody liked Alicia Parker, who smoked in front of her daughter and was always away. The Parkers paid well, and they never took Ashley on their trips or social weekends, so there was plenty of work for Sophie when she wasn't teaching. She and Ashley played house in the rambling apartment the Parkers owned, heating up TV dinners and grilling hot dogs in the state-of-the-art kitchen ("the fancier the kitchen, the less likely that a meal ever gets cooked in it," Sophie told Mark). Like sisters, they romped in the living room, which was roped off with a twisted swag, museum-style, to prevent any such romping. Dropping Toni off for play dates, Mark estimated the furniture had cost a half a million. Another point against Alicia — she'd hired a decorator, which was okay on Park Avenue but not Riverside Drive, which harbored indignant populist ghosts even in ten-room apartments.

Househusbanding was a good beard for Mark's infidelity — after all, he and Sophie were park buddies. The New York Public Library helped, too. The business library in the old B. Altman building on Fifth was the hangout of the unemployed, a quarry of information: how to start a business, find a job, understand

the bond market, gain computer skills. It was open some evenings. If he wasn't working at the liquor store, Mark left for the
library as soon as Maggie came home, only sometimes he went
straight to Queens.

Sophie had a fourth-floor walk-up in an asbestos-shingled
house in Astoria, a respectable immigrant neighborhood near
LaGuardia Airport, no high-rises, a tar-papery look, no Ralph
Lauren, no Starbucks, no nail salons, not much crime, and af-
fordable rents. On their first trip to Astoria together, they had
brought the little girls, eaten crispy fried sardines in a Greek
restaurant and a ton of French fries and baklava. The next time,
Mark went by himself to Sophie's sunny, bare room. Her sofa
bed, which she never closed, butted up against the armchair.
Four steps took you from there to the refrigerator and eight steps
to the bathroom. Handles fell off the doors, and the hot water
was unreliable. She had offered him a glass of wine—a ghastly
jug Chardonnay. He resolved to teach her something about wine
one of these days. The mattress had aggressive springs, and the
linens were not exactly pristine. He got a slight chill, thinking
of Maggie and HIV and wondering if other men had recently
vacated this bed, but he went ahead anyway.

"If you're wondering if I have a lot of guys here, I don't. I
haven't had a boyfriend in a year, haven't had sex since last September. I was scared of that guy, and the condom broke, you
might know. I had to wait six months to get tested. I am clean—I
don't have HIV. Or anything else. I assume you don't have HIV
either, being married. I'm on the Pill again. But you have to use
this." She took a package of condoms from the dresser drawer.
Incredible girl! Making love to her in this dilapidated room
brought back delirious memories, or at least ancient wishes,
from his junior year abroad in Paris. Sophie was as natural, as

expert, as playful, as he had expected French girls to be, years ago, except that they weren't. She was different in every way from Maggie, always so anxious, and you yourself half dead with anxiety because it had been two weeks since you touched her and you couldn't think about anything but the job hunt and would Toni hear the orgasm. At 7:30 he bolted out of Sophie's bed, wholly focused on consequences—he had promised to be home for dinner. The library closed at 8:00; Maggie would expect him before then. He was at least an hour from home. He pulled his clothes on as Sophie sat against the pillows, the sheet around her chest. He wondered what she would do for dinner: he knew there was nothing in the fridge. He should be inviting her out for fried sardines. But she was happy, unconcerned. She got up and put on shorts and a shirt, and at the door handed him a set of keys. "Come back whenever. Just let me know in advance, no surprises. And try not to run into the landlady. She hates me enough already."

"No landlady. No surprises." And when he finally got home, no fireworks. Maggie was dicing vegetables for a casserole she meant to freeze, and she smiled and kept on dicing. "Anything interesting turn up?" Toni, all bathed and fed and curly, was at the kitchen table drawing flowers and cats on kids' art paper. "Hi, Daddy," she said. He'd read a John Cheever story about a man who survives a plane crash and when he gets home, nobody notices that anything has happened to him or has time to listen to anything he is saying. And he felt like that, that he had just had the most important experience of his life and nobody had the slightest idea.

Absorbed in Sophie's pre-Raphaelite beauty, he wondered how he could ever solve this. Sophie was only a child herself . . . he had no business . . . how could he leave Maggie and Toni? How would he ever pay child support? Sophie had begun to pack up the toys, the water bottles.

"Oh, Christ, Sophie." he said. "You shouldn't be here with me. What if somebody notices?"

"Notices? Are we not allowed to occupy the same park bench? What are we doing wrong?"

"You'd get fired if they knew you and I slept together. The Parkers would fire you, the school would fire you. You'd be evicted from your studio, hanged for a witch."

"They wouldn't fire me. Not all these West Side parents. They'd probably hang you first. Even Alicia Parker would stand up for me. What would she do without me? I'm the only baby-sitter who hasn't quit or been canned. But tell me. Do you really think you'll get that job next week?"

"How do I know? I'll try. It can't hurt to have a job—I mean I have a job, the liquor store, but you know what that pays. Money solves a lot."

"But is it what you want, Morgan Stanley, for the rest of your life maybe?"

"What I really want. I don't know what I want. Maybe just not to have to torture myself anymore about schools for Toni. You know, Maggie's already talking about her ticking clock. An-other baby."

"Another baby. And you don't know how to manage with the one you've got?"

"Yeah, I see myself trembling in a wheelchair, and Toni will be getting her Ph.D. from Harvard, and Antonia will be there, too, a crone of ninety, and we'll all be uncorking the champagne. School, from one end of life to the other. It was better, maybe, when women weren't so thirsty for schooling. Education. Debts. I haven't paid off my own debts."

"Right. I am about to default on mine." Sophie had no parents, except a mother who lived with her fourth husband in Miami Beach and hadn't sent Sophie so much as a birthday card for three years.

"I don't suppose Morgan Stanley would be any different from Grumple. I'll just do what I do, cook the books or whatever. But like I say, having a regular income, in the six figures, can't hurt. Especially with this endless highway of tuition stretched out in front of me like the New Jersey Turnpike, a toll road with the tolls getting higher at every gate. And then there's the two maxed-out credit cards. I guess there's some point to this."

"But let's say you don't get that job next week. Have you ever thought of going away with me? I don't have any big ambitions. I just want to live. There are nursery schools all over America. I make twenty-five thousand five hundred dollars a year. I owe fifty thousand dollars to the government. I could clerk in Walmart's for what I make at Parkside. I could stand to live someplace where rents are cheaper. And where it's warm. Where I could have a backyard. Keep a dog, maybe. Have an old car, even. We could go together. Florida. It's beautiful around Fort Myers."

"You're crazy. I can't leave Toni and Maggie. You mean, just run out on them?"

"Well, I can't imagine you're making Maggie so happy. Maybe you could get a job somewhere else, send them money. Maggie could marry somebody else. Toni could come spend the summers. I came to New York for the glamour. You're the most glamorous thing that's happened to me, an older man. I think I love you. I know I love you. You hate your life, but you're going downtown Tuesday morning to interview for a job you don't want. You're barely forty. I don't understand you guys, you Parkside Montessori dads. But if running away is too scary, can't you get away tomorrow? I don't have to work. The Parkers are coming home tonight."

"There is no way I can get out there tomorrow. Tomorrow's Sunday. The library is closed. Anyway, I haven't seen Maggie in a week. I have to think about that interview. And you're wrong. I do want that job. It would solve a lot of problems. . . . If I get that job, maybe in a year we can work something out."

"Like what? You come to Astoria once a month when you don't have to work late? I don't want to be your mistress. I want to live with you full time." She stared across the park, unsmiling.

"Okay, listen, you have to forget me. I have to forget you. I can't run away with you, leave my wife and child. I never said I had any idea of that. Older men are not glamorous. Married men especially are not glamorous. I'm entangled, don't you see, hopelessly. That little kid over there means something to me. I should just walk off from her? She loves me. This is stupid, wrong. You need somebody who can belong to you."

"I have to go back. Ashley needs a bath. I have to get dinner for us tonight. I want her to look tip-top when Alicia and Kevin get home. Well, here comes the ice cream guy. I'll get us all Popsicles and then go."

"No, listen to me. Listen just one minute. Let me get my life together. If I make a few paydays, real ones, maybe I can think clearly. But I don't want to just take it on the lam, run out. What could I do in Fort Myers, clerk in a liquor store? What would we do for money? Give me a break, I can't just abandon my family. You must be patient. You're so much better off without me. But I keep thinking that if I had an income I could get a real divorce." He was exhausted, dizzy. His hangover had come back.

Disheveled and dirty, Ashley and Toni ran across the park

chanting, "Ice cream man, ice cream man, did you bring the money?" He should have taken Toni home an hour ago. Maggie would be pissed.

"Okay," he whispered. "I'll phone you when I can. Next week, after the interview, I'll be able to see you, somehow. Won't you be getting off early one afternoon? Can I phone? Will you wait for me?"

She shook her head. "Hopeless. You were probably right the first time. I need to get you out of my life." She seemed about to cry. Oh, Christ, maybe she did love him.

The foursome climbed the concrete path, the kids dripping Popsicle goo, toys and sand pails rattling at the back of the strollers, the dog crying *quack quack.*

"I'll call you," he said, at the corner. Sophie shook her head and walked quickly away. He needed some food, a whole bag of potato chips, maybe, a whole pint of ice cream. When would Maggie be home? Toni whined. "Tired, Daddy, hungry, Daddy." She tugged his hand. "When is Mommy coming home?"

9 Arty

HE WOKE UP stiff and apprehensive on the lounge, his left arm pinned under Greg. The temperature had dropped, and an evening breeze rustled the rose bush. He eased his right leg off the edge of the cushion, bent his knee, stretched his foot. Oh, God. That helped. A hot shower, yes, nice hot water running over his legs would be heaven, and it was cool enough for long pants. Might pop one of those pain pills of Greg's. Celebrex. Smart aspirin, they called it. Smart for the drug company, definitely something to celebrate, even if it ate up your stomach lining and brought on GI bleeds. Then some fluish malaise crept through him. Not a virus. Reality. The doctor's phone call. Good news, bad news. Yes, the MRI had shown, no question about it, that double knee replacement surgery would be a good idea. A splendid idea. Only six months of rehab and Greg would be dancing in musicals again, the doctor joked. All that remained was to set the thing up. But the CT scan had brought the bad news, news so bad the knee replacement would have to be postponed. There was something on Greg's lung. Some goddamned anomaly. Some shady patch with something lurking inside the shade. And that meant a lung biopsy. Not fun. Major stuff. Late next week. A lung biopsy. What if it were positive?

Well, there was all that. But also, Ian. Another one of them. If not Ian, Troy. Kyle. Felipe. Jesús. Dangerous, Gregory's bad habits. He swore to Arty that he practiced safe sex. "Or usually I do. It's really only 'safer' sex, the experts say. No sex is safe, according to them." Monogamy was perfectly safe, he replied, and monogamy was natural to Arty, a gene on his Y chromosome. Yet he put up with Greg's philandering. He was married to this man, deeply married, not in any paltry legal sense but in the only sense, having nothing to do with legality. Nothing to do with possessiveness. Dear naïve Greg, who could not resist the beautiful young body. "This boy is so lovely," he had said to Arty each time. "You mustn't begrudge me, my dear. It isn't like you to be conventional. I don't want to replace you. It's my twenty-year-old self I seek in them. They make me young again. Futile, of course. But poetic. Does it not enrich us when I return?"

Ian was a musician. An organist! Greg and Arty had been introduced to him by the Reverend Canon Barry T. E. Courtly, of the Church of the Celestial Redeemer, the landmark Anglican church that Arty and Greg had attended for years. At a sedate dinner party that included a couple of lesbian ladies from the parish, Barry had presented Ian, the new organist, with the long eyelashes of a boy-child and little to say for himself, a ravishing youth, and Arty knew at once that either he was a very talented musician or that his relations with Father Courtly were exactly as the dinner guests surmised, or both. The reverend canon refrained from coming out of the closet because that might have cost him his post. But the closet did not severely restrict his activities. Arty had always been grateful for reticence of this sort, as it saved a lot of squabbling. It was better simply to be mum. Don't ask, don't tell; Clinton had at least been right about one thing. He and Gregory had lived together all these years, but did they go about kissing each other on the street? No. Did they take to the streets about gay marriage? Did they intend to split their church wide open by demanding matrimony? They did not. Marriage was for straights, for squares.

It had been a quite stupid evening, with the conversation dominated by one Harold Quimby, a British writer and an old friend of Barry's, whose books went by such titles as *Cats in Manhattan, Royal Dogs, A Brief History of Absinthe,* and *The Postmodern Cocktail.* Who could possibly read such things? While Quimby had expounded on his allergy to shellfish (in fact, all fish, he specified) and the indifference of the typical French cinéphile to the *Wizard of Oz* and Judy Garland, generally, and which Saudi princes own race horses, and who his great-aunt's fifth husband was, Arty watched Ian make eyes at Gregory, having learned, no doubt from Father Courtly, that Greg was a famous dancer and, as was plain to see, black—a combination that thrilled pallid youths like Ian.

Well, a biopsy. Arthur's arm was numb, useless. He could never lift it again. He slid it from under Greg's body, which was bonier than ever. "Wake up, old darling. Gangrene is creeping up toward my elbow. And Antonia is due. I'm stiff as rawhide. I need a hot shower. My feet are ice cubes. I need some pain pills. I need a drink. Rise and shine."

The sun was hidden behind the buildings on Bleecker Street, dropping into the horizon beyond the river. He squinted at his watch: 6:30. "Oh, dear." He was sorry he'd asked Antonia to come for drinks. Should they tell her about the lung? He supposed they must. Should he tell her about Ian? No. Once, he had told her about another boy of Gregory's. "How can you endure it?" she had asked. "Why don't you throw his ass out of here?" Women didn't get it. Arty could bear it because it meant nothing to their basic relationship. Simply Greg's residual childishness.

Greg blinked awake, his eyes watery, his lips dry. He sat up and hung his arm across Arty's shoulders. "Call her and tell her we're late. Oh, hell, she won't care." His smile, at age seventy-two, was innocent, shining, his frailty that of a boy, not an old man. No doubt this was what attracted the procession of Ians. The sweetness. Not celebrity but true fame. People who mattered in the business knew who Gregory was.

Arty went barefoot toward his bathroom, through a gallery lined with treasures. He was an autograph dealer, a marginal business but he made money at it, selling the letters and mementos of the famous and distinguished, their signed photographs, their Christmas cards, often framed in gilt. "The authenticity of all material offered for sale is genuine," proclaimed the flyleaf of his catalogue and the home page of his website, "and this guarantee to refund the purchase price is without time limit."

Just like him. Genuine. How did he know the fake from the true? How could he pick up a letter in some collector's trove, look at it, and know for a certainty that Theodore Roosevelt, or for that matter Madame de Maintenon, had truly held that paper in his hand, her hand, and signed it. But he knew. He knew from a thousand details, the paper, the feel and scent of it, the quality of the signature. He knew the quirks and slants and curlicues in the handwriting of perhaps two thousand people whose autographs came regularly to market. Knew John Adams's hand from John Quincy Adams's. Knew that Flannery O'Connor's letters were very desirable now and G. B. Shaw's were not. Poor Shaw, ousted by a newcomer whose works he would have detested. (Arty detested them, too.) Had only recently identified an extensive musical autograph of Donizetti: bars of music resembling a length of lace, in a light, nervous hand working at top speed, and with a bit of study he realized it was a passage from *Roberto Devereux* (opera was his other passion), and then he spotted the signature, very faint, in the margin. It had brought $6,500, a handsome profit. Genuine.

Of course, Gregory was genuine, too, just duplicitous. Arthur's customers ranged from libraries to collectors with special tastes, the rich. They, too, were genuine. But among his clients a few chiselers always turned up, with rubber checks and bogus credit cards, willing to commit fraud in order to gain access to the famous—for was not owning the Queen of England's Christmas card the next thing to receiving an invitation to Buckingham Palace, and a lot less bother? Ah, he was content with small things; he would have been content with one lover forever. And yet Ian had come here yesterday afternoon while Arthur was uptown at a meeting; had greeted him politely when he came in the door. The three of them had drunk tea together. Ian was only a boy with a crush. No threat, no major threat.

Even now, crushed with apprehension about Greg's lung, he took comfort in dwelling among his notables. The beauteous Edna St. Vincent Millay, Eleanor Roosevelt in her crumpled hat and crumpled face and fabulous buck teeth, Duke Ellington beaming at his piano, W. H. Auden wispy with cigarette smoke, above one of his letters. He had the presidents, from T. R. through Clinton, something of each man. Arthur had never met these people nor desired to. He simply wished to be the curator of curiosities, of small things, ephemera. A librarian, a sweeper up of tidbits, a conservator of trivia. He possessed their signatures, the most intimate of identifiers, the most personal, except for a fingerprint, which was less

interesting. Their deeds and decisions, their music, art, and politics, had faded in the public memory, along with whatever good
they might have done. All that remained were these curios.

Gregory, you scoundrel, causing me all this heartache. He let
the shower run until it was reliably hot (you could never trust the
water in these old buildings) and eased his aching shoulder and
leg under the warm flow. He allowed himself to weep—very efficient to weep in the shower. For years he had tried to save his
tears for the shower. You simply let it all run down the drain, and
your eyes didn't swell up. He had never thought of growing old,
of being widowed. Surely neither he nor Greg would ever grow
old and die. Arty contemplated his own wrinkles and flab, his
droopy pectorals, his thinning hair, his thickened toenails. Well,
what the hell, Gregory still liked this wreck of a physique. Ever
the optimist, old Greg. And Arthur would never tire of his lover's
body, no matter if he had to have both knees replaced and lost
every hair on his head. He dried himself roughly, made a hideous
face in the mirror. Total cholesterol below 180, HDL 65. Triglycerides okay. Blood pressure of a thirty-year-old. A bit of the old
benign prostatic hyperplasia, meaning in plain English that he
had to pee a lot, but manageable, meaning you just put up with
it. But if Greg were going to die of that thing in his lung, Arty
wished for high cholesterol and blood pressure, atrial fibrillation.
Maybe some worm was chewing his interior, too.

It was too early to panic. The lung biopsy would be negative.
One had to struggle through these piles of shit, otherwise known
as health care—having little bits of yourself examined under various instruments, waiting days and even weeks for some secretary
to call you up and inform you your balls had to be cut off and
she'd schedule the surgery at Mount Sinai. Or perhaps she would
merely say they weren't completely certain about the matter, and

you needed another MRI in six months. Watchful waiting. And do be carefree while we're watching. Make plans.

He did his usual rumba to dry his tush, and then he wrapped the towel around him. The phone was ringing. Where was Gregory? The machine switched on. He picked up when he heard it was Candace. "My dear, forgive me. I'm just out of the shower."

"Uncle Arty, I won't keep you. Alison and I were wondering if you and Greg might come to dinner next Tuesday evening, the eleventh, it is." Greg's niece, the only child of his sister Mary.

"My dear, we'd love it. We are ever at your disposal. Simply say when and where." He should have checked with Greg but he didn't. Greg loved Candace like a daughter. Alison of course was a splendid girl, a newly made partner in her law firm—and perhaps the third or fourth in a string of lovers that Candace had introduced them to. She moved pretty fast, had even had a husband for a while. Well, these gorgeous highly educated black women knew how to get on, indeed they did.

"Oh, our place. Toward eight? And I hate to bring it up, but did Uncle Greg hear anything from those tests?"

Arthur told her the news—a lung biopsy. She said shit. She said not to worry, that it would be okay. She asked where the biopsy would be done. She offered to come and sit with Arty at the hospital. But he declined. "It won't amount to a thing, dear girl. Not a thing. The knee operation will be the big deal. We'll want you around then. We'll be old bears. Tired old bears. We'll need a hand."

He hung up, and sobbed silently once more. The dark green walls of the bedroom were hung with Gregory's things: Gwen Verdon, in a gilt frame and her Lola the vamp regalia, one mus- cled leg propped on a chair. "Dearest Gregory, I wish I could dance with you forever."

"I do, too. That's all I ever wanted. I'm scared," Arty said aloud. He picked up a *Pajama Game* program from the table, with a picture of Greg in a trio of dancers, in black tights, clutching bowler hats, hips cocked. SSSSSteam heat. Greg's bio: "Born in Chicago, he studied tap and ballet as a youngster, excelling until required by his father to quit dancing and take up basketball, an activity at which he did not excel. His first encounter with professional dancing was a performance by a traveling company of the Sadler's Wells Ballet in 1954 (later the Royal); he sat in the colored section of the theater where the performance was held. He left for New York shortly after . . ." "Where he found me," Arty always added, for himself, "and I loved him and took care of him and made him a home so he could dance. It doesn't say that on the damn program, but there wouldn't have been a Gregory without me. He would have killed himself somehow, walked in front of a truck, smoked himself to death, taken drugs. I gave him context. Ought to say that on the program, never does."

A photo from Bob Fosse: "To Gregory, the very best there is or will ever be." One from Paul Taylor and another from Jerome Robbins. Gregory arm in arm with George Balanchine, the stars, the geniuses who claimed the Tonys, or Drama Desk Awards, or Lifetime Achievement trophies or whatever. Gregory had simply taken their ideas and made them visible— "the very best there is or ever will be." If his name made it to the marquee or the theater poster (and sometimes it did), it was in small letters. He was only famous, only a star, among those who really knew what dancing was.

And among the public faces, private things: Gregory and Arthur in their swim trunks at Fire Island Pines, arms linked, the summer they had met almost fifty years ago. Greg had a cigarette stuck swaggeringly between his lips; it took ten years to persuade him to quit. They grinned radiantly in the sun, one of them thin and muscular, the other with a softer body, stocky and square and hairy. Arty could remember exactly how Greg's skin felt that day. He had always been a cynic, a classicist, but he remembered being overwhelmed and certain he would never love or want another human being the rest of his life. Being gay had been so natural, so easy. There was no other way to live. And yet in those days, psychiatrists still classified homosexuality as a disease.

In the next photo, taken by Antonia, the pair of them wore tuxedos at their thirtieth anniversary and brandished a champagne bottle. In 1969 gay men at the Stonewall Inn, two blocks away, had erupted in violent rebellion because the cops broke in and arrested men for dancing together. And Stonewall had triumphed: no longer did the police stage brutal raids on bars and clubs, and after that, men found they could do anything they wanted. The Golden Age arrived. Then came the Black Death. Arthur and Greg had never taken part in club life, bathhouse life. They had not fought for gay rights. Better to be aloof.

The doorbell rang, and Greg was on on his way to answer. With his emotions under control, Arty put on new chinos and a black tee and slipped his feet into loafers. New cotton clothes— what could be more satisfying? He found Antonia in the living room with Greg; she looked fifty, like a kid. She could be Maggie's older sister. Love did people good.

"You look splendid, dear. How'd the big confession go? Maggie okay about Sam?"

"It went okay, I guess. Well, she was pretty shocked. You know young people—prudish as can be. I hate feeling like some sort of slut in front of my own daughter. I'm the naughty teenager, she's the mom. She's overworked, weighed down with care, married to a flake. No job. Drinks too much. Maybe he's an okay guy.

But it's a hard time, and he hasn't been very good to her lately. I think she was a little jealous of me. God, how do you keep this place so beautiful?"

They had the same three-bedroom layout as Antonia's five floors above. But here there were gilt rococo mirrors, a real Boucher drawing, fat brown leather, and in the corner a majestic floor clock ticking its majestic tick. Impeccable taste, and she had always mistrusted impeccable taste.

"We deeply care about home décor, like all Village queens."

"Stop calling yourself a queen. Why have people taken up all the old hate words and applied them to themselves? Gay men calling themselves queens and queers, black people calling each other nigger. Will Sam start calling himself a yid?"

"Well, darling, it's all just among friends. What'll it be?" Arty moved toward the kitchen. "I have a very cold white Bordeaux. And bourgueil, a French red you serve cold. And the usual. Or would you like a martini?"

"Wine, please. The Bordeaux."

"Do you want me just to hire a hit man for Mark?" Arty asked. "I could ask them down for dinner and just bump him off. I never wanted Maggie to marry him."

"Right. But don't poison him yet. He has a job interview soon at Morgan Stanley. Maggie says he'll get the job. I don't have any idea why she says that, do you? She believes a decent job would fix their problems. It would be pleasant to think so, Lady Brett."

"Well, what the hell. He might get the job." Greg uncorked the Bordeaux meticulously, almost ceremoniously, and set out three glasses and offered Antonia a taste.

"It'll do. Did you hear anything?"

"About what?"

"Don't kid me. You know about what. I meant to ask you Thursday when we talked."

"Hadn't heard Thursday. Heard yesterday."

"What did they say?"

"Biopsy. Lung biopsy. They saw something suspicious. Two weeks from now." Arty's face threatened collapse. But Greg was smiling.

"I'll be fine. The doc said ninety percent of these things turn out to be nothing. Some shadow from some childhood infection. Or nothing. It puts me in a good category that I quit smoking so long ago. What are you two croaking about? I have to have the knee done. This is just one more thing."

"Where? Is it overnight or walk-in?"

"NYU. Yes, overnight. It won't be fun. Nobody said it would be fun. This sort of thing is part of growing old and having Medicare. I'll be okay."

Antonia couldn't think of anything to say. "Well, it will all be fine, fine. What are you guys doing for supper? Sam's coming tonight, but I have no idea when. How about I whip up a little pasta? Arty could go get a movie. I was thinking about *Bicycle Thief*. How long since you saw *Bicycle Thief*? Remember when we all first saw *Bicycle Thief*?" Ah, the years they had spent on art films in art theaters, the tiny cups of espresso they had drunk in lobbies. Art films could somehow save the world. Only they hadn't.

They chose *Umberto D*, De Sica's old man on the edge of homelessness. Arty went to the video store on Greenwich Avenue, and he promised to bring some dried porcini mushrooms from the fancy new grocery store.

Once he was gone, Antonia asked, "What do you think this thing is going to be? Really nothing?"

"Not nothing. I think I have lung cancer. I've been coughing for six months. I can't get my breath. I hurt. They say cancer doesn't hurt at first, but my chest hurts. The doc did not say I was in a good category. He told me to expect the worst."

"Oh, honey. Don't say that."

"Well, I have to say it: it's true. Antonia, you've got to help me with Arty. Will you take care of him? I am not indispensable, I have no illusions about that, I'm a burden and a cripple and a pain in the ass, and I cheat on him, but if he died, I would die, and he feels the same way."

"Well, why do you cheat on him? Why do you hurt him?"

"I don't know. It keeps you young, and it makes sex better when you come back. And anyway, I think he likes it."

"Well, whatever you say. But stop harping on lung cancer. You know that if anything should happen to you—such as you get hit by a Ford Explorer on Seventh Avenue—I will take care of Arty. We'll take care of Arty. Sam loves him, too. I don't know why we all love him, the rotten little conservative."

Arty came back with the mushrooms and the movie, and she started dinner. She knew their kitchen as well as her own, enjoyed cooking there. She struck a piece of garlic with the side of the knife blade. The shiny clove burst out of its papery skin, lay plump on the chopping board, its fumes rising. Life. Garlic was life. The lovely stench of garlic on her fingers meant supper under way. Another day, a normal day, the passage of time denied, or at least dramatically slowed, because garlic was always the same.

The number of garlic cloves she might expect to chop was finite. Must she decline into the misery of monitoring every bodily twinge, every ache and cough? Should she gaze greedily at those bottles in the vitamin section that promised to boost resistance to macular degeneration or Alzheimer's? Oh, the cruel foreshortening of years! And it happened just as you finally understood yourself, had at long last perfected the vaginal orgasm, had a grandchild to love, and could make a delicious dinner in twenty minutes or less. She sautéed the garlic lightly, soaked the dried mushrooms, added some oregano from the garden, with chopped fresh tomatoes. It would be delicious, with grated cheese. They would watch the movie. Not count the days or think about the diagnosis looming down the road.

10 Maggie

S HE STARTED TOWARD Sheridan Square. Mother has
a lover. And why not? Old people get to play, young
people must work. It wasn't fair to her or to Toni, or to Dad, but
then, after all, he was dead. She remembered an old play title: *Oh
Dad, Poor Dad, Mama's Hung You in the Closet, and I'm Feeling So Sad.* It had come true. At the corner a bike was chained
to a lamppost. A working bicycle, not smashed as it would have
been ten years ago. Marc Jacobs and Ralph Lauren had replaced
the Laundromat and the bookstore, and in some of the new
name-brand buildings down by the Hudson a few million dollars
would buy a river view and bedroom-size bathrooms and your
private wine cellar, stocked by somebody on the building staff,
since you yourself were too dumb to stock it. Thank God for rent
control on West End Avenue.

The afternoon light mellowed into haze. She had the rest of the
day to herself—Mark was taking care of Toni until suppertime.
She might go to the office and finish editing that puffball's first
novel, which she must release early next week, and she had 150

pages to go. She might look for bargains at Filene's. She hadn't bought anything for herself since Mark got fired. And then were school clothes . . . a new coat for Toni. More on the credit card. Clothes could wait. Maybe she should surprise Mark and Toni in the baby park. No. Something told her she would be intruding. She said hello to Juanita, the super from the brownstone next door, who was packing up the garbage bags for collection Monday. An old gentlemen tottered toward her, leaning on the arm of his black nurse. The aging population. Not everybody around here was young and rich, no matter what Antonia thought.

She decided she'd stop by the library, check out a book for story time tonight. Go to Brooks and get Mark a new shirt for the interview? Too pushy, overanxious, too good luck charmy? And the credit card problem, but should he not have a new shirt? How uncertain she was of him, after all these years. She still could hardly believe she had married this handsome man with an MBA, her dream man after her scraggly suitors at Wesleyan, smacking their lips over the imminent demise of capitalism, its death rattle audible only to the elect, looking for a woman to wash their socks while they got their doctorates. How gratefully she had abandoned them for Mark Adler, financial planner. And he had gone off the rails. Unemployed. Depressed. Slipping into a frame of mind where a man is permanently unemployable. A misfit, like the guys with utopia in their hearts.

Toni, Daddy, and Mommy must sit down together tonight. Disorder had overtaken her family; she must set things to rights. Dinner, a bath, stories. Mommy doing mommy things, togetherness. She inventoried her depressing home pantry—pasta, tomato sauce. Could they eat spaghetti again? She had promised herself not to shop at Fairway again until payday. Anything over $2 would have to go on the credit card. That, again. But without it, there'd literally be no money for supper. Some dark missile zoomed into her air space carrying a payload of rage, but Maggie deflected it. If Mark could get that job, they would gradually pay their debts. This was like waiting for an illness to pass. You had to keep the ship steady, not panic. She crossed the street at Sheridan Square, grubby crossroads of Seventh Avenue and West Fourth, with its ancient newsstand at the mouth of the subway stop and the cigar store across the street. At one end of the tiny triangular park that made it a "square," General Philip Sheridan, in bronze, Grant's lieutenant, stared in his stoic soldierly way at two pairs of life-size white plaster figures, a male pair and a female pair, looking somewhat battered, placed in the park to commemorate lesbian and gay liberation. She went into the subway.

She missed a train because her metro card wouldn't work. PLEASE SWIPE AGAIN, the turnstile advised. Red taillights disappeared toward Fourteenth Street. All was silent, and the tunnel coming up from Houston Street was black. A track sign warned about rat poison, and she saw a gray, boneless body prowling sniffily. A nest of gray, boneless babies must be nearby. Poisoning rats, Maggie had read, stimulated reproduction—they had some group wisdom about what the size of their population should be. The rat raised its head and stiffened, trembled, and vanished under the railing like liquid. She peered southward—yes. No sound yet, but the silvery rails gleamed, slashing the floor of the black tunnel in a dark underground sunrise. She felt a surge of excitement, pictured herself on the track where she had gone to retrieve some fallen object, perhaps her handbag or the keys to her apartment. She would hear the approaching roar, see the rails set on fire by the eyes of the train. Seconds, only seconds to escape. Would brave Maggie make it? Yes, yes, plucky Maggie is scrambling to the edge of the platform, folks, pulling herself up by her own thin arms. Ah, hear the screech of steel upon steel, see the sparks as the motorman desperately brakes, and cannot stop, but our Maggie is safe!

Or there was the Anna-Karenina-on-the-subway scenario. The train, folks, thunders into the station, and—Oh my God!—our Maggie Karenina is hurling her beautiful body in front of the oncoming engine. *Smack. Crack.* Squashed. Now Count Vronsky is really, really sorry. Now old man Karenin feels like a schmuck. But think, folks, what happened to the children? Tolstoy never said what happened to them. The dear little boy, the baby daughter by Vronsky. Novelists are so profligate with children. Mothers vanish or kill themselves in novels, and nobody ever bothers inviting the orphans to the funeral. No, folks, Maggie isn't going to do it. Maggie has her little suicide fantasy, but don't call the social worker just yet. Maggie is Toni's mom, and she is going home to get dinner on the table.

The train came and ceremoniously opened its doors, and Maggie stepped quietly on board, sat down, and opened her newspaper.

She stopped by the library for Toni's books, shopped at Fairway, an act of faith, of hope—more debt on the credit card, but a better dinner. Tofu for the spaghetti sauce, a bunch of fresh thyme, good olive oil, and a salad. She stopped at the liquor store (not Mark's) for red wine. The formality of wineglasses on the table, the good plates, civilized conversation. It was past five when she went through the door with her bouquet of plastic bags and called out, "I'm home," and "Mommy!" sounded from the bathroom. Toni hurtled into the tiny foyer, dripping and naked, wrapped her arms around Maggie's legs. "Mommy, I washed my own hair." Maggie let the bags fall, risking broken bottles.

"Oh, you're getting me all wet," but she landed a kiss on head and cheek and shoulder. Mark brought a towel—he did not offer a kiss—and they dried Toni's back and head, rubbed the thin legs while Toni clung around her neck. Chipped purple polish on the toenails. Green on the fingernails. Bubble-gum-scented bubble bath, silken skin, hair tumble-curly, the heady fragrance of clean child. The imprint of it on Maggie's dampened T-shirt.

"How was the park, darling?"

"Good."

"Who did you see down there?"

"Well, we saw Ashley, and I played in the water with her. I didn't know anybody else. Brittany is still in her country. And we saw Sophie, my teacher. Pretty Sophie."

"Oh, yeah? Is she babysitting Ashley again?" Mark retrieved the plastic bags from the floor, led the way into the kitchen.

"Run along, find your nighty. Get dressed for bed. I'll have supper in a few minutes. Mommy is making spaghetti. Grandma sends you oodles of hugs and kisses and wants you to come cook with her soon. Mark, help her find her nighty."

"Don't need any help, and can I have mac and cheese from the package? You always make spaghetti." Toni headed for her bedroom, dragging the bath towel, to which a dust ball clung. Need to mop. Need to clean. Need full-time cleaning help. She retrieved her chopping knife from the rust-stained, pockmarked sink. The landlord had offered to remodel—for a huge rent increase. Of course, they refused, and he resumed his efforts to eject them. He failed to call the exterminator. To repair the leaking faucet. To unplug the toilet. Mark was no good at any of that.

Five days a week Maggie went to a pristine cubicle on the fourteenth floor of a new skyscraper, with corner offices for the editor-in-chief and director of publicity. She had a job most erstwhile English majors would kill to have, editing smart new novels, and one of her writers had already published in the *New*

Yorker and posed for his picture with his arms draped on the back of a Victorian settee in his Brooklyn Heights apartment and his legs splayed above a white fur throw rug under his feet. This guy might have the kind of baby face that sold books these days, but he sure could not spell. She was thirty-five, and her yearly salary was 15 percent of his advance and unlikely to improve; indeed, she was menaced by possible cutbacks, downsizing, belt-tightening, and other ugly justifications for firing employees who had showed up on time every day, plus some Saturdays. If the book failed, she might be out. But maybe it wouldn't fail, since the guy had friends at the *Book Review,* which would pronounce his work chilling and superb. And then there was her other genius, the one whose cocaine habit ("Bolivian marching powder," he called it) made enchanting reading in his first novel (briefly a best seller) but had put him two years behind his contractual deadline for the second. But his name was always in columns in various magazines. She was Somebody, wasn't she, and she didn't want to start dinner at a rusty sink. But she'd make the best of it.

"Sophie seems to have turned the Parkers into a permanent job. Lucky for them. Lucky for her. Teachers don't even make as much as fiction editors. Where are the Parkers? Don't they know school starts Tuesday?" Public schools had started the first of September, but Parkside followed the principle of all private education: the higher the tuition, the fewer the number of school days.

"Uh, in L.A., I think she said. They went out right after Labor Day. Coming in tonight. You got wine, aren't you the extravagant one."

"Yeah, I thought we could have a glass with dinner. I tried to pick something good."

"Didn't Tommy steer you right?"

"Well, I didn't go to your store." She had gone into the one farther up Broadway. He smiled.

"You and Antonia have a nice tea party? Did you settle my hash?"

"We hardly mentioned your name. Why do you say that? She does know about your interview. She wished you luck. We talked mostly about her. She had big news for me. She's taken a lover. Can you imagine? A woman her age with a lover."

"A lover. Holy shit. Her personal trainer from the gym?"

"Not. I'll let you guess who it is."

"Arty has gone straight?"

"Oh, Mark."

"Sam. I knew already. Who else? He's been hanging around ever since your dad died. The celebrated Sam Mendel. Is he going to divorce his wife for her? Lots of dough. Shitloads. They could have a pretty good time, with what she's got already"

Toni came into the kitchen just then, wearing a nighty. Had Toni heard 'shitloads'? Why didn't he watch his language? Him down in the park with Sophie. Him talking about her mother's money. Where would they get the tuition for this year if not from Antonia? Her fingers, clutching the chopping knife and grasping the onions, suddenly looked to her like spider legs. Mad Maggie. You read about jobless men going violent. Out-of-work bus driver murders wife, kids, self. How about underpaid editor stabs hubby, kid, self?

"Mom says not. She's like an infatuated teen. His wife might take his country estate away from him in the process, and he couldn't bear that, Mother says." Anger was not the answer. She had to make Mark understand that she loved him, that they could have what they wanted, if only he would want what she wanted.

Order, calm. Mozart on the hi-fi. Two nice kids. A nanny. Vacations. She threw the minced onion into the sizzling oil, added the tofu.

"God, the wonders of Viagra." Mark opened the fridge, then decided not to snack. "But what's to worry? Be happy for her." He opened the pantry where they kept the Scotch—knowing he had finished it off last night. Maybe there was a drop left.

"Daddy, what's Viagra?"

"A pill for tired old men."

"Mommy, are you fixing my mac and cheese?"

Yes, she was. "But you have to have some carrots with it. And a banana." She remembered the laundry, overflowing in the basket in the bedroom. Toni had no clean clothes.

"Mark, honey. Could you take the laundry and put it in one of the machines? There's really a lot of it. We could have dinner when you get back, and then you could go down and transfer it to the dryer." Outside the kitchen window was a brick wall, some fifteen feet away, and on the sill her spider plant, rather than keeling over from lack of light as you might expect, had grown leggy. A cockroach shot across the counter and she smashed it with a wad of paper towel.

"Mark! Did you hear what I asked you?"

"Oh, for Christ's sake, Maggie. Start a laundry at dinnertime? I've played househusband all day. I'll do the laundry tomorrow, but can you give me a break? Get off the obsessive-compulsive routine. Anyway, you said you wanted us to be together. How can we be together if I'm in the basement?"

"What's a househusband, Mommy? Do houses have husbands?"

"No. But they should. Mommies and daddies and little girls like you should have a husband to do the dishes and the cooking and the shopping and the laundry, and then wouldn't everything be nice? We could play games and read and sit in the park all the time." She was racked by the prospect of her daughter in dirty underpants.

"I'd like that. We could hire a maid. The Parkers have a maid. At least sometimes they do. Why are you so cross about the laundry, Daddy?" Toni carried her mac and cheese to the table and began to stuff pasta in her mouth without sitting down, ignoring the carrot and banana. "You make the best mac and cheese, Mommy."

"I dunno why I am so cross. Daddy will try to do better. Sit down, baby, and put your napkin in your lap. Here's your glass of milk." He would teach her manners, which might make up for his shortcomings in the laundry department.

"I don't want Sophie to be my teacher anymore."

"Why not?" Maggie turned around. Toni was being cunning, trying to stir something up. What? Why? Why was Sophie always in the conversation lately?

Mark stepped in fast. "She is such a nice teacher. Remember when your rabbit broke his leg last spring? Remember how sweet she was?" The rabbit in the school menagerie had been injured when a bookcase collapsed, and Sophie had taken it to the vet and personally paid the bill. X-rays, anesthesia, a splint. A few hundred dollars she didn't have. She became a hero, at least to the children. Mark had taken up a collection to reimburse her.

Eating with her fingers, Toni said, "I guess I do like Sophie. I like her okay." Inexplicably, the child stopped eating and clammed up. Minutes later she fell asleep at her plate; Mark carried her to bed. Oh well, no story hour.

After dinner, Mark left the kitchen with a glass of wine. Maggie wrestled the heavy laundry basket to the elevator. Better to do the laundry while Toni was sleeping and Mark home, so she didn't have to drag Toni to the basement. It took two jumbos to hold all the stuff—oh fuck, only quarters enough for one machine, so Maggie had to knock on the super's door to get change for a five. Against the rules to bother the super at night except for fire and flood, but maybe the super's wife wouldn't mind? Maybe she would know what it was like? No, she was furious. "Why you not get change at the grocery, madam? Why you bother me at night? Time to watch TV. Not time to wash clothes." She had a sumptuous figure and sumptuous black eyes. Maggie felt old, anemic. But the woman gave her the change.

Upstairs an hour and a half later, she put away the clean clothes in the dark without waking anybody She wasn't mad at Mark anymore, did not suspect him of cheating. He had left a little wine in the bottle, good boy, and she drank it. She brushed and flossed. Toothpaste and red wine made a funny taste together. She thought of getting into bed naked, but put on a thin floral shift, with little straps, tight over the breasts. The sort of nightgown you bought after discarding the honeymoon finery because it was silly and you wanted to sleep naked as always but then after you had a child, you wore nightgowns again. Maggie snuggled against his back and put her arm over him, pressed her abdomen against his behind. She wanted him. No, she wanted him to want her. She wanted him to find her delectable, as he once had. He was not asleep. She could tell by the tension in his back and legs. She waited. She touched his shoulder, and his breathing regularized, a veritable scientific demonstration of delta slumber. And he curled a bit further into the fetal position, drawing up his legs.

She ought to put her hand inside the shorts, rouse him, insist. She should massage his back. But she was timid. Once, in arcadia, he had been the suitor, she the suitee. A funny word. Was it really a word? Where had it come from? What did it remind her of? Oh, yes, suttee. She saw her body, clad in a sari, atop a huge pyre, and the flames licked skyward while crowds below chanted prayers in Hindi. Her hands were passively folded on her bosom. She was not even strapped down. A videocassette of the mind, which she quickly and firmly switched off. Her last thought as she fell asleep was of her daughter's socks folded in matching pairs. Tomorrow her family would have clean underwear. And it would be her turn to take Toni to the park. And another week would begin the day after that, and then on Tuesday he would have his interview, and once he had a paycheck again . . . arcadia.

11 Antonia

THE ANSWERING MACHINE was flashing when she got home from downstairs. Sam? Why couldn't he have called earlier? He must have known she was at Arty and Greg's. He should have called her there. She never called him, even on his cell phone: Edith might hear. This was part of their understanding, one of many unspoken arrangements. He had never told her not to phone.

She allowed the light to go on pulsing. What if it was not Sam? Or what if he couldn't make it? It might be Helen Mulcahy making her round of fund-raising calls to purchase more elaborate street lamps for Perry Street, fancier than the ones on Charles. Or complaining that Antonia had been putting glass bottles in the wrong bin. Or wanting her to vet the financials of the poor chap hoping to purchase 2A. It might not be Sam at all. Oh, where was he, why had he not called her at Arty's?

The street lamps, which in Antonia's opinion were quite good enough, cast a little light upward into the living room, onto the hulky sofa, the marble mantel, the stacks of books and CDs,

Fred's big ugly TV that she meant to move elsewhere. A crumpled plaid throw on the club chair could have been Fred himself. Fred had worked thirty years' worth of Sunday crosswords in that chair. Five days at the paper, and then on Sunday he read the paper and worked the puzzle. She could see where his slippers had worn the carpet, she could see his gleaming bony ankles, his sharpened pencil at the ready. The capital of Albania? How do you spell Hormuz? A five-letter word for boredom, a ten-letter word for disinclination? The man in the bathrobe, plain, calm, steady, the man Maggie still saw at the kitchen table, the father she loved.

She'd had a very long time to mourn him: the five years of his decline, after he'd had to quit his job, that bitter end game called premature old age, when everything got worse and never better. Bed pans, potty chairs, injections. The kind, capable, muscular EMS guys carrying him to and from St. Vincent's hospital. Pain, shortness of breath, and six bottles of pills to keep track of. Sometimes she had simply hated it, and him, too, and sometimes his suffering was her own, and she had wept hysterically in the hospital corridor, as terrified as he. There had been a sort of love between them. Even after she had moved into Maggie's bed—Snoopy sheets and all—the day Maggie left for Wesleyan.

A low flicker like summer lightning passed through the room, a bulb about to go out. Soft sounds arose from the street, an angry conversation on a cell phone, footsteps, canine toenails *tick-ticking* on the sidewalk. The understated *kafunk* of a car door closing, an engine igniting, the car pulling out of its parking spot, and on Bleecker some Village partying. Down by the river, she supposed, people exchanged sex for money or drugs, or were contemplating murder, but not on Perry Street. Far away, a train whistle. The ghost whistle—all tracks in Manhattan were underground. And yet she heard the train, as she heard the hoot of the vanished *Statendam* from the Holland America Line pier at the foot of Christopher Street.

She could no longer resist the answering machine. "Hello, Antonia. Sorry to miss you. Sam Mendel here." So very formal, as if Fred might still listen to the message. Or Edith was within earshot. He never said "darling" or "dearest girl," and the messages always left her slightly chilled. The same with his e-mails, correct, not X rated. "Lots to do here, couldn't get away early, but I can escape after dinner. Should reach you by midnight. Go ahead to bed if you're tired." She played it twice. Yes, he would find her in bed.

She checked the fridge. The new batch of pear sorbet. Smoked salmon. A loaf of good bread, a cucumber, crème fraîche, dill. She made some treats, peeling and chopping the cucumber into little sticks, wrapping the salmon around them with the crème fraîche, scissoring the dill over everything, covering the plate tightly with plastic wrap. She put a white wine to chill. He would want it.

She undressed, wrapped herself in the sheet, and hugged his new pillow. Greg did not have lung cancer, surely. He was just frightened. Maybe it was nothing. A scare. And if it wasn't? Well, they'd deal with it somehow.

Hurry, Sam. He had told her that he never lay down without taking her in his arms, curling around her. He was hers, up to the point where the real estate began. Property is love. She could certainly compete with Edith, but not that house. Was her happiness about to vanish, like the *Statendam*? She hugged the pillow tighter, closed her eyes, and drifted into a dream. Sam, Maggie, Toni, Mark. Cancer. Greg dancing before her eyes, "sssssteam heat, I got sssssteam heat, but I need your love to keep away the cold." After a while she heard a key in the front lock, got out of bed, ran to meet him, took him in her arms.

"Exhausted, darling? What a long drive! Where did you park?"

"It was a long drive. Down at the garage on the corner. No place on the street, and I hadn't the patience . . ."

"Something to drink, love? I have some little things in the fridge. You must be starved."

"Well, not so much. Not so much starved for food." Starved or not, he took his time undressing, detouring to the bathroom, peeing, washing. She heard him brushing his teeth. Lovely sounds. Then he came to bed. She was in no great haste, why should she be? The prelude was more delicious than the act itself. "You make me happy, so happy. You please me so." She had never been so aware of another's pleasure, could not say where his pleasure began and hers ended. Much later, when they had gotten hungry and needed a drink and their mouths were dry, she kissed him, thanked him, for truly she was grateful. (Was it Ben Franklin who said that old women are always grateful?) "Thanks for what?" Sam said. "Thanks, yourself. You make me feel like myself again."

Toward 3 a.m. they opened the white wine, ate the salmon and cucumbers. The taste of food, the smell, was as erotic as sex, synesthesia. The idea of losing him crossed her mind. Would she ever be able to cook and eat again? Certainly she would never be able to make love again. They went back to bed with a bowl of pear sorbet, fed it to each other with a single spoon, and fell asleep.

12 Mark

A T THE NEWSSTAND at West Eighty-sixth Street, Mark bought the *Wall Street Journal* and went into the subway, fighting a loose feeling in his rectum. The local rolled in; a woman in high heels outmaneuvered him for the last seat. It was election day. Eight equally unappealing candidates running for mayor. Why vote? He clung to the steel bar, scanned the front page, growing faint, fearful of soiling himself. At Columbus Circle he edged out a black woman for a seat, ignoring her contemptuous glance. By Forty-second the threat had eased off. He closed his eyes and dozed, missing his chance to change to the express train, which was what he needed, but at Fourteenth Street he crossed the platform and got on the 2.

Fifteen minutes later, at Wall Street, he climbed sweatily to the light. He must not appear dank and rumpled. On the side of a building the names Charles Schwab and Donald Trump, in big brass letters, assaulted him. Here was where the gods walked. Where, if you had money and swagger enough, you put your name on the side of a building. Would this ever happen to Mark

Adler? Across the street Starbucks was an open door in the impenetrable stone façades. You didn't have to be anybody to go to Starbucks, just have $3.50 for a coffee. He shouldn't spend the money. Yes, he must, and he waited in line after shouting his order, ignoring the sticky buns and bagels.

Sipping scalding liquid through the slot in the plastic, he stopped at the Morgan Bank to observe the pockmarks in its north wall, tiny holes so small, so old, like weathering, but he happened to know that a hundred years ago an anarchist had set off a bomb, killing bystanders but no bankers and scarring the façade. John Pierpont Morgan had indignantly refused to repair it. Morgan had walked from his bank to Trinity Church every morning and prayed, certain that God, too, was a banker and trader who took risks with other people's capital, a high roller who counted only his gains. Across from the New York Stock Exchange stood a huge bronze George Washington, in cloak and tight britches showing off his incredibly good-looking, heroic legs, like Caesar Augustus extending his divine hand here on the site of his inauguration, the spirit of America, the father of his country positioned at just the right spot, a step from the stock exchange, ten steps from one of the wealthiest churches in the world (Trinity owned a lot of land around town). Two blocks uptown and west, the World Trade Center, Mark's destination, pushed its aluminum bulk skyward, gleaming like the hard drive of some huge server, the direct or indirect handiwork of NYSE, Trinity Church, and George. Was Morgan Stanley, to which he was applying, connected in some historical way to J. P. Morgan? He should have looked that up. Stuff like that could make a difference in an interview.

It was only 8:30. He had come early to stroll around, get used to the idea of working in this area. He was sweating less than in the subway, and his gut felt reliable. He thought ahead: this was his first interview. For his second, which might take place a week or two hence, he'd buy a new suit. For the hiring interview, even further on, they might take him to Windows on the World, way up there, where the white linen napkins were so stiff you could hardly wipe your mouth on them. Grumple had had a Christmas lunch there, and the thought set his bowels to cramping again.

He squinted upward. At Windows on the World, people might be enjoying business breakfasts. He'd bring Toni and Maggie for a treat one of these days. Tourists must be lining up to get into the observatory—a fine day for the view, you could see to California, nearly. Glancing at a plate glass window, he saw he looked good: gray suit, white shirt, dark tie, shined shoes. Yes, he would do as a bond analyst, a valued new member of the middle management team. He'd had an expensive haircut yesterday, in lieu of a new shirt. He had drunk nothing last night, had deferred the discussion about how to pay Toni's tuition. But, really, if Grandma wanted to pay, why not?

Maggie's dream might come true. The fat paycheck. The second baby. Not so bad, really, what Maggie yearned for. He could live that life. Toni, sweet Toni. Summers at the beach. Private school. Little smocked print dresses at two hundred dollars apiece. Dancing lessons, a violin. He would break off with Sophie. But how could he say good-bye to her sweetness, her carelessness, her long, silky body, her appetite for love, a woman without unpaid bills, grocery lists, and maxed-out credit cards that he was responsible for? Oh, perhaps he could keep her. Was not that the way gentlemen did things? Was it not almost the norm?

At the foot of Wall Street, Trinity lifted its pure Gothic spire in the lair of Mammon, but Mark bypassed it, turning north on

Broadway toward Liberty. The ad he'd answered had been for a research analyst in the fixed-income group to make investment decisions for high-grade industrial or telecom corporate bonds. He'd need to analyze financial statements and reports. Sure. One financial statement was pretty much like another. A tissue of lies, possibly. Loans disguised as income. Quarterly earnings nudged this way or that. Expenses downsized. Earnings inflated. The ten-million-dollar home recently purchased by the CEO with company funds tricked up to look like a corporate purchase. The cost of stock options for executives carefully hidden. It was the exact opposite of what most people did. Most people tried to downsize income in order not to pay taxes. Companies, on the other hand, only wanted the share price to rise.

They asked for five years of experience, which he had, more or less, and he had enhanced his resume only a bit. They'd never check anyway. His old boss at Grumple would recommend him—that had been the deal. The ad he was answering claimed they would consider talented up-and-comers with a little less experience than was required, so he wasn't really lying. "Excellent communication and analytical skills are a must," they said. The base salary was $100K plus bonuses and stock options. That should get him out of the baby park. Wouldn't stretch to a mistress and a second home, but it was a start. Antonia would not live forever.

Jackhammers chattered down the street. The World Trade Center was closer than he had thought; no problem at all to get over there, Two World Trade, the south tower. He would arrive at exactly 9:30. He would allow five minutes to get from the lobby to the sixtieth floor. He walked up Broadway, past the sushi joints and pizza parlors and McDonald's and the Payless shoe store and the sausage vendors, all the cheap stuff on streets where powerful people rocked the universe, made decisions that caused tuna fishermen in the Philippines to starve or prosper, to take home adequate paychecks from the canning factory or lose their jobs, or allowed young women in Malaysia to earn their keep by disassembling old computer components instead of working in a brothel or young men in Calcutta to be on the other end of the line when you called about your credit-card bill. Life was made here, this was where the money lived, flowing in and out, bestowing and denying life all over the planet. He could be an important cog in this grand engine, which maybe was God.

At the corner of Maiden Lane, he realized that he was standing on a clock, and he leaped off it as if it had been a snake. A big white clock, three feet across, with Roman numerals, 8:45. He had time to kill. Why not backtrack and visit Trinity Church? If J. P. Morgan could manipulate the market from a pew, Mark Adler could ask the Great Engine to help him get a job. "Dear God, I want to be part of this Thing which Thou has designed for the nurture of thy children. Enclose me in the tents of industriousness."

The church always retained its serenity, its holiness, in spite of its location, the endless traffic through its doors. He knew that he could step inside and be quiet—maybe that's all he needed, maybe he would not ask God to get him a job. A tour group was assembling at the door. Mark threw his coffee cup in a trash can and went inside.

13 Antonia

A TRAFFIC HELICOPTER above lower Manhattan reported that all was well, a perfect day, everything was moving. Traffic flowed up- and downtown on West Street, no tie-ups, no breakdowns, pouring toward the Brooklyn Battery Tunnel at headlong speeds, weaving in and out ferociously, pedals to the floor. Cyclists, skateboarders, joggers, walkers, dogs, all navigated the concrete paths and parks along the river. Every little open space that politicians created was soon jammed with human bodies. A gorgeous, majestic landscape: the wide river named for the explorer who had arrived four centuries ago in the *Half Moon*, the sprawling skyline of New Jersey — Hoboken, Weehawken, Jersey City — and to the east the great bridges from Manhattan to Brooklyn. At the tip of the island, the financial district rose like teeth in the jaws of *Tyrannosaurus rex*. Well, another day, another dollar.

Later that week, Antonia realized that she and Arty and Sam had set off from Perry Street on their customary walk along the river at the same time that security at Logan Airport, famous for its inattention, had casually failed to vet ten young men with one-way tickets to Los Angeles, ten men who had traveled from Portland, Maine, very early that morning. No doubt they were whispering prayers and promises to the god who had sent them on this mission, a vengeful god, and perhaps they had swallowed holy water from Medina to give them strength, holy men about to commit holy acts, at least in their view.

Antonia, Sam, and Arty crossed the West Side Highway in leaps—the lights were set to favor the cars and trucks. Alongside the traffic artery lay flowers, fields, gardens, playgrounds. Ferries crisscrossed the waterway to New Jersey; the Statue of Liberty, like a table ornament at the mouth of the harbor, lifted her torch. As they made their way southward, the gardens grew more lavish. A pool brimmed with purple and white lotuses and water irises and with orange fish. In the soaring palaces of Tribeca that lined the park, everybody was rich. Fit. The Promised Land. The cold war was over. Maybe all wars were over; History itself, according to a famous political philosopher, had ended.

Blatant prosperity, blatant spending, were everywhere, evidenced by orange cones and heavy machinery and teams of workmen digging new parks. In the autocratic way of New York City, these projects simply happened. Nobody voted on it or knew where the money was coming from. All these years later, no one, least of all Antonia, quite understood how the World Trade Center, a little farther downtown, had gotten built . . . something about the Rockefeller brothers and Chase Manhattan and the Port Authority, all inexplicable to her, all completely insulated from the wishes and desires of the likes of Antonia and Arty, or even of Sam. New York worked this way. It was not a public enterprise. Except it was the public's money, funneled off into the usual pockets and reappearing in the form of skyscrapers.

Antonia had hated the twin towers at first, ugly monuments to big money that drove out the little merchants on the streets around. People had protested, marched. It was all forgotten—and the towers had become the very symbol of New York. Graft and hidden power made democracies work, Antonia had come to see. The towers *were* democracy or capitalism, however the pair mated.

At the slip north of the yacht marina, a ferryboat unloaded two hundred people from New Jersey, who crowded down the gangplank, poured past the basin with its enormous commercial vessels, toward the World Financial Center, a glass skyscraper with a half moon on top, the City of Oz. Behind, the twin towers soared upward, making the ground tilt, like a trompe l'oeil painting that narrowed and curved and widened on its way to the sky. Nobody, of course, had any idea that something was screaming due south down the Hudson river. Words were in the air, to the north, words that had broken a long and troubling silence. The pilot of an aircraft that took off from Logan, Boston, should have been talking with the air traffic controller. But he was not talking. Not to worry, thought ground control, a glitch. It happens. "American 11, where are you, come in please."

And then, something broke the silence at Logan, something so unnerving that the ground could not grasp it at first, a voice from the cockpit but on the wrong microphone. "We have some planes. Just stay quiet and you'll be okay. We are returning to the airport." And the ground replied, like a sinner skewered by the voice of God or a man who thought he'd seen a ghost, "Who's trying to call me?" And then the pilot of United 175, also out of Boston, came on the circuit and told the ground in New York that he'd heard something strange, and the controller said, "Okay, I'll pass that along," and the pilot said, "It cut out," meaning American 11, and then he, too, cut out and that was the last thing the

THE FUTURE OF LOVE

ground ever heard from him. It was a few minutes after 8:30. A person named Marwan al-Shehhi, late of the United Arab Emirates, had entered the cockpit and placed his hand over the pilot's face in order to draw a blade across his throat.

Antonia made her way to the iron fence on the landward end of the marina, where a quotation from Walt Whitman had been mounted in big brass letters. She always made a point of reading it.

" 'City of the world! (For all races are here. All the lands of the earth make contributions here:) City of the sea! City of wharves and stores—City of tall façades of marble and iron! Proud and passionate city—mettlesome mad extravagant city.' "

"Bloody old Walt Whitman," Arty said. "All those exclamation points."

"Damnit, he was a great poet, Arty. And a gay man. You ought to love him. And it is a mettlesome mad extravagant city." Why was Arty so contrary?

"And Whitman was a big whiskery faker."

Sam laughed at them. Antonia's eyes watered, for some reason. She wiped away the tears, but they came again.

Again the silence overhead was broken, though no one near the World Trade Center could possibly have known how close the next voice was to them. "Okay. My name is Betty Ong. I'm number three on flight eleven." The woman who spoke into a wireless phone in the back of the big jet was a high-cheeked Chinese-American, the flight attendant from central casting, the one who found you an extra pillow and was kind to bratty kids and impatient old ladies.

"Our number one got stabbed. Our purser is stabbed. Nobody knows who stabbed whom and we can't even get up to business class right now because nobody can breathe. Somebody's got mace or something. And we can't get to the cockpit, the door won't open." She reported these facts to the ground. Betty Ong was entering history, like Edward R. Murrow broadcasting from London in the blitz, except that Betty Ong's transmission was fated to be brief. She neither screamed nor wept. She would have gotten up to help the slaughtered and the terrified, the slashed, she would have administered first aid and located extra pillows and blankets, murmured comforting words, as she was trained to do, but there were five killers aboard, with razor blades and knives, and perhaps she had looked into the eyes of Mohammed Atta of Cairo and Hamburg, who had boarded her plane in Boston. In the cabin, where passengers had recently awaited Ms. Ong's arrival with the coffee cart, at least three people were dead or bleeding to death, and the cockpit door was locked.

"Our first-class attendant and our purser are stabbed," she specified, with Shakespearean clarity. Shakespeare knew nothing of flight attendants and pursers and death in the confines of an aluminum tube hurtling through space, but he understood murderers, and he would have understood Betty Ong. And what of the crew behind the cockpit door? She could not say. Dead, or bleeding to death. Was there a doctor on board? inquired the ground, stupefied, as if a doctor could have made a difference. No, no doctor. And out the windows of the plane, a great city flashed by in the morning light as the plane went past the speed of sound, flying low, screaming, and yet no one looked up and noticed. Betty Ong stopped speaking. But the voice of another attendant came out of American Airlines 11 just before the end, and after calmly naming the seat locations of three of the hijackers, and saying they were of Middle Eastern descent, she said, "We are flying too low. We are flying too fast. I see water and buildings. Oh my god, oh my god." Those were all the words that escaped from the plane over Manhattan that morning.

A noise. A roar. Antonia went to the public fountain for a gulp of water; the noise grew louder. A big plane, and something was wrong. Arty and Sam were staring upward, trying to locate it. This was the lane for incoming flights to LaGuardia. There always was a plane. But this one was going the wrong way, shrieking and roaring so that it drowned out the honks, squawks, roars, thuds, sirens, whistles of the normal day unfolding. They saw it, above them, and then there came a deadly sound, like a bomb exploding far above, an earthquake in the sky, the fire and the black smoke bursting from the top floors of the north tower, an instantaneous inferno a mile above them, as the plane plowed into the building like something out of a video game. From on high a clutter of paper, fragments, powder, and plastic debris burst into the air and began its long, fluttering descent.

The crowds gaped upward. Oh shit. No. No. No. Oh shit.

"It was a big plane," somebody screamed. "A plane hit the tower."

The inferno roared above, and the particles showered, some borne up on the wind, some dropping like stones. From far away sirens began a low whine, which soon merged from all around, downtown, uptown, a mass cry, as the protective mechanisms of the city went into action.

Antonia said this wasn't true. This was some practical joke. All her life she had hated practical jokes, had been the last one to laugh, the last one to get it. "Be a good sport, Antonia," the kids had said to her. "This must be some major screwup at LaGuardia. Reagan broke that air traffic controllers' strike. They've been understaffed. This is what happens." She groped for the simplest explanation, but a diabolical rage hung in the air, along with the fire and the smoke and the mysterious falling trash.

"Antonia . . . it isn't Reagan. Or anything like a mistake. No pilot would run a plane into a building. We have to get out of here. Don't think about air traffic control. It's the second chap-ter—those bastards." Sam took her arm and Arty's.

"The second chapter of what?"

"It has to be the terrorists, the Arabs, another blind sheik wearing a goddamn tablecloth on his head. They couldn't blow it up from the basement a few years ago. Now they are starting at the top. It's them, that's all it can be. There must have been a bomb on that plane. Maybe it was a nuclear bomb."

Why was Sam ranting about nuclear bombs? This was Tues-day and they were taking their walk. Antonia heard something she could not identify . . . a *thud*. A *thwack*. No word for it. They looked skyward. From the smoke high above, a human being was dropping at the speed of light. "Look," Sam said, "somebody's up there on the edge of that burning hole." Antonia saw. Arty saw. They had not imagined the sound a human body would make hitting concrete from a mile up, but now they knew.

"Sam, what are you saying? What do the Arabs have to do with it? Why are you saying Arabs?" Ah, God, Morgan Stanley. It was definitely in the World Trade Center, but which tower? "Mark is in there. He had an interview this morning. At Morgan Stanley. Where is Morgan Stanley, up there in that building?"

She jerked her arm out of Sam's grasp. Another body hurtled to the ground. "Oh, don't jump, don't jump, they'll come and help you, don't do it, don't do it!" And once again that sound against concrete, causing the fragile skin and bones to vaporize.

"I don't know where Morgan Stanley is. Try not to think about Mark. We'll find out about him. We have to get out of here. We must go home."

They joined the stampede of pedestrians, cyclists, women wheeling baby carriages. And as they ran, a second plane came in—from the east?—and the south tower exploded. Antonia saw only smoke and flames, a white fog. "We've been bombed," she shrieked. "New York City has been bombed. We'll all die." She was breathless, screaming. They had to stop every block or two to catch their breath. Later, none of them could remember the walk — how they had come all that way without being trampled, the mob pressing northward with organic unity, the highway a stream of rescue vehicles streaking southward through the red lights. At Christopher Street they dodged across the stalled traffic and dived into the maze of Village streets.

City of the sea! City of wharves and stores! All races are here. Who would want to blow it up? It was the best city there was, the very best in the world. What have we done? What have they done? Antonia wanted to protest, wanted to go on TV, make a speech. Mark! Where was he? How would he ever get out? That terrible sound, that crash onto the pavement, could that have been Mark?

When they ran into the kitchen, Greg was still in his pajamas, reading the paper at the table, his last moment of quiet oblivion.

14 Mark

INSIDE THE CHURCH, he sat down halfway to the altar, admiring the carved ivory altarpiece with the Apostles in hieratic rows. Sunbeams lit up the wall of stained glass behind the altar: Jesus and the Disciples, Moses and the Prophets, in the sacred gleam. The group of schoolchildren, in private-school uniforms, came giggling down the central aisle until they, too, found their seats in the front of the nave. One day Toni might be down here on a tour. Maybe they could get her into Dalton, and Maggie would forget about the suburbs. `

Mark had grown up part Jewish, part Protestant, and part nothing, attending both synagogue and church depending on the habits of his friends. One summer he had been baptized as a Methodist, because he had a crush on a Methodist girl, but the conversion lasted only as long as the romance. He was always open to some spiritual poke in the viscera. He wished that he had a proper god to steady him. All the great robber barons had been religious, not just Morgan but John D. Rockefeller, Carnegie . . . Somehow Mark must get hold of all this. He pictured his family at worship on Sundays, but probably they would go sailing.

If only he could pray for fifteen minutes and then sit here in the silence, he would proceed to the south tower and prepare to meet his interviewer. Clutching the pew in front of him, he bowed his head, pulled out the velvet prie-dieu, knelt. "Oh, God, I need this job. I need it so much. I promise to learn to love my wife. I'm talking family values. Come across for me."

Then he heard an odd noise, which he first imagined as some sort of sardonic reply from on high. Others in the church had begun looking toward the ceiling, as if expecting to see through it. Whatever it was, the roar of jet engines, growing louder and more aggressive with every instant, shattered the serenity of the nave. Then came an explosion, a catastrophe overhead. Trinity church shivered. Shuddered. Rocked on its ancient foundations. A fine cloud of dust descended from the ceiling, as if from angels' wings. Then more roaring, and cries and curses in the street.

Leaping off the prie-dieu, he ran down the aisle, past the uniformed guards and out onto Broadway. Debris, dust, a kind of snow fluttered earthward. A wad of singed paper fell toward the sidewalk right under his nose but wafted to his shoulder. Furiously, he brushed it off. My God, the north tower was burning. Coming down in splinters and chunks, like a huge crate demolished by a sledgehammer. Flames and black smoke, hellish smoke, poured out of a deadly wound high up. "A plane hit the tower," somebody screamed.

Jesus, he thought, there are people in there. I could have been one of them. And then way up, he saw something beyond his powers to take in—an object hurtling from on high. No, it was a human body. He could see the arms. He was sure he could see its arms. Mark heard the body land but could not see whatever could conceivably have been left of it on the ground. "Oh, God." He had an interview in the other building in less than forty-five minutes. Did he dare go there? Did he dare get into an elevator?

Would they just conduct business as usual, maybe even look out
the window, while the occasional human being fell from the upper floors next door? "Yes, Mr. Adler, and what exactly did you
do in your last position? Please tell me more about it. And what
precisely do you think you can bring to our company to make it a
stronger, more profitable company?" He must not fail to show up
for his interview. He could hear himself telling Maggie, "Well,
damnit, I *am* sorry, but there was a fire in the next building
and I was scared to get in the elevator. I mean, who knew when
another plane might hit *that* tower." And Maggie would look
hopeless. And Sophie would think him a coward.

Yet the menace, the strangeness of the event, the heaviness of
the black smoke, the falling body, told him that the fire would not
be out any time soon, and that business would not be conducted
as usual. And he felt . . . what was it? Relief. Some lunatic had
run an airplane into a building, and he didn't have to interview.
Like a kid waking up to a blizzard, blinding white flakes falling
outside the bedroom window, the sound of shovels way down
on the sidewalk, traffic at a standstill: oh boy, no school. Trying
to squelch that sudden triumphant feeling, he considered doing
something heroic: walking the two blocks over there, maybe,
and volunteering to help. Maybe he could climb the stairs, lead
people out. But the sirens were deafening—help was coming.
People in asbestos suits, with training. They'd be going up there,
hoses at the ready. The air was thick with debris; people poured
out of the eateries. "It was on purpose," someone shouted. "It
was a plane, and they did it on purpose." "Bastards, shits." "It's
the Arabs again. Fuck 'em, fuck 'em!"

Mark recoiled. Arabs. Yes, Sheik Abd der Whatever, the blind,
white-eyed terrorist mastermind now in jail. And the dumb fuck
who went back for the deposit on his van, the van they used to

carry in the explosives, a move so sublimely stupid that the FBI was able to catch them all. But why think of Arabs? Not Arabs! Always blaming Arabs. He tried, and failed, to imagine how a person could seize control of an airplane, run it into a building. How a person could wish to do such a thing.

The sense of relief gave way to sweaty, irrational fear. What if a falling computer hit him? What if something worse was on the way? He wanted to run, but he had to hang around and see what happened. The church. He could wait there. Then he heard it, again the sound of a buzz bomb, a plane coming in from the east, over Brooklyn, too low, too fast, no way to stop the damned thing. Was the guy crazy? The jet slammed into the south tower, and a volcano erupted. He could have been in the elevator, heading toward the sixtieth floor, prepared to sit in the waiting room until he was called. As he looked upward through the smoke and fire, he thought he saw people clinging to the beams. He squinted hard. Not his imagination! They were there! He had always suffered from a carefully repressed vertigo or acrophobia. On the one helicopter ride he had ever taken, years ago, looking down from that peculiar height, so close to the tops of tall buildings, so different from an airplane, he had collapsed, unconscious, in his seat, and the pilot had radioed the EMS to be there at the landing. He pictured himself clinging to the crumbling, red-hot aluminum siding, ninety stories up. It could be him. Another few minutes and it would have been him.

He shut out what he had witnessed, and returned to the equally terrifying thought that his future, as he had construed it only this morning, had exploded before his eyes. He would not have the chance to come out of the Wall Street station, clutching his newspaper, every morning at nine. Morgan Stanley was no doubt a mass of bent metal and plastic, a lungful of ash, an air pollutant floating past him. Maybe the man who had agreed to interview him was dead, or was clinging to a ledge up there. Maybe his phony resumé was in the man's hand. He made his way back to the church through the choking air. Fire trucks and police cars pushed into the narrow streets, their shrieks sounding from far away, from way across the Brooklyn Bridge, across the East River. The guards at Trinity were urging people to get out, to go uptown. Someone shouted that the subways had stopped running.

Mark shoved past the guards and fled down the aisle. In the front pews the children sat in a defensive little group, unsure what was going on. One little girl was wailing. Why wasn't somebody clearing them out of there? Four women, apparently in charge of the kids, were buzzing together. One said it was better to wait things out, wait until the fire trucks and the cop cars and the ambulances got clustered around the towers. Wait for a police escort. One was calling the police on her cell phone, but she couldn't get through. It wouldn't do to take these children outside to be trampled or have burning computers or desks fall on their heads. "I think you're right, lady," Mark said. "I think you'd better wait it out. You wouldn't want these children to see what I've just seen. It's bedlam out there, and I heard somebody say the subways aren't running. There's no way to get out. Bodies are in the air, human bodies."

He retreated and sat down. He ought to phone somebody. He sought out the men's room—the need had grown urgent. Not a soul was in there. He peed. You have to pee even if they're raining bombs on you. What was he to do? He couldn't sit in Trinity Church all day. When the air cleared up, he would leave. But where would he go? This could be a sign, a sign that the life he was living, the life that Maggie wanted them to be living, was a fake, a phony, like his resumé. God's way of telling him that analyzing bonds was not his talent, with His usual knack for overstatement.

He thought of broken bones, people burning alive up there. Maybe those bodies would fall down, too. Who knew what would happen next? Maybe a bomb, maybe an invasion. He knew of war mainly through movies or history books—Vietnam had been less real to him than the London blitz, which he had read about in school. He had never been in the army or had any military training. He had no idea how to use a gun, not even a .22. He realized he was talking to himself. "I don't even know how to load a gun." He fumbled for his watch. It was almost ten o'clock.

He heard a rumble, like the beginning of the coda in a massive symphony of destruction, a roar unlike any other, a volcano, a rumble greater than that of the roaring planes, working to a crescendo. This time there was no doubt—the church trembled, faltered, rocked, shook. The ceiling quaked, threatened to dislodge itself, to break into pieces and crush them all. Had another plane hit the spire? Something huge was falling. Without going out, he divined what it was. One of the lacerated fiery towers was caving in, maybe both of them. God knew why or how. Maybe part of them would hit the spire of Trinity. "Oh, God," he pleaded, "don't let it hit the church. Don't think of me, think of all these kids." At the front of the church, the children screamed. As he started toward them, a guard grabbed his arm.

"Listen, sir. Get out of here. There is nothing you can do to help these children. We got the cops. Two police vans are on the way to pick them up. You'll do well to save yourself. There are no subways and no phones. One of the buildings has just fallen down, all the way down, all of it. I got it on my radio. It's a nightmare out there, but go outside and follow the crowds. People are walking toward the Brooklyn Bridge. It's the best way out. The fewer people around here, the better. Go on. Don't be a hero. We'll get the kids out. You are just another problem. Get out. Get out while you can. There is no telling what's coming next. Just run."

So Mark went out into the evil air. The chaos reminded him of footage from France in 1940, with refugees running along a road and a Nazi plane strafing them. He could not see the other side of the street. Shielding his nose against the thick fumes, he hardly noticed that the roar had stopped, was aware only of the gray stuff falling all around, silent snow, a blizzard to put an end to all school days, a snow day that might last forever; the twin towers must have been made of paper, and it was all out in the street. He picked up one of the pages that were drifting like ghosts through hell, and to his horror he found it was a sheet of Morgan Stanley letterhead. Perhaps on this sheet they might have sent him a letter of rejection. . . . Thank you so much for coming in to talk with us, but we feel . . .

In the gutter Mark noticed a few odd shoes: a woman's red sandal, a man's brown loafer. Had they fallen from above, or been lost in the flight toward the river? Why odd shoes rather than pairs? He picked up the red sandal. The label in the instep was Italian, expensive. Surely he could find the mate. Possibly he could find the woman who wore the sandals, could return her shoes to her. She would need her shoes, want her shoes. Where was she, fleeing barefoot or in one high heel toward the Brooklyn Bridge? He would carry it along, he might catch up with her. Along the streets cars were covered in the gray avalanche, their windows blown out, parked forever, no cops to write out parking tickets and no tow truck clanking up these streets. On his junior year abroad, he had gone from Paris to Pompeii, had been shown the casts of twisted Roman bodies, agony rendered eternal, roasted bodies. Someone should throw plaster over these shoes, these dead automobiles, put them in a museum. He took off his jacket and covered his mouth. His hair was saturated with dust and his suit was white. Turning back, he saw black smoke and flames curling furiously from the upper floors of the north tower, a fire that no firefighter, no matter how courageous, would ever bring under control. No, they would all die.

And beside the wounded tower, which used to have a twin, there was nothing. Nothing. He could not even see the top of the rubble. The north tower was doomed. He was certain he could see the struts beginning to yield, back there in the gray storm. He was carried along by the crowds pushing their way toward the Brooklyn Bridge. Firefighting equipment, screaming, was flowing across it, in the opposite direction. Hart Crane's bridge, the bridge so many men had died to erect, simply to enable people to go quickly, and on foot or bicycle, if they chose, from Manhattan to Brooklyn. Maybe on the other side he would find a bus or subway running. If not, he'd walk to Astoria. He had Sophie's keys. It couldn't be more than five miles. He knew the way. This was a new life, a new epoch. The tears poured from his eyes — it didn't matter. He had just missed being crushed to death or incinerated. The idea of jumping from the ninetieth floor overpowered him once more, gagged him, and he had to stop and rest in order to keep from fainting. What if his interview had started at nine? He wanted no part of J. P. Morgan's world, or even George Washington's. Sophie wanted to go away. He would go with her.

How would he tell Maggie and Toni? What would they do? They'd be better off without him. This hollow life — he needed to be finished with this hollow life. His insurance policy! That was the key. He had wanted to let it go, but Maggie had fought him, had borrowed money to pay the premiums. Well, it was all worth it. All he needed to do was vanish. Simply not call, not show up. He would be numbered among the missing. This would all work out for the best. "A far, far better thing . . . than I have ever done." But wait, didn't the damn insurance company require a corpus delecti before it would pay off? He tried to remember all the murder mysteries he'd read as a teenager. He tried to remember the law. A death certificate would surely suffice, and by tomorrow they'd be handing them out like jelly beans.

He paused to look back at the burning building, and as he neared the center of the great bridge chaining the two cities together, he saw the north tower tremble. In the throng, it was impossible to run. He took his wallet out of his breast pocket, salvaged the cash (so little of it!), which he put into his pants pocket with his change, and threw everything else—the maxed-out credit card, Toni's school picture, his ATM card, his driver's license, all his other ID, as well as the wallet and his cell phone—into the East River. Rest in peace. Mark Adler had just gone to the bottom of the river, a suicide. He pressed onward across the bridge, wiping the dust from his face with his suit jacket, shielding his nose with it, unaware that in one hand he was still carrying a woman's high-heeled red sandal by the strap. He turned once, to see the north tower fold up like a cardboard box and sink to the ground. He ran on.

15   Antonia

SHE FOUND THE phone and dialed Maggie as Arty switched on the TV. Gregory shrank from them, their hysteria, their dust.

"Oh, Mom, what is it? Mark, are you calling about Mark, do you know where Mark is?"

"Have you seen what's happened? Sam and Arty and I were down there. Do you have the TV on at your office?" Antonia heard it blaring in the background.

"Mark left early this morning. I don't know where he is. I don't know if he got there. I am going down there. You must help me. You must get uptown and pick Toni up at school. Mark was supposed to pick her up today. Please say you will, in case . . . in case Mark doesn't make it. Maybe he didn't get to the appointment. I have to go now. I'll call you when I can."

"No, you mustn't go down there. It's too dangerous, you'll be killed. They won't let you near there. Fire and steel are falling out of the sky, people are jumping. Both towers are hit. Police and fire trucks are swarming. Darling, they will never let you near the place." Maggie had hung up.

"I'm going down there. I can find them both."

"No, you bloody well are not going." Sam said. "Who'll look after Toni if you and Maggie and Mark are all down there at that inferno? You and I must go after Toni, I heard Maggie ask you. We have to go after her, bring her here."

"Candace," Gregory burst in. "She works at 120 Wall. Are they dead? Is Candace dead?" Stunned by Maggie's dilemma, nobody had thought of the women.

"Call them, call them right now." The line was dead on the first try, then yielded a dial tone, followed by a busy signal.

"It will take time. Don't panic. They have to be okay. Neither of them had any reason to be in the World Trade Center." The four of them stared at the screen, as if watching an event in farthest Asia, though they heard sirens and shrieks and the dust rained down. The north tower swayed, buckled, shuddered, exactly as its mate had done only minutes earlier, and turned into dust and smoke and steel and debris, and its struts and supports and I-beams and its famous aluminum walls roared toward earth in a heap of particles. Sam bent his head. Antonia had never seen him cry, and she laid her hands on his head. It seemed as if the south end of Manhattan was about to break off and float away or simply sink into the harbor.

When Antonia and Sam left to go uptown it was noon, and the keening of sirens filled the emptiness of Perry Street. Two blocks east, St. Vincent's Hospital readied itself to receive the injured, the bleeding, the broken. A TV crew was setting up, a gorgeous blond anchorwoman, just opposite the Emergency Room where Antonia had sat with Fred in several cardiac and diabetic crises. Today the medics were outdoors, waiting with stretchers. But nobody came. Around the corner, a line of would-be blood do-nors had formed. It disappeared around the block toward Sixth Avenue and West Twelfth Street. Antonia thought of the abat-toirs of the world: Stalingrad, Hiroshima, Nagasaki, Antietam. The Somme, Normandy, Cambodia. And now the abattoir had come to Manhattan.

The air stank of burning wire, molten steel, pulverized con-crete, and perhaps burning bodies. Thousands of computers had been crushed and ground up like pepper. A woman hastened past wearing a white surgical mask. The neighborhood was bar-ricaded, and civilian traffic was shut down. Nobody was walk-ing dogs or standing outside the house on Perry Street where AA meetings convened. Charley was gone. Nobody was double-parked. No FedEx truck blocked traffic. Everyday life had been vaporized.

Oh, God, let Mark be okay. How would they tell Toni Mark had been killed? Who would tell her? How do you explain this to a four-year-old? "Your daddy died this morning, crushed in falling steel, burnt in the fire." What was today? September 11, 2001. "Daddy isn't coming home. Something bad happened to him, and he cannot help it." Was that the right way? Should you just use the word *dead*?

Police emergency tape blocked the subway entrance. She and Sam headed toward Fourteenth Street, and Sam put his arm around her, the one time they had publicly embraced except dur-ing the vacation in England. She felt frail, like a child, and vul-nerable in the rank air, the void of the familiar street. If they had to walk all the way to Toni's school, they knew they could. But at Twenty-second Street they found a cab.

16 Edith

SHE AND THE TWINS ate scrambled eggs and bacon for breakfast, and their company made her feel like a child again. No arguments about relining the pool or whether to sell the Gramercy Park apartment. Viv and Adri were deep into a dozen aching knees in Brooklyn, with a few bits about chronic fatigue syndrome and the food additives that certainly caused it (Viv) or did not cause it (Adri), the anomaly in Martin's cranium revealed by the MRI and whether it explained his irascibility toward his grandchildren. Viv thought so, definitely. Modern medicine had opened up new worlds for them. Chatting comfortably about it all, they ate their eggs, their toast and jam, and drank their caffeinated or decaffeinated beverages, diluted with soy milk or regular fat free, sweetened with sugar or the newest artificial crystals.

"Never felt so well, he says, since he went on the Atkins." Viv was alluding to her younger half-brother, who lived on one of the Georgia Sea Islands. "Says he lost thirty pounds, his cholesterol dropped to normal, blood pressure of a young kid."

"Well, I don't know how he gets along on all that fat and no vegetables," said Adri. "I go by heart healthy. But no beef. Mad cow, hoof and mouth. It's full of antibiotics. I don't believe in that Atkins. He's a fat man—did you ever see his photo?"

Edith promised that everything on their plates, including the bacon, was organic. No antibiotics. No pesticides. The eggs from cage-free hens. She even got up and retrieved the packages from the refrigerator, made them read the labels. They each swallowed a multivitamin.

"Is it true," asked Viv, "that you're sending out engraved invitations from Tiffany's for Alison's wedding next June?"

"What wedding?"

"What wedding. Who are you kidding? Alison and her roommate are tying the knot, as best as two ladies can tie the knot. We all know it, Edith. Why are you so squirrelly about it? Two hundred people. A dance band. Are we invited? Are you really doing engraved invitations? Sam said so, and the girls will be in white satin gowns."

"No, they won't be in white satin gowns. I have been dragged along into this mess by Sam, as usual, and Alison and her father. Why are you so interested? "

"Are we invited?"

"Don't be crazy. Haven't you been invited to every single party we've ever given? But I don't want this to happen, or at least not here."

"What, Edith. You're a homophobe?"

"A homophobe! Where did you hear that word? Anyway, you and Viv aren't homophobes? You had the same upbringing I had. Men in pairs are bad enough, but two women? Well, okay, if they want to live together and say they're just friends. But getting married—when they can't even really get married? They have to call it commitment? Stop and think. What would our mothers say? Can't you imagine?"

"Well, what about us? We've lived together all our lives. So what? And it's been hard, too. People think we're crazy. Maybe they think we're . . . ," said Viv, and giggled.

"People just think we couldn't get husbands. We could have had plenty of husbands. We just didn't care for it." Adri said.

"What difference would it make what our mothers would say? Our mothers took in sewing so we'd have decent school shoes. They came from the old country, lived in a strange city, got used to strange money and strange food and the Irish and Ukrainians and Russian Jews rubbing up against them. What's gay marriage compared to all that? Wake up, Edith. Why can't Alison and Candace wear wedding dresses if they want? They're lawyers, rich lawyers. They go into court and mow down the prosecuting attorney. Or whoever. Just like on TV. I think our mothers would be proud of them."

"Oh, Viv. Oh, Adri. How can you say such terrible things? Marriage is for men and women."

"Yeah," Adri said, "according to the Torah, a man can have as many wives as he wants, can sell his daughters into slavery. Go with the flow, Edith. This isn't ancient Sumer. And who knows what they did there, probably worse than us."

"Oh, hush. I was looking forward to some peace, with Sam gone, and you've got me upset."

The small TV in the kitchen chattered at low volume. Edith noticed something odd that she could not quite ignore. A movie. They were showing a thriller. Two very tall buildings, yes, it was the twin towers in lower Manhattan, the World Trade Center, and in this film the towers were burning, smoke pouring from their upper floors. It was that old movie about a skyscraper fire. The firefighters would struggle up the stairs.

"Pass me the jam, won't you?" It was Adri. "No, the blueberry. What is that? Why are they showing a movie like that at this hour of the morning? . . . Edith, turn that up, it *isn't* a movie."

"Hand me the gizmo." She held the remote out toward the set, pumped up the volume.

". . . the World Trade Center, both the north and south towers, struck by hijacked aircraft, an American Airlines flight apparently out of Logan Airport, Boston, and a United flight also from Logan, both headed for Los Angeles originally, it is believed. The planes plowed into the towers at about eight forty-five and nine, respectively. No definite word from Washington yet, but it is assumed to be a terrorist attack." The voice was hysterical.

Then the scene changed, to the Pentagon. Smashed, burning. "There has also been a similar attack in Washington. No word on loss of life at either site. Firefighters and police are reporting to the site of the attack in force. Eight other commercial airliners are thought to be under the control of hijackers, headed for unknown destinations. Air traffic control is grounding all air traffic in the U.S. or headed toward it. A fire is reported burning on the Mall in Washington, and a car bomb has been discovered outside the State Department. President Bush has been in Florida traveling on Air Force One, but the plane has whisked him away and his whereabouts are unknown. A direct threat against the White House and Air Force One is said to exist, as well as the Capitol building. Government buildings are being evacuated."

A pain, like an oncoming heart attack, swept from Edith's chest to her head. No, this could not be. She flipped channels. My God, some had no picture.

The announcer said it was the White House, they were going for the White House. "But who is it? Who is doing this? Who's 'they'? Have people lost their minds?" The word *terrorist* forced itself into their vocabulary.

"Oh, my God," Viv said. "They are coming to kill us all."

In a blistering vision Edith saw a close-up of planes crashing into the George Washington Bridge, the Brooklyn Bridge, the White House, the Capitol. "What if they kill Bush and the whole Congress?"

"Well," Adri said, "I've often thought of that but I wouldn't like it."

At 10:12 a.m. one of the towers—it was hard to tell which one—boiling with flames and smoke, let go its moorings and collapsed. The picture quivered. The announcer's voice went dead. People on the ground were screaming "Shit!"

"Look." Edith was calm. "The other one is going to fall down, too. You can see it in the picture." One lone tower, desolate against the ruined sky, smoldering and pouring foul waste.

"Sam," Edith said. "Alison. Oh dear, Alison lives down there, she lives right down there!" She dialed several numbers but nothing went through. What if lower Manhattan simply crumbled and sank into the sea. Who knew if Viv and Adri would have a home to return to? The attackers probably had a plane to send to Windsor Terrace. Many lethal aircraft were in the sky, many hijackings had taken place, more were coming. The three women forgot their buttered toast and stared at this thing on TV.

Edith kept dialing. On the fourth try, she got Gramercy Park, and Sam's voice said, "We're unable to come to the phone just now, please . . ." Oh damn him, where was he? And Alison. If that horrid black Candace had gone to work on Wall Street this morning, what would have become of her? She suppressed a wish for Candace to be dead. No, she'd rather have the commitment ceremony.

Sam had to come home. There was a war on. A wisp of satisfaction, of comfort, crept into Edith's heart. Manhattan was finished. Sam would have to come home, be content with this house, this land, her company. She had foolishly allowed Sam a long leash. This attack was an omen, or a portent. Things had to be set right.

17   Mark

Unsure of the way to Astoria, he soon got lost in the labyrinths of Queens, but just as the day ended and twilight came, he began to recognize the names of streets, as well as subway stops he knew, and at seven o'clock he rang her doorbell, looking nervously around him. No answer. Luckily, nobody was on the street. The ladies who might have been sitting out on a fine fall evening were sitting slack jawed, no doubt, in front of their TVs. He must not be seen—a hundred reasons why not to be seen. He knew he had the keys. He had put them in his pants pocket that morning on his way to the interview.

The place was gloomy, and he wondered if it was wise to turn on a light. Sophie lived like a duchess whose maid was expected to appear at any moment and tidy up. Books were here and there on the floor; they slid out of her grasp and stayed where they fell. Lacy bras, in various colors, hung on the backs of chairs, along with matching little thongs, brazen and flimsy. A laundry bag bulged in the corner. Water, he was dying of thirst. She always put off washing dishes until every dish was crusty in the sink, but one clean glass was in the cabinet. He filled it from the faucet and drained it in gulps, spilling a bit down his shirt front. He'd drunk nothing since the latte at Starbucks, eaten nothing. He was still carrying the red sandal, and he set it down on the coffee table. He needed the bathroom desperately, urgently, and he crossed the room, undid his trousers, and sat down. It must have been nine hours since he used the toilet in Trinity Church. He looked around him at the blissful, childish disorder. Towels here and there, the shelves a thicket of tubes and spray cans, bottles of nail lacquer, lipsticks, moisturizers, pink and tan and black things, eye makeup, products to remove the eye makeup, products to thicken hair and make it lustrous. Sophie was beautiful with nothing on her face or body, and yet she creamed and combed and powdered and groomed, tweezed and depilated, exfoliated, moisturized, drew her eyebrows in with wispy lines. A magazine rack under the sink held bouquets of magazines folded open to half-read articles, so that you could not tell whether it was *Glamour* or *Vogue*. It was heaven to be here. Secret. Safe.

He zipped up, and washed his hands, and felt his knees buckle. A moment later he collapsed on the open sofa bed, to the tune of a loud creak. But, horror, the mysterious white ashy grit that clung to his only good suit and tie was flaking off on the sheets and blankets and floor. Pulverized steel and plastic and possibly human flesh. Poisons, toxins! It would kill them both! And there was a trail of it from the front door into the toilet.

He had brought the disaster with him. Brushing the stuff off himself and the sofa stirred it up more. The red sandal was covered in it. He had never found its owner and he never would. Then, unable to stay upright any longer, he stopped worrying about his dirty suit and the dust and fell asleep. It must have been near midnight when he heard Sophie's key in the lock. "Sophie, darling, it's Mark." He had hoped not to terrify her, but she flipped the light on and began to scream and sob.

"I thought you were dead, I thought you were dead," she cried over and over, clutching him in her arms. How good it felt to hold her, kiss her, assure her he was alive, that he had not gone into the tower, that he had escaped unharmed. That his first thought had been of her, that he had walked straight here. He kissed her again and again, only to have her recoil.

"Your suit, my God, your suit. You're covered with stuff!" Almost clawing him, she pulled off jacket, tie, shirt, and he removed his trousers, both of them trying to brush away the sticky white stuff.

"No, don't scatter it around," she pleaded, "it's poisonous, it will kill us. You mustn't touch it ever again. Find a plastic bag. Look under the sink." And so at possibly the most dramatic moment of his life, he knelt in his shorts and excavated the chaos under Sophie's sink for a plastic bag, which he finally located way at the back behind two identical rusty cans of roach spray. She dragged her vacuum cleaner from the closet and began frantically hosing up the debris.

"I want to get that suit of here," she wept, once they had wrapped it in the black bag. But he could hardly offer to take it to the trash can below, since he'd nothing left but his underwear, and had no intention of allowing her to do it, so they shoved it in the bottom of the closet, leaving the displaced vacuum cleaner in the middle of the floor. As if handling a murder weapon, she wrapped the red sandal in newspaper and laid it in the garbage. "Why did you bring that? You just picked it up? Oh, Mark, poor darling. How utterly weird, how weird. Who could it have belonged to?" He had no answer.

"Have you called Maggie? Mrs. Blass came to pick up Toni at school this afternoon, you know. She was with some elderly gentleman. She said she didn't know where you were. She said Maggie had gone down there. Toni didn't hear her say you were missing."

"No, I haven't called Maggie. Or anybody. I'm unclear about things. I go to a job interview, the building falls down before I can get there, my life is ruined. Only maybe it isn't ruined."

She said nothing, trying to construe his meaning.

"You came here?"

"I came here. I came to you. I never thought of going any-where else. Tell me what happened at school today. Where have you been all this time?"

"Oh, Mark. It's Ashley Parker. I was with her tonight, and her grandparents. Kevin worked in the south tower, Alicia in the north. They're both dead." And Mark remembered sud-denly, with a pain in his gut, that Ashley had talked about it, had pointed to the towers way downtown, had told Toni very proudly that her parents worked in those tall buildings.

The teaching staff of Parkside Montessori, some ten miles north of the burning towers, had taken turns going up to the rooftop gym to witness the diasaster. "All we did, mostly, was try to keep the kids from seeing anything on TV or hearing anything about it. We just wanted to get them home. Susie did nothing all day but phone parents and babysitters, a tough job because the phones mostly didn't work. Of the Parkside parents, only Kevin and Alicia Parker had jobs in the towers. I took her down there a time or two. We visited both offices. They had big offices, sec-retaries, fine views."

"Oh my God."

"A nightmare day. Susie kept the TV on, where none of the children could see it. I kept sneaking in to watch. I knew you were down there, Mark. I played games with the kids, read stories until lunch. Then they ate their sandwiches and drank their milk. Toni Adler and Ashley Parker, both in my class, the tragic little girls, not knowing. You know everybody thought you were gone, too." And she broke down once more.

Around noon, she went on, teachers had escorted a large group of children to the playground. But the enormous columns of smoke could be seen from Riverside Park, and the children smelled doomsday. Around three, an hour after Antonia Blass and the elderly gent had come for Toni and only Ashley Parker remained at school, the phone call had come. Susie Falcon had gone almost crazy and had been unable to stand on her feet for a few moments. It was true: Kevin had phoned his parents in Forest Hills moments before he died. Alicia Parker called whatever housekeeper she had just hired and told her to carry on as usual and be sure to pick Ashley up at school. Then she called Kevin and told him she couldn't get out, and found out he couldn't, either. Kevin's mother had collapsed and was in the emergency room in Queens Hospital. So his father called a car service and came to Parkside to get his granddaughter. The new housekeeper had fled some time after Alicia had made her final phone call.

"Ashley knew already, I know she knew. And she wasn't budging. Getting her in the car with her grandfather was like feeding her into an operating room. She was so bewildered. She fought me. I felt monstrous, monstrous. I had to go out there with her. I was the only person in the world for her. And you know, she never cried. Ashley never cried. Once we got there, I helped get her to bed. Afterward Mr. Parker sent me home in the hired car. Otherwise I'd never had gotten home. He begged me to stay, but

I had to find you. Oh, Mark, what are they going to do? What will happen to Ashley? What are we going to do? You have to call Maggie."

"I don't know, I don't know. Wouldn't you like us to have a future together? Sophie, darling, let's think. No fast decisions. I have a plan. . . . At least give me a chance to explain. But come here. Undress. I'm half dead. You're half dead. I need you, I need you to hold me." They clung to each other until they fell asleep.

18   Antonia

SHE SHUT THE bedroom door behind her. She stopped to get her bearings. Maggie and Toni were in the other bedroom; Sam was in her bed, still asleep. That man's photo was on TV last night, the one who had put an end to order: Mohammed Atta with a flat, square, dark face and bitter black eyes like the black holes somewhere in space. He was the mastermind, had contrived all this, had cut throats, and had died in the holocaust he had engineered. In American Airlines 11, from Boston, he had hurtled toward her as she stood far below reading Whitman on the side of that fence.

All night she and Sam had tossed and squirmed, dozed and wakened, escaped—but only barely—from debilitating dreams. In one dream, she'd been deep in conversation with Mohammed Atta, who insisted, "I didn't do this." Toward 3:00 a.m. Antonia had awakened Sam. "Where is Mark? When will we know?" She was too tired to cry. Sam took her through the scenario, Mark leaving home early, dropping Toni at school, the interview scheduled for 10:00, Morgan Stanley in the south tower, below the line of attack, the impossibility of Mark having gone up there. He must have arrived on Wall Street around 8:30, maybe later. Surely he did not go into that building. He would have been on the sidewalk when the first plane struck. He was lost in the chaos but would turn up.

"Right." She turned her back to him, reached back and pulled him to her, hooking his leg between hers, arranging his right arm on her hip and up onto her chest. This way they could generate warmth, which would in turn generate sleep. He stroked her, curled up to her as close as he could get.

"I ask you, would he go into a building that's being torched by jet planes? You said he didn't want the job at Morgan Stanley anyway. He'd run in there and be barbecued or crushed for a job he didn't want in the first place?"

"Why hasn't he turned up?"

"Amnesia?"

"Yeah, like in the romance novels. Oh God, I wish I had amnesia. I wish I'd taken a sleeping pill. Too late. We have so much to do tomorrow. I'll be a dead person. "

"No, darling. We'll sleep."

And they had, until about five, when he had wakened her. She had tried to fend him off, ah, God, she was so tired, but he had parted her legs, slid down below her hips. She was greedy for his need of her, greedy for his desire. This was medicinal. Human. Commonplace.

Antonia took two aspirin with orange juice, and she told herself that Mark was dead. Otherwise he would have called. What would Maggie do? Maybe it was better he was dead. Then Maggie could start over, somebody else would come along, somebody wanting a widow with a charming child, and it would all be fine. But, oh God, right now her eyes burned, her knees ached.

A hangman's knot tightened beneath her left shoulder blade. On such a fall day, she would usually have opened the terrace doors, inspected the treetops. But the attack had revoked autumn. Stuff was still settling on the leaves, the terrace floor. The radio advised sealing doors and windows with duct tape—but the city had run out of duct tape, as well as surgical and construction masks. Most people on the street looked like scrub nurses. Antonia measured coffee into a filter, poured the water, set out cocoa and tea bags. The coffee pot gurgled, the milk on the stove started to scald, the electric kettle creaked. Breakfast aromas triumphed over the dirty air.

Toni came to the kitchen whimpering, barefoot in her pajamas, and Antonia lifted her to a stool, hugged her close.

"Grandma, I don't want to stay here today. I want to go with Mommy."

"Yes, you and I will both go with her. Of course we're going with her. I told her so last night. Come, Grandma will make you some pancakes."

"Don't want any pancakes. Want to find my daddy. I want to go to school." Antonia patted the mass of curls, swiped her fingers toward the spurting tears but Toni hid her face. Antonia captured the trembling chin in one hand, dabbed at the cheeks with a clean dishtowel dampened in warm water, a gesture that reminded her of her own childhood. Practical, motherly solutions to grief. Like burying your face in an apron, then having a good cup of tea.

"Of course you do. And we will find him. It's just a little confusing. That's why there isn't any school. But there will be school again tomorrow, or at least next week. It's sort of like a holiday. If you don't want pancakes, would you like some toast? I think I have some bagels."

"Don't want a bagel. Don't want toast."

Sam came in dressed and shaved, as if they had slept eight hours. "Good morning, all."

Toni eyed him. She could not figure out who he was. "Did you spend the night here with my grandma?"

"Yes, yes, indeed I did. I had a very good sleep. Did you?

"Are you my grandpa?"

"Well, not the way people usually get to be grandpas. But I could be your grandpa if you want. That would be okay by me. If you need one, I'm applying for the job. We can give it a try today if you like. You can test me out. You can decide later. It is all up to you. Maybe we could play a game together after breakfast. Do you know any card games? I could teach you one. Ever play go fish? You look like a gin rummy player to me."

Toni did not answer, but at least did not refuse. She watched Sam dissolve a cube of sugar in his cup, and then slipped out of Antonia's arms. "Would you like another one? Can I put it in for you?"

"Well, I only like one lump. But I am going to have another cup of coffee pretty soon, and you can put the cube in. Would you do that for me? Are you really not going to eat that piece of toast over there? Can I have it?"

"No, I am going to eat it. I want some jelly. I don't remember my other grandpa, the one who lived here one time. He was grumpy a lot of the time. I think he was sick."

"Well, poor grandpa. I remember him, you know, and he was very sick, you're right. And that does make old guys grumpy. But if you let me fill in for him this morning and afterward, I will try not to get sick or grumpy." Antonia found a deck of cards in a kitchen drawer, and Sam dealt them on the kitchen counter.

Edith wanted him home. He had spoken to her three times

in the past two days. He was quite safe, he had assured her; he had been safe in his apartment when it happened. Alison was perfectly safe. She and Candace had been late starting to work that morning, and had suffered no ill effects. They had moved in on Perry Street, with Candace's uncle. Their building in Tribeca had been evacuated, sealed up, and no one knew when or even if it would be declared safe for occupancy. But Gregory's apartment would hold them, not to worry. No, Alison did not want to move to Gramercy Park. No, he could not come straight home because the garage where his car was parked was closed. (That was a lie, and he hated lying—not so much the lie itself as being forced into that position.)

Still, it was true that the drive to his house in the Catskills would be hard indeed: the cops were stopping cars at the bridges and tunnels. It was sort of true that he wanted to make sure their friends were okay. Maybe they needed to offer refuge to somebody, it was so difficult to get hold of anyone. Edith had said, Oh. She didn't believe him. At the end of that particular conversation, on Wednesday, he had promised to be home by Friday. Now it was Thursday. After allowing Toni to win two or three games of go fish, he excused himself, and in the privacy of Antonia's bedroom checked his phone messages. Edith's voice, as he expected. He called her.

"Sam, why are you still in New York? We need you. Viv says there are helicopters patrolling the Croton reservoir down the road. Those awful people are going to put arsenic in New York City's water. Viv and Adri are never going home—the air is poisoned down there. The air is going to kill everybody in New York. Viv says Mayor Giuliani is under orders from Bush not to tell anybody about it. The air-conditioning under the twin towers has put tons of some chemical into the air and it may even get as far as Margaretville. And Adri says the next target is that nuclear power plant on the Hudson. The Arabs are going to blow it up. Indian Point. They're going to turn it into an atomic bomb. Just like that movie with Jack Lemmon."

"Edith, I don't think it can be that bad."

"It is that bad. You must come home. We're out of things, and I'm afraid to drive to Margaretville. Adri says our cars may explode when we start them. She wants you to leave your car in the garage and get a bus. I'll pick you up in Margaretville."

"How can you, if you're afraid to drive because the car may explode? Tell Adri to rein her imagination in. Nothing is going to harm you where you are—no toxic fumes, no terrorist attacks, and no nuclear bombs. The reactor at Indian Point is buried in a thousand tons of solid concrete. Things are bad enough without making stuff up."

"I'd come that far for you. Of course I'd drive to Margaretville. Sam, three women have no business alone up here. There might be terrorists hiding in the woods, for all we know. This would be an ideal place for them."

"Nobody is hiding in the woods, Edith, for the love of heaven. A few bears, maybe, and those arrogant deer you were complaining about. And what would I do about terrorists if there were any? I don't even own a rifle. I'd be as helpless as Viv and Adri if a terrorist came across the field. I'm an old man. I couldn't even handle a slingshot.

"I told you I'd come home tomorrow, but I will try to get there today." His mood darkened. He felt ill. "I am not coming on the bus. The air is pretty bad here, I admit, and it's chaos. Well, not chaos. Grief. Confusion. Did you stop to think that three hundred fifty firefighters and cops were killed?"

"How can you stay there?"

"Because the city is taking hold—you can't knock New York down. If Adri and Viv are never going home, you and I may have to move back to the city, so brace up. But in the meantime, Edith, we have two people on our payroll, the gardener and the housekeeper. It may not be part of their job description, but can't you persuade one of them to do some grocery shopping for you in Margaretville if you are afraid to drive down there? Just a thought."

How tired he had grown of reasoning with Edith, of dealing with a lifetime of her crotchets! She was at home, as safe as a brick of gold at Fort Knox. With two servants, and she couldn't figure out how to get a quart of milk from the village. Yet pity and guilt arose in him. She was, after all, his wife.

"Edith, please be calm. I've been doing the best I could. We have many friends to be concerned for. I am hoping to be of some use."

"Sam, what is it? Why won't you leave that death trap and come home?"

"It's the death trap I love above all others. Remember, I'm from here. You are, too. But I like it here. Don't fret, Edith, I'll be at your side very soon." He returned to his card game in the kitchen. Bad dog, naughty puppy. Go home.

19 Maggie

A T NINE SHE AWOKE in her old bedroom, with her ragged teddy bear and dilapidated sets of Clue and Monopoly on a low shelf. It was Thursday. Two days into the new world. Wednesday had been a tangle of uncertainty capped by the news that Ashley Parker's parents were dead. Ashley's grandfather had somehow made it in from Queens late Tuesday afternoon to pick her up, and Sophie had gone with them—and the news made Maggie sick, weak. If the Parkers were dead, Mark must be, too. She had spent Wednesday with her mother and Sam, waiting for the phone to ring, trying to get through to hospitals. He had been taken somewhere, surely, and would come to himself and call her. Years ago, when they were dating, she would count to one thousand to make the phone ring. This time, even after the countdown, it did not ring.

Today she meant to start searching, taping posters to every wall. The stories were taking shape on TV, on street corners, in the paper, fiery deaths, suicides, strangers joining hands on hot steel girders and jumping into the air. A man with a mop bucket and squeegee had pried open the elevator in which he was trapped, cutting the thin plasterboard wall with the only tool he had, the metal rim of his squeegee, and he and the other occupants of the elevator had escaped down the stairs, passing firefighters on their way up, just before the building collapsed.

Had Mark been in that elevator with the squeegee man? Wounded or burned, perhaps? People had stumbled down flight after flight, carrying disabled colleagues. Maybe Mark had carried some person down and was wandering around dazed. Or alive but trapped under a pile of twisted steel, wounded, thirsty, desperate, unable to cry out! (At least that would be some excuse for what he was putting her through.) And maybe he was dead. She saw him leap off a melting aluminum slab, and she imagined his funeral. His memorial service. Where would they hold it? Who would speak for him? Would she herself have to speak? It struck her, horribly, that Mark had nobody to speak his eulogy. His boss at the liquor store? Oh, no! She would be in a black dress. Toni would bury her head against her mother's leg. Toni in a little blue coat like Caroline Kennedy at her father's funeral in those long-ago photos. She went into the bathroom to splash her face with cold water.

A funeral would at least be clear. Cleaner than the torment that nagged at her—not merely that he had been crushed by falling steel but that he was alive and hiding from her. With Sophie, in Astoria? No, he was incapable of that. He could not make her suffer so. She and Toni were widow and orphan. With a substantial bit of life insurance. Mark had wanted to let it go. "Goddamn it, how can we rake up this kind of money?" he had shouted. She had borrowed the money from Antonia and paid the bill, two days before the grace period expired. Well, she had no choice but to start looking for him. She dressed in jeans and an old shirt.

"Good morning, everybody." She felt like being polite when she walked into the kitchen. She patted Toni's back and inserted a slice of bread in the toaster. She scarcely knew this man who casually shared her mother's bed, who was playing go fish with her daughter, as if he had the right to be there drinking his coffee from Fred Blass's old mug. Sam Mendel was having breakfast with the family, while Fred and Mark were missing. Maggie wished Edith Mendel would order him home. She hated her mother for allowing him to stay. Gross! as she used to say in her youth. Gross. And yet the man was kind. Sam knew somebody at Morgan Stanley and had phoned him, but there was no way of ascertaining whether a man named Mark Adler had shown up for an interview on Tuesday morning. All the records at that office had gone down in the crash. However, the tower had been hit at 9:00 a.m., and why would a guy expecting an interview at 10:00 be sitting in the reception room that early? "Tell your young friend nobody would come that early. He was on the ground. He'll turn up." Maggie had been grateful for the effort.

"We have to get ready, Toni. Come get dressed. Mother, are you ready?" She took Toni's hand and led her out of the kitchen. "Mother, can you pack a bag?" Antonia had already begun packing it.

"Do we really need to take the stroller?" Maggie called down the hallway. Antonia answered yes.

She and Toni brushed and dressed and came out of the bedroom into the hallway, Maggie pushing the child ahead of her, wondering if they'd need jackets and where she had put the package of tape she'd bought yesterday. Should she pack juice for Toni? And then she noticed that Sam was at the front door with Antonia, holding both her hands. Her mother was white-faced. Quickly, Maggie detoured into the kitchen, dragging Toni along.

This was not a conversation she wanted to overhear. But though his voice was low, Maggie heard it.

"Dearest girl, I have to go. I won't be here when you get back. I have to go home. I'm needed there. I can't put it off any longer."

"Right now? Today? I thought you meant to stay until Friday."

"Right now. I'll phone you tonight. I don't think e-mail is working. If you get news of Mark, be sure to call me."

"But is your cell phone working? I can't call you on your regular phone. Edith might answer. Without e-mail, I am cut off from you." Maggie heard the bewilderment in her mother's voice. Then silence.

"Antonia. Don't do this. You know what the deal is. I have obligations. I have to go."

"I do know what the deal is. You aren't coming back, are you?"

"I don't know if I am or not. Damnit. I have three terrified women in my house, all dependent on me, and I have no ready excuse to be in the city. What can I dredge up at this point? A lunch with my old buddies at the club?"

"Sam, don't."

"You mustn't say don't. You mustn't look at me that way. You'll be fine. You have obligations the same as I do."

Maggie and Toni reappeared in the hall at that moment.

"Grandpa, where are you going? Are you coming with us to look for my daddy?"

"No, Miss Toni, I have to go away.

"Then let me hug you bye."

He bent down for her—"I'm so happy you wanted to tell me good-bye"—and he kissed her.

When he straightened up, his face had hardened, and Maggie

saw that Antonia's was crumbling. Sam was leaving. Really leaving. Perhaps her vengeful wish had been granted.

"My dears, I wish you success today. Please don't push yourselves too hard. I promise you there'll be good news by this evening. And Maggie, please do phone me. I really want to know. And if there is anything I can do . . ." He looked less confident, not quite so tough. Slightly pale. Was he about to cry? It was hard to tell with an old man.

"You're very kind, Sam. I won't forget all you've done."

"I'll see you when I see you," Antonia said, as they started for the elevator, laden with two tote bags and the stroller. They left Sam in the doorway, as if he owned the place, Maggie thought. Oh, well, he did have keys.

20 Antonia

THE SIGHT OF THE Sixty-ninth Regiment Armory, a cavernous old landmark on Lexington Avenue and Twenty-sixth Street, inscribed all around with the names of Civil War battles, somehow lifted Antonia's black mood as they exited their taxi and organized their baggage. The Union Army had stored ordnance here. In 1913, on the eve of another war, European modernism had paid a visit here in the shape of the Armory Show. An outraged New York had gotten its first look at the *Nude Descending a Staircase* and Picasso. Swords could be beaten into plowshares, or at least into paintings, she reflected. On September 13, 2001, the armory had been turned into information central for those seeking missing persons.

"I remember coming to a performance here years ago," Antonia said, strapping Toni into her stroller and hanging a heavy bag on the handles. "Remember Happenings? You wouldn't remember what a Happening was, it was back in the sixties. You'd probably call it performance art. There was a Happening here in this armory, with a lot of painters doing crazy things before a huge crowd. Your father refused to come."

"Well, Mother," Maggie said, "I guess this is our Happening. Something has finally really honest-to-God happened."

Lines had formed inside and out, the desperate and exhausted, clutching manila envelopes, waiting their turn at the row of tables, desks where volunteers with computers took down information and filled out questionnaires, churned out the bales of paper generated by so much death. They took their place at the end of a line, and Toni began to fidget in her stroller, then whined, then wailed. She spurned Antonia's offer of a sip of juice and discarded her cookie. Antonia retrieved it and found a trash can.

"Hush, Toni," Maggie told her. "We have to do this. We are looking for Daddy. Sit still." Toni hid her face.

"Maggie. She doesn't understand. This is no place for her." This echoing cave of hope-against-hope was no place for Antonia, either. As she stroked her granddaughter's hair, the complaints from behind the ten little fingers let up, and Toni accepted another cookie.

"Grandma, I hate this." Antonia unfastened the stroller straps, walked Toni around the perimeter of the vast room.

They waited an hour for their turn. Name of the missing person. Relationship to you. A detailed description, in addition to the photo, and what was he wearing on the day in question, and his whereabouts, so far as you know, that morning? Identifying scars, moles, features? Did he have a pacemaker? No, too young. A tattoo? No, too old. Jewelry? A wedding ring, engraved From Your Loving Wife Maggie 6/5/94. Did she have a hair sample? What? Cells? The detritus from a toothbrush. The mucus on a handkerchief. Dandruff. That sort of thing. For DNA testing.

The woman behind the desk explained that these might offer the only way to identify a body, since bodies, even if recovered, might be in small pieces. "You know," she said, "they aren't finding so many bodies."

"No, I don't have anything like that."

"Well, you'll have to come back with it." She handed Maggie a tissue.

"Honey," Antonia said, "try not to cry. You're scaring Toni silly."

"I feel for you," said the woman behind the desk. "My sister was down there at the north tower for an interview, too, that morning. Blue Cross. And we haven't heard a word about her."

Maggie and Antonia pushed through the crowd at the exit. "Mother, you and Toni go home. I want to put my posters up. And a little time alone wouldn't be so bad. I need to get this done, and I can't have Toni watching. Toni, you and Grandma go for a walk, maybe Grandma would take you to the park. I'll come and find you later." She headed off eastward. She could manage to keep herself together if she could only be alone.

Antonia wheeled the stroller toward Madison Square Park, once the neighborhood hangout for druggies and mental cases but spruced up with plantings and a fancy playground and now the equal of any along Riverside Drive. Antonia dusted off a bench and freed Toni from her stroller. "Let's run around a bit, sweetie, stretch our legs."

"You come over from the armory?" It was a short, fat man, leading a pug on a leash. Both man and dog were equipped with white masks, the dog's taped over its muzzle. The dog danced on its hindlegs, excited by the child, eager to get acquainted. Toni put out her hand but stayed close to Antonia.

"You come from over at the armory?" the man asked a second time. "Too bad, too bad."

"Yes, we did." How could he tell? Did some visible angst cling to them? Some ashiness?

"Yes, my daddy didn't come home from the explosion, and they are going to find him. It will be okay. He will be home by tomorrow, Mommy is sure of it. Why is the doggy wearing that white thing? May I touch him?" The mournful eyes above the mask gave back a kind of smile as she stroked the flat head. Antonia, alert for the slightest sign in Toni of nervous collapse, or the beginning of an aggressive move from the pug, was amazed that the curious, eager, opinionated Toni had suddenly replaced the sorrowful child cringing in her stroller. The man handed her the leash, and Toni darted around the park, coaxing the dog to run along beside her. It yapped, twisted its fat body with glee.

"I buried my wife six months ago." His dark brown eyes were mild, rimmed in red, above his mask, and he spoke with some unidentifiable accent. "Cancer. Brain tumor. Only six months ago I put her in the ground. And this morning up by Macy's a delivery van went wild and killed three people in the street. Did you know that?" His eyes lit up. "TV said one of the people killed had escaped from the World Trade Center on Tuesday. Now he's dead. Guess his number was up. Ha, ha. Ah, the dying, the dying everywhere. They will have us dying. We have allowed them to die, and now they will have us dying."

"Well, that's terrible about your wife. And I'm sorry about the accident up by Macy's. I didn't know. I hadn't heard. But who is it that would have us dying? I don't understand." If he stripped off that mask, what would be under it? A gaping hole, maybe, like in a horror movie.

"Why, the wretched of the earth. The dispossessed. The angry, the hungry. Those that hate us. We have brought this on ourselves."

"Sir, please keep your voice down. I don't want my granddaughter hearing about dying. She's been through enough these past two days. And I cannot agree with what you say. I never hurt anybody or dispossessed anybody that I know of. And she even less. We did nothing to deserve this."

"But you did. By being who you are, you dispossess others. You commit your sins and grasp after money. You commit your adulteries and tell your lies. You made the Arabs pay for German crimes against the Jews. Why didn't you make the Germans pay? And you voted for the men who did the evil. You never asked what or why."

Antonia stood up. He probably lurked around here waiting for victims emerging from the armory. "Well, I sure didn't vote for the current bunch, though I did try to elect some of the others. I've done the best I could." How did he know about the adultery? "And our country has tried to do good. Think of the Marshall plan. Think of a democratic Germany. A peaceful Japan. You can't mean the Israelis don't have a right to their country. Of course they do. Toni, come here. Bring the dog and come here. We have to go. "

"Did you say the little girl's father was dead?"

"No, I didn't. I am sure he isn't dead. We just don't know where he is. Toni, come over here."

"Yeah? Did he work down there in the towers?"

"No, not at all." The man was clearly disappointed. She and Toni were one more item in his litany of misfortune, of sins and crimes. He was collecting discards from the house of the dead.

Toni handed him the leash, and Antonia fastened her into the stroller and said good-bye. Walking fast, she noticed the pall of grit and particles on the leaves and benches. Oh, God, maybe it was her fault that terrorists had knocked down the World Trade Center. She was committing adultery, or at least Sam was. Or fornication. The Taliban didn't recognize the difference, probably. That man said everybody hated us. Why did they hate us? She was trapped in her little corner of New York, her own little set of delusions. Just like most people on the planet. And anyway, everybody did not hate us. He was crazy.

And at last she allowed herself to think of Sam. He would be at the wheel, in the thin northbound traffic on Third Avenue. Or maybe crossing the George Washington Bridge. She wished she were in the passenger seat, asking him what he'd like for dinner. Speeding down the autoroute in Sicily, looking for a place to stop and picnic. Did she not need him more than that spoiled, rich, indolent woman in that huge house? Did she not love him more? This morning, when he woke her up, he needed her. Like food. Like wine. He was gone, back where his obligations were. She could not even phone him without fear of having Edith answer. "You know what the deal is." Yes, she knew.

But he would come back to her, to Antonia. He belonged to her. He'd be back in a few days, after he got those terrified women all tended to at the mansion, got them all calmed down. He wouldn't break off with her, he couldn't. He loved her so, he had never had a life until now. She had restored his youth. She had given him the virility of a thirty-year-old. Oh, God, could she have fallen for a line like that? The oldest story in the book. And she had eaten it up. Have some madeira, m'dear. Heh, heh. She was a fool. Men! He was gone.

The traffic was so scanty she hardly needed to look before crossing the street. Her knees hurt. Toni had fallen asleep, and she tried to cushion the skewed, dangling head, to arrange the little arms. Downtown the sirens screamed and moaned, the noise relentlessly normal. Fighter jets swept the sky, looking for killers and rogues; helicopters battered the air. No passenger jets made their careful descent toward LaGuardia. When she crossed Fourteenth Street, she had to show her passport—her passport! Her home was in no-man's-land. Black smoke billowed from the hole downtown, the corridor to hell.

21 Maggie

S HE SAT DOWN on the stoop of a brownstone on East
Twenty-eighth Street and blew her nose on her last
tissue. She took her Xeroxed photos of Mark out of her pack
and wrote MISSING in red marker across each one. Her dream
man, silly teenage phrase, but he was or had been, and his image
smiled at her in multiples. The photo was four months old. In
the confusion of the past year, she'd forgotten to take pictures,
except a few at Toni's birthday party. Love, pictures, fun. Family
outings. It had all dried up at the state unemployment website a
year ago. Though she didn't mean to be ungrateful for unemployment. God knows.

She stood up and looked around. Where to put these pictures?
The law of averages was against her, against all these pathetic
posters on fences and lampposts, in store windows. The streets in
the twenties were papered with them, as if the city were throwing
a giant block party. Votive candles burned beneath vast disor-
dered displays on the fences. Where were the eyes that would ex-
amine these faces, the fingers that would dial the phone numbers

below the photos? She fumbled for her roll of tape and began walking. Her first spot: the subway entrance at Park and Twenty-eighth. She left Mark there. MISSING. Next, the window of a pizza joint on Third Avenue. Mark's face looked strange to her, not his at all, the colors off, the smile somehow alien.

In Union Square Park she found a spot to rest among the vigil keepers. Young people sat in a circle on the grass, holding hands and singing. She taped Mark's picture to a fence at the edge of the park, among a hundred other faces. Had all these kids in the circle lost friends and lovers? No. They just wanted to be part of the scene—imagine sitting indoors while all this was going on! She heard the strains of "Amazing Grace" from a guitar. The kids sang and wept. She sang a few bars with them.

Her next stop was St. Vincent's Hospital, where she added her poster to those on the Eleventh Street wall: the faces, the same faces again, hundreds of faces, beloved young men and women. Would they ever be found? What about the people with nobody to put up pictures of them? Immigrants, maybe, workers without papers. Who would send the news to China or Cambodia or Mexico? The faces were beginning to break her will. Maggie fell into a trance of anguish. "Am I a widow? Is my little girl an orphan?" At least the firefighters' widows knew for sure. And they'd have the pensions.

She went into the hospital lobby, past the line of waiting blood donors. "Type O only," an orderly told her; they had enough of all other types. She persevered to the main desk and inquired about admissions—no, Mark Adler had not been admitted, nor any unidentified person. Outside, she found that CBS was still waiting for a bit of news to happen, and the medics waited in the ER doorway, but the emergency vehicles screaming in the distance did not head for St. Vincent's.

She walked over to Washington Square, where a memorial with many more posters and many votive candles had been assembled around the perpetually scaffolded arch. Okay, Mark is dead. How does a four-year-old deal with losing her father in a bombing? Well, lots of children in this town had to deal with it. Ashley Parker, for one, who now had only her aged grandparents. And millions and millions of kids in the world had had to deal with it. Boom, your mother, and maybe your dad, too, is gone, blown up, shot, skewered, smashed, beheaded by some red-eyed, slavering teenage soldier boy with a machete.

Her heel had blistered. Goddamn, it must be the socks. She was practically crippled, ill, and thirsty. She went into a coffee shop, sat down at the counter, asked for tea with milk. (Who cared if it was herbal, or where the water came from? She would drink out of a ditch.) The counterman, a black youth in a white apron, brought the tea and offered a box of tissues. She thanked him, wiped her eyes, and added two envelopes of sugar to the tea. For the extra energy. She had to rest her head on the counter.

"Who you missing?"

"My husband."

"Poor lady. I don't know nobody who got killed, nobody who even lost anybody. Make me almost ashamed. The people who come in here, they cry a lot. And it took me two hours to get to work this morning. Had to walk part of the way."

"I know. It's awful trying to get around. You're lucky, though. Don't be ashamed for not knowing anybody. I wish I didn't know anybody either."

The syrupy tea soothed her like Valium. Well, maybe she had to take another angle on it. Maybe it wouldn't be all bad, Mark's death. Besides the $250,000, she might be able to get reparations. Based on his liquor store salary? His earnings to date?

Divorce had been lurking in the shadows for months. In their last real fight, Mark had yelled "divorce" so loud that Toni had overheard, got out of bed at eleven o'clock, and pleaded with them to stop. Her poor little girl! Maybe widowhood would be better. At least there'd be no shouting matches. She could remember the sweet parts, forget the rest. A widow starting over. A young widow, not a hard-bitten, hard-working, bread-winning wife. I am Maggie Adler, widowed tragically in a terrorist attack. She paid for the tea and left a good tip.

She had ten photos left. She should post them around Riverside Park, Roosevelt Hospital, the pizza joints close to home where somebody might possibly recognize the face. When would news ever come? Where was he? Once again he had failed her. Left her to pick up the pieces, if she could find any pieces to pick up. As she walked along West Fourth Street and crossed Sixth Avenue, the idea came to her. It was as plain now as a newspaper headline—the only theory that explained everything. He was not dead nor wandering around in a pitiable amnesiac haze. Mark was on the lam.

Sophie. Whose name intruded on breakfast and dinner, who lived in Astoria. A faraway place. A stopping place on the way to Tahiti, Pago Pago, Guam. Guam, where the snakes uncoiled out of the treetops and fell on you. It was because ecology was out of control and they had let the snake-eating birds die out. Or something of the sort. Maybe he would run away to Guam. She had considered it occasionally herself. He was in Astoria with Sophie. Yes, the bastard. Leaving her in limbo. For if he were still alive, how could she collect the insurance, or apply for reparations, or have a memorial service? You can tell a kid her father is dead, but how do you explain "on the lam," a deserter? How do you frame a sentence with that information?

At Sheridan Square, weak-kneed, she went into the park and found a place to sit down between the plaster same-sex couples (God, how sad they looked) and General Philip Sheridan, scourge of the Shenandoah valley. Oh, if only he were here! There should be a statue for angry, abused wives. She rummaged in her bag for her phone. The bench was rough and mercilessly hard through her jeans. She stuck her legs out. Surprisingly, the phone had a signal, and she dialed Parkside Montessori. Susie Falcon answered after only two rings.

"Oh, Maggie, how are you? How is Toni? Is there any news?

"I have no news. I have spent the afternoon pasting up pictures. Toni is with my mother. Don't ask me how she's handling it. I don't know. I don't know anything anymore. I need to talk with Sophie."

"Oh, she isn't here. She did come in this morning. We're having a trauma counselor, you may have heard. Our children are utterly traumatized, as you can imagine yourself. But everybody left half an hour ago. Sophie was going to the Parker home in Queens. Poor little Ashley has no one but her grandparents, and her grandmother is still hospitalized. Shock. They thought maybe a stroke. Oh God, it is too terrible."

"Yes, simply unthinkable. Susie, I need Sophie's address and phone number."

"Oh, dear, we don't usually give out our teachers' addresses, not even to parents." Maggie heard wariness coming into the director's voice. Protecting that bitch! I'm either a widow or my husband has abandoned me and my kid, and the head of the school is following rules.

"Look, Susie, I know you don't usually do a lot of things. I understand your policies. But Toni is upset. I am sure it will help her to talk with Sophie. I wouldn't bother her at the Parker home. She has her hands full. But just let me have her phone in Astoria."

"Well, I suppose I could. Let me find my Rolodex. I can imagine how upset Toni is. What have you told her? Ah, here it is." She dictated it and Maggie put it into the phone. "Give my love to Toni and your mother, will you? I know everything is going to be okay. . . . Don't worry, Maggie. He'll be home soon. And you phone us the instant you have any news. Our hearts are with you."

22 Mark

HE AWOKE AT NOON Thursday, naked under the
sheet, groggy, disoriented. He remembered telling
Sophie good-bye early this morning. She was gone . . . where?
Why wouldn't his mind work? Yes, she had gone to Parkside
Montessori. Since she had come home Tuesday night, they had
not looked at the clock, let alone the TV, but had held each other,
made love, slept. Sometime Wednesday morning, Sophie dressed
and went out for groceries. Nothing was open but the deli two
blocks over, and she had come home with eggs, oranges, butter,
jam, bread. They had eaten ravenously. Afterward he had tried
explaining his plan. "Honey, let me tell you what we'll do. We
have to make a plan."

"No, it's too soon. I don't want to think about the future.
Look, I thought you were dead. I thought you had been killed
down there, and I wouldn't even have the right to hear the news.
Except maybe some official announcement from Susie Falcon.
Think about today, this minute only."

How odd that interlude had been, Wednesday, eating and sleeping when you needed to, having sex when you wanted it, which had been frequently. About three o'clock, as they were recovering from a bout of passion, both of them sticky with love, worn out with it and yet somehow desperate for more, as if it would cure some disorder in them, Susie Falcon had phoned. The school was still closed, Susie said, but a crisis counselor had been hired, and a trauma specialist. Or perhaps this was all one person; Sophie hadn't got it quite straight. Who would have imagined that the fall of the World Trade Center downtown could bore so deeply into a school for little kids far away uptown. One child orphaned, another possibly fatherless. Margaret Adler possibly a widow. As he listened to Sophie's side of the conversation, Mark wondered if it had been the Parkers' bodies he heard falling to the sidewalk, that whacking noise he'd never get out of his head. Whatever the case, Susie's call subtly altered the texture of the day. Sophie was not quite the same afterward.

"Susie says it's too early to give up hope for you," she reported blankly. No trace of emotion. "She says Maggie is checking hospitals. She and Toni are downtown with your mother-in-law, and they're sure you'll turn up." She was still standing naked by the phone. Had she really decided to become his accomplice? She found an old bathrobe and put it on. Was that a sign of something? "Anyway, you'll have to get along without me tomorrow. I'll be off to meet the crisis counselor in the morning, and then I'm going to Forest Hills." Not long afterward, Grandpa Parker phoned. Mrs. Parker was still in the hospital, suffering from shock and atrial fibrillation. Ashley was having a terrible time of it, numb, unable to cry or even ask questions, not eating. He asked Sophie to come to work for him full time, told her to name her salary. He broke into tears. Ashley came on the phone—the

first time she had opened her mouth, according to her grandfather. She begged Sophie to come. "Of course, sweetie, I'll be
there right after I get done at school."

This morning Mark had awakened long enough to kiss her,
hoping to bolster her will . . . and his own.

"Sophie, I love you. You have to do what you can for Ashley.
Of course you do. I wouldn't want it any other way. But don't
forget, this is our chance. This is the tough part. We can work
it out. I have to stay here. For the moment, there's no place else
to go." She had returned his kisses. But her mind was clearly
somewhere else.

"Poor darling. Poor darling. Of course you must stay here. I'll
be back. I'll phone you."

Now that he was awake and cognizant, he realized he was a
prisoner but was grateful to be within four walls, four flights up,
in a quiet place in which to contemplate the black hole of opportunity, the ferocious singularity that had opened in his life.
What a beginning for their new lives, two nights and a day in bed
together, sex that shut out the disaster downtown, duty, decency,
Maggie, even Toni. He sat up, trying to formulate some plan
of action for today—difficult amid the seductive clutter around
him. His main problem was that he had only a few dollars and
no clothes.

No, his main problem was that Sophie had still not listened to
his plan. He had decided that as soon as public transportation
was back in order, they would leave New York together on a bus,
heading for a warm climate: California, Arizona, Florida. She
had mentioned Fort Myers. Or maybe Las Vegas. How about
Vegas? The economy was booming, anybody could get a job,
they were desperate for teachers. He and Sophie would arrive
unnoticed, after a long ride that he would somehow turn into

fun. They could stop off and do some sightseeing, clean up, have a decent meal at two or three spots along the way. They could rent some nice little place in Vegas. Or wherever it turned out to be. He had heard it was no problem to get new social security cards and driver's licenses. Birth certificates might be a problem, but he could figure it out. All you had to do was phone some state agency. He'd use somebody else's name. He would find a job, anything at first. Then he'd set up as a retirement planning consultant. Financing this whole venture was going to be difficult. The money he had taken from his wallet before he tossed it off the bridge came to $19.55. But, as he well knew, Sophie had $10,000 in a money market account somewhere, a legacy from her aunt. Surely she would be willing to invest it in him, in their new life. He would repay her many times over.

He might never see his home again on West End Avenue, the shabby apartment Maggie kept so tidy. He thought of Toni's room, the bed she slept in, her toys in plastic crates. Himself in front of the TV with a can of beer, the out-of-work dad. Mark Adler had an opportunity to be elsewhere, to be other, to be antimatter, the positive image of his old negative self. Did he have the courage?

He parted the curtains at the front windows and rolled up one of the frayed straw blinds. The sun poured through the opening. Nobody had seen him enter, he was quite sure. And the streets were still vacant, nobody perched on the stoops, no chairs set up on the sidewalks. So far he was invisible. Only Sophie knew. He could discard his identity—one of the unemployed already expunged from the statistics, holder of a valueless MBA, a father unable to support his kid. Mark Adler had died tragically, looking for work. Toni could hold her head up when she said that. He tried to consider himself dead, an involuntary suicide. They were talking about twenty thousand lives. Maybe more. If his old life were among them, who would know the difference?

He flipped on the TV. The anchor people were struggling to find enough vocabulary in which to couch the city's losses, to enunciate the sorrow and rage and grief and bewilderment — "Why did they do this? What do they want?" — while downtown it was dawning on the rescue teams that the bodies had been squashed, reduced to nothing. Yet among the orphans, the widows, whose lives had been changed forever, there were surely a few for whom this event created a new life. He thought about the fireman's widow (who surely existed) still bruised from a beating last weekend. She'd get a lump sum instead of just lumps, and the bastard was gone. Only a few people would know she was rejoicing under her black veil. A husband who discovered that his wife was still alive because instead of going to work that morning, she had gone to a hotel room with her lover. And he would divorce her, and be glad of it. The widow of an accountant who knew her husband was embezzling, and she would not have to watch him go to jail because all traces of his crimes had been effaced, and she knew the number of the account in the offshore bank.

Among the dead were surely those about to be diagnosed with throat cancer or Parkinson's or beginning to show the signs of Alzheimer's, and they had been spared a more terrible death. Others like himself, on their way to interview for jobs they didn't want and probably would not have landed anyway. And they did not have to wait two weeks and then get a turndown by e-mail. If this attack turned out to be a war, if disaster struck somewhere else tomorrow, Los Angeles, perhaps, or the Golden Gate Bridge, if the city air were sown with smallpox virus, what would Mark Adler's tiny package of deception mean in the face of all that?

He would get a fresh credit card without a scintilla of debt on it. Well, that did bother him, leaving Maggie with the credit card debt at 20% interest. Maybe they'd forgive the debt. Would they stick her with his college loan payments? Was a spouse responsible for those? This was a turning of the path, an opening of a door. Maggie could collect the insurance. She would find another man, probably a better man than he. He'd been on his way to interview for a high-paying job. She might be entitled to a tidy sum. Even if all they counted were his liquor-store earnings and his contributions as a stay-at-home dad.

Ah, Toni, the only thing he had ever done right, and he pictured her, in her pinafore, leading her wooden dog down the path to the baby park. He wrestled with the thought that she'd be better off without him. Was there any chance Maggie would collaborate with him in this, would understand how neat the deal was, might allow him to see Toni occasionally, or at least keep up with her in secret? He'd show up at her college graduation. She would forgive him. No, that would never work. Anyway, a daddy who committed insurance fraud was hardly an asset. He would have to vanish. He wondered what the statute of limitations was on that.

Other men had abandoned beloved children, had simply walked off. One of his coworkers at Grumple had been the son of such a man, a serial monogamist, who had strewn offspring by five legal wives around the United States. Yet, in spite of this heritage, the Grumple guy had done okay. Lived in Greenwich. No apparent scars.

But like the AA folks say, take it one day at a time. He needed clothes. All he had were his dirty shorts and undershirt. He should wash them, but he put them on as he waited for the water to heat for coffee. He was hungry. They'd eaten all the eggs. Drunk all the milk. He wanted milk for his coffee. New clothes.

Sophie would have to go and get him some pants and a shirt. When would she come home? She had promised to phone him after the session at school this morning, but she had not.

He went back to the TV. Meaningless numbers rose and fell, along with a parade of false news. A truck loaded with explosives had been apprehended on the George Washington Bridge, and the cop who stopped it and made the arrest was up for a medal already, was to get his medal tonight on TV. A myth. The area around the Empire State Building had to be evacuated because of an imminent attack. Again, false, false. Rudolph Giuliani appeared with his commissioners, solid, square-bodied toughs looking more or less like the lineup behind Brezhnev on the parapets of the Kremlin long ago. You could see they knew their jobs. The mayor promised swift and lengthy jail terms for pranksters and scaremongers. "People who make bomb threats will be tracked down and jailed," he said, and you knew he would damn well do it. Mark wondered what the mayor might do with a man who went on the lam under cover of a terrorist attack. Well, Rudy had his own marital scandals.

Again and again they ran the film of what he had seen with his own eyes: the plane slamming into the north tower, the burst of flame, and minutes later the second one slamming the south tower, the south tower collapsing, the north tower collapsing, the same crowds fleeing eternally northward on Broadway and West Street and across the island toward the Brooklyn Bridge, the same cries of "Oh shit" in the sound track, the same black woman weeping, the same blanket of apocalyptic smoke. The firefighters climbing toward their deaths with ninety pounds of gear strapped to their backs. The heroes who would never return. Oh, the lucky bastards—he wished he had been among them. He was grateful that they did not show the bodies falling. They spoke only briefly of them, and of the living human bodies in the lobbies, set alight by jet fuel seeping down the elevator shafts.

Each time, he searched the footage intently for his own face—how easily a video camera might betray him. But he did not spot Mark Adler in the streets or in the crowds thronging the Brooklyn Bridge. Early this morning he had dreamed of his interview. As Mark made his pitch, he had felt a burning sensation in his lap, had realized that his pants were dissolving, disappearing, as though acid had been poured on them. His privates, his naked knees, and his sock tops were clearly visible. Easy enough to see where that one came from. Whatever he decided to do, he had to have some clothes to do it. Would Sophie never phone? Maggie appeared, like an apparition in a seance. He rehearsed the confession he might be forced to make:

"I am safe but have been suffering from amnesia. I went to a motel. I'll be home tomorrow."

"I ran away, Maggie. I want to come back. Will you take me? I will try to be a father to Toni, at least. I will try to be better than I am."

"Go get the damn insurance money. I'll play dead. All you have to do is let me hear about Toni occasionally. This really is the better way."

No, none of that would work. If only Sophie would phone, if only she would opt for Key West, or Mendocino, or Phoenix: lovely warm places. They could even pretend to be married, or could really get married. Bigamy was nothing compared with the rest of it. Anyhow, who would know? If Sophie would only phone and say yes, they could move quickly. He couldn't risk being seen, discovered, here in Queens. Maggie would need to be able to prove him dead if she ever wanted to collect that life insurance. Would Metropolitan Life take her word that Mark Adler had disappeared?

The phone rang. Sophie. He picked up.

"Mark. How are you?"

"Oh, Jesus, honey, so glad to hear your voice. I am trapped here. I need you. Please come home. I am going nuts."

"I won't be coming home tonight. I have to stay here. I am going to work for Mr. Parker permanently. I may give up my apartment. Even my job soon."

"But Sophie, have you thought about our future? Sure, you need to help the Parkers and poor Ashley. You're all they've got. But what about . . ."

"Yeah, I have thought about it. Ever since Tuesday night, I've hardly thought of anything else. Mark, you have to go home. You have to go back to Maggie, to Toni. You must know what it does to a child to lose a parent in a holocaust. You've heard of that, I know. I can't believe you ever thought of . . . what you thought of. How could you, really? I look at Ashley. You don't want to do that to Toni. You and Maggie will have to sort things out. I am ashamed that I am any part of her problem. You can tell her that."

"Sure, yeah, I'll tell her. Oh, Sophie, don't send me back into that. Let me just explain. Toni will be better off, Maggie much better off. I love you. I am offering to give up everything I have for you, even my name. There must be some way. . . ."

"There isn't any way. I have to come home tomorrow and pack some things. It would be better if you were gone. I mean, you have to be gone."

"Yeah. Yeah."

"You're a sweet guy, Mark, but all fucked up. And me, too. I am all fucked up, too. You sort of have a criminal mentality."

"Sophie! Don't call me a criminal."

"I didn't. I just meant you aren't thinking straight. You've been through a trauma. But I am thinking straight. Good-bye, Mark." And she hung up.

He loved her, really loved her, her beauty, her disorder, her gaiety, and most of all her intuitiveness with Ashley and Toni. Something magical about her, disconnected from the ambitions that drove most people. What he had proposed was dishonorable—even criminal, as she said—but wouldn't it be fraudulent to go back to Maggie? Sophie, I am not a criminal! Men have committed worse deeds to escape an unbearable life. Of course, the guy who absconds to Rio always gets caught; just as he is ordering the second martini and thinking of seducing the cooch dancer at the night club, the police inspector catches up with him. That's the way it goes.

He stood in his underwear and contemplated his options. Toxic or not, the suit had to be resurrected. And the socks. And the shirt and tie. He pulled the bag from the closet, laid the wrinkled, ashy clothing on the floor and used the vacuum cleaner on them. Which did not help much. The bag was bulging, and he knew there was no other. Well, he couldn't go naked, and it was a long way home. He washed his face and hands and hair, and shaved with the tiny electric razor that Sophie used on her underarms.

The phone rang once more. Maybe it was somebody for Sophie, somebody who didn't know he was there. But maybe it was Sophie. Perhaps she had thought things over, was coming home for at least one conversation. Finally, when he thought he could not bear the suspense, the machine clicked on. Sophie's recorded voice. Maggie.

"Hello, Maggie." He could just not have answered. But it

hardly mattered. It would all come out anyway. This was as good a time as any to begin.

"You're alive. You know, I knew you'd be there. I registered you as a missing person at the armory. I went around town today putting up posters with your picture, and then coming up West Fourth Street, it all came clear to me, and I knew where you were. I got Sophie's number from Susie Falcon." She was breathless.

"How is Toni?"

"How is Toni? I don't know how she is. Scared. She wants you to come home. How are you? I assume you want a divorce."

"I don't want a divorce. I do want to come home. I was about to call you."

"You have to tell Toni you aren't dead. I don't know if I can tell her. We have to think of some story and stick to it. You want me to tell her you ran away to sleep with her teacher?"

"Where is Toni?"

"At my mom's. Where would she be? She won't talk about you. She knows we think you're dead. I guess you know about Ashley."

"Where are you?"

"On a bench in Sheridan Square. I meant to go home and get some hairs from your brush or your toothbrush or something and take them back to missing persons. That's at least one job I can forget. One errand I don't have to do. Were you down there when it happened?"

"Yeah, I watched the first plane, and then I didn't know what to do about the interview, so I waited in Trinity Church, and then I ran. I ran here. To Sophie. I thought maybe it was a way out. For me. For you. I had some idea you could collect my life insurance and I would go away. I even thought of telling you about it. Not a very good idea, I guess."

"You're sick. Crazy. You're crazy. You need help. Do you think I would lie, say you are dead when I'm talking to you on the phone and you're shacked up with your girlfriend? You are a cheater in ten different ways. What am I supposed to do? Beg you to come back? I hate you, you prick. Prick. Die in the street!"

"Right."

"You should have been killed instead of all those brave men who died saving others. I'm too stunned to cry. You and that slut. Fucking her pupil's father. What are we going to tell Toni? Greg and Arty? The school? Anybody? I can't even imagine what my mother will say. You can wander around the streets for all I care. What do you want, Mark?"

"Oh, Maggie. Try and understand. Don't call Sophie a slut, she's only a kid. She's not a slut. She's already told me to get out. I meant to get out anyway. I was coming to my senses. You don't know what it was like. I never should have . . . I never would have gotten that job. I wanted it for you and Toni, but I wouldn't have got it. I ran across the bridge and I thought maybe it was a sign, a sign I should just drop out, get out. I just ran to the first place I thought of. Tell them . . . tell them I've been sick. Tell them I've been hiding. Tell them I just came to. Tell Toni I'll read her a story. Maybe we can figure something out. I will come home tonight if you'll let me. Don't ask me to come to Antonia's. Not today."

"Okay, okay. I can't talk to you anymore. You call Toni now. You call Antonia now. You talk to them before I get there. You make up a story. You were hit on the head and some kindly person took you home to Queens until you figured out who you were. You lost your cell phone and your wallet. I don't care what you say. I'll come home tonight. I wished and prayed all day for you to be alive. And now you are. Be careful what you wish for, the wise man says." The signal failed.

He buttoned his soiled shirt carefully, then put on the trousers and jacket. He folded his tie and put it in his pocket. He was able to restore his shoes to a respectable shine, but the bathroom mirror showed Lazarus, with the dust of the grave upon him. Mark let himself out of Sophie's apartment, locked the lock, and slid the keys under the door.

23 Antonia

S HE SAT UP in the dark, shivering.

What had awakened her? She had been lost in a maze of narrow cobbled streets, squat white houses, unsure what she sought, frightened because her face was naked and men were watching, and then she had ascended some stairs, had transmigrated to a room, which she had entered without knocking, like a spirit called up by a Ouija board. The room contained, or rather was contained by, a morbidly obese sofa upholstered in swirling pink-and-green flowers on black, a sofa descended from the sphinxes and the temple of Hatshepsut, massive, authoritarian—and in its depths sat Mrs. Atta, mother of the hijacker. They could have a chat, two mommies, and Antonia tried to embrace her.

"I'm so sorry, Mrs. Atta, your son, he's gone in a pillar of fire."

But the woman pushed her away. "My son is not dead!"

"You should have stopped him. You should have told him those virgins waiting for him in paradise were a lie."

Mrs. Atta grew angry. "Not a lie. But he is here, not there. You deserve all you got. Infidels!"

"How can you be proud of somebody who murders?"

"He is my son, he is not dead. You lie. He did not murder."

Mohammed, Antonia saw, was staring at her from the bedroom ceiling: dead eyes, the cartoon-slash mouth, the black hair, backlighted as if on a scrim. Once more he had hijacked her dreams. "Vengeance is mine," he cried, "and I forbid any women to attend my funeral because women are dirty." He vanished—all but his black eyes.

She hoped the sick bugger was up there with the virgins and couldn't get an erection. She tried to shake off the mother, the sofa, him, and return to where she was, in her own bed with her own granddaughter. A low light glowed around the edges of the window blinds, not the dawn. She rubbed her eyes until she could read the numbers on the clock: 2:53, 2:54, 2:55, digital blinks. Oh, God, the worst of all possible times. Toni slept deeply, one arm curled on her pillow, the comforter up to her chin. These things, sensible, real things, had awakened her. The need to pee, the need to drink. The roof of her mouth was cracked leather, she had rhinoceros breath. Fluids out, fluids in. Something to be grateful for. She bent over the child, who might also be dreaming of monsters. Surely not. Antonia tidied the covers, patted the brown curls, forced herself out of bed into the chilly room.

Mark had brought Toni to Perry Street yesterday afternoon. Mark and Maggie were undergoing marital therapy, and the counselor had prescribed an evening out for them: dinner, a movie, a night alone together in their apartment. Toni needed a break, too. Particularly since the grandmother was always willing. For this you paid $200 an hour. At any rate, Antonia paid it.

Mark was no longer in the job market—he needed to heal, the therapist said. He was working part time at the liquor store as he had been for months. Well, God help him. At first Antonia had opposed Maggie's taking him in again. At least in the privacy of her heart, she had opposed it. Not having been asked for advice, she did not offer any. Why a marriage should be preserved after a man had disgraced himself, devastated his wife, and terrified his child was a mystery. At least his pathetic circumstances brought Toni frequently to Perry Street.

"Grandma, I'm having a sleepover with you," Toni had explained when she and Mark arrived, clearly impatient for her father to leave. Toni exhibited such symptoms of anxiety as nightmares, sulks and tears, and a disinclination to go to school. Maggie blamed the deaths of Ashley Parker's parents for Toni's problems. Sophie had continued as Toni's teacher at Parkside Montessori, and in theory Toni knew nothing about Sophie and her father. But she knew. That evening, when she and Antonia had cooked dinner together (pancakes, bacon, puddles of maple syrup) Toni said, "He hid from Mommy and me, on purpose." She said nothing about Ashley, only her own betrayal.

Remembering another among the vanished: "Has my new grandpa left? Will he be sleeping here tonight? I liked him. Are you going to keep him, Grandma?"

"No. I decided not to keep him."

And on top of all this, Gregory had been diagnosed with lung cancer. On the last day of September, surgeons had removed a large piece of his right lung, and he had almost died two days later from the trauma to his heart. Antonia had sat outside the ICU with Arty and Candace for two days, off and on, waiting their turn for a glimpse of him. It seemed only a straw in this hurricane of troubles that George Bush had become a hero with poll ratings near 100 percent. With his cowboy talk and his bluster. And Mark had survived.

Sam and Edith were in therapy, too. She knew from his e-mails. The terrorists had created a workers' paradise—for social workers. Post-traumatic stress disorder, PTSD, what people used to call shock and grief, was as heavy in the air as chemicals from the explosions. The whole city had PTSD, according to the diagnostic manuals, and the grief counselors were working overtime. Why not tell Maggie that Mark didn't have PTSD at all, he was a two-timer and she ought to divorce him? Why didn't Sam tell Edith he was in love with another woman? Thinking such bitter thoughts, Antonia wondered if she herself needed grief therapy. Losing your lover was a minor inconvenience in the context of such massive grief, the thousands casting flowers into the great pit downtown. But it hurt. Physically. Like an asthma attack, those nights when she woke herself moaning "No, no" and had to get up and find the Scotch and sit for hours staring into the dark. No Scotch tonight. Toni was here.

She put on her bathrobe, went barefoot across the cold hallway. The terrible change in things, the paranoia. A woman down the street called the cops about some pieces of discarded carpet she had seen by the garbage cans—"terrorists' beds," she feared. And in Brooklyn the firefighters and police, as well as the FBI and Homeland Security, had spent an entire day ransacking a building, at a cost to the taxpayers of $2 million, because the janitor had seen a child's toy resembling a bomb in the basement. On the other hand, the crime rate had plummeted. Nobody had the heart to commit murder or burglary these days. The site downtown swarmed with engineers and bulldozer operators and sanitation trucks. So much stuff had been donated, blankets and boots and coats and gloves, that they had to hire somebody to

haul it all away. Teams of volunteers had materialized to cook
and serve meals to the workers, who spurned the healthy food
they dished up and demanded Big Macs. Cheerleaders stood on
West Side Drive, hailing the trucks as they rolled downtown,
yelling words of gratitude, waving signs. Oh, city of wharves and
stores, mettlesome, mad, extravagant city! Well, it was showing
its mettle. Walt Whitman would have recognized it. He'd have
been down there eating Big Macs.

Antonia sat on the toilet, her feet freezing on the bathroom
tile. She wiped her bottom, washed her hands in the icy water of
2 a.m., went back to bed. Toni was radiantly warm, but Antonia
thought of Sam in bed and turned away. How could he have left
her, how could he?

Her next attempts to sleep were trumped by Maggie. The
counselor advised not to worry about the job. After all, he had
work, work he said he enjoyed, and the financial industry was
reeling. No point in reapplying to Morgan Stanley. Maggie urged
him to start a new life, go back to school. Teaching, perhaps, a
purposeful life. Antonia wondered if he was still seeing Sophie
on the side. Part of the healing process. No, that was forbidden,
except for the unavoidable meetings at the classroom door.

As for herself and Sam, they had closed the road between
them, dynamited the bridge. And yet nothing was final. Hope
crushed to earth shall rise again, shall shamelessly apply for a
reentry visa. They would travel together again. As she had last
June, she would meet him at the airport. He would be smiling at
her in the split second before she spotted him. They'd eat wonderful dinners together, drink wine together all over France,
England, Spain. But then she mocked him as a sorry poltroon.
"You are nothing but a sham," she shouted in her fantasies. "You
care only for property." She composed epitaphs for Sam Mendel:

"The man of property." "He loved his mansion more than life."
"Food is not love but real estate is." "Here lies a cold cat."

Revenge, she wanted revenge. Just you wait, 'Enry 'Iggins. But
she remembered every hair and muscle and line, the body she
had caressed in every way she knew, and if only he would come
back, she would do it again. Be his mistress, his concubine, his
lady of the shadows. In autumn, at twilight, one had no time for
scruples.

She got up and raised a blind. A helicopter chattered overhead.
Never a shortage of helicopters. A car alarm bleated, briefly, far
away, and she heard a man shout. Somewhere below her, beside
a stoop, Charley lay in Maggie's old sleeping bag, his filthy backpack by his matted head, newspapers spread beneath him. It had
been a week since she'd staked him to a meal. The attack had
hurt the homeless, increasing their ranks, decreasing the few city
mercies available to them. Who had time to run soup kitchens,
except to feed the brave workers downtown? Why hadn't the
block association done something for Charley last year instead of
planting all those goddamn petunias? Helen, you jerk.

A war raged in Afghanistan, where many people hardly knew
the name of the next village and had never heard of the World
Trade Center. Years ago, she had promised herself a visit to the
Kabul Museum, where the lovely ancient marble and bronze ar-
tifacts testified to the first meeting of Greeks and Chinese, Ro-
mans and Steppe dwellers, strange princes and warriors of the
Hindu Kush, whose court artists, seeking a face for their god,
had carved Buddhas in the shining earthly image of Apollo, god
of the sun and of the muses, so that each time you saw a Buddha
face, you saw the face of idealized male beauty. An import from
the west. She had yearned to see these things. But the Taliban
had pulverized everything in the Kabul Museum, had gone into

the desert and dynamited the giant stone Buddhas carved into the crags and cliffs of Bamiyan. The Buddhas had once observed the Silk Road caravans lumbering past, processions of camels carrying luxury goods from China to the west. The Taliban had demonstrated that only murder and ignorance and stupidity matter. And George Bush would help them carry the game even further. Young warriors from Wisconsin and Tennessee, wearing the hard-won insignia of Green Berets and Rangers, tramped through the ferocious mountains, the razor-sharp terrain where the word *assassin* had been coined centuries beforehand, where murder had been reliably begotten throughout history. These young men, as so many before them, must wonder what had drawn them into the mountains of death. But like the soldiers in Thucidides, they went on. And from the icy Afghan sky, robots fired missiles, and airplanes had electronic eyes so that they could identify a man from twenty thousand feet and kill him with one pulse of a computer. Everyone said the war was good, necessary. "Bring 'em on. We want 'em, dead or alive."

The clock blinked 5:00. Perhaps there was no organizing principle for the chaos, the irrationality of history, the malign indifference of biology, the inevitability of war. All that she could think of was what, as a young student, she had believed to be the organizing principle of the world: grammar and syntax, iambic pentameter, the rhyme schemes of sonnets, the only reliably beautiful thing at one's disposal: words. Words that imposed order. Syntax that forbade ambiguity. That made things clear. In the beginning was the Word, and the Word was God and the Word was with God.

She crept back into bed. Toni had kicked off the covers. Antonia banked the comforter around her. Sam should be here, coming to bed with her, warming his cold hands against her flesh. And as they fell asleep together, he would tell her that she had given him the rarest gift. I do love you, Antonia. She could not find a comfortable position. The clock blinked 5:15. Antonia at last fell asleep.

24 Sam

H E AWOKE EACH MORNING and told himself Antonia was gone. This was the new world. Edith was everywhere. She entered his office without knocking when he was at the computer. A most annoying habit on her part, since he was always hoping for messages from Antonia, which appeared unpredictably. She might be philosophical: *We were crazy. We should have realized it would all blow up one day. Maybe if we were French . . . but we aren't.* Contemptuous: *Why tell me your troubles? Fuck off. You made this mess.* In a panic about Edith's snooping, he deleted Antonia's e-mails almost before reading them, then tried to reconstruct them in his head. He deleted his e-mails to Antonia. But didn't deleted e-mails always survive in some electronic purgatory? Finally he fell upon the expedient of changing his password daily to keep Edith out, but then he would forget the password himself. Would she read his mind?

Edith watched him as he sank into his English leather chair and grimly pretended to read Chekhov. She watched him watching the snowfall. He took comfort in snow, imagining animals asleep beneath it. He no longer used his cell phone, for his wife examined every incoming bill. The company sent a full disclosure each month, all the numbers. Would she follow him into the bathroom, watch him pee? He was under house arrest. He might as well have been the twentieth hijacker. Still, he had betrayed her. She was, after all, his wife.

Vivienne and Adrienne settled in for the winter, and for once Sam was glad to have them: two kindly faces at mealtimes, Edith's antagonists, discounting her rage, tamping down her outrage at his infidelity, at his having preferred another woman's company and, obviously, bed to hers.

"So what's so terrible?" he heard Viv ask Adri one afternoon when they had borrowed his computer to look up hoarseness on the website of the American Academy of Otolaryngology. (How had anyone managed to be a hypochondriac before the advent of the Internet?)

"Right. What's her kick?" Adri answered. "She has what she wants." Such trivia as a husband's philanderings could never compare with vocal-cord polyps, chemicals in foods, nuclear power plants, and other threats to public health. Out of daily contact with their circle in Brooklyn, the twins ran short of medical news—whether certain biopsies had been positive for malignancy, whose triglycerides refused to go down on any diet or regimen, who had switched from Fosamax to Calcitonin, who was having good luck on the okra-and-tofu diet—but they kept up as best they could.

Edith's attack had been frontal, monetary, and lethal. "You are welcome to a divorce if you want one. I will take this estate away from you, every acre of it. The house. Everything in it. The paintings. The china. Your eight-burner cookstove. All of it. You think I don't know how to fight you, or how to find a good

attorney, but I know. You'll never see this place again. I'll deed
it to Stephen. I will see to it that Anna and Stephen and Rachel
never speak to you again. You can have the apartment on Gramercy Park. At least for the moment. You can go there today.
I will pack for you. And then you can pack *it*. I want to sell it.
Please remember that it is half mine."

"A bit harsh of you, wouldn't you say, my love? Don't you think
we need to cool off?" He saw himself wandering the Manhattan
streets, weeping in Antonia's arms. She would have to care for
him. He would be a sick, poverty-stricken old man, dependent
on his mistress. His children would shun him. Edith would see
to that. Ah, poor Antonia. He could not saddle her with himself.
She would grow to hate him. But why in the name of god could
he find no voice for himself, no brief for his side of things? Sometimes, in private, he wept over his smashed sense of rightness,
of entitlement, of passion, of mutual orgasm, of deliciousness
achieved in Antonia's arms, bed, or kitchen. "This is love, what
we need, we all need," he had said. He cringed, lied, like a prisoner under interrogation. Edith would bring in the glowing grate,
the pincers, and the iron maiden. He was starting to believe his
story, and the more he believed it the less easily Edith fell for it.
"I haven't done anything so terrible, really. Formed a friendship.
Pursued intellectual interests. Good God, Edith, I have always
had friendships apart from you. You were quite clear about not
wanting to share my other life. It bored you, taxed you. What are
you so angry about?"

"You creep. You were sleeping with her. At your age! There is
no fool like an old fool."

"Edith. How cruel. Not to mention that the phrase is a cliché."

"Supercilious bastard. Don't pull your New York intellectual
stuff on me, your afternoons-at-the-Century-Club face. What's

next, a quote from Shakespeare? The famous publisher and ac-
tivist playing around with an employee. And at age seventy-two.
You're the cliché."

"No, I am not. No, I didn't. She wasn't my employee then.
It was only dinner. . . ." He went on cringing, lying, denying.
When the truth threatened to emerge, he quickly repressed it.
They had somehow reached a stage where Edith believed he had
been Antonia's lover, but he did not. No, he had never really been
her lover. No, he had not had sexual relations with that woman.
He understood how Bill Clinton had felt, why he had said such
a thing. If, for a trifle like sex (it never seems trifling at the time,
only later), they threaten to deprive you of all you esteem, of
course you say you never did it. He and Antonia had been mere
traveling companions, mere dinner companions. What point was
there in speaking the truth, the paltry little flaccid truth?

*Every time I turn on this machine I hope to see a message
from you. Humiliating. And sometimes I do see one. We should
stop e-mailing. You have purchased stability and respectability.
You can't even tell Edith the truth. No, we cannot have dinner in
November. How can you even suggest it? Would it be with her
knowledge and permission, or without? And one thing would
certainly lead to another.*

He pleaded, sporadically, for just one evening with Antonia,
just a few hours of relief from this new life. Edith bored him,
made him feel like ninety. But could he walk away from a wife
of almost fifty years? No, he had never intended such a thing.
He had thought of traveling from Sicily to the Scilly Isles with
Antonia, and on to the Outer Hebrides, but never of abandoning
Edith. Or at least not of abandoning his house. The house hung
him from his thumbs. Lose this house? His creation, in which
Edith had acted as a naysayer at every phase? What would she

want with this house? How would she ever care for the property? The gardens would turn into a weed patch, a deer preserve.
Was he to be reduced to fighting Edith for it? Possibly seeing her
win it? No. Never. Never. Never. Going through World War III
with Anna and Stephen and Rachel? Imagine Rachel, praying
over him! And thus he would circle 'round himself, until pure
longing for Antonia silenced the uproar in his mind and he could
wrap up in his comforter and nap. Did he not owe Antonia
something, too?

New York City, so brutal and indestructible yet so vulnerable,
had become the chief target for the enemies of modernity. They
had come to crush all that Sam stood for, all that made life worth
living. If they got their way, Antonia would be put into a pit and
stoned. Along with half the American female population. But
the city fought back, cursed the enemy even as it wept out loud,
counted its dead, brought in its heavy machinery; its teams of
burly guys who knew what to do, and always did know, began
to excavate the dreadful chasm downtown, from which chemical
horrors were still expected to emerge and poison the population.
The city was tougher and more resilient than most nations. New
York luck had not entirely run out: a breach in the retaining walls
under the towers would have allowed the Hudson to flood the
subways and turn them into giant irreclaimable sewers all the
way up to the Bronx, but they did not break; the electrical system
and the telephones were not damaged beyond repair; after all the
horrendous losses, there were still police and firefighters left, and
hospitals and ambulances.

And yet it was too much to bear. On the news every night one
heard the piercing whine of the pipe bands, the slow march of
death: 347 firefighters and police dead, and somehow they all
had to be buried or memorialized, and there were not enough

bagpipers in the world to do it. The dozens and dozens of obitu-
aries in the paper day after day. Sickening, how very young the
dead were, how sweet their faces, these stockbrokers and traders
and clerks. Burned, crushed, finished. Like the firefighters and
cops, they left children behind for grandparents to raise. Oh, the
butchers, the butchers. Death was all around, way outside the
city limits, way outside the confines of Manhattan. Hundreds of
funerals in New Jersey, on Long Island. Even in Massachusetts.
Delaware County had already had two memorial services: the
parents of one dead firefighter lived in Margaretville; a guy who
had a summer house down the road and worked as a financial
analyst had died in the north tower.

Sam despised himself for hiding out in the Catskills, marveled
at how the losses radiated outward from the city, penetrating
almost the entire world. Brits had died, Chinese, Filipinos, Ma-
laysians, Africans. New Jerseyans. Manhattanites. If New York
was suffering, he was suffering. If the air stank, he wanted to
smell it, fill his lungs with it. If the sky was filled with choppers
and fighter planes, he wanted to hear their roar. He wept when
he watched the *News Hour*. How dare they do this to his town?

What was happening to Antonia and little Toni? Were they
breathing fumes that would take their lives one day? What of
Mark and Maggie? How could they possibly piece things together again after his appalling behavior? Running off to Toni's
nursery school teacher, for Christ's sake. How could anybody . . .
But then he remembered exactly how a man could do that. He
was needed there, Antonia needed him. He needed her. Plus he
had work to do: committees, boards, meetings. Things had not
shut down. But at the first suggestion that he might return to
Manhattan, even for a night, Edith bristled, started in again.

Sam took to napping fitfully all day, and reading all night, in a crisis of insomnia that neither pills nor whiskey could touch. He paced the floor of his bedroom, stared at the pages of a score of books, whose printed words somehow made no sense to him and dissolved before his eyes, leaving Antonia's face. He thought of making love to her, tormented himself with detailed and lubricious fantasies, the taste of her labia, her mouth on his genitals. But also the pure comfort her companionship provided, unconnected with carnality or sex. Sometimes this would put him to sleep toward morning. At least staying up all night saved some confrontations—Edith was always in bed by ten. She the early bird, he the wounded nocturnal animal.

One day in November, with the four of them at lunch and Sam despondent before his salad, Vivienne had announced, "Sam, you're depressed. Practically anorexic. Eating is your pleasure and you never eat anymore. This is terrible. You need help. What kind of help?"

"Yes, you have to decide what kind of help," Adri continued. "We've been talking about it. You both need help. You could just get separate lawyers and end it all. I mean, get a divorce. Sam, maybe that would be the best. Edith is eating you alive."

Viv next recommended an arbitrator, "to help you decide how to end it. Help you do a nice fair property settlement. Or you could get a marriage counselor and decide if you ought to patch things up. That's three different kinds of help you could get."

"I wouldn't like to see you divorced," Adri said.

"On which I beg to differ with you, sister. I think you'd both be better off," said Viv. "Edith, I wish you'd let up a bit. Don't you care about Sam? Sam is seriously depressed."

"What about me? I'm facing the end of my marriage, and I have been betrayed for no reason, and I'm not seriously depressed? And you, my own cousin, tell me I'm eating this man alive? You should go home."

"Edith, don't say such unkind things." Viv was always calm.

"We are trying to help you," Adri said.

Sam revived a bit. "You pick your favorite health-care or legal professional, my dear. What'll it be? Doctor, lawyer, rabbi, or priest?" Edith chose the marriage counselor a week later, and with their connections in the medical world Viv and Adri soon located someone in New York, since surely there was no suitable person in Delaware County. Edith refused to spend the night in Manhattan, so Sam drove them to and from the sessions, often seven or eight hours round trip, with inbound delays at the George Washington Bridge. The counselor was a Dr. Steiner, who reminded Sam of Heinrich Himmler, the same secret smile and the same drab coloration. He was semifamous and the author of an oft-reprinted book on marriage, *Until Death Do Us Part: The Sacred Promise.* Sam recalled seeing him on some talk show. He had expected at least a neutral stance, but neutrality had gone out of fashion in psychiatry. Rather than sophistication and tolerance, the profession was intent on strangling secular humanism, if that meant some louche tolerance of wandering affections and legal separations. Had the damn White House taken charge of marriage counseling? Sam would have been better off with a rabbi, who might have had some mercy and some sense.

"My goal is always to save a marriage, and most especially when an elderly couple comes for help. I am opposed to divorce on moral and, yes, religious grounds. It is particularly damaging for those who've been married a long time. So be warned."

"We are not elderly. Or at any rate, I dislike being called elderly." He tried not to sound as hostile as he felt.

Steiner smiled. Sam soon learned there was no point in trying to outwit Steiner. What was the use? He stuck to his story. Antonia was only a friend, only an intellectual companion. Yes, he had secretly made a trip to England with her because she was such a knowledgeable traveler. And they had had a legitimate business meeting to attend. Edith had lost all interest in traveling. He was simply trying to protect Edith, to be considerate of her feelings. To be an honorable man. Yes, he had been with Antonia on the morning of the attack. Why not? They often took walks. He had come from his apartment at Gramercy Park early that morning, and gone walking with her friend Arthur. The autograph dealer. There was soon to be a family connection between them, since Arthur's partner, Gregory, had this lovely niece, an attorney, who was about to team up with their very own granddaughter, Alison. It was simple, simple.

Edith set in angrily. "You hear how he talks? A commitment ceremony. If they can't help their sexual choices, they should live quietly. How have they gotten so brazen! Barging around, wanting to get married. My lovely little Alison, my petted grandchild, exploited by this social-climbing black person. And they are going to do it in gowns with trains. Yes. And veils, in the name of mercy. Everything according to *Modern Bride*. Yes, that's what Stephen said they said! Is one of them to have a bachelor party in advance? Which one?" Steiner said nothing, waiting for Sam.

"Well, if they're going to do a commitment ceremony, what do you expect them to wear? Sackcloth and ashes? Okay, okay. I have to admit it's a little over the top. Like some kind of parody. They are listing at Tiffany's and Michael Fina. Picking silver patterns. If you're striking a blow for gay rights, maybe you should invent your own customs. But hell, I don't know. I guess it might as well be satin and lace. If the caterer calls it a wedding, and Macy's and Williams Sonoma don't object to two women listing in their registry, who are we to object?"

"I do very much resent your saying yes to Stephen and Alison without telling me what lengths they intended to go to. I'm not religious, but this goes against my religion. It is disgusting, physically disgusting. And now I'll have to stand in a receiving line with two women in bridal gowns. Pairs of lesbians in evening dress dancing it up all over my house!"

The lesbian wedding took up all forty-five minutes of the first session—not a word about Antonia. They drove home in silence.

"Perhaps Candace and Alison will be happier than we have been," Sam had ventured at the beginning of the second session. Dr. Steiner warned him not to be negative. Edith next revisited the subject of Sam's whereabouts on September 11, and what she called his friendship with Antonia. Then a whole lifetime of resentment bubbled up: his critical, even cynical, attitude toward his children; his bullying; his refusal to understand her views of life. She slashed at him for abandoning her, for isolating her in the country while he gadded around in New York. At the end of what proved to be a very long monologue, she claimed that separate sleeping arrangements and their mutual lack of sexual interest for the past thirty years had been his idea. He had left her bed. He had never liked sex. After the first ten minutes, Sam stopped trying to get a word in.

As the analysis progressed, from one week to the next, Sam tried to defend himself against the charge of child neglect: "I was only doing what fathers did in those days, trying to make a good living. How unfair it is of Edith to bring up charges like these, as she was the most zealous of mothers. She would have slapped my hand if I had tried to change a diaper. She wanted me out working hard, making money. She has definite views on gender roles. She thought I should earn enough to hire help for her—and God knows I did, and she hardly had to wait for it. She never wanted me to come into the kitchen and do dishes, though I did that, too. I'm a better cook than she is."

He wrote to Antonia:

We're seeing Steiner tomorrow at 11 a.m. if I survive the getting up and leaving by 7. I don't know if there's wisdom in continuing to see him, but leaping off the cliff has been avoided—or postponed. I think avoided because everybody seems to be glued to everybody else and to everything else. Husbands to wives they don't love, wives to husbands they don't love, husbands to houses they love and hate, etc., kids to the prospect of inheriting money, and all sorts of lesser but real currents. The thing that I can't figure out is the profession's insistence that truth is, if not essential, then helpful, clarifying, and also, in the end, therapeutic. But once you let certain truths—and some of them are awful, awful truths—out of the can, you can't shove them back in. Where does it get me to tell Edith I love you? She will only screech more loudly.

Sam was unable to raise his voice in his own defense. If Edith failed to cut him off, Steiner always did. How Sam hated them both, yearned to blurt out that he was only lying in order to coddle Edith. That he was lying because he was afraid his entire financial structure was about to be struck by screaming jet planes and burned to a cinder. That he was trapped by age and the threat of dying, that he was ill from insomnia, loneliness, from pure confusion. From lack of conviction. From combining sedatives with alcohol on many a night. He thought of writing a long, impassioned letter to Steiner, setting forth the true situation, setting forth his raw emotions and confusions, telling him what a splendid woman Antonia was and that he did truly love her. That in fact there had been moments when he knew his only hope of living another ten years was with Antonia, who delighted his heart, eased his aching body, took years off him more surely than all the antiaging nostrums currently in the marketplace. Why was he reduced to this humiliating double confessional known as marriage counseling, in which neither party could possibly tell the truth? But he could utter no such cry. Speak no such truth. Steiner would use the information as a murder weapon. Antonia grew severe.

You've asked me many times what could be gained by your telling the truth. Only this: If you and I had been mere dinner companions, a book club, and I was simply more interesting than Edith, that makes you a snob. By telling her and Steiner that we are lovers, you lend yourself, and me, some gravitas. You were not just out for sex. And yet I know how difficult it is to extract the words "I love" from you when one is not speaking of a plate of oysters. Love that arrives late in life is a thing of dignity, an event that creates its own rights, just as property creates its own rights.

But since you want peaceful coexistence with her, you will have to abide by her rules. One of those rules is to leave me strictly alone. As you say, ego is involved there. You are an ornament to Edith's life, her entree to respectability and comfort. For all I know she loves you. Love goes under many guises. It might break up the logjam if you told the truth: you and I are partners in a way that you and she were never partners. But given your true desires here, it isn't worth it. You must be content to live by her rules. I love you, in spite of it all. In spite of property. Which is, as they say, theft.

After ten miserable trips from the Catskills to Manhattan, Sam apologized for his failings, agreed to meet Edith's demands. He would move permanently and live with Edith, close the apartment in New York, sell it eventually. He would resign from the various boards, give up the Century Club, cut all ties with Antonia, indeed, he had already cut them. (He did not mention e-mail and thought privately that e-mail might be an exception.) Steiner looked so pleased with himself that Sam had to stare at the floor. Another marriage rescued! Another sacred union pulled back off the end of the plank and anchored firmly to the poop deck. And at that moment, Sam wondered, just for one moment, if Antonia had perhaps been right, if the truth might have served some purpose even if the outcome had proved the same.

In this debacle, he did make one condition of his own. They must proceed with plans for the commitment ceremony. Edith must lay aside her homophobia—Steiner had cut in to remind him that "homophobia" was a pejorative, a loaded word, that millions of people, for good reason, and with the approbation of their priests and ministers and rabbis, saw matters exactly as Edith did. Sam countered that Alison was their granddaughter, their beloved first-born granddaughter. They could not insult Alison, could not cravenly withdraw their commitment to commitment. People went every day and took part in ceremonies they hardly approved of. Literary prizes, for example; half the time, as most insiders knew, the winner scarcely deserved the prize. And yet everybody flocked to the cocktail party. Half the weddings anybody attended, same sex or not, were looked upon as folly by at least a few of the guests. But people turned up anyhow. "This," he said, trying to tamp down his despair, "is what civilization is. Keeping your mouth shut."

Edith, it turned out, was ready to make concessions. It wasn't really the ceremony, she said, just Sam's handling of it. His insensitivity. She could go through with it. Disgusted with himself and with her, he promised to make things as easy for Edith as he could. She promised that she would find a way go through with it. Her daughter Rachel certainly was opposed to it, and many others in the family, but they would just have to put up with it.

Steiner was adamant that they needed further counseling, that they must rebuild their marriage, and even their sexuality. But Sam could see that Edith was as indifferent to this project as he was. And so they bade Dr. Steiner farewell. All this had cost only five thousand dollars.

The drive home that afternoon brought a new tranquillity. Sam felt it even as he beat through the brutal traffic over the George Washington Bridge and onto New Jersey 17. Borrowing Sam's cell phone, Edith managed to press the right button to ring home and let Viv and Adri know they'd be there for dinner. "It's all settled," she said. "I think we should eat out," and suggested the twins make reservations. Sam had agreed to stay home and live with her, and if the price of this was having this big party with a lot of lesbians, okay. She would buy a new dress, get those gorgeous diamonds out of the safe. And let Sam arrange the house party, with all her children there. It might be worth it.

AS THE WINTER rolled on, Sam took full charge of the party. Stephen's caterer was a pudgy middle-aged man with two cell phones, a beeper, and a Blackberry. Not much time left to plan the thing—a rush job, and he made it clear there'd be extra charges for the haste. He insisted on major revisions to the old barn, to render it a suitable, insurable venue for a huge reception, with dancing—work must commence at once. He wanted to dig up part of the lawn and turn it into a field of wild flowers that would bloom in June. No, Sam said. No wild flowers.

"There will be plenty of flowers by then: roses in bloom, and you can gather mountain laurel from the woods." It would cost thousands to get the barn in shape, but there was no choice. He couldn't have dancing in the house. Edith would never permit it, trampling her carpets, spilling drinks on her furniture. And there was not enough room. He had no idea what the bill would amount to. He didn't care.

None of their children had gotten married here. Anna eloped. Stephen and Camilla got married at her home in Cleveland, of course, as was fitting and proper. Rachel held her wedding in an enormous Baptist church in Little Rock, where Sam and Edith felt desperately uncomfortable. They felt even more uncomfortable at the reception at a country club, in which Sam and Edith were the first Jews ever to set foot. But he paid for and put up with everything with a good grace. No alcoholic beverages, lots of praying.

He thought a bit anxiously about caterer's trucks in the driveway and fellows in white aprons seizing control of his kitchen, setting up grills in the yard, waitpersons in formal dress passing silver trays lined with exquisite nibbles. The house would be a hotel: Candace's mother. Camilla and Stephen, Anna and whoever she happened to be living with by next June. The twins. Rachel and company (she had refused to come to such a thing, but he knew she'd come anyway). But if nothing else came out of it, he would get one more glimpse of Antonia. She was, of course, essential—she and Mark and Maggie and Toni—because of Arthur and Gregory.

Antonia wrote, *You ask me not to flay you alive with my words, but how can I do otherwise? My friend is gone, my lover. Edith won the case with her tears and indignation (after 30 years of a sexless marriage, for which she blames you, at this late date) and her eternal house. She won you with your marriage vows of so long ago, and because her suffering counts more with you than mine. I hate her. Injured Dignity Placated by Numerous Concessions. Sounds like a bad Victorian painting. I hate you, too. You were too great a coward even to acknowledge me in the seclusion of a psychiatrist's den. You are happy and content. It makes me feel cheap and worthless, but I feel sorrier for you than for me. I am glad it's winter. I keep hoping for snow and ice. I hate to think of June. Greg may be dead before June.*

No, no that could not happen. Greg would come. He and Arty, of all people, must come. He would do special things for Toni and the other children who might come. They should be allowed to dance, not be shut off in the house playing board games or something. He would hire some musicians, a couple of clowns perhaps. He dreamed of lavish entertainments. He would hold Antonia in his arms, on the dance floor, to be sure. Exactly what might happen after that evening he had no idea. His life as a prisoner could not continue forever. The truth . . . he could always resurrect the truth.

25 Antonia

IN NOVEMBER THE CITY had lain under a fog of depression, and the vacancy in the skyline was dispiriting and astonishing, like two front teeth suddenly yanked from one's own mouth. Bits of bodies came to light regularly in the hole, halting the excavation while workers knelt and wept, swamping the medical examiner's office. Rage broke out among the firemen, who feared the remains of one of their own might be carted off to Fresh Kills, the aptly named garbage dump in Staten Island. Clean snow fell occasionally on the ruins but did not stop the work. Smoke and ash still rose from Ground Zero, as it had been christened, which was still under heavy police guard. One sunny afternoon Antonia went down to watch, and was not surprised to see pushcart vendors selling postcards and T-shirts and NYFD caps and photos suitable for framing. And why not? They were probably selling souvenirs in Jerusalem before the body was off the cross.

In December things picked up a bit. Though every envelope might be filled with anthrax, people began to write and mail greeting cards. Churches made their concert plans. The pipes of Trinity Church had been choked by the grit of the explosion, and the organ now lay in pieces in the storeroom, but Trinity had dusted off the stained glass and the pews and floors and planned to provide Christmas music somehow. Tourists were scarce in the hungry city, despite give-away rates at hotels, despite the glittering Christmas tree heroically set up, as if nothing had happened, at Rockefeller Center. The mayor urged people to go out and eat, get tickets to the Rockettes, spend money in restaurants, and cheer up because if money didn't start flowing, the city would die another death.

And Christmas arrived. Along the Village streets greengrocers and small merchants displayed Christmas articles on the sidewalk, potted poinsettias and small standard-issue circles of evergreen tied up with a shiny red ball or two and little plaid bows. Upscale florist shops had sprung up alongside the spas and nail salons of the new Village, so that there were dozens in a six-block area, competing energetically for trade with huge pots of scarlet amaryllis and exquisite trees decorated with birds and satin bows, as well as leggy orchid plants in torpid blossom and flowers so exotic Antonia could not guess their names. Fruit-cakes in tins were stacked in grocery-store windows, and boxes of clementines from Spain and Morocco. Caviar and foie gras and black or white truffles could be procured on order. Fresh figs, pomegranates, and blood oranges were plentiful, and genuine free-range organic turkeys could be reserved, or suckling pigs if you preferred, and tofu turkeys for the vegans. A small tree in the condom-shop window on Bleecker Street was hung with prophylactics. An odd kind of war, this war on terror, with the home front so handsomely provisioned.

On Seventh Avenue, right on schedule, the tree man in parka

and earmuffs strung up his lights and built a fire in a small stove amid his evergreen forest, which was stacked in clumps like a hedge along the narrow sidewalk, the boughs bound tightly in white plastic twine. He set up two or three shapely trees in metal stands. The price went up every year, but nobody seemed to notice. Early in the month, earlier than she usually bought a tree, and earlier in the morning than she usually was out, Antonia selected a big Douglas fir, the branches of which unfolded into perfect symmetry like a hoop skirt once the man untied them. She paid extra for delivery. Rushing home, she searched the bottom of her closet for the ancient metal stand with its little basin for water. They had bought it when Maggie was three. She unfastened the rusty bolts, dragged it into the living room. Somehow she and the deliveryman got the tree standing. She tugged ruthlessly at the branches: it stood solid. Toni wouldn't pull it over, as she had done when she was two. Antonia's hands were lacerated and pitch-stained. The ornaments for the tree would come later, at the party she was planning. She still had every historic bauble, even the frail angel Maggie had made in first grade.

A week later, deep in party preparations, Antonia forced herself to take pleasure in what she was doing. The unhealthy mix of emotions Sam's absence aroused in her (anger, shame, lust) sometimes combined with grief over Greg like a migraine. She had lost ten pounds, looked pale, bony. Older. One could be too thin, no matter what the Duchess of Windsor thought. She had angrily thrown out the stash of pear sorbet, watched it melt away down the drain under hot water. Today the complex aromas of shallots and garlic, mushrooms and herbs, the other slightly earthy, dirty smells of savory herbs and roots made her queasy. The beef fillet was repellent and bloody in its paper wrapping; but she knew how to turn the red hunk into a splendid thing. Slender green beans were on the menu, tomatoes stuffed and broiled, a chestnut puree, brussels sprouts with walnuts. A side of mac and cheese, made from scratch, for the two children (Ashley had been invited). She intended to make a gratin of potatoes, Grenoble style; she resurrected her wine-stained first edition of Julia Child, banished a decade ago for fear of butter and cream. She sliced the potatoes and grated the cheese. She made a marinade of olive oil and vinegar and fresh tarragon and thyme and sank the roast in it, refused to think of the chemistry, the actions, that were tied up with Sam, the meals that were drawn-out pleasures themselves as well as preludes to other pleasures. This was the first real dinner she had cooked without him.

She had made stacks of cookies; Maggie was bringing more. Arty was supplying the wines. And Candace was bringing a bourbon cake, the recipe her mother had used in Chicago, the very same recipe Antonia's mother had used in Mississippi. Both families, Antonia had discovered, had come from the Delta, and if you made whiskey cakes by the same recipe, Antonia thought, you were the same flesh, sisters.

Sophie had brought Ashley to spend the weekend with Toni. Antonia tried to imagine her arriving, wondered whether it was Maggie or Mark who had answered the door. Magnanimity and forgiveness reigned. Did Maggie speak to Sophie? Sophie to Mark? How did they all manage?

And there was to be a surprise—Maggie had a surprise, something she was saving for the Christmas party. News. Could it be that Mark had had an interview or gotten a new job? He was still clerking at the liquor store; it suited him, really. If only it paid a little more and offered a benefits package, Antonia wouldn't have minded. Maggie was still pushing him to go back to school, get his teaching credentials. There was a city program he might qualify for, teaching and studying for a degree at the same time. She had never seemed more devoted to this man than after he had betrayed her. She seemed almost to have forgotten the whole episode, content with struggling along as usual, as long as Antonia paid the school bills. Well, okay, okay. She brought out the real silver and the real glasses and set the table carefully. Some of the silver needed polishing. And the disreputable-looking red napkins needed washing and ironing, all of which Antonia undertook, as well as the wrapping of the small gifts she had bought to set beside each plate.

Greg rang the bell first; he was undergoing chemotherapy twice a week, in hope of killing the tumor that still sprouted in his chest, and elsewhere, even after the surgery. Antonia settled him on the sofa, piled pillows behind him, and wrapped his legs in a quilt. He smiled, said that he felt okay today, that the news from the MRI had been fairly encouraging, and he did not really need his morphine patches this afternoon and expected to be able to hang an ornament or two on the tree, maybe even eat some macaroni and cheese, though the thought of anything else filled him with apprehension. Cinnamon toast was his favorite food. His eyes were bright with something Antonia could not connect with health. Arty came in next, with a load of bottles, which he quickly stowed in the kitchen. He plumped up the pillows and fussed around his lover as if the problem were a bad cold.

Alison and Candace, who were still living with Greg and Arty, waiting for their residence to be reopened and declared fit for habitation, carried a substantial bourbon cake and put it on the sideboard. Antonia tried to feel affectionate toward Alison, Sam's own granddaughter. But she thought her a featherhead and could not imagine her as a trial lawyer. The two women settled in close to Greg, Candace on the floor and Alison at the end of the couch.

The two little girls, arriving with Maggie and Mark, were in a party mood. Toni was in navy velveteen, Ashley in green, both with white tights and patent leather shoes, like children out of some fantasy about children. Antonia had an idea that Ashley didn't miss her parents severely—they'd traveled so much that she might imagine them away on another business trip. Today, at least, Ashley had no hint of the traumatized orphan about her.

"Oh, how glamorous you are," Antonia told them. "I had no idea you'd come so dressed up! Are you too beautiful to do any work?" She had set up a low table in the dining room, with craft paper, glue, scissors, a bowl of popcorn, cotton poufs, old Christmas cards to be cut up, crayons, and glitter. Ashley went to work at once on a popcorn chain. Maggie quickly shrouded the kids in aprons in case they smeared glue. Mark declined a drink and took over the supervision of the children. He even made a popcorn string himself. Good boy, best behavior.

The afternoon passed in the pleasant way of such family parties: the too warm room, the excitement of decorating the tree and turning on the lights at last, the scent of the fir, the children falling into disagreements, the smell of beef roasting, the dishes carried to the table, the admirable crunch when Antonia broke the top of the gratin, Arty opening and serving wines, the cake and cookies waiting, the coffee afterward, with brandy. Antonia presided over it all with mounting satisfaction, dishing up and serving the food and later clearing the table, bringing out coffee cups and dessert plates, turning on the lamps midafternoon when it was getting dark. Normalcy achieved. No point in thinking of Sam, or of Greg's impending death. And indeed, who would or should pity her, in ease, in comfort, surrounded by her family? Two gay men, two women about to be married to whatever extent the law allowed, Maggie and Mark in therapy, probably for life, Toni and Ashley content with each other and with the day. A true American family, archetypical not in spite of but because of terminal illness, adultery, sexual nonconformity, a not-too-merry widow, and a newly orphaned child. Would it play in Kansas? China? Kenya? In Saudi Arabia? In Congress? The White House? Definitely not. Still, here they all were. Bush and Cheney did not always win. The Taliban did not always win.

After the feast, Antonia helped the children out of their fancy dresses, gave them soft, old T-shirts, and put them down for naps on her big bed. Gregory had fallen asleep. Everyone had eaten bourbon cake and cookies; Arty had served brandy. Antonia had had very little to drink and couldn't relax in the after-dinner torpor. There was, heaven knew, plenty to do in the kitchen. She recognized her daughter's plate on the kitchen counter—practically untouched, not even the vegetables. Was there some hidden meaning in the rejected dinner? She scraped it into the garbage. It occurred to her that Maggie had refused the wine, and then the brandy. As Antonia bent over the dishwasher, Maggie stepped into the kitchen.

"Mama," she said. "I want to tell you before I tell everybody else." Antonia felt used up. Done in. Terrified. She knew the secret already, knew it by the look on Maggie's face, her smile. Antonia sat down on a stool.

"Maggie. Honey. You're pregnant."

"Yes."

"How pregnant?"

"Must have happened the middle of October. I just saw the doctor. I'm due early August."

"And Toni?"

"Toni doesn't know yet. She will be happy. You know how sweet she is about things. She has adjusted to Mark's return, I think. She'll be five soon. That's close to the age of reason, I guess."

"And Mark?"

"Oh, a bit overwhelmed. With this, with everything. Doesn't know where he stands, or what he should do, but that's who Mark is. Not ever knowing. Maybe he feels a bit, well, a bit trapped. But the therapist is helping. This will make us a real family. He will simply have to find his way. Mama, I'm so happy. I'm the main one who's happy. Please be happy, too."

Happy! Had Maggie lost her mind? Had Mark? Was it some accident? No, obviously not. Maggie didn't have such accidents. How would she manage, how could she want another child by a man who had betrayed her, taken the first steps toward fraud and desertion? Not to mention who was going to pay for it and what kind of maternity leave would be forthcoming and where would they live, they hadn't even enough space for a crib. All this skidded through Antonia's mind and crashed. It was unutterable, and in the end she did not utter any of it.

"Aren't you afraid he'll have a tough time with it? I mean, you said the therapist thinks he has PTSD or something and needs a lot of time to adjust. A new baby doesn't allow the parents a lot of time to adjust."

"The therapist is helping him with it. The baby will get him through it. He needs more responsibility, she says. But how do you feel? You don't sound thrilled, dear mother."

"A new baby. A new grandchild. I am happy." It was a lie, yet she felt better, even euphoric. "Yes, another grandchild!" A baby born out of the shock and despair of September 11. Odd, now that she had said the words, she was happy. Hell, she might as well be happy, and she tried to remember the sensation of a new baby in her arms. There'd be things to buy. Maggie had a lot of Toni's things stored here. She would have to go over them, wash them. Maybe Toni would want to help. She smiled. She followed Maggie into the dining room to hear the official announcement, deliberately avoiding Mark's eyes.

By eight o'clock, except for Greg in a drugged slumber on the sofa, everybody had gone home. "Let him sleep here," Antonia told Arty. "I'll take care of him. You get a little sleep yourself." She covered Greg with the quilt, put a glass of water on the table. If he woke and called for help, she'd hear him.

She opened the curtains and looked down into the street. There wasn't much foot traffic on Perry this cold evening. One December long ago when Maggie was home from college, she had gone to visit a friend uptown in Washington Heights. Antonia and Fred had expected her home by six, but she didn't come. Two hours passed. Of course, she was a grown woman. She might have gone into a bar. Gone out with her friend. But Maggie was the kind of kid who phoned. The more Fred refused to worry, the more Antonia did. The weather had turned bitter during the afternoon, and Maggie had only a light coat and no gloves.

At ten, Maggie came in.

"Do you know what happened to me? I stayed uptown later than I thought. And then the A train didn't come for a long time, and when I got out of the subway I walked in the wrong direction. I don't know how I could have, but I did. And then a car skidded up onto the sidewalk. I didn't have time to blink or dodge. It smashed into a mailbox, and then a storefront. I just missed being smashed into the store. I had to brush glass off my coat. The police came. They took me to the station. It took forever to do the paperwork. The fellow driving the car was drunk, and he died in the crash. He nearly killed me, too."

Antonia herself might have died from that.

Luck was also a terrorist. If Mark's interview had been scheduled an hour earlier, at nine, he might have died in the south tower. Luck intervened in the form of a Morgan Stanley appointment schedule, and the keys to Sophie's apartment in Mark's pocket. Next August there would be four Adlers—and that was not luck, it was Maggie's wish. She could almost mourn for Mark. Healing and closure. Forgiveness and renewal. All the sad jargon of therapeutic living. And the poor chap who had tried so ignobly to escape was trapped forever. A second baby never did anything for an unhappy marriage except make it unhappier. Choose life, Mr. Bush and his heavy contributors were constantly preaching. Well, Maggie had chosen it, so Antonia had no choice but to choose life, too.

26   Greg

THE CLOCK WENT OFF at eight, and he opened his eyes. He slept in bits and pieces around the clock, no day or night, with the TV on. Its mutter kept him from swinging off into dope-powered fantasies. This morning, as always, two people chatted merrily about the weather. It is Groundhog Day, they said. He was alone on the sofa, where he had all but taken up residence. Arty or Antonia sat with him in turn, held his head, his hand. Brought him thick, sweet drinks to try. He would open his eyes, unsure whose face would swim into view. Sometimes Ian's face, Ian's hands. Ian sometimes held him, dear boy. The point of being alive was to have no pain. Pleasure was what we wanted. He could scarcely lift the morning paper. Doorknobs, faucets, and the tops of peanut butter jars, car door handles were obstacles in the roadway. He was using up his morphine patches too fast.

Why had they set the clock? It was doctor day. Antonia's turn to take him. And just as he figured it out, she appeared, smiling, helped him upright, assisted him toward the bathroom, asking him if he wanted to shower. Yes, he could manage that, had enough dignity and strength to shower alone, and she went away and he undressed and shivered under the torrent of hot water. He managed to enjoy it after a moment, and then to turn off the faucet and towel himself dry. Excellent. But the mirror showed a bag of bones. Antonia handed him a pair of undershorts through the doorway without looking, and then helped him into a pair of new khakis and a blue striped shirt and sweater in the smaller sizes he now required. He was exhausted and had to sit down. She clipped the tags off his brand-new camel-hair coat with the fur collar. "Let me wear my old down jacket," he said, "I'm too weak for a new coat," but she held it out to him, and he slipped his arms in. It felt heavy on his shoulders, but comforting, even in the warmth of the apartment, and he turned the fur up around his ears.

"You look wonderful, years younger. Just look at yourself in that outfit!" Lying Antonia. But he saw that really he did look younger, and his black eyes in the mirror shone, like a dying poet's. His skin was lighter, his face fuller. Edema, no doubt. Where had his muscles gone?

He had begged Arty not to order all that stuff from catalogues. No room in the closet for all that stuff. Why did he need all that stuff? Oh, Arty, busy man, running his business more efficiently than ever, talking about the money they'd need for the long vacation he was planning after Greg got well. Would he prefer the Dordogne or Brittany? Greg picked the Dordogne. How could a person with half a dozen new pairs of trousers and a thousand-dollar coat and renewed subscriptions to the *New Yorker* and *Antiques* and a three-month lease on a villa starting next July be rude enough to just up and die without using any of it? Not Gregory Johnson, certainly not he.

In the kitchen, in the coat, he drank a glass of pineapple juice, the only thing he could think of swallowing. Vitamin bottles littered the kitchen counter, antioxidants, believed by Arty to possess special powers. Brave warrior molecules that went after free radicals, the bad guys, and squelched them. Yes, squelched, quenched, stamped them out, according to the *New York Times* science section. Terrorist, enemy molecules that made you old, sick, threadbare, weevily. Greg swallowed a few antioxidants daily. Also on the counter, submerged in a bowl of tea, was a giant blob of kombucha, a mushroom that turned the tea sharp and vinegary. The guy at the health food store had sold it to Ian as a cancer cure. "Better, cheaper than what they are doing to you," Ian said, for he disapproved of chemotherapy. Arty and Antonia said it was bullshit, but Greg drank his daily dose anyway. Why not? It smelled like healing powers to him, and it hurt less than chemo.

Arty had wanted to come along, too, this morning, but Antonia forbade it. "I brought you a sleeping pill. Get some rest. You look like the one with lung cancer."

And so he and Antonia went out into the street. A mild day for early February. At Perry and Hudson a school bus rolled up and waited at the red light. A scrim of mist rose from the river, from Hell Gate and the sea, and the pale hibernal sun burned through in one patch, lighting the dirty brick and brownstone façades, turning them mauve and gray. Gregory unbuttoned his coat in the false spring: there might be news today. Real news.

There were no taxis hurtling up Hudson Street. Foolishly, he had refused to let Arty call a car service. He leaned heavily on Antonia, he, Gregory who had once leaped and tapped from one end of the stage to the other, had turned himself into an S curve. Well, he had other interests. He was otherwise. Very otherwise.

Inside the the school bus that was waiting for the light to change, kids yelped and yelled and threw spitballs, and the driver yelled back at them. Whatever happened to him this morning, that school bus would stop here every day with its load of raucous kids. He admired the survival capacity of the city, of Antonia, of Arthur, of these children. Of Groundhog Day. The ferocious nineteen from Riyadh and Cairo had knocked us down, and we bloody well got right up again. He sighted down Hudson Street as if it were a gun barrel. Overhead a jet plane floated, headed toward LaGuardia, at a normal speed. Some nice pilot at the controls, backed up by his copilot and navigator. Not some nut intent on mass murder.

Where were the taxis? Crawling into the backseat of a taxi was more than he could do, maybe. "Let's wait for one of those big taxis." Certain consonants, such as *t*, caught in his throat. "Those vans. Where you can sit up straight. It'll be better for your legs, too. Why don't we have those nice London taxis? Where you just step in?"

"Because this is a democracy, not a class-ridden decaying monarchical system with a rich old queen at the top where taxis are made to please the customer. This is America. It shouldn't be more comfortable in a taxi than in a subway, should it? Also, this is New York: it should cost three times as much." Plucky Antonia, trying to amuse him, and he laughed.

His knee hurt more than his chest. "I ought to have had the knee replacement instead of the lung surgery. It would have been less of a nuisance. I'd feel better now."

"Don't say that. You'll have the knee replacement soon as you're better." Ah, brave Antonia, uttering stout falsehoods. But her optimism pushed his mood upward again—mood swings being an essential part of this curious process of illness, as he had discovered. Maybe, by God, he would get well. Somewhere along the rest stops of this morning's trek from radiology to oncology there could be good news. Dr. Lopez, in his white coat, might look up from his charts and pictures and say remission. For the last six weeks, Greg had taken a magic pill every morning. Some people, taking this same experimental pill, had recovered, to all intents and purposes, said Dr. Lopez, their breathing restored, their pain abating, and what intents and purposes could there be beyond that? Lopez, Professor of Oncology at New York University Medical Center, thought it might be the new cure for lung cancer. He had developed this agent, as he called it like a CIA station chief, and he was testing it. Today I am the groundhog, Greg thought, the lab animal. I will see my shadow today and . . . What was it? Winter would be over? Was that the way it went? Or you saw it and winter lasted forever? Which way did it go?

The assignment today was to pick up X-ray films from a radiology office in the east sixties, and then proceed downtown to where Lopez the oncologist was. There had been three oncologists, plus two surgeons, a cardiologist, assorted radiologists, and a couple of other experts and specialists. He could no longer keep track of the names.

At last the traffic spurted toward them. A flock of cabs ran northward, their roof lights shining, and in response to Antonia's imperially stiff-armed gesture, a van taxi, with plenty of legroom, stopped for them. The lilting voice of Beverly Sills, opera star, admonished them to buckle up. Greg couldn't do it, but Antonia wrestled the belt around Greg' s coat and then fastened her own. Thank you, Beverly, and thank you, Ralph Nader, and Mayor Guiliani. A dying man still fastens his seat belt.

The traffic on Eighth Avenue thickened, clogged, halted. Two days earlier on East Sixty-fifth Street, they had locked Gregory in a tube, peered inside every hollow and crevice and tissue and organ, every bone, everything. The pictures would be methodical, sheets and sheets of film, frame by tiny frame, hundreds of frames on heavy black sheets, the inventory of one's body, everything but the pubic hair, which had fallen out anyway. This morning the photos were ready for analysis, dispatches from a war inside Gregory's body. Lopez's secretary apologized for the detour but said it would save time and money if Mr. Johnson picked up the films. A bloody nuisance, but sick people had to go and collect things. It kept them busy. It gave them a job. Being sick was full-time employment.

The trip took forty-five minutes, at least ten minutes inching across Sixty-fifth Street, which was barricaded with construction and double-parked cars. The meter read thirty dollars by the time they got there, and Antonia phoned ahead to Lopez to say they were going to be late. Inside, bedlam, every chair taken, a long line curling around the desk. "We are just here for a pick-up," Antonia shouted, but no one looked up, so they took their place in line.

A middle-aged woman with red hair and thick makeup sat behind the desk. "Sign that form," she repeated, like a monomaniac, making no eye contact. "And move on, and sit down. Your name will be called." On the wall, a laminated sign advised, "You must bring the proper form from your insurance company—or pay in cash today." Sign and sit down. Sign and sit down. Present the form or pay. The signatories, once they'd gotten past reception, stood in another line where a nurse was dispensing orange Kool-aid from a plastic pitcher into plastic cups. "Drink this," she commanded, her orders blending, like a fugue, with "Sign that form and sit down."

"I'm here," Antonia yelled from the back of the line, "to collect

Mr. Gregory Johnson's X-rays. We have an appointment downtown in fifteen minutes. We are going to be late. The oncologist
sent me." Nobody heard.

"Steinberg." "Mankowitz." Greg told Antonia to press forward. She waved at the receptionist, who directed them to sign
in and sit down.

"No, you don't understand. I'm merely here to pick up film
that's ready, and I've been waiting fifteen minutes, and . . ."

No, she was too damn polite, and Gregory felt a surge of
power and croaked out authoritatively, "I want my X-rays. I've
been waiting fifteen minutes. Give them to me. I can't stand here
any more. I am going to collapse."

All eyes turned to them, a white-haired lady in jeans and a
down jacket, a spindly man who clung to the side of the desk
to keep from falling. The receptionist looked up, she who daily
faced a roomful of women with lumps in their breasts, children
with broken bones, teenagers showing symptoms of brain tu-
mors, young fathers with metastasizing cancers, grandfathers
and grandmothers with the same. Transfigured by radiation and
chemotherapy and experimental drugs, Greg could have been an
archangel with a trumpet.

In seconds a woman in a white coat appeared from the back
office, carrying a huge, heavy manila envelope filled with sheets
of film measuring two by three feet. Antonia took the package
in her arms. Greg started for the door. Antonia came on behind
him like Eurydice following Orpheus out of hell, and the nurses
resumed with "Sign this" and "Drink this." He cursed Watson
and Crick for discovering the structure of DNA, Marie Curie
for inventing X-rays, the FDA for certifying radiation centers,
and the National Cancer Institute just for good measure. He was
scared shitless of what was on those films, and he knew Antonia

was, too, and he knew she was also scared that she would be here next. Never send to know for whom the bell tolls. O Lord, send us both the ischemic infarct.

The fare, when they reached the towering glass boxes of NYU Medical Center half an hour later, came to another thirty dollars. Better to be rich if one had to be sick. Better not to be Charley, better to be the cherished partner of Arty. Greg and Antonia made their way through the crowded lobby and rode the elevator with a twisted woman in a wheel chair, and a man carrying a boy of three with a swelling on his cheek. On the tenth floor where they all got off was a jungle-canopy of signs: ONCOLOGY, PEDIATRIC CARDIOLOGY, PAIN MANAGEMENT. All the layers of Purgatory. How would a person manage pain? Greg wondered. What could they be talking about?

"The doctor will only be a few minutes, Mr. Johnson," the receptionist promised, looking away from her computer screen. "He understands why you are late. Do have a seat." A lavish room, botanical prints on the wall, plenty of magazines, today's *New York Times,* and ten floors below them heavy traffic on the FDR Drive, the East River glistening, and the borough of Queens lumbering off toward Douglaston and Little Neck and Manhasset.

Dr. Lopez brought his patient in quickly. "Ah, Mr. Johnson. Mrs. Blass, how good of you to come in with Gregory. Let me take that heavy box for you." He opened it, riffled impatiently through the heavy sheets of film without looking at them. In his hand he held the reports, which had been faxed ahead. Greg stared past him, out the window at the silvery river. The sunlight was dim. The stream of cars flowed as steadily as the water. Is all locomotion really the same, he wondered, from blood vessels to traffic? Little particles hurtling along and sometimes sticking together? Were we large-scale versions of single cells, pasted together with chemical bonds but still just wiggling the great primordial wiggle as in the sea ponds and shallows of millions of years ago, our sense of self and our sorrow a grand illusion?

Like an art director inspecting a fashion shoot, Dr. Lopez examined Gregory's interior in scores of the little images on his light box. Gregory and Antonia looked, too, tried to decipher the rows and rows of images, a vacation on which you'd taken too many pictures. Was that white thing a cancer, or something you needed? They watched Lopez for any hint, their hearts sinking.

"Ah," he said at last, and switched off the light box. "I had such hopes. Such hopes. It is not unusual, however, for some new modality to work magic for a few weeks, and then for the disease to gather strength, to come back in double force. This is what appears to have happened here." He spoke to Antonia, as though he expected her to deliver the message, avoiding Gregory. But he found his courage.

"I am so sorry, Gregory. You have been most heroic in joining my trial, and I scarcely know how to thank you. But I'm discontinuing the medication as of today. . . . Seems only to be making matters worse. I have no choice."

Dr. Lopez shuffled his papers. Then, as if he might be able to figure out one final rescue mission, he busily seized each faxed report in turn, trained his daggerish gaze on first one and then another. His eyes pierced the papers, almost set them to smoldering.

"Yes," he said.

"Yes, what?" Yes what, you handsome young Spanish genius with the beautiful wife and three lovely children framed in silver on your desk?

"Everything is progressing."

"Progressing? Are you rooting for me or the cancer?"

"Our pill worked, then it quit. Now all is definitely in a state of

progress once more. Yes, I suppose it is in fact only progress from
the point of view of the illness. So, we must look at our options."

He smiled, inspected yet another sheaf of papers, and closed
the fat dossier. Some Lopez assistant, Greg knew, would copy the
data into charts for publication of the trial. It would appear two
years from now in a prestigious cancer journal. He would be a
set of numbers in a column. Nameless. Well, that wasn't so bad.
Immortality, indeed, more so than tap dancing. He just hadn't
gotten the part in this particular clinical trial.

Our options are to go home and die. "Yes, what are our
options?"

Well, the options might include a new course of chemotherapy,
there was one other chemotherapeutic drug that had not yet been
tried in this case, but since everything else has utterly failed, the
outlook was hardly hopeful.

What would the side effects be of this one remaining drug?

Deprive him of every remaining hair, and it would never grow
back. Reduce his white cell count further, make him a target for
any passing bug. A cold germ could kill him. Protracted vomiting.
Neuropathy, that is, the fingers will turn numb, so the patient will
be unable to pick up a spoon. There had been one clinical trial
showing that it could lengthen the life of a patient in Greg's . . .
condition.

"How much?"

Dr. Lopez swallowed. "Two additional months of life in about
thirty percent of those who've tried it."

"And if I do not?"

The physician could not speak of death, so he spoke of time.
"Six months. We are talking months, not years. On average. I
cannot predict for you. Maybe six months. Maybe less. Maybe
weeks. I cannot say. I simply cannot say, sir."

"This is it? You said options. That is only one option."

"We cannot give you any other form of chemotherapy. We cannot order any more radiation. You cannot take any more of the experimental drug. Indeed, you must give us what remains of the last bottle." He looked helpless, and his glance ceased to flash intelligence and fire.

Greg understood what the other option was. "I will think it over," he said.

"Yes, yes, think it over. This is no emergency. You can decide next week. You can let me know. It is an FDA-approved drug, this agent. We know what to expect. A thirty percent chance of prolongation . . ."

Antonia rose, opened her arms to him. The refuge felt momentarily safe. But he must not waver. "Good-bye. And thank you, Dr. Lopez." They shook hands all around.

The receptionist left her computer and her glass cage and came out to shake hands with him as well. And she kissed Antonia lightly on the cheek. "You may telephone the drugstore for morphine," she said, "and you can have all you need. Don't hesitate." She thrust a prescription into Antonia's hand. "Have this filled at the drugstore downstairs." But Gregory, when they reached the first floor, was too tired to wait, so they went on without the morphine.

"I am fucking mad," Antonia said. Just then Gregory had another of his mood swings, back to empathy, disinterested observation. Poor physician, yearning to heal, and having to do his dagger-eye routine, having to look extremely brisk and businesslike, having to speak of options and progress, having to invent a way of never mentioning death, pain, suffering. How many hands has he shaken in this doorway, after telling the patients he has nothing to offer? He drives his Mercedes home to his wife and kids and says, Guess what, I lost one more poor bastard. He thinks, Oh God, one day I will find something. Or he just feels happy the day is done and goes home to dinner.

In the taxi Greg stared ahead. "How are you?" Antonia asked. "Were you expecting that?"

"What else after all this torture? But no, I thought there might be better news. I thought of hearing the word remission."

"What you do think about that chemotherapy he offered? Do you think you should do it?"

"Guess I'll have to think about it." That's what you say to crazy people who want you to get well. That's what you say to doctors who know you have a week to live but talk of desperate measures and mention six months.

To be among the living and the well is, perhaps, to be crazy, to be timid, to deny, to equivocate, to speak in euphemisms. For some reason, the traffic thinned out a little and they sped downtown. The driver tailgated, swerved, skinned past buses close enough to scrape the paint, and screeched up to red lights at 40 mph. He told them he had learned to drive in Izmir, his home town, but he was glad to be here, in New York. Loved America. Muslim guys driving taxis made a point of sounding patriotic these days. Gregory liked his style. Maybe the guy would catch the American virus and lose his religion, fight his way through to the good life. Locomotion. That's what organisms do. Once, for a biology test, Greg had had to memorize the duties that fell to all organisms, from paramecia to jellyfish to us. Locomotion, digestion, elimination, respiration, and reproduction, and he couldn't remember the rest of the obligations of living organisms. Pay their taxes, probably. Learn to dance.

"I'll tell Arty what Lopez said. I'll tell him when we get there. I want you to be with us. He'll want me to do the chemicals. I'll have to tell him no. You back me up. The time has come."

"Of course."

He took her hand. They passed the armory. "Here's where Maggie went to sign up for widowhood," Antonia said. Only it didn't work out. Well, you took what you got. "Death to the Infidel," Mohammed Atta had said. Well, okay. Death.

Greg remembered who he was, even so, the dancer flourishing a black bowler. For Antonia's sake, he grinned, did a Bob Fosse bit, lifting an invisible bowler from his head and peering out under the brim.

"Do you know what's so bad about it? Arty. Leaving him. I'm a traitor. He has always taken care of me. That's his modus vivendi. Who will he take care of now? But what pisses me off the most is that the last time we made love was July. And it wasn't any good. You get so careless when you think you're going to live. I was sort of bored with him. I figured I could make it up to him later. Why didn't some angel come out of the ceiling in a white robe and tell me this was the very last time? If I could fix just one thing, that would be it. I would go back and make it good. Imagine, he will have only that to remember of me now."

"No, no. He will remember the other times. The first time. You remember the first time, they say. I remember the first time, with Sam, I mean. Oh, I miss him so. How can we handle all this loss? You're rotten, Gregory Johnson, to do this to us, and Sam is rotten, too. Don't imagine I will forgive either one of you." The world had turned to a sea of pain. The groundhog had seen his shadow, and it would be winter forever.

27 Mark

THE PROBLEM TROUBLING him most was seeing or not seeing Sophie. He took Toni to school early most mornings because Sophie and Ashley came late; on other days he and Toni arrived late so that Sophie would already be busy in the classroom. That took care of avoidance, but he hoped daily for a sighting. At least in theory, Parkside teachers were required to greet parent and pupil each morning, or nanny and pupil, to ask how things were at home. But Sophie had often skipped the greeting, even in the old days. Thus a whole week would pass without a glimpse of her. She was avoiding him, too. Evenings, he and Maggie talked of the new baby (not of job searches or money, as those had been declared off-limits by the therapist: Mark must get his bearings), and Sophie gnawed incessantly at him, him, Mark Adler, for Chrissakes, the father of one and a half children. The Mark Adler who, about to enroll in a birthing class with his wife, stood on windy corners and in icy doorways hoping to waylay his lover.

She now lived full time with Ashley in the Parker apartment, except for commuting to Forest Hills on weekends. According to

Toni, Ashley believed her parents were coming home soon—and Toni did what she could to reinforce the fantasy. "You came home, Daddy, and Ashley's mommy and daddy will, too." Mark lacked the energy to dispute her. Maybe they would come.

The therapist had forbidden any contact between him and Sophie, except the unavoidable parent-and-teacher kind. Nobody at the school knew about them, and when he had come home from Astoria last September, Maggie had given out the amnesia story. Post-traumatic shock from watching people jump from on high. Because of that, he had lost his wallet, wandered around a couple of days until he got his memory back and phoned home. People seemed to believe it; at least they asked no probing questions. The therapist said he and Maggie had serious wounds they must work daily to heal. Being a pathetic casualty of life was better than being a coward and a heel, nurturing a fraudulent scheme against Metropolitan Life. Cowardice and larceny had no remedies, but PTSD did. In December he left a message on Sophie's phone:

"We need to talk." It was a lie. All he did was talk. Curse Freud and all his tribe for supposing that talk was of any use. He wanted to see Sophie. In private. To touch her. Just her hand, or perhaps her hair. Well, all right. He wanted to be in bed with her, just one last time. To make sure she, and he, existed. She did not answer the message.

In early January he saw her at school: she was greeting her pupils at the door. Out on the street moments later, choking, he left another message. No reply. Two days later she came into the liquor store with Ashley, looking for a white wine. He found her a good cheap Vouvray and was careful not to touch her hand when he made change. With whom was she planning to share the wine? In the hour after she left he managed not to break down, not to quit his job, not to go to Port Authority and board the next bus.

A month after that, she approached him while Toni was in the cloakroom taking off her mittens and boots. "I have the afternoon off. The class is going on a field trip with another group, and I am off the hook. I could meet you somewhere this afternoon. Somewhere public. I mean just for a few minutes. Or maybe you'll be working."

He was supposed to work, but he would tell Tommy he had a dentist's appointment.

"How about the playground?" she said. "One o'clock?"

At 12:45 he dusted off the bench and sat down next to the bronze hippos. Nobody was there. The empty swings creaked in the sharp wind. He checked his watch and his phone every five minutes, and finally it was one o'clock. He stamped his feet, jogged around the playground to keep warm. Another quarter hour went by, and the time slid toward half past. Forty-five min-utes in this bloody wind, and she had dissed him. How well this rhymed with everything else in his lousy life. Did she hate him this much? And he saw her through the bare trees, almost run-ning down the path, saw her boots and jeans and pink, tight-fitting coat, and her silky hair blowing in strands from around her earmuffs.

He had decided not tell her about the baby. Anyway, he did not really want to believe there would be a baby, and summer was a long way off.

She came right up to him, as if they saw each other every day, and held him for a moment.

"Sophie, Sophie." He clutched her tightly, his fat parka puffy against her flimsy wool coat, kissed her cheek, and dived for her mouth. She pushed him away.

"We mustn't start anything, you know. Sorry I'm late. Susie Falcon stopped me at the door to chat about something. I couldn't escape."

"It doesn't matter. Tell me how you are."

"Rich. I'm rich. Mr. Parker has even paid off my credit card. He pays me twice my teaching salary, and I still have that, too. I can make my loan payments. I am letting my apartment go next month—no living expenses. Ashley and I have a car service to take us back and forth to Forest Hills. I live on Riverside Drive now." She laughed. "Me in a ten-room apartment. With antiques! Good thing Ashley has wealthy grandparents. And she'll be getting a lot of money from the government, they think. They've hired a lawyer."

They sat facing each other on the bench, at arm's length.

"Yeah." He tried to imagine Sophie rich. No longer lounging around in lace bra and panties in the crappy, dysfunctional apartment in Astoria. Where would she keep all that stuff? Where would she live her life? In his September fantasy, he had pictured the two of them, under assumed names, looking for jobs in Fort Myers, Florida, or Arcata, California. Living in some apartment with a sofa bed, wondering if that was all they'd ever have. "You really like this arrangement? How is Ashley?"

"Like it? Well, the money's nice. Ashley is pretty confused. She loves me, you know. She's an odd little bundle, even if you don't count all she's gone through, which would make any kid odd, I admit. We see a grief counselor every week, and she tells her counselor some ugly stuff about her mother. I don't know if it qualifies as child abuse. Alicia never read to her or anything. And sometimes she hit her. Or locked her in her room for hours. But then Ashley will cry hysterically and say that she misses her parents and wants them to come home. I wonder how much of it is true. She's almost too good at getting people to feel sorry for her. But she isn't kidding about not believing Kevin and Alicia are dead. The shrink tries to explain things, and Ashley says she understands, but she doesn't. She's just humoring the shrink. And you know what? Sometimes she gets mad at me because they haven't come back. And she gets mad at them, too. The shrink says that's normal. It's tough."

"So you're the mother. With a kid blaming you for something that isn't your fault. What are they like, the grandparents? Move this way, Sophie. It's cold." She slid an inch closer.

"Oh, you know. Old. They are old. Mrs. Parker is a cranky, nasty old dame. She's got heart disease and knee arthritis. She watches TV all day. He is in pretty good shape, but Kevin was all they had. They'll never get over this. They were old when he was born; they thought they would never have any kids. They were so proud of him, an attorney and all, a big job in Two World Trade. She can't say his name without breaking down. They've got her on antidepressants. The Parkers never liked Alicia, and they hardly knew Ashley before September 11 because Alicia made sure they stayed shut out. She looked down on them, thought them trashy, and they knew it. But this is the last thing they needed—their son dead along with the bitchy daughter-in-law, and not even a body to bury. Plus a child to raise. They were thinking of going into assisted living."

"How lucky they are to have you."

"Right. Yeah. They don't approve of me, though. They just don't know what else to do."

"Why are you moving in with them? Do you have your own room?"

"Oh, sure, they have space for Ashley and space for me. Kevin's old room. They have this big ugly house in Forest Hills, with oriental carpets on top of the inlaid carpets and fringe all over everything, and they never open the drapes. Custom-made by B. Altman in 1975, she keeps telling me. Everything smells old. You know. Old. The fridge is full of soda pop. They don't drink alcohol. They don't eat vegetables, unless you count potatoes. At night, for jollies, they play Lawrence Welk and old dance-band stuff. It's hard being out there on weekends. I only have Sundays off, and most Sundays I take Ashley somewhere with me. She hates it out there. She doesn't like her grandmother. So I guess we are in the same position as Alicia—they're a pain in the ass, just like she said. But I take their orders. And you, you're expecting a baby. Congratulations."

"How did you know?"

"Toni, of course. She talks about it at school. Says she wants a brother."

"I wasn't going to tell you."

"What do you mean? Not tell me! You want me to say I feel betrayed? Well, okay, I feel betrayed. One day you want to run away with me and incriminate yourself for me and have me as your accomplice, and a couple weeks later you're making a baby for your wife. But okay, it's all in the history of the world, it has happened before this. I am looking for a new boyfriend." She did look hurt. Betrayed, even.

"Sophie, I still don't believe she's pregnant. I keep thinking it will go away. Sort of like Ashley thinking her parents will come home. I don't know how we'll manage. Two kids in one tiny bedroom? But Maggie's happy. She seems to believe that the genie in whatever magic lamp she rubs will grant wishes number two and three: a house in the burbs and a good job for me. She's a ten-man support group all by herself. That genie in the lamp doesn't talk to me. I'm the lumpen proletariat. The serf. Lucky to sit at the table, to sleep in the bed of her evolving life. I don't have a vote."

"Do you ever think of your great plan, us running off together? Do you think it would have worked out?"

"Think of it? No, it probably wouldn't have worked out. I think of you, anyway. I sleep with Maggie, but I sleep with you. One day I'll probably call her by your name. You don't know how bad this is. You were right to throw me out, but this is bad." He put his hands in his pockets and stood up. "Oh, Sophie, goddamn it. How did I get in this trap?"

"You know how. You had to go back to Toni. I had to take care of Ashley. And what would we be doing now, jobless, broke. Yeah, it would have been fun, at first. It's always fun at first. Free, starting over. But we'd have been scared all the time. Every ring of the phone. . . . The insurance company would have tracked you down. You know they would. They don't just give the widow a big check and walk off. You did the right thing, and this way I am earning big money. Maybe one day. . . ."

"There isn't going to be a one day. If I couldn't leave Toni, how will I ever leave Toni and Frederick? Or Toni and Frederica? We don't know if it's a boy or a girl, we chose not to know, or at least Maggie chose for it to be a surprise. Don't tell us what you see on the sonogram, doc! But she's got the name all picked out. Her dad was Frederick Blass, and the baby will be named for him. It's okay with me. I don't want it named for my parents." He sat down again.

Her hand rested on her knee. He picked it up, pulled off the glove, and kissed her fingers, the soft palm. "Your little hand is cold. Mimi, my Mimi." He sang a couple of bars from *La Bohème,* off-key, and she laughed. He hadn't been sure she would get the reference.

"At least, Sophie, you'll always be able to tell yourself that a man once loved you enough to commit a crime in order to have you."

"Yeah, I guess that counts for something. Only you didn't do it." She pulled her hand away, took back her glove. But she was rattled, undone.

"I could not love thee, dear, so much, loved I not honor more. The shrink says Maggie has to forgive me. Maggie says she has forgiven me. The shrink says I have to forgive myself. I have forgiven myself. We're into healing. We're into closure. Moving forward. And our fully certified social worker can no doubt dig up a few other hackneyed expressions for what we're doing. And I'm back in Antonia's good books. Anyway, she speaks to me."

"Yeah, I guess that matters."

"Look, let's go up to Starbucks, baby. I'm freezing my ass off. You must be freezing yours, too, in that coat. I'll buy you a coffee. That's permitted. I can even tell our marriage counselor about it. We won't be alone. Lots of people in Starbucks. If Maggie comes by, we'll wave at her and invite her in."

"No coffee, thanks. Not a great idea to be together. You may not think this hurts, being with you. But it does. Anyway, I have to go. You know there might be a day, there could be a day. My rich times won't last. Mr. Parker wants to move to Florida. He has this big condo lined up in Boca Raton or someplace. He said we could all live together. I'd be the au pair. Or I could get my own place after a while. He thinks Ashley could go to public school down there. It would be cheaper, simpler. Warmer. Once he gets legal title to the Parker apartment, he'll sell it. He sees no point in maintaining an apartment in Manhattan for Ashley and me. This is only to let her finish the school year. Granny Parker is all for moving."

"My God, are you going with them? Sophie, it's no life for you."

"Right. I also know they are thinking of dumping me. I am only the governess. They could throw me out tonight. I overheard the dear old souls last week; they were in the living room with the TV on and they thought I was in bed. 'A young kid like that,' she told him, 'looking for a husband, she'll be bringing boyfriends in before we know it. Don't say I didn't warn you when you run into some juvenile delinquent in our bathroom. She's not fit. . . . We need an older woman, somebody settled.' If I ever showed up with a date, I'd be out on my ass the next morning. She hates my clothes, tells me my jeans are too tight. In her day a teacher wouldn't have been allowed to dress that way. So I have to make the most of this windfall. For Ashley, not just myself. But I don't feel permanent, and in her young life Ashley will have a lot of adjusting to do. If they want her to have a middle-aged woman for a nanny, somebody in a white uniform, that's what she'll have."

"But she loves you. Why don't they make you legal guardian?" In piercing clarity, he pictured a scene on a beach somewhere, sand pails and a striped umbrella stuck in the sand, him and Toni, Sophie and Ashley, in bathing suits and sun hats. A blended family. The two little girls now sisters, and Maggie definitely not part of the picture, not pregnant with Mark's child, Maggie married to some other guy and pregnant by that guy in a suitable house in Long Island, a guy working on Wall Street. Maggie divorcing Mark. Maggie dying in childbirth. No, he could not go that far.

"Appoint some stranger, some slut in tight jeans, the legal guardian of your son's only survivor? Ashley is about to become rich. An orphan heiress. Do you suppose they'll let me manage all that? Not likely. I have no control over it anyway. I thought at first that Alicia's family would take some interest in Ashley. She has a sister in Montana or somewhere. But she never even phones to see how Ashley is doing. She never came to the service. I love that little girl. I'd adopt her and raise her if I could. But Grandma thinks I have poor judgment. She caught us watching *Sex and the City*. She made me turn it off. Ashley called her an evil old witch right there to her face. Which only made me look more like a failure. My problem now is not to get too attached to Ashley. I'm a servant. When is your baby due?"

"August 17."

"You still like Hammond's, selling the fine wines?"

"It's a paycheck. Sort of. Maggie begs me to talk to Morgan Stanley, to take up where I left off. But there's no job there. Even if I wanted that kind of work, the financial industry is in shambles. New York City may not even be the big financial center anymore. Who wants to work in a town where lunatics come and blow you up? They talk about dirty bombs, you know, nuclear weapons in the street. Smallpox, anthrax, whatever. And this notion she has about me getting an M.A. and teaching—another big debt to Uncle Sambo. And I'm no teacher. She has these hallucinations. I'm lucky to be a retail clerk. Antonia pays the tuition. Maybe she'll find us a decent place to live next summer after the baby comes."

"Oh, Mark, you give up so easily. I have to go now." My God, she looked defeated. "I did love you once. But you're right, there isn't going to be a day."

Grabbing her shoulders, he kissed her. "Let's get out of this cold park. Let's go somewhere. We can go to the Parker apartment. The kids won't be home for a couple of hours. Come on, let's go."

"Oh, you're crazy. You low-life. It was stupid to meet you. Get out of my life. Let me go. Don't walk up the path with me. You stay here. You go in the other direction. I don't want to be seen with you. Don't leave me any more messages. It ruins my whole day to get those messages. It makes me want you. Well, I don't want you any more."

He offered no further resistance. All he had wanted, after all, was to touch her, kiss her hand, her mouth. It would have been a grave mistake, the other thing he had asked for. And if only she had said yes. Just an hour of her. He could have lived on that for a long time. He sat down on their bench and watched the pink coat flickering away from him among the bare trees.

28 Arty

HE WALKED FROM room to room, unable to endure the deathbed vigil. "Deathbed" annoyed him, irritated him. What an idea! Gregory would always be the dancer, the body in motion. The beauty of the male body in motion. For now, the dancing man lay quiet, a small figure under the sheet, his head wrapped in white, an oxygen mask over his mouth, a morphine drip in his arm, his eyes half open but sightless. The drugs, Arty supposed, were at fault, and he hated them for inducing this near-death. But to be sure, Gregory's screaming three days earlier had been hard to bear, searing. It had echoed through the thick walls of the building, had brought neighbors to the door. One had to call for morphine, more of it. Soaked with sweat and tears himself, Arty had given up insisting that Greg was going to get well, or at least had given up saying it, and had ceded control to Antonia. Prepare for death. Do it the best way you can.

Hospice nurses were here around the clock now, far superior, Arty knew, to having Greg in a hospital or even a hospice. More humane. And you didn't have to run uptown in a taxi. The nurse on duty today (Clara, her name was) had the good taste to dress in classic starchy white and proper shoes, for which Arty was so grateful. You should not be a hospice nurse, he felt, in polyester pants and sneakers. Or blue jeans and a checkered shirt. You should have a costume, and Clara understood this. A perfect name, Clara. The name of a saint, light, illumination. She knew all about dying. She had washed Gregory's body, cleaned him as gently as she would an infant, disposed of the grievous evidence of incontinence, the fluids and mess of dying, had swaddled him in white, lined the bed with thick disposable pads, placed pillows in such a way that she could guarantee his comfort. "He is comfortable now, " she said, "I am certain he is in no pain."

She had liberated Greg's right hand from the sheet and tubing, arranging it so that Arty and Antonia, Candace and Alison, could hold it whenever they liked. She urged them to hold the hand, to talk to her patient. "You may not see any sign of it, but I am sure he can hear you. Tell him you love him." Arty had managed half an hour at Gregory's bedside, cradling the cooling, limp hand in both of his, patting or squeezing as the urge arose, but he could not rationally conceive that Greg knew of the patting and squeezing. Or heard Arty chanting "I love you." Lord, he wouldn't have chanted even in their palmy youth, half drunk, at Fire Island Pines! Antonia leaned over the poor body and whispered, "Do you remember the crème caramel I made you last month, and I finally got the crust to crack under the spoon, the way it should, and you loved it so much?" Greg's eyebrows lifted. He blinked. His lips almost formed a smile.

"Arty, come here, come here. He knows. He remembers the crème caramel!" But before Arty could get across the room, the face went blank once more. Not the crème caramel at all but some twitch at his interior, some wave in the morphine.

Arty wandered across the room and sat in the worn-out wing
chair that he had wanted to replace with something better — particularly last fall when he was struggling to provide future benefits that Greg would simply not be able to leave behind. Maybe
if he had bought a new chair . . . It was the chemotherapy, plus
wretched Dr. Lopez's experiments, that had brought Greg to this
low state. He told himself that Greg would get past this, once the
poison had drained from his body. His lungs would heal on their
own once the poison was out.

How could Gregory die with handsome Ian sitting at his bedside (Arty had permitted him to sit there as long and as often
as he liked) and the members of the Church of the Celestial Redeemer holding regular prayer sessions for him, and his lover of
forty-odd years guaranteeing him a lifetime of pleasant journeys
if only he would stop this craziness? He grew angry. Oh, damn
you Greg, it was to have been a negative biopsy and a knee replacement and that was to have been it. Foolish, foolish boy. Get
hold of yourself. Why did I allow you to try that crazy treatment
at New York University Hospital? What did Dr. Lopez know?
How to kill people, that's what.

Clara came to the bed, rearranged the bedclothes once more,
patted Gregory's arm. Antonia held the limp hand. "It won't be
long now," Clara said. "If you have anything to tell him, this is
the time. I believe he will hear you. And if I were you, I'd make
those phone calls. . . ."

Antonia whispered, "You'll be great, baby," in Gregory's ear.
Well, he might know. He might know he was dying. Maybe it
was like opening night. He used to tell her how he sat in misery at
his dressing table, sometimes even vomited, how he stood weak
and sweaty in the wings, unable to remember his steps, and then

the cue came and he was out there dancing. His muscles took over, his bones propelled him, his fear did not count. Maybe it was like that. A performance, or at least you thought it would be a performance until oblivion set in. Boom. Curtain down.

Arty did not wish to be there, so he went down the hallway. Here were his treasures, all to have gone in an orderly fashion to Gregory after Arthur's death, which should by all rights have come first. Here were Edna St. Vincent Millay, Eleanor Roosevelt with crumpled hat and crumpled smile, the joyous Duke Ellington, W. H. Auden with his cursed cigarette. Arty took that picture off the wall and turned it backside out. He took a moment's pleasure from the queen and Prince Philip's invitation to a weekend at Balmoral. Not an invitation addressed to him, to be sure, but it did not matter. He thought, briefly, of sending a long-delayed reply, in his and Gregory's name, to Buckingham Palace. The queen often invited famous dancers, why not Gregory? Most gracious majesty, Arthur and Gregory are honored to accept your invitation of thirty years past . . . no, no. One did not address the queen that way. Surely Emily Post would have advice on proper forms of address for the queen of England. . . .

In his office at one end of his bedroom, he sat down in his comfortable executive chair, began rummaging. Through these difficult months he had kept the business going. No choice, really, he couldn't quit. They lived on his income. What would they do without it? He hadn't put away very much for them. The money seemed to evaporate, and the mutual funds he chose often went down. Gregory, of course, had always been broke. Too bad Greg hadn't been a singer, there might have been some royalties from recordings. And songs to keep. . . . But dance vanished utterly, at the instant of its creation. The body moved, the art was lost. You could not resell it, no residuals, and the clips from famous musicals that you sometimes saw on PBS brought nothing in the way of income to Gregory, though he was always the best dancer on the screen. Arty opened his newest catalog—response had been poor. Did his customers sense his distraction? An earlier listing, published last winter, had failed to attract many buyers either. Was his trade falling apart? There were bills to pay. . . .

And yet, here were all his people, in the pages of his catalogues, carefully captioned by his own hand, out of his own knowledge, the great and famous mingling with the less renowned, the dead with the living, all circulating happily as though at a cocktail party. Wanda Landowska, effusive about the joys of playing Mozart on Paderewski's own Steinway—"a marvel!"—and one could own such a document for only $750. Why had there been no takers? He pictured the famous harpsichordist with her large nose festooning her plain-as-dirt countenance, her smile, ringing his doorbell and entering, and he presented her to Paulette Goddard, also in the catalogue, along with Betty Hutton, both these film stars represented by signed photos. One so diminutively elegant; both of them, when the role called for it, excellent clowns. And excellent company! Wanda and Paulette and Betty would find a great many things to talk about at this party. He would bring them martinis on a tray. He opened the large folder where he kept poems in the hand of Philip Larkin, who had spent his whole life in terror of dying.

Larkin could come to the party. Here, among the papers, was a Confederate poet, one Paul Hamilton Hayne, who, after his home had been burned by General Sherman's troops, had copied this quatrain into a letter, now offered for $1,000:

> And thus for evermore, till time shall cease,
> Man's soul & Nature's—each a separate sphere—

Revolve, the one in discord, one in peace,
And who shall make the solemn mystery clear?

Arty had never believed in souls. Or solemn mysteries. You were all one piece, and when your body was gone, you were gone, and all that remained of you were your little scraps, your letters, your unfulfilled contracts, your unpaid bills, if anybody bothered to keep them. Well, now he might have to start believing in souls. Or ghosts. Perhaps he could arrange for Gregory to haunt the house. Damnit, Greg, you owe me this much! But it was all silly because Gregory wasn't going.

His little gilt desk clock chimed three, and Arty realized he had been sitting in the same position for at least an hour, his head echoing with the dissonant music of Maurice Ravel's "La Valse," played by Wanda on the harpsichord, while the dead whirled in the room, Betty, Paulette, Philip, Paul, and even Isabella II of Spain (1849, two hundred dollars) and Christopher Isherwood (1971, five hundred dollars). But all he possessed was their ephemera and trivia. He wished to burrow deeper into his things. He did not wish to return to Greg's side. Because if he died, well . . .

Oh, a hand on his shoulder. It was Sam Mendel. The real one, not Sam Mendel as the author of a memo about the future of publishing, written out by hand (1985, $600) or his face in a well-chosen frame. Antonia must have phoned him. Or maybe Alison had. He was, after all, her grandfather. Alison must have known that Sam belonged here. She must understand by now that Antonia loved him.

"Arty. How are you, my friend?"

He looked upward, blank-eyed, unable to shake off the reverie of his familiars. Perhaps Sam had come to reclaim Antonia, so despairing since the events of September 11, and one of the events had been that Sam left her, which, if not the doing of Al Qaeda, she had taken as an outcome of the attack. Arty had never quite presumed to think of himself as a friend of this mannerly, amusing, duplicitous lover of Antonia's, the Important Man, member of Important Clubs, at his ease in a kind of uptown male Manhattan society that Arty and Gregory could never have been admitted to. Nevertheless, to Arty's surprise, Sam bent over and embraced him.

"Alison called me this morning. She and Candace are here now. We all wanted to be here. Dear friend, it's time. Today seems to be the day. Perhaps we can help." And Arty saw the young women standing behind Sam. Candace was calm, Alison weeping, ever the unstable partner. "Oh, Uncle Arty," Candace said, and he realized why they all had come.

"No. It isn't time."

"Uncle Arthur, you must say good-bye. It is time. The hospice nurse says so. Come, dear, we'll go with you. You mustn't let this moment pass. Uncle Greg wants you there, I know he does."

And so Arty went quietly with them, with Candace and Sam on either side of him, down the short hallway, into the bedroom where the starched white nurse and Antonia stood like sentinels beside Gregory's bed. He could hear the rasping, uneven breaths. As Arty neared the bedside and bent over the form under the sheet, Gregory opened his eyes, seemed to see.

"Look," Arty shouted jubilantly, "you're all wrong. Look, he sees us, hears us. He is coming around." Clara had another look at Gregory, just in case. But when she pulled the sheet from around the legs and feet, she found, not to her surprise, that they had gone cold.

"I love you. I love you." Arty said it mechanically, because it was expected of him, and also because it was true.

"Yes, say that," the nurse commanded. "It might do him good."

"There's no point," Antonia said. "No point at all." Sam seemed to be holding Arty upright, and she positioned herself on the other side of him. The interval between breaths grew longer, and after three more, there was only silence. Then a rattle in the chest. A kind of cough. Then the breaths stopped. After a brief interval Clara disconnected the morphine drip and the oxygen and pulled the sheet gently over Gregory's face.

Arthur, a crushed old man, sank into the ratty wing chair. He did not weep, nor could he think of anything to say. Gregory gone? Lines from Matthew Arnold, memorized so many years ago, sprang into his mind:

> Ah, love, let us be true
> To one another! for the world, which seems
> To lie before us like a land of dreams,
> So various, so beautiful, so new,
> Hath really neither joy, nor love, nor light,
> Nor certitude, nor peace, nor help for pain;
> And we are here as on a darkling plain
> Swept with confused alarms of struggle and flight,
> Where ignorant armies clash by night.

Arthur got hold of his dignity and his sense of reality, stood up and recited the lines. "Dover Beach," he said. "Well, it applies to Gregory and me. Antonia, my dear friend, I leave you to take charge. May I just sit beside him for a moment?"

29 Antonia

ANTONIA AND SAM and Candace and Alison adjourned together into Gregory's little study and began to take care of the details. A death certificate would be needed: Clara's duty; the cremation must be arranged. One afternoon last December, Antonia and Gregory had made a list. "Arty won't know what to do," he had said. "You'll have to help him. He'll just sit there stunned. He'll be angry with me, you know. Dying is the ultimate infidelity. Even worse than Ian." Antonia found the list. She called Ian first, then Maggie. Sam advised her on who might undertake the cremation, made some phone calls himself. The church people; there would be a memorial service at the church. Arty must pick the date. Later. Sam talked to a producer friend of his, and they decided on a memorial in a Broadway theater next month.

Antonia and Sam sat quietly together, not touching. She lacked the energy to be angry. Grief had made her docile. Perhaps Edith needed him more than she did. Well, that was all right. She,

Antonia, was strong. She, Antonia, had her own family. She needed no one. Having made arrangements and phone calls, they persuaded Arty and the others to come to Antonia's apartment upstairs for something to eat and drink. Maggie and Toni and Mark would soon be there.

But after one cup of coffee, Sam said, "I have to get back to the country. I'll come for the memorial services, when the dates are set. And I'll expect all of you at the commitment ceremony in June. You must come. You mustn't let me down."

"Let you down!" What a fatuous request, but she was unable to resist him when he put his arms around her and kissed her. The comfort of it, the need she felt for him! She loved him, wanted him to come upstairs with her right now, not to go home. She tried not to kiss him but did. He gently disengaged himself and left her standing alone at the door.

"Oh, Sam," she said. "Oh, Sam." She sobbed as she had not done in many years. Sobbing is for the young. Older women lose the knack for it. They have sobbed enough, and their tears, if any, wet their faces in silence. But now she had a cry. Not a good cry. A bad cry. She could not tell which loss she minded most, Greg or Sam or something else. Her optimism, perhaps. The idea that had informed her life, that if she worked hard, read the Op Ed page and the *New Yorker* and *Harper's* and once in a while the *New York Review of Books*, watched the documentaries on PBS, served on committees and rode buses to Washington, marched on Pennsylvania Avenue, and voted right, all would be well. Progress. Her country was now at war, anthrax had killed innocent people via the U.S. Post Office, the pundits were talking about weaponized smallpox. Science had vanquished a disease, and now the warriors had revived it. Laws were being written authorizing spying and tyranny. Everybody but a few old cranks like Antonia seemed to be in favor of these laws. Or too afraid to speak against them. And another thing had now vaporized: her certainty that it had been just fine to fall in love at an advanced age, that it was right to have had a love affair with Sam, who was another woman's husband. Love was not the ruling force. Perhaps she was not entitled to it, even though she was about to die, never having known it, beyond this one encounter.

All this had come about in only six months and three weeks. It was as if Mohammed Atta and his gang had put an end to tolerance and hope. Had destroyed our beliefs. Had caused us, a great nation, to behave like the bullies and knaves he believed us to be. The particulate matter emitted from Ground Zero consisted not only of pulverized concrete and plastic and tattered office paper but pulverized ideas, liberal ideas. Ideas about making things better via goodwill.

Religion had not vanished from the earth or changed into something personal and benevolent, a Buddhist teaching, something closer to the teachings of Jesus, something that insisted on kindness and abhorred revenge and greed. It ruled in its most virulent forms, authorizing self-interest and conquest and Inquisition, plotting Armageddon, condemning all adversaries as evil and satanic, trashing international law, inciting violence, condoning torture. And now it was time to bury Gregory, her dancing man.

From deep in the crater, now, on certain nights, the beacons from two powerful spotlights beamed the phantoms of twin skyscrapers into the night sky. You could see them from everywhere, from surprising angles in Manhattan, in Queens, New Jersey, just as the Twin Towers had been visible from fifty miles away, and people all over the city stopped in the streets to marvel at the lights, silent and pure as shafts of ice in the moonlight. Perhaps these beams meant something. Perhaps they pointed to a less lousy, less rat-infested time than the present.

30 Sam

RAIN, DREARY, ENDLESS mountain rain, low skies, at 7:00 a.m. on what ought to have been a prime June day. He burrowed deep into his bed. Wet shoes this afternoon, raincoats, umbrellas to be disposed of. Dripping guests. The girls' satin gowns dragging through soggy grass. A heavy chill in the vast barn, and no heat. Him in his goddamn tuxedo, shivering over a plate of filet mignon. Perhaps he'd wear an undershirt. Wool socks? He had counted on a midsummer night, moonlight, fireflies, zephyrs.

He arose. The house was silent, even though twelve people were abed in it, counting him and Edith. An army encampment. Across the hall were Alison and Candace, in the large bedroom, spacious enough for two women and two formal gowns, and next door in the room with twin beds, Viv and Adri. They had been wonderfully loud in their adoration of the gowns, which they had insisted on pressing themselves and arranging on hangers. This afternoon Viv and Adri would help Alison and Candace dress, an honor the bridal mothers had ceded. Sam felt that at the earliest opportunity he should treat the twins to dinner at Gramercy Tavern. If they could find anything pure enough on the menu, and if he could lure them back to New York, which they had forsaken last September.

In the next room, Stephen and Camilla Mendel were presumably asleep in the king-size bed, and Sam hoped they still had a use for a bed besides sleeping—but he suspected that his son and daughter-in-law had fallen into the same sexless détente he and Edith lived in. Maybe Stephen, like his father, had looked elsewhere. Steve and Cammy never touched each other in public, that's how you could tell. Sam had overheard Camilla telling Edith, "I don't mind lesbians. I don't even care anymore that my daughter is one. I mean, one has to be supportive, and it's better than her being alone, I guess. Or with some really bad man. I do object to them getting married in bridal gowns, especially at the family estate."

Oh, yes. An offense to the house, the universal love object.

Candace's mother, Mary Johnson, after refusing to attend Greg's memorials or the commitment, had changed her mind and driven in from Chicago. She was bedded down in one of the smaller rooms. Sam had imagined her as a well-spoken, light-skinned lady, as indeed she turned out to be, insistently middle class, pretty if a little dumpy, and he could imagine her swept into an affair by Candace's father, the Ghanaian diplomat. He, of course, had not even bothered to reply to the invitation. Sam tried and failed to put Mary at her ease—and he was a master at the trade, the smoother-over, just sincere enough. She gazed at him from a distant cloud, would not chitchat. Was it race or class? Gender or religion? Would she have been happier if her daughter were marrying a black man? A black woman? As a librarian invited to stay in a rich publisher's house, did she feel ill at ease? Had Edith been an ass to her? Sam's poor-boy past should have been a bond between him and Mary, but it wasn't. She was as rigid as her daughter was adaptable. The whole thing upset him. He had wanted to be her pal.

His Rachel had arrived yesterday from Little Rock—without her insupportable Baptist husband, who, to Sam's relief, had refused to attend. Rachel was reserved. Composed. Tall, dark, thin. Frightening. He asked himself yet again if his own secularism, his theological sleaziness, had led her into the arms of Jesus. Rachel had taken on a gospel gleam: something implacable, unshakeable, something that made her eyes shine as if she were engaging in inward prayer. She would stand on the other side from him at the Rapture, marching up to heaven with other Christians while he went in the other direction with the Muslims, Buddhists, secular humanists, and assorted democrats. At least they could hardly send him to hell for being a Jew, since he had been so desultory about it. Well, think of the Nazis.

Sheep from goats.

Rachel had begun squabbling with her brother the moment she arrived, scarcely waiting until Sam had gotten the first drinks mixed. "I'm here out of family loyalty. I am a forgiving person. I want to keep in touch with Alison, because she needs me in her life. And she will need me more later, when, God willing, this phase is over. Someone should offer help here. If nobody else will, I will."

Stephen boiled over. "You say one word to her or go around preaching your twisted gospel at this ceremony, or saying anything to upset her and Candace, and I'll throw you in the goddamn lily pond."

Edith had threatened to have a nervous breakdown. "I have done all I could to make you happy, to get us all through this, and now you come in here yelling. Rachel, it is so unjust. Stephen, you are a rude boy, as always." Sam had squelched the conflagration as efficiently as he could. He had even put his arm around Edith, had led her to the sofa. It was the first time he had had his arm around her in years. It was her fault, this eternal warfare. She had raised them according to neo-Darwinian principles, survival of the fittest, like Naked Apes. And no wonder they continued to strive, and to hate one another.

"Rachel, it's a joyous occasion, and we don't want any speeches. Let him who is without sin among you cast the first stone. Judge not that ye be not judged. You follow a man named Jesus who said those things. And who was good to his mom. So, have a care for your mother. Stephen, for God's sake. Try to be civilized under this roof." My God, he should have laid in smelling salts.

But that was on the first evening, and things had been fairly civil since. His children had always hated one another. So this was just one more family feud. One more chance for the heirs to assess the value of the silver service and china and survey the grounds and promise themselves that when they got hold of it all they would uproot the pachysandra and enlarge the swimming pool and redo the living room in black leather.

Anna, his Orthodox daughter, had arrived two days ago—with Martin, her live-in (though living in was hardly Orthodox), whom she called her fiancé, who had only come along, as he explained, because he'd never been to one of these. Martin and Anna were houseguests number nine and ten, still asleep this rainy morn, or at any rate Sam had not heard their voices. They were probably the only couple, apart from the brides, who still had sex. A melancholy count in these magnificent accommodations. Edith never ever ran out of fitted sheets and monogrammed towels and pillows and little bottles of perfume, and cotton plissé covers for the blankets. She even had engraved notepaper, and stamps, for Christ's sake, in every guest room. Sam wondered exactly how much she had invested in guest comfort—it might as well be a ducal manor.

Now, at the window and in his bathrobe, he could hardly make out the south pond, the willows, the lush border of irises and lilies, the lawn rolling easily toward the meadow and the back gardens, the giant oak now dripping water, so thick and gray was the air. He sized up the dark western sky. He figured it would clear up. Give it till early afternoon.

Was all the planning and money going to waste? Out of 150 invited, he feared only half would show up. The young people, of course, were showing up: the friends and law partners and business associates. It was the old guard that disapproved. There were some Catholics-by-marriage and so forth lurking around the edges of both families. They, of course, had declined. Chairs would be empty for other reasons. Certain relatives and certain friends who had agreed to come would be unwilling, in the end, to appear. They would cancel their reservations at the nearby country inns, the B&Bs with canopied beds and ruffled skirts on the dressing tables. Some of the acceptances had surely come from people like Martin, who planned to dine out on the story. "You won't believe this, but . . ."

Surely, Sam hoped, a few would come with love and respect. How could Jews say no? Hadn't the Jewish people suffered enough from the fact that most people were always on the look-out for something to scorn—and then to murder? Would the world be any wickeder for two women pledging their troth?

He sat down on his rumpled bed and stared at his feet, the tendons running down to each toe, the bony ankles, the ropey veins.

A knot of insomniac fatigue tortured his upper back. He pictured Antonia behind him in the bed, half-asleep, cuddling up, pressing her fingertips just below his scapula, massaging the knot into submission. If she were there she would do that, and then, perhaps, he would fall asleep in her arms. He lay down once more, trying to doze off on this fantasy. O my love, why have I forsaken thee? She had been so wise about his aches, his calf cramps, the agonies of muscle and bone. Love was part medicine, a way of patching things up. Sex, the great healer. Tenderness, an analgesic. He had abandoned the comforts of Antonia's bed and body, her voice, her pear sorbet, her manner of handing him a cup of tea and always asking "Sugar, darling?" because sometimes he wanted sugar and sometimes not. If he went about it in the right way, he might have her once more.

For she would be here. Today. Arty was to escort Candace down the aisle, or at least to the altar, in place of Greg. Maggie and Mark Adler and little Toni were coming, for Gregory's sake and for Arty's, and he had arranged the seating charts so that they had the best table, in the center of the room near the dance band. He had made elaborate arrangements for the separate children's party. Several youngsters besides Toni were coming.

Would Antonia dance with him? Suppose he went to her table, asked her to dance, and she refused? Or, perhaps, on the excuse of bad weather, or out of pure rage, she did not come at all. Her place at the table, with its array of wineglasses and cleverly folded napkins and the party favors (miniature flashlights and small sterling silver picture frames), and the cooked-to-order fillet and the al dente vegetables, the smoked salmon flown from Scotland, the wines, and all the other paraphernalia of the lavish wedding table would remain untouched. MS. ANTONIA BLASS, the place card would read, but the chair would be empty. Ah, no, she would come. Arty would bring her. He would insist on her coming, and Maggie and Mark and Toni would, as well. He would take her hand, lead her to the dance floor, and hold her in his arms. How he missed her. And for what? Edith hadn't known the difference. How could he be faithful to a woman like Edith? He had thought all winter about leaving her. He was almost certain he would do it. He was sick with loneliness in this overpopulated house.

He rose and pulled on pants and socks, relieved that he could still do this standing up, buttoned his shirt, and slipped into a sweater. Out the back windows he saw caterers' trucks, lined up in the back driveway, which led to the barn; they were well into the setting up. Regiments of catering staff, piling up hay in aesthetically pleasing ways in the old barn, getting three bars ready to serve any kind of drink a person could dream up, arranging the tables to perfection, setting up the temporary kitchen where the meal would be cooked and the exquisite little hors d'oeuvres piled on silver trays, which would then be passed among the guests by squads of young persons in black and white who looked like movie stars. Did caterers ever hire any plain-looking waiters? No. Sam thought of the waste, the trash. The flowers fresh this morning and wilted tomorrow. The mounds of linen to be washed, the tables to be refolded, the chairs to be stacked. A local charity would come and collect the leftovers for hungry people in this area who had never seen endive wrapped around shrimp or beef.

Downstairs he found Alison, touchingly beautiful, a fine tennis player, too. She pleased him in every way. She turned from the coffee machine and kissed him.

"Nervous, honey?"

"I guess. Afraid I'll stumble over that stupid dress. I didn't sleep much last night. Did you?"

"Never do, my love. Haven't slept in years. The dress is beautiful. Why do you say stupid?"

"Sometimes I wish we'd done it differently. It's been a battle at every stage. Grandma is plenty mad about the dresses. She told me that if I were really happy with myself, I wouldn't want that kind of wedding dress. And I told her if she felt that way she should think it over. That what we want is support, not criticism. But maybe she's right. I wanted to go all the way. We're just as good as anybody. Why can't I be the whitest, silliest bride that ever there was?"

"Indeed. You can be. And what were you supposed to wear, my dear, jodhpurs? A caftan? What's wrong with bridal satin? Where's Candace?"

"She went to her mother's room for a talk. I came down to make us a breakfast tray."

"Well, some girl talk should help. It's a lot to go through. It's just very hard on you. Do you kids ever wish you weren't obliged to be so demonstrative?"

"Maybe if people like Candace and me make enough noise, every queer in America will be able to go into deep debt for their weddings. They'll have to legalize it. The caterers of America will lobby Congress for it. The whole wedding industry will insist. The issue will swing presidential elections, once the honeymoon-hotel lobby gets in there with its muscle. Think of the upsurge in honeymoon business. God knows lawyers will like it—think of the divorces to handle. The custody suits. The adoptions to be arranged. The property settlements. This is a little like a protest march. In white satin with a train."

"Ah, matrimony is an honorable estate, as well as a boon to the GNP, and you are entering it as best you can, to the extent the world as currently constituted will permit. I'll be damned if

I know why anybody wants to get married, gay or straight. But since you are forbidden to do it, that's enough reason. Are you planning to make me a great-grandfather?"

"Sure, Grandpa, would you like that? You're so cute! Dad is okay on the kid idea but mom looks like a prune when I talk about it. I think we'll go to Africa next year and get a baby. Or maybe we'll try Vietnam. We can just go there and sit in a café in Ho Chi Minh City until somebody offers us a child. I know a couple that did it. Or maybe we'll find two gays to partner with. Do artificial insemination. Two mommies and two daddies. There are many possibilities."

"I like all those ideas. Will one of you quit work and raise these kids?"

"Me. I hate being a lawyer. And I'd love to raise some kids. A stay-at-home mom. How did you get to be so wise, Grandpa? Grandma's scared of scandal, Mother is pissed off because she had to tell her girlfriends in Dallas. For Rachel it's hellfire." She handed him a cup of coffee.

"Is the *Times* going to publish the picture and the story?"

"I don't know. But they said they are seriously discussing a change in policy. A union is a union, I told them. I also told them I was an attorney. Maybe they were afraid we'd sue."

"They really ought to publish it."

"I wish you were giving me away. It isn't every girl who has a choice of her father and grandfather to give her away at her commitment ceremony. So great that Candace has Uncle Arty, now that Gregory is gone. I loved him so much, so much. Such support."

"Yes, he was a fine fellow." He took a breath. He understood the white gowns, but why did they need men to give them away?

A mystery. After a pause he said, "I hope you know what you're getting into. The woman you marry today may not be the woman you end up with, even if she looks more or less like the same woman. I mean, commitment changes people. The years change people.

"I sound like an old grouch. All you have to worry about is this weather, this sodden grass. And the smart money says it's going to clear off."

He kissed her, and she left the kitchen with a tray of coffee mugs and oranges.

Sam sat alone, watching the western ridge. Did he see a patch of blue? No. He heard stirrings upstairs, flushing toilets, running showers, footfalls. Then a familiar pair of voices, murmuring together. The twins, in yellow chenille bathrobes and bunny slippers, came into the kitchen.

"Well, you're up early," Viv said.

"When did you come down? I thought we were the early birds."

Sam got to his feet and embraced Adri, then Viv. "Coffee, ladies?"

"Decaf." Ah, decaf for Viv. He searched for the decaf beans.

"Oh, espresso for me." Adri always wanted espresso. "One of those café lattes you do with that machine. But it has to be soy milk. I'm lactose intolerant."

With her it was a moral imperative to be lactose intolerant.

"Adri, you aren't," her sister said. "You aren't, you aren't. How could you be lactose intolerant all of a sudden when you've drunk milk all your life? And don't start in about celiac disease, either."

"I do have celiac. They say fifty percent of us have it and don't know it. I know it. Anyway, Vivienne, if you have no sympathy, just spare me."

"Give her the soy milk. I want nonfat."

Soy milk. Horrid, unnatural, overprocessed, Sam thought, and sure enough, Edith had laid in a supply of it. Ah, the decaf beans. God bless the twins, even if they did talk endlessly about herbal remedies for toenail fungus. They were all solidarity; they would have sided with a Mendel embezzler or serial killer, had there been one. Sam set out five kinds of sweeteners, three artificial ones plus white and unrefined sugar. If necessary, he could find some honey. Did the health industry advise a person to sweeten coffee with honey? How had the middle class learned to fear everything on the grocery shelf?

"Ladies, I love you. I may have been a headache and I may have been a bore. But thanks for putting up with me over the years. Thanks for being here. I am grateful for the support, as Alison and Candace keep saying. Endlessly. Christ, *support* used to be a word applied to stockings. Or what daddies did for their families."

And the three of them embraced once more, Viv and Adri nestling happily in Sam's arms, their arms around his waist. Over their matching gray heads, Sam could see that the fog lying on the mountains was lifting. "Look, a patch of blue up there!" He whispered a command to the skies. All at once most of the upstairs population surged into the kitchen, Anna and Martin in supercilious smiles and bathrobes, Rachel in skirt and shirt and inner light. Stephen and Camilla in jeans and battle readiness. Almost like old times: family breakfasts had always been fend-for-yourself, with plenty of provisions, even when the kids were small. Edith came in last, the dowager duchess in dressing gown and mules. Sam set about manufacturing coffee to every prescription.

"Rachel, isn't that a bit much?" It was Stephen, rebuking his sister for saying grace over her bagel. "Practicing for when you inherit the house and turn this place into a church camp?"

"Shut up, Stevie," Anna chimed in. "She can pray if she likes. But she isn't likely to turn the old manse into a church camp, because you're scheming to get it yourself. You can set up head-quarters in the barn and laser every eyeball in Delaware County." Martin snickered.

"Show a bit of respect for your brother, darling. You may want your vision corrected one day, too," said Cammy.

How Sam hated his daughter-in-law. And Anna's boyfriend, as well. He hated them all, if he got right down to it. "For the love of God, stop this. You've come here for a joyous occasion. Rachel, stop praying over the damn bagel. It only provokes your brother. You two had your mother on the verge of collapse the other day. Can't you show more manners and a little less public piety? I am a bloody secular humanist, a devout one. A born-again one. Yes, I am a born-again believer in the principles of the Enlightenment. I worship Voltaire. Don't pray over the food. It offends me."

Ah, the penalties of being an excellent provider, of acquiring property, of sending your three offspring to the best schools, of having the means to give an elaborate party for 150 people, of having a distinguished career. Of sticking to one wife for forty-five years with only one lapse. And he had mended the lapse, sacrificed his own inclinations. He hoped that Antonia would not let him down. He hoped that the weather would not let him down. In late morning, as though some force in nature were bending to Sam Mendel's will, the sun broke through like Apollo driving his chariot over the mountains, brightening the green hues and sending the fog away like smoke up a chimney. The irises and the phlox and roses and lilies and lilacs lifted their heads and dried to brilliant colors. The blueberry bushes on the hillside fluffed out their leaves, like fat birds. It was an excellent omen.

31   Commitment

B Y 5:30 THAT AFTERNOON, when the procession of automobiles began turning in at the wrought-iron gate by the road, the air was crisp, the sky blue, with only a few scudding white clouds. Sam's talent as a master gardener was evident on all sides. Sam the master publisher had almost reclaimed his own identity after these horrid months of being handcuffed to Edith and that wretch Steiner and the caterer and the hordes of party planners, a prisoner in his own house.

And the family had not fallen into open warfare since the little breakfast skirmish. Nobody, not even Anna's boyfriend, had gotten drunk—yet—though cocktails and wine had been offered at the family lunch. Edith had been polite to everybody. She had even, at one point, quite cordially taken Mary's arm, and the two of them had spoken warmly with Candace.

The family had retired to bathe and dress after lunch. The coiffeur who charged Edith one hundred dollars a cut came at two to do the girls' hair, and cut Viv and Adri and Camilla and Anna, as well, all part of the girlish fun. A cosmetician followed

him and made up the bridal faces. The smell of creams and lac-
quers perfumed the entire upstairs. Two manicurists had minis-
tered unto all.

Edith had come down the stairs right after Sam, giving him
an opportunity to watch her descent. What a showcase for a
woman, stairs, even a woman of seventy. She had chosen a long
black gown—"appropriate, I think"—and retrieved the diamonds. One carat twinkled in each ear, plus a choker at her neck
and a thick pavé bracelet on her wrist. On her left hand a siz-
able square-cut rock sparkled aggressively as Edith picked up
her dress to descend the stairs, revealing the high-heeled sandals
she was wearing (dangerous for a woman her age). She had had
them sent up from New York—eight hundred dollars. Her white
hair curled thickly around her ears. Sam, at the foot of the stairs,
feared she needed a bodyguard for the ice. Edith had always said
the diamonds would go to Alison, the first granddaughter, but
she had changed her mind.

The brides came down last, clutching hands, tentative in their
finery, but regal, so regal that Edith forgot to cry, and Camilla
and Anna and Rachel forgot their shock and disapproval. Grand
creations of satin that showed off the breasts and fine waists and
swept to the floor—perfectly cut upper-crust, in-excellent-taste
bridal gowns, not identical but similar in design as well as price
tag. The dresses had, in the end, been purchased at the famous
Brooklyn bridal shop rather than Lord & Taylor. Viv and Adri
had dressed the brides as they had promised to do, buttoning
them into the tight bodices, arranging the trains. The twins, in
matching blue gowns, came along behind the brides.

At the photo session (still photography and video), Mary had
warmed up to Sam, remarking on the beauty of the dresses. "If they
were marrying men," she said, "they couldn't be more beautiful.

You know, when my Candace married David, she wore just a plain old suit. I knew that marriage wouldn't last. Oh dear, I hope this works out for her. Oh, Mr. Mendel. . . ."

"Sam."

"Sam, I do like your granddaughter. Alison is a fine young woman, a fine partner, but oh dear. Oh dear. I hope I can manage to introduce her to my friends when she comes to Chicago. This is very difficult for me."

"And for me. Any time we marry off our children, we can only hope. I know you expected different. Maybe I expected different. Alison is my pet. Her choice is my choice, and I could hardly love or respect Candace more than I do. They are going to adopt a child, you know. Maybe children. We'll all love that. Maybe it will make up a bit for Gregory's loss." It annoyed him that Mary had not come for her brother's memorial services.

"Oh dear, Mr. Mendel. Sam. Please forgive my saying this. If I could tell you, if I could tell you what my parents would think to see us all reduced to this, my brother gone leaving no one, an old man who spent his life with another man. You don't know what it did to my father when he knew what Gregory had chosen to do—all the fame and Broadway lights in the world didn't make up for it to him. He said the white race was trying to stamp us out. He said if they couldn't do it with drugs and alcohol and prison sentences, they'd do it by seducing our men, raping our women. And now Candace. You know, that's the hurt of it. Not Alison. Who wouldn't want Alison in their family? But how will we African Americans survive if we all turn queer? And then there's me, of course. I didn't do right. I never married Candace's father."

"Mary, don't cry, my dear. You mustn't cry." She was wiping her eyes. "Who cares if you didn't marry her father? So what?

These are great times we live in. Humanity throwing off its chains. People doing what they always wanted to do but couldn't." He knew he sounded like that song from *Chicago,* the musical, but so what? "Think of the two beautiful young women. Think of the babies they may adopt. Or have. Think how happy Gregory was with Arthur, the beautiful dancing Gregory has given the world. Whom have they harmed? Nobody. It's all been good."

Her tears were splashing over. He patted her shoulder energetically, offered her his handkerchief.

"Mary, I am ham-handed. Be calm, my friend. Be happy. Wait till you have the grandbabies. Who knows, maybe they'll decide to do the artificial insemination bit, as Alison calls it, if you're not so hot on the idea of adopting in Africa or Saigon or wherever. One of them can become pregnant. Both of them, why not? They're both big earners, they can do what they want. And by the way, we'll all be family now." He prayed that something he said would comfort her. What did he expect, after all, that she should be beaming with gratitude because Candace was joining this so distinguished family of his? Or was he simply impatient with this anxious lady from Chicago? Sam tried, once again, to deconstruct himself. What kind of shit was he? As bad as Edith? As bad as Antonia had told him he was? An arrogant, selfish, overly entitled, blind bastard trampling on the rights of women? Ah, his darling, his heart's darling. How he longed to see her. He would kiss her feet in front of them all if only she would take him back.

The party was brilliant. Undeterred by the dismal skies of the morning or their patriotic duty to defend marriage as a sacred bond between a man and a woman, 110 people showed up. Not bad, really, even if it had been a straight-laced hetero affair. There were more than enough bodies to fill the big barn, occupy its twelve beautifully appointed round tables, to make a gala. The altar near the lily pond wore a floral blanket, something like the draping for a Mafia casket, Sam thought, but it was what the brides had wanted. Tiny white roses, masses of them. Wearing a precisely cut new tuxedo, Arty accompanied Candace down the aisle between the rows of chairs set up outdoors by the caterers, and Stephen brought Alison in. A string quartet played Schubert, quite lovely. An attorney of Alison's acquaintance officiated. Alison had written the ceremony, making her own palimpsest out of the Book of Common Prayer and her poetic inclinations, with pauses for the reading of Shakespeare sonnets as well as two interminable poems some girlfriend of theirs had produced for the occasion—the whole thing as relentlessly conventional as the wedding dresses. The brides kissed each other afterward, then sprang into the arms of waiting relatives.

They formed a receiving line: the brides, their parents, Sam, Edith. Sam craned his neck for his first real glimpse of Antonia, and his hands were shaking when she finally reached Edith and shook hands and then turned to him. He appreciated her grace, the way she managed not to look guilty or confrontational, merely polite and respectful, just another guest at the wedding. She was, he saw, as slim as ever, with her straight-cut white hair, and a pale gray satin suit. He hoped she had bought the suit only for him. Behind her came Mark and then Toni, who recognized him, and to his delight demanded a hug. He saw, to his astonishment, that Maggie was pregnant, very much so. "Congratulations to all of you, what splendid news," and he kissed her, though he knew she hated him for loving Antonia as much as for abandoning her. What would a new baby mean for Antonia? As for Mark Adler, poor boy, he went from one mess to another.

He was grateful to Edith for her forbearance, as well. Edith must, in the end, have decided to believe his nonsense about the book club, the companionable relationship, and the separate rooms when he and Antonia had made the trip to England. All his expedient lies. It was all worth it—he could not have handled it if Edith had been rude to Antonia. Today sufficient numbers of people choked on their true thoughts, so he could not have unleashed his own. Still, he had to go slowly, gently. It would not do to enrage Edith, to act a cad. There had to be some decent way out of this, some honorable way. ("Edith, I have invited Antonia to come on a long voyage with me, and she has agreed. Since you dislike travel so much, I thought you would be better off just staying here. What do you say, my dear?") Oh, why could he not devise some way, some plausible way, to have his cake and eat it, too? Why should everyone get hysterical? They were all alive. In the past nine months, the predicted squadrons of terrorists or bioterrorists had not smashed the city and broken their hearts. Gregory was dead—a reminder that life was too precious and too precarious to be wasted. Gather ye rosebuds!

Cocktails were served for an hour or more, and finally the guests sat down, and the orchestra played and the waiters circulated. Candace danced with Arty (who couldn't dance) and Alison danced with Stephen (who could), and then the brides danced together, so happy with each other and so perfect in their gowns that even Edith beamed approval. Sitting beside his wife, Sam grew euphoric. He claimed his dance with Alison and then Candace, and after the first course was served led Edith out to fox-trot. He was an accomplished ballroom dancer, and Edith wasn't so bad either, but she was listless and complained of headache, and so they resumed their places at the head table. Eventually the fillet arrived, and after two bites, Sam took a gulp of the splendid red Burgundy he had chosen, crossed the floor, and invited Mary to dance, then Viv and Adri, carefully working his way through a number of women, until he felt he had earned the right to approach Antonia.

"May I have this dance?" She might have refused. But she smiled and took his hand. He followed her to the dance floor.

"Can I see you in New York?

"No."

"We mustn't let our relationship die."

"You killed it. It's dead already."

"No, I can't live without you."

"You are giving a pretty good imitation of it. I never saw you in formal clothes before. You look ridiculous."

"I concede the point. I never intend to wear formal clothes again."

"You bastard."

"Yes."

"You prefer this to me. And why not? The gardens, the pool. The magnificent dwelling. I tried to go upstairs, but one of your servants politely told me there were bathrooms on the ground level. It really made me laugh. As if I really cared what the upstairs of the Mendel mansion looks like. What a joke. And you vote Democratic."

"Antonia, I will take you upstairs and show you whatever you want to see. Now, if you'll come."

"No. I don't want a tour. And I assume you aren't making an indecent proposal. But I do want to imagine you here. I want to know how much everything is worth. I want the total to be high. You made your choice. I wouldn't want you to dump me for a dump."

"Stop it. Don't talk like this. I want you to allow me to come back."

"You are crazy. How can you?"

"I made a mistake."

"You'll have to live with it."

"Damnit, Antonia, you stepped on my foot. Did you and Fred never go dancing?"

"No. Fred was no dancer. And I was always out at political meetings. Meetings where women talked about what shits men are. And how men care only for themselves and their erect pricks. I should have listened more attentively at those hate-men meetings."

"No, you should listen attentively right now. I'm sorry. I can never explain what I did, not really. It seemed the right thing at the time. She was so forlorn, and well, her threats were pretty terrible. I can only beg forgiveness. I know I fail as a lover sometimes, and as a friend most of the time, but I need you."

"What are you proposing? You're going to get a divorce, or I can expect you one night a week at Perry Street, under cover of some phony committee meeting? And I must be cautious about phoning you lest you be in Edith's presence?"

In fact, they were standing still, at arm's length, at the edge of the floor. "Whatever you want to say to me, I deserve it. But let me come back. I miss you so. We could go to France this summer."

"What, another sneak-away?"

"Just say you'll come along. That will give me the motive to break free." He put his arms around her, thinking she could hardly resist the pull of the music. Just the way you look tonight. "Love me, never never change. Keep that breathless charm," he sang. "Antonia, at least relax enough to dance with me. You are a terrible dancer. But don't stand still. You are beautiful tonight, you know. But I don't love you for your looks."

She yielded. Just a few steps. "Sam, you hurt me so much."

"I know, my love. I want to erase it. It will take you a long time to trust me, but you can learn. I will be trustworthy now. Worthy of you now.

"Sam, I love you so much. I love you so much I will probably forgive you. Damn you, I probably will go to France with you."

"You will? Say you will."

"I don't promise. But I will see you. Lunch. And I just mean lunch. No touching."

"Oh, Antonia."

"I could back you up to that swimming pool of yours and throw you in it and hold you under till you drowned, and at the same time I want you to kiss me, but don't do it here. I hate you, I love you. I freeze, I burn. Guess this is what the young folks mean by love. Oh, I wish I had learned to dance."

32   Edith

THE MUSIC GREW LOUDER. She was bored. The main course had been served, eaten, and at some tables, removed. Nobody looked drunk, but Edith could sense the ease brought on by rich food in four courses and more wine than reasonable persons ought to drink. The barn was warm. She hadn't needed the shawl she had draped over the chair back. Most people were on the dance floor. In one corner the kids were gyrating. She reckoned it would be hours before the cake was cut and the other desserts offered. She pushed back from the table, feeling dizzy. She had not eaten the shrimp and calamari or the salad with figs and Gorgonzola, and only a few bites of the fillet, because each course looked increasingly inedible. She regretted the few sips she had taken of the champagne and of the heart-stoppingly expensive wine Sam had selected for the steak. Her head began to ring and ache, as if a pair of ice tongs were embedded in her temples or a balloon were inflating inside her head. When the server came to remove her plate, she laid her fine, thin hand, decked with the heavy stone, on his arm and asked for some aspirin. Quickly, solicitously, he brought two tablets on a tiny silver tray.

She swallowed them with water and thought she felt the fire in her head abate somewhat. Sam was on the dance floor with that woman—he had said he meant to dance with all the ladies over fifty; it was merely a cover-up for dancing with Antonia, as he was now doing. He had danced with her first, and she had been glad when it was over because the sandals were agony, and she had been wrong to put her aged feet in such gear. Antonia did not look so threatening. Not nearly as pretty as Edith herself and subtracting the decades, Edith imagined that Antonia would not have been much competition for her fifty years ago. But at least she was not young. Sam was not the trophy type. His trophies were all on the wall in his library: the prizes, the awards, the photos of him with Faulkner and John Cheever and Joan Didion.

In the softness of the June night with the full moon rising (the morning rain now present only in a flowery essence in the air), people were pushing out of the open-ended barn into the garden, dancing on the pathways and lawn. Contrary to Edith's nightmares, it was just like any party. No women in tuxedos boogying across the dance floor, no gay men writhing suggestively. Well, there were, in fact, same-sex couples on the dance floor, but so what? The ceremony had been dignified, seemly to an extreme, and Stephen had danced the first dance with Alison, and that poor sad fellow from Greenwich Village, Gregory's partner, they called him, had led Candace to the floor. Then the two women had danced together, and it had seemed as sedate as any society wedding. Perhaps all this would not put an end to civilization as she knew it.

The music segued from Rogers and Hart to a Beatles song, and then to what she might have ventured to call rock, and the dance floor was suddenly peopled by the young, writhing and shaking. I'd better get away from this, I'd better go into the house and lie down.

She felt unsteady on her feet. She was alone at the table. Viv and Adri had gone across the room. Oh, these sandals, these ankle straps. She made her way around the edge of the dance floor and exited the barn, relieved that she had escaped unnoticed. The air was cooler outdoors, and she nodded to several people she saw who were swaying to the music and drinking wine on the pebbled garden paths.

All at once her memory was bereft of proper names, as if she had had brain surgery. That gentleman under the grape arbor, for example, had been an associate of her husband's . . . Who was called what? What was her husband's name? That name had vanished too! She was as innocent of proper names as a newborn babe. She smiled at him, whoever he was, and moved on. It was a very long way to the back terrace of the house and the door. She wanted to lie down in that nice thing one could rest in, what was it? People called it a . . . what? There was one in there somewhere, with a warmer. Not a warmer, not a warmer. A, a throw. But *throw* was not a noun. Whatever it was called, this resting place was miles away, but she promised herself not to hurry. She could easily remember that there were plenty of places to rest downstairs, inside the house and out. All at once, a large supply of nouns came back to her, like chickens crowding around to be fed. Ah, yes. She would take a little nap in the library under one of those lovely cashmere throws she had bought from one of those fancy catalogues. On the leather chaise longue. A chaise longue, not lounge, she had finally learned. Only the ignorant said chaise lounge.

And then she heard the voices. Loud voices. Her younger

daughter's voice. Her son's. Her first-born daughter's voice. Anna, Stephen, Rachel. Names, names, names. They were squabbling, squabbling in public, how could they, how could they lack all breeding? Naughty things, they had always quarreled, she had never been able to stop it. Odd, they were her children, and she knew their voices, but once again their names went out of her head. Well, the names would come back, don't you worry, your proper nouns will come back. She looked around: way over by the lily pond, she saw a crowd of well-dressed people, women in gowns, men in dinner jackets. A phalanx of moving backs, of gowns and dinner jackets in a circle. The voice she heard belonged to her daughter—what was her name?—who was shouting before a lectern. Unfair, said the voice, to bring children into such a situation, godless. Godless. Laughter erupted. Bad enough for the community, the voice continued, and a sin and a crime to rear children thus. Edith wondered which children. She had not reared her children badly.

Bullshit, the male voice yelled. Ah, Stephen, her son, the doctor, and he fixes ladies' eyes so they can read the luncheon menu, five thousand dollars for each eye. And he is the father of my granddaughter, who wore a satin bridal gown today and married a man from Harvard, only he is black. And it wasn't Harvard. Oh dear, it wasn't a black man, it was a black woman, but how can a woman marry another woman? It isn't done. Edith called up the thoughts like images flashed across some big screen, safe from the pounding of the blood. Something was happening in her neck. She wanted to go toward the lily pond, put a stop to the fracas. Unfortunately, she was choking.

She felt for her necklace clasp, unfastened it, and it dangled from her hand, but the choking sensation did not go away. Bullshit, came the cry once more. Rachel, I told you not to start this crap at the ceremony, and I meant it. Oh, Stephen, don't, an unfamiliar male voice said. Alison will thank me some day when she has returned from all this, the woman's voice shrieked. Stephen, you must support me in this—for she will be redeemed. I am praying for her. A hundred people in Little Rock are praying for her. I haven't much time to convince you, I am leaving tomorrow morning. I have prayed and prayed. Alison is my niece, your daughter. How can she meet her God with this stain on her life, and a black woman, too? Just ask Mary what she thinks of all this—it's a tragedy. She says it's the end of their family. You think people like you have done black people a favor to bring them to such a pass?

All this talk was crazy. Edith started once more toward the wall of bodies; she must tell them that everybody was happy; we should all try to be happy, there was so little time. The crowd was thickening, and her efforts to go in that direction were not getting her anyplace. She saw that she was simply hanging desperately to the stone wall by the azalea bed. Her diamond choker was dangling from her hand, and she let it fall to the grass. She could find it tomorrow. She saw, out of the corner of her eye, her husband—ah, once more his name had gone up in smoke—lunging toward the crowd at the lily pond, shouldering his way through. More loud voices, angry voices. Followed by a splash, a heavy splash, a squawk of rage, then another splash, and another, to more cries and wild laughter. Oh dear. She wanted no part of this.

And then, easily, unaware that she had crumpled, Edith was on the ground, next to an azalea bush, voiceless. She could not cry out. She managed to sit upright and rub her ankle. She unstrapped one sandal and freed her foot. She could not manage the other. It would just have to stay on her poor blistered foot. Ah, how wonderful and cool the grass felt. It was dewy. Heavenly. She must have turned her ankle, the way she did in the woods last fall, before the towers fell, before the terrorists made everyone realize they ought to behave. Good heavens, would she have to give up walking? These thoughts, she realized, were formless, no words to them, just clouds of thought like the flames rising from burning buildings.

Oh, the shouts, the commotion over by the pond. All about the house. The upkeep. A man insisting furiously that if Alison wants to marry a dozen women here and keep them all in the upstairs bedrooms, she can do it! Fuck you! Oh, shameful, saying that word right out in front of guests. She must put a stop to this right now. She heard another splash, saw the splattering, heard the laughter and the yelling.

Unbearable. But though she was pressed to the ground as if by stones, as if someone had stacked stones on her chest, her head had cleared. There was no pain, no pain at all. The aspirin had taken hold. She would not, after all, need to go inside and nap on the library couch. She could nap here, among the flowers. She took off her ring, because it seemed so heavy, and then her brace-let. She laid her jewels on the grass beside her head, as though tucking them under a pillow. They would be safe there.

Looking up, she was not a bit surprised to see that deer, with its noble antlered head, positioned just behind the wall, the very same deer that had accosted her when she had fallen in the woods last September. Why, here he was again. His eyes were shining black, shimmering with the shadows of trees. His white-flecked brick-brown coat glistened. Brown, not black, Edith had always believed, was the true color of death. And she was right. Here it was. The deer spoke politely. First put your hand on my neck, and then swing up on my back, and we'll be gone. It will be easy, Edith, you are light as air. She nodded, wafted easily into the saddle on the deer's back, and picked up the embroidered reins. Ah, a reindeer. The nouns poured suddenly into her brain, released in a magnificent flood, every noun she had ever known, ever thought of. Reindeer. Azaleas. Coleus. Pachysandra. Rachel. Stephen. Camilla. Anna. Alison. Sam. Weddings. Diamonds. Caterers. This was what it must mean to be free, to die, to have an endless supply of nouns, never again to have to grope for words or try to remember where you put anything or what you had said just a moment ago or to take your calcium pills at breakfast and your Fosamax on Saturdays. To be barefoot, free of your terrible sandals. She clicked happily to the reindeer, and away he ran, galloping as if he had been a Mongol pony and she a princess of the steppes.

IN THE END, it would be difficult to assess the events of the day. The stories told at dinner parties would grow more complex as the next year passed. For the spectators at the lily pond, witnessing an entertaining sibling fight, a fight that had by far outshone the dancing and the filet mignon, the Burgundy, the ceremony, the testimonials from friends, and certainly the poetry written especially for the occasion, this was the high point of the day. God, when the Mendel brood got going at the pond, it had been a magnificent little microcosm of the American electorate, one analytically inclined guest pointed out. Rachel, the evangelical, fueled only by mineral water; Stephen, the influential doctor, drunk; and Anna, the hippie rededicated to Orthodoxy, also drunk, but not as drunk as Stephen. They had gone at one another gloriously, at first with words; then they began to flail away, and it all degenerated into a matter of property, this grand estate where the three of them had grown up, and which they were each determined to have for themselves, chiefly to prevent their siblings from possessing it.

At the peak of it, Sam raced across the lawn, bellowing. Rachel and Stephen then wrestled each other into the lily pond, and Anna jumped in after, or maybe they yanked her in, making a great splash that ruined several pairs of trousers and two silk skirts in the vicinity. In the knee-deep water, the story would go, the three got entangled in the lotuses, pulled up the serpentine roots, wallowed in them, a perfect Laocoön, and two other people had jumped companionably in. Sam arrived in time to see them do it, five vandals destroying his cosseted lily pond, pride of his garden, brought to perfection with his own hands and patient efforts, hours of digging in the brown mud, and there they were, festooned with lotuses and lotus roots, wet and muddy and drunk, except for Rachel, who was drunk only with zeal and hatred. He stared in horror, forgetting everything but the lotuses, including Alison and Candace and his great-grandchildren, and Antonia, whose allegiance he had hoped to recapture, whose bed he had hoped to reenter. It all fell away.

"My God," he cried. "My God. You have murdered my lotuses." And then a louder wail drowned out his own. Candace and Alison, hand in hand, their gowns billowing around them, had left the party and headed toward the fracas, guessing what was going on and ready for battle. "That bastard Aunt Rachel, I might have known she would stir up something. Let's get her!" Alison had said as they left the barn. Then, halfway to the lily pond, Alison had stopped cold, had stopped Candace. She saw a pair of feet, human feet, sticking out of the azalea hedge by the stone wall. One of the feet was bare, the other in a high-heel sandal bound on by an ankle strap.

"Candace. Look. There's somebody there. Good God, help me. It's Grandma." It was this that put an end to Sam's hollering about the lotuses, the cry for help from Alison that, in fact, probably kept him from jumping into the pond himself and thrashing the five vandals.

Candace and Alison discovered Edith's body, in its shroud of black chiffon, among the azaleas, with her diamonds placed carefully beside her still carefully coiffed head, as if in a royal burial. Alison dropped to the ground and took her grandmother's bare foot in her hands, groped for the limp arms. "Help!" the two women screamed. "It's Grandma. Get a doctor, get an ambulance." But the chill of that poor elderly foot in Alison's palm told her it was too late. On their knees, the brides tried to extricate the corpse from the bushes. It seemed weightless and yet they could not lift it.

"No, we mustn't move her. Wait for the medics."

"No, no. We have to get her out of these bushes. She must have had a heart attack, a stroke, out here all by herself. Oh no, oh no, oh, how could this have happened?" Alison collapsed on the ground, and Candace tried to raise her. "You have to get up, you must get hold of yourself, darling. Maybe she's not dead."

But Alison began screaming. "Oh, Grandma, it's my fault. We should never have done this. I've killed my grandmother."

"You haven't killed anybody. I haven't killed anybody. My sweet God, will somebody call the hospital?"

Sam arrived only steps ahead of the legions from the lily pond, and behind them lumbered Stephen, Rachel, and Anna. Dripping. Disgusting. Sam fell to his knees beside Edith. "What is it?

What is it?" And then he saw. Alison was sobbing out of control, and he wanted desperately to comfort her, to tell the child not to cry. But he could not speak. Looking up in bewilderment, he saw Antonia's face in the crowd that had gathered, and irrationally he wanted to go to her, to bury his head in her arms, to ask her please for Christ's sake to sort all this out for him.

Two or three cell phones emerged from dinner-jacket pockets, and two or three men frantically dialed 911. The ambulance had to travel miles from Margaretville. Sam stood up, calmly directed people to move back, not to crowd around. Sam took charge.

"I think that we won't be serving wedding cake tonight. I think it would be best if the party were over. My dear friends, I apologize, but my wife appears to be seriously ill. We must take her to the hospital. I beg you to find your coats and hats and go home. We are waiting for the ambulance." His voice, his orderly and seemly consideration for his guests, took on the quality of a recorded announcement. "Do go home, my friends. We must take care of this." After forty-five minutes the ambulance, its lights flashing, pulled silently into the driveway. The EMS team bent over the body, but there was little to be done except to load it onto the gurney and be gone. Sam and Stephen, Alison and Candace in their voluminous gowns, now slightly muddy and damp, accompanied her.

They would have to make arrangements. The orchestra had packed up and was loading and leaving, and the caterers had begun clearing. All this would have been done soon anyway. They had served their time. This would make a story. "The hostess stroked out, poor old lady. We got off an hour early." The guests had cleared out, most of them, by the time the ambulance arrived, though several had stayed to rubberneck or in hope of being useful; a group gathered in the house with Vivienne and

Adrienne, who needed medical attention themselves. By eleven o'clock the garden was quiet, and nighttime had settled in. In the barn all that remained was the elaborate wedding cake, left uncut on a big round table. Two bride dolls, one white and one black, in white satin and veils, stood smiling at the pinnacle.

33   Antonia

S HE LEFT BED and bedroom without making a sound. Sam had finally fallen asleep toward 4:00 a.m. His insomnia was a contagion, his malaise a reproach. Rain, distant thunder in the night. They had tried to make love, and after a couple of false starts she was beginning to feel good, but he softened and drooped, and his mood turned surly. At 1:30 he got up and took a ten-milligram hit of Ambien. At 2:30, wide awake, he went to the kitchen for whiskey. She turned on the lamp so that he could make his way safely back to bed without stumbling on a discarded shoe or a chair leg. Red-eyed and as cranky as he, she watched him cross the room. He was an aggregate of parts: the long legs and arms, the abdominal muscles, the refractory and obstinate penis, the territory she knew so well, every hair and mole and muscle of it, a pocked and cratered landscape. Her territory.

The rattle of ice cubes in the glass exasperated her, but she took the sip of Scotch he offered. What she had craved for months and months was here next to her: Sam naked. Taking more than his share of the sheet and comforter, two pillows beneath his head and one beneath his right knee. Antonia had never wished Edith dead, but at least she had died easily and fast, as we all hope we may. Suppose she had lived, after her stroke that evening, and Sam had been obliged to nurse her for years? It could have ended that way, and Sam would have stuck by her. And Antonia would have wanted him to stick by her. They should rejoice in fortune's handiwork, which had ruled differently, but Sam could not rejoice. And so Antonia could not rejoice. You get what you want and don't know what to do with it.

Now, at eight o'clock, she was grateful for the light. Her shoulders and neck were in knots, her head a howling cave. Her brain must be thinning out, as well as the cartilage in her knees. She started the coffee, peeled an orange. Could she build the rest of her life on rituals of this sort? Forget Sam, be a grandmother, now that there were two little girls. Antonia and Frederica. Maggie needed a full-time servant, maybe more, and Grandma would have to be it. A month ago she and Toni had waited all afternoon outside the birthing room, and had been allowed to hold the new baby when she was only two hours old.

"It's a kitten, its eyes are not open," Toni had said, her own hazel eyes filled with sadness beyond her years. She wished she could have gotten a kitten instead, she told Antonia. Mark, at his wife's bedside, had looked haggard, as if he, too, would have preferred a kitten, and he was sneezing and complaining of sore throat and nasal congestion. Antonia pitied him—not unusual these days—and had held him tight for a moment. A trapped animal. Did he dream of Sophie? Of some other life? But this was his life, a wife and two children. Maggie had labored only five hours, no anesthesia, no epidural, the way a proper modern mother was supposed to deliver, and she was glowing with new-mother pride, the unmedicated natural birth, no episiotomy, and she put her baby to her breast with the sweat of parturition still on her face. Antonia's fears and anxieties momentarily dissolved, replaced by pure giddy love as she held the baby, swaddled in a cotton blanket, the eyes still looking inward in their bewildered newborn way, the tiny face battered from the long headfirst journey. Who could this be? No wonder people hesitated to give new babies a name.

So the four Adlers were crammed into their dilapidated apartment on West End Avenue. At least the liquor store had increased Mark's hours as well as his wages. It wasn't enough. Maggie had no intention of living on the earnings of a retail clerk. It either had to be something with lots of money, like investment banking, or something socially commendable, like teaching. But it couldn't be selling booze. Antonia had asked Sam if he could do anything; he had friends at First Boston, at Citibank, an interview maybe, now that the financial industry was recovering, could that be arranged? But Mark had lost interest. Anyway, his resumé would reveal a two-year gap. Nobody would hire him. Maggie's maternity leave would end in November. She was frantic about the problem of pumping and storing breast milk at the office. She imagined herself at an author conference: "Sorry, I have to go and pump. I'm tight. I'm leaking." All these worries Antonia shared with her, and she thought of offering to support them for a few months. But Maggie would lose her job if she delayed. The motherhood bar had been hoisted up many notches since Antonia's time: you couldn't have any pain medication, you had to breast-feed for a year, even if you had to pump the milk and give it by bottle, and you had to get back to your job after three months' leave. Unpaid leave. They put you on disability. But America loves families.

From the moment they'd come home from the hospital, Antonia had provided dinners, suppers, casseroles for the freezer, dishwashing services, had taken laundry to the basement, had administered back rubs, foot rubs, bought a year's supply of organic nipple ointment and a huge supply of diapers, disposable but ecologically okay. (Touching, she had to admit, this determination not to dirty up the world or be dirtied up by it, even if in Maggie's heart this had replaced all other politics.) She had washed and folded clothes, accompanied Toni for long afternoons in Riverside Park, had brought her to Perry Street for overnights, had seen to it that she had new shoes and jeans for her first day at Parkside Montessori, and had paid the tuition. Mark had called her the "perfect grandmother." The statement, as always, had its acrid edge.

She fetched the *Times* from her front door. September 11, 2002, was the date. Yes, today. She noticed the special section, Resilience and Grief. She extracted it, glanced through it. Mayor Bloomberg advised the city to grieve today but take hold of tomorrow. Right. She could think of nothing she'd like more. The second lead on page one said the Bush administration was determined to go to war against Iraq, though "intelligence officials acknowledged they had no accurate assessments of that country's arms and capacities." But, yes, there would be a war. Bush had stood on top of the smoking ruins, had promised revenge and justice, as if those two ends could ever coexist. Americans wanted to be safe, whatever that might mean, and the president had to make them safe. In spite of what the sages had promised, we had not seen the end of history or the beginning of the long, stately future of peace and democracy. Those sages had somehow forgotten about the Middle East. Africa. That the majority of people on Earth lived in hunger, thirst, fear, and dirt from birth to death and thus hated the well fed and the clean. History swept ferociously onward out of Antonia's ken and control. She understood nothing.

She threw open the terrace door: mist in the urban rain forest. Arty's garden was cloudy, wet: its rows of bushy-headed purple and pink mums, the cherry tomatoes ripe in September, the bed of lemon balm, where, on hot summer days, matching yellow butterflies had quivered over every fragrant sprig. Arty had folded up the old double lounge where he and Gregory had napped together so many afternoons. There was only a single chair. Arty lacked the energy for selling letters and photos and old shopping lists; his business was crumbling. But his garden flourished. Besides the lemon balm, he had planted thyme, basil, marjoram, and dill. Six new rose bushes for Greg. A mockingbird was flicking its spiky tail and mimicking the persistent beeps of a backward-moving truck far away on West Fourth Street. Mockingbirds had invaded Manhattan, and they made it their business to satirize the sounds of traffic. Arty claimed he'd seen a hummingbird around his flame plants. Greg talked with him every day, too—another claim Antonia saw no reason to dispute.

The coffee had only made her headache worse. Sleep, she must sleep. But who could sleep at 8:30 in the morning? She saw the face of the specter, Mohammed Atta, as clear as if some quick-sketch artist had Magic-Markered it on the garden mists. A year ago today, almost to the hour, he had hurtled down the Hudson, aiming his stolen airplane at the north tower, his heart bursting with self-righteousness.

"You again. You have ruined the world with your jihad, and what good has it done? They take tweezers away from people at airports. They look into people's shoes. Does that help you? Our army is out killing Muslims with Predator missiles. You should be ashamed of what you've done to your mother. I talked with her, and she isn't proud of you for being a martyr. Not at all. She says you have broken her heart. You are a criminal and a lunatic, that's all. And now you know there aren't any virgins in heaven, either. They send the virgins to the other place.

"Listen, I will tell you something you ought to know. It will help you, help us all. A Japanese court is holding hearings about the atrocities they committed in China during World War II. You weren't born then, and you have no idea what went on then, what kind of killing there was—enough to make your act fade into nothing, enough to make you a dilettante. The Japanese killed ten million Chinese. That's always the figure, isn't it, ten or six million, when the butchers start out to butcher? Of course you, Mr. Mohammed Atta, only got three thousand with your crazy crew. But the Japanese, not to mention ourselves, were real pros at killing, and one way they killed the Chinese was with medical experiments. They dissected people alive. Took men, women, and children and tied them down and cut them open. They said it was for science, but it was for fun, in fact. They liked it. After the war was over, we Americans pretended we didn't know.

"So the other day this elderly Japanese man came and presented himself to the tribunal. He didn't have to come, but he wanted to tell his story. As a young soldier in China, his job was to scrub down people who were going to be dissected. He didn't see the operations, but he knew what was happening, because he heard the screams and saw the tortured bodies afterward, but he just took his hose and washed the people, and passed them on down the line into the huts where the butchers were working.

"After the war, he went home, became a civilian, got a job, led a life, raised a family, grew old and arthritic, and had to take pills for his heart. But he never forgot. And when he heard about the

court, he came on his own. Bought his own train ticket. Somebody asked him, 'Why at your age do you come forward and
confess to these horrors?'

"And he said, 'Because if no one comes, we shall just go from
darkness to darkness.'

"So one day you will come forward to confess, in some court
somewhere. Maybe we all will regret the darkness. But we shall
all see it. Finally. We shall see the darkness. Maybe that is the
best we can do. Maybe that is all that progress can ever mean."

The mist cleared. She was only talking to herself like a dotty
old woman. Mohammed Atta was gone. Aspirin, she must take
two aspirin. She could get through the day on aspirin. She went
back into the kitchen and searched the medicine drawer. She
heard Sam head toward the bathroom. It would take him a while.
Perhaps when he came into the kitchen she would send him away
for good. What did history teach, except that war is the way of
Homo sapiens, and love an illusion?

34 Sam

HE SHOWERED IN very hot water, lots of lather. He'd been an agent provocateur last night. Some horrid contrariness had inhabited him, some wickedness. By now, three months after the funeral, he should already have planned a journey for himself and Antonia, should have booked plane tickets to France, to England. People were traveling again, after all. The terrorists had not put an end to travel. He thought of Scotland. Scotland would be lovely. He thought of heather, single malts, a journey to the Outer Hebrides. But he was happy nowhere. His home, his grounds, his gardens were empty, their tranquillity destroyed. His lily pond had been ripped apart. He would never replant it. The discarded sandal, the diamonds in the grass by the azalea bushes, Edith's terrible pallor. What had she been thinking as she lay down to die?

Vivienne and Adrienne had stayed with him into July and August, protecting him as tenderly as ever. Monitoring his mental health. Proposing a visit to a grief counselor, then withdrawing the suggestion when he looked annoyed. So much to be done. So much to be carted off! They had taken charge of Edith's bedroom, sorting through her perfumes, combs, hand mirrors, dresses, monogrammed stationery, panties, stockings, the expensive nightgowns and negligees, all of it. Sam had hardly realized she possessed these things. The dressing table of a leading lady, a diva: bottles of nail polish in a dozen shades of pink, a regiment of bottles just for the cuticles. An army of lipstick tubes. Most of it unused. Viv and Adri sorted patiently, made bags for the thrift shop, refused to give up even when Sam begged them to abandon the project.

"A shame Anna and Rachel aren't looking through their mother's things," Viv said.

"Stephen, too, what about him? And Camilla?"

"They'll want their mother's things one day."

"I doubt that," Sam said. "But let's finish up. Let's forget it. We need to get back to New York. I'll have the housekeeper come and check up once a week. I'll ask her to put white sheets on the furniture. No one's going to be here. I can't bear the place."

The diamonds. He had needed to do something with the diamonds. Viv and Adri had gathered them so carefully from the grass the night Edith died (the undertaker had removed the studs from her ears and returned them to the family), had locked the jewels away in their proper box, thinking they would belong to Alison. But to Sam the solution was obvious: he gave the diamonds to the twins. And felt relief, even joy, that they were gone. Perhaps he would feel relieved if the house and land were gone. Perhaps he would sell it, this showy container for his financial and social capital, this creation of his vanity. He would walk off from it, indifferent to its value. A good idea. A plausible idea.

In Antonia's cramped shower stall, with the water scalding hot, he energetically soaped his scrotum and then his head and chest.

Antonia. Dear optimistic Antonia. She still gave money to that poor old man on the street. She still imagined that who you voted for mattered. The little that was left of liberalism after the fall of the Soviet Union had vaporized along with the concrete and plastic and paper on September 11, 2001. The brief epoch when the poor had gotten the upper hand in this country was long gone, had been replaced, inevitably, by the might of money. The other side had been in charge for years. There had, indeed, been a class war, and the rich had won. And they would run things to their liking. There was no stopping them. War paid them handsomely, so they would have war. Well, at least Antonia was interesting. You could have a conversation with Antonia. At the dinner table of the rest of his life, she would be able to think of something to say.

Did he love her? Did he know what love was? He could not recall loving Edith, though he must have. He must have thought he loved her, before it turned into a business deal. He had loved his babies. Stephen, Anna, Rachel. And he still did love them, he supposed, even when they were tipsy and screaming and tearing his lilies to shreds while Edith died in the azaleas. If his children were greedy, perhaps they only followed his example. Maybe that was love, the refusal to hate your offspring even when they not only refused to honor their father and their mother but coveted the real estate, as well.

He recalled the first rush of loving Antonia, the delight, the lust. Women as they aged could become proficient at sexual pleasure, sometimes they were easy and wanton, whereas men needed coaxing and patience and had to make do. In youth you came too fast and too often, in age you were fortunate to do it at all. But out of their abilities and limitations they had invented a love-making that surpassed the passions of youth, made youthfulness appear clumsy, at least in recollection, not to mention the routine sexuality of marriage. Eros dies last. At least if you are fortunate enough to have a partner.

He shampooed his head, massaged his chest, observed the white suds running down his legs and into the drain. He dried himself with tender care, ran Antonia's comb through his hair, what there was of it, flossed and brushed his teeth for two whole minutes. He felt a thrill of satisfaction at his own cleanliness, the smell of plain soap, his old seersucker bathrobe on the hook as if it belonged here. He was not as destroyed by insomnia as he had expected, and the whiskey had not harmed him, nor had the sleeping pill, though it said plainly on the label not to mix pills and alcohol. He felt rather fit. Locating a razor, he shaved his chin and cheeks and upper lip. In the mirror was an old man. He could still see, breathe, walk. Today might be the last day, or maybe he had ten more years. Perhaps if he and Antonia walked downtown, down to the site, he could find a way to reconcile the contradictions of love, his terror of tying himself to another woman and starting another life.

"Listen, my love," he would say to her. "We have only a few years left. Maybe a day left. Old age is dangerous country. We should get hardship pay for living here. Old age is a minefield, and we shall each step on a mine. If Al Qaeda doesn't get us, our bodies will. Our eyes will stop seeing, our ears stop hearing. There'll be some massive screw-up in my plumbing, some abdominal mass that presents itself. Too much calcium in my arteries and the chambers of my heart, not enough calcium in your bones. I shall need to help you cross the room. One day—I pray not today or tomorrow—I won't be able to get an erection, no matter how loving you are, how wise. One day I'll look at my bookshelves, at the titles of all the books I've published and all the books I've read, and I won't remember a one of them. One day all that will happen, my dear. No use to deny it. Do you think we might lie together in the same bed each night until death do us part?"

35 The Two of Them

WHEN HE CAME into the kitchen, he said only, "Good morning." She stood by the terrace door with her back to him, intent on the scene outdoors. She had not heard him enter. When he approached her, put his arms tightly around her, kissed her neck, she gave quite a start. "Didn't mean to scare you." He turned her toward him. Kissed her mouth. "You taste like coffee and oranges."

"You taste like toothpaste." She smiled. She did not tell him that she had given up hope, had resolved to send him away. The aspirin was beginning to take effect. She did not need sleep, she felt buoyant. They were as close as two people could be.

"Shall we take a walk this morning?" The question was tremulous—she could not have borne his saying no.

And he said yes, they would walk to Ground Zero. They would place flowers for the dead, observe a moment of silence. They could sit for a while in Trinity Church. Perhaps there would be music. A commemoration for this day. The sun rose over the rooftops and turrets, the cornices and the water towers, the disorderly, haphazard, law-unto-itself ragged skyline of the Village.

ACKNOWLEDGMENTS

Sooner or later a writer turns to friends and family. ("Tell me what you think. Pull no punches. But don't hurt my feelings. And by next Monday.") My thanks are due to my daughters, Katharine Rubick and Elizabeth Tomkievicz, for their valuable insights, patience, and love; to Brett, Robert, and Angela Averitt; to Barbara Welch and Joan Corell; and to the novelist Fenton Johnson. All these people are or have been teachers, in addition to other accomplishments, and they had much to teach me. Gary Combs, an autograph dealer and friend, picked out the themes of this book from casual conversations we had and urged me onward, reading two drafts. He was not the model for Arthur, but I took material from his elegant catalogues. My friends Suzanne Ruta, a writer, and Huguette Martel, a painter, were always there to say "bon courage." I thank Patricia Thomas and Meriwether Rhodes for a positive reaction to an early draft when I was about to delete the whole thing. Anna Bodine also saw something promising in early drafts. I am happy to thank Joe Spieler, my agent, for his hard work and excellent advice, and my editor and publisher Elisabeth Scharlatt, who years ago was my editor on *Womenfolks*. I am glad to be reunited with this wise and creative spirit.